# LIEGE

## O-MEN: LIEGE'S LEGION

## ELAINE LEVINE

Published by Elaine Levine
Copyright © 2018 Elaine Levine
Last Updated: November 27, 2018
Cover art by The Killion Group, Inc.
Cover image featuring Dennis Mulbah © Roy MayH
Editing by Arran McNicol @ editing720
Proofing by Carol Agnew @ Attention to Detail Proofreading

Print ISBNs:
ISBN-13: 9781790485529

# LIEGE

O-MEN: LIEGE'S LEGION, BOOK 1

He's not a robot. He's not a human. He's both.

Liege, changed against his will into a super soldier by nanotechnology, is driven to protect humanity from the evil intent of his enemies. But the deadly focus he was wired for comes to a crashing halt when he sees *her*, a female who ignites in him a very human hunger, one he no longer thought himself capable of feeling.

Summer Coltrane is oblivious to the powers swirling around her--light and dark, evil and good--until the veil between both worlds is ripped open and she's plunged into a terrible power play between a darkly tempting warrior and his ruthless enemies.

To stay alive, she must join forces with Liege, a man who kills without remorse to save those he loves in a war no one in her world can know about.

## OTHER BOOKS BY ELAINE LEVINE

### O-MEN: LIEGE'S LEGION

LIEGE

### RED TEAM SERIES

(This series must be read in order.)

1 The Edge of Courage

2 SHATTERED VALOR

3 HONOR UNRAVELED

4 KIT & IVY: A RED TEAM WEDDING NOVELLA

5 TWISTED MERCY

6 TY & EDEN: A RED TEAM WEDDING NOVELLA

7 ASSASSIN'S PROMISE

8 WAR BRINGER

9 ROCCO & MANDY: A RED TEAM WEDDING NOVELLA

10 RAZED GLORY

11 DEADLY CREED

12 FORSAKEN DUTY

13 MAX & HOPE: A RED TEAM WEDDING NOVELLA

14 OWEN & ADDY: A RED TEAM WEDDING NOVELLA

### SLEEPER SEALS

11 Freedom Code

**Men of Defiance Series**

(This series may be read in any order.)

1 Rachel and the Hired Gun

2 Audrey and the Maverick

3 Leah and the Bounty Hunter

4 Logan's Outlaw

5 Agnes and the Renegade

# DEDICATION

*I've been meaning to tell you, Barry, that I love you like I love a deep-fried bacon-wrapped Twinkie. But more.*

Dear Readers,

This is it! Our new adventure in the Red Team/Omni/O-Men world begins with Liege's story!

For those of you who haven't read the Red Team, you're in the right place--Liege's story is a great entry point. No prior Red Team knowledge is assumed in this series. There will be some appearances in Liege's Legion of Red Team characters, so if you have time and interest, there's another whole series waiting for a binge-read!

For those of you who have read the Red Team, you'll notice that this story is on the same timeline, starting back in September, roughly at the end of War Bringer.

Liege's story **doesn't have a cliffhanger**, but it does end with a peek at the next story, which is Bastion and Selena's. Selena was the lone warrior left unmatched from the Red Team series. I've been dying to write her story, but she needed to be paired with the perfect-for-her hero, and I think Bastion is just that guy!

For now, I hope you fall as deeply in love with Liege and Summer as I have!

Elaine

# 1

**M**usic spilled outside the bar every time the doors opened, beating a pulsing rhythm. Liege stood by his bumper, waiting for a break in traffic so he could cross the street to join his men.

The Fort Collins college crowd was heavy now that the university was back in session. Tired of waiting for a break in traffic, Liege was about to force cars to a stop when something drew his attention.

A man was standing two lanes away, not entirely out of the road. Cars rushed by, driving through him, but nothing diverted the monster's focus from Liege.

Chills like mini razorblades cut through Liege's nerves.

*The Matchmaker.*

They stared at each other on the dark street, hidden from the eyes of regulars. "Matchmaker" was a piss-poor name for the fiend. He should be the

Reaper. The image he projected of himself was skinny and tall, at least seven or eight feet. His bright orange hair was combed straight upward so it stood a hand's length from his skull. His red eyes, lit from within, glowed victoriously in the thickening shadows.

The late September night was overcast. A fog crept close, twisting about the Matchmaker's feet. He slowly lifted his arm and pointed a long finger toward Liege, whose heart began to hurt. He rejected the monster's message, refusing to accept its implications, but no shield any mutant had yet created could resist the Matchmaker's truth.

Liege felt a wave of sorrow. The Matchmaker's singular purpose was connecting a mutant with his mate, even if that meant the death of one or the other, as it always did.

Liege leaned against his SUV's bumper. His life-mate was near; she had to be if the Matchmaker was here. Liege knew with perfect certainty that he would meet the woman, come to know her, love her, and then lose her.

Or so the legend went.

The only way Liege could avoid that outcome was to let the Matchmaker take his life.

The pain blossomed across Liege's chest as he continued to resist the message. He flattened a hand over his heart, trying to halt the pain from spreading up his neck, down his arms. Tears welled in his eyes. He didn't want to die, but better that than to live with the terrible price of the Matchmaker's curse.

Liege couldn't breathe, couldn't support his own weight. He closed his eyes and hit his knees on the wet road, then slumped forward, his arms folded around himself, his forehead pressed to the ground.

He thought of the men he led. How would they get along without him? His mind went to the lifemate he would never meet, the woman his soul apparently already loved.

The pain ended instantly.

He gasped and pulled a ragged breath, then turned his head, shooting a look across the road. The apparition was gone. Liege collapsed on the pavement. The shield he had in place protected him from the rush of cars. Each one in his lane slowed then moved over to avoid him. He was making a traffic jam, and none of the regulars even knew why they couldn't drive near him.

He needed a minute to get his breath before getting out of the road.

The motherfucking Matchmaker hadn't accepted his surrender. And now Liege's fate was sealed.

A long few minutes later, he hoisted himself to his feet. Leaning against the side of his car, he took inventory of his body and mind. It seemed he was himself again, just wiped out.

Forget searching for Omni World Order operative Brett Flynn; Liege and his men should hunt the Matchmaker and send him to the other side.

Liege crossed the street and headed to the bar where his men waited. But instead of entering, he looked farther down the sidewalk where there were more shops and restaurants. For some reason, he felt drawn to that area. He couldn't tell if he was operating under his own volition or via an external compulsion. There was only one being who could exert that control over him: the Matchmaker.

He had a bad feeling about what he was heading toward. *Her*. His lifemate. Fuck, he'd wanted to ignore the Matchmaker's message. He'd survived the encounter. He wanted to just get back to the life he'd been living. He didn't want to meet the woman, didn't want the metric fuck-ton of pain loving her would bring him—or the death that loving him would bring her.

He stopped outside a bar and grill that served reimagined American cuisine, resisting the pull to go in there. He told himself he had no intention of seeking the woman out, though he knew she was inside. Her energy called to him. He had to resist—he couldn't destroy her by joining their lives.

Maybe he should just find out who she was so he could stay away from her.

He wrapped his energy in a mirage that caused anyone looking at the space where he was to see it as it had been before he was there, effectively making himself invisible. Inside the restaurant, he shut his eyes and felt for the woman's energy.

He heard a familiar female laughter at a table; his daughter was here.

He went over to her table. She looked happy, but

he could also feel an undercurrent of tension inside her. She was with two friends. A pretty brunette and a white ball of light.

What the hell?

Liege glared at the luminous woman sitting on the opposite side of the booth from the other two. He forced himself to see beyond her brilliant light to the aura it hid, a bright pink with touches of gold and green. He looked beneath that to the woman herself. A white female with blond hair, blue eyes, and fading freckles on her nose and cheeks.

Aw, fuck. The Matchmaker was right. She was his light. Unless…she wasn't. She was friends with his daughter. What if the Matchmaker and the Omnis had gotten together for this new trick?

If she was working with the Omnis, then his daughter was in danger.

Liege turned and stumbled out of the restaurant, only to slump against the wall outside. He wasn't going to die because of the Matchmaker, but the Omni female was—and soon, before she could harm Liege's daughter.

*Yo. Liege. You coming in?* Acier asked via their mental link. *You parked fifteen minutes ago.*

Liege had blocked out everything on the link he shared with his men from the time he saw the Matchmaker.

*No*, Liege said. *Change of plans. Have fun without me.*

Liege waited outside the restaurant for the women. Took another hour before they spilled into the dark night. They laughed and hugged, then went their own ways. Liege followed the ball of light, keeping himself from being seen, as he had all night. She got into a beat-up Subaru wagon. He got in too, sitting in the back, hiding from her the fact that he'd opened a door in her car and the dip it made when he got in. He wasn't a small man. His legs were folded to his chin in the crowded back seat.

The woman shivered and waited for the heat to come on. It didn't. Liege closed his eyes as he let his energy mingle with hers. Dammit all, the Match-maker had chosen well. Her energy felt like a balm to his soul. And he loved her sweet scent.

What if she really was his light?

He could fight himself, but he couldn't fight the truth of the way their mingled energy felt. The danger was that if the Matchmaker had been able to discover his light, Liege's enemies could as well.

He didn't like to believe in fate, but what if he couldn't avoid what was coming?

THE WOMAN HAD an apartment over a garage in an older area of town, not far from the university. She was in there now, settling down for the night. Liege had taken a cab back to his SUV and returned, waiting for her to fall asleep.

He set an illusion that his vehicle was a large trash dumpster. He didn't want neighbors to take note of his big SUV. There were no cameras to disable in the alleyway, nothing to do but wait.

After a while, when all was calm inside, he went upstairs then unlocked the deadbolt telekinetically, pausing to listen inside the apartment. Had the sound of the door being unlocked awakened the woman?

No. All was quiet and still. He opened the door and closed it behind him without touching it. Her energy hit him like a wall of water, surrounding him, drowning him. He spread his arms wide, absorbing as much of her as he could, like a starving man at a buffet.

She was his perfect match. Right now, in the quiet privacy of this dark apartment, he could give himself the peace of belonging to another, of having a life-mate, of feeling love that was reciprocated.

Only he knew what he indulged in, so it was safe to pretend for a few moments that this woman wasn't an enemy here to harm him or his daughter.

And, of course, it was that thought that sobered him. He focused on his purpose in being there: recon-naissance.

Any mutant could fake an energy signature. Though she was a regular, she could be under someone else's control.

Her studio flat was filled with colors and clashing patterns of textiles. She had a four-poster queen-sized bed. Mosquito netting was draped down each poster. The ceiling was open to the rafters, giving the room a sense of greater space. Shiplap covered the exposed wood, painted a pale seafoam color on the walls and white on the ceiling. The floor was a dark stained wood. A faded antique flat-weave Uzbek carpet in red and other bold colors—a style he'd often seen in Afghanistan—covered most of the main room.

A tall nightstand and a dresser, both antiques, flanked the bed. A futon couch was between the bed and the kitchen, with a long coffee table in front of it. A TV took up a chunk of the opposite wall on top of a long credenza.

Set in a nook next to the front door was a small kitchen. It had a retro-looking turquoise fridge, a narrow four-burner stove and oven, and a sink. A short peninsula separated it from the rest of the room. Three tall barstools, made from wood and black iron, stood at the counter.

A small stack of mail was in a file holder affixed to the wall. He took out a couple of envelopes. The woman's name was Summer Coltrane.

*Summer*. The name suited her perfectly. Saying it reminded him of a warm, sultry breeze.

A short hallway led off the main room. To the left was a small bathroom; to the right was a long and narrow closet. He checked out the bathroom. There were no toiletry products that belonged to a man. The relief he felt actually hurt his chest. Geez, what the fuck would he have done if he found she was in a relationship?

Nothing. He wouldn't have done a damned thing.

She couldn't be his, so it was best if she found someone who made her happy.

Reality check. He didn't give a damn about her happiness. She might be an Omni operative, and if she was, he was going to have to end her.

Her long closet was half household storage, half clothing and shoes. Here, too, nothing belonging to a man was stored.

He returned to the main room. The woman still slept. He'd learned what he'd come to learn, but he couldn't quite make himself leave yet. This was the closest he'd been to her, and he wanted to linger.

When he concentrated, he could see through the bright glow surrounding her to the peaceful colors of her aura.

Humans had perfected their ability to twist the truth with their expressions, words, and even behavior, but only mutants knew how to extend that to their auras.

This close to her, Liege knew she was a regular, unchanged human. He slipped into her dream world. She was in a garden, tending to flowers. A spider crawled across her hand. He felt the deep revulsion in her reaction, which was quickly followed by a calm acceptance that each creature had its place in the whole of life. She moved her hand over to a nearby plant and let the spider slip away.

He pulled out of her sleeping mind, only to be broadsided by emotions and the uncomfortable knowledge that he wasn't here for purely reconnaissance purposes.

He was here for her. For himself. For a future they could never have.

His enemies had chosen their operative with expert precision. Whoever was controlling her seemed to know all of his dreams and hopes and desires.

If he weren't careful, his loss of control would have a devastating impact on his daughter.

He straightened and forced himself to leave the woman. He went out the way he came, locking her apartment behind him.

LIEGE SAT in his SUV outside a garden center on the north side of town. He'd followed the woman here, where she apparently worked, which confirmed his suspicions.

Briscoe's Garden and Landscape Design Center was one of several businesses in the area that were fronts for the Omni World Order, the secret crime organization Liege and his team were fighting.

The Matchmaker only ever matched human females with warriors who were in the Omni resistance. Liege had long wondered whose side the fiend was on, and now that he'd connected Liege with a female employed by the Omnis, perhaps he had his answer; Summer's bright glow wasn't a natural occurrence but one manufactured by the Omnis to trick

Liege into believing he'd found his light, a subterfuge that wouldn't have worked without the Matchmaker.

Liege had learned long ago, in the mutant camps, to expect that any and all mind games were always in play.

Perhaps Summer Coltrane was a trick to distract him. Who knew what she really was or whom she was working for? Maybe she herself didn't even know.

Liege watched her move around the outside the garden center. She was bright, like a free-floating ball of lightning. She stopped to talk to a customer near a stack of hay bales loaded with pumpkins. The man she was talking to didn't glow. Nor did the other staffers who were watering the mums and rearranging outdoor displays. Only the woman glowed.

He could see the auras of the regulars. Nothing unusual in them. Nothing alarming, either.

Liege camouflaged his SUV with a blanket of energy, making it appear to regulars as one of the garden center's utility trucks, parked and empty. Once again, he hid himself behind a compulsion forced on any who might look his way, causing them to see the space where he was as it had been before he was there —a small trick that took little attention to create. The electromagnetic pulse he emitted to interfere with the security cameras was more of an effort, but it was worth it.

Up close, he could see that his female was young. Those faded freckles that dotted her nose fascinated him. Chilled by the autumn air, her skin was pink and white. She wore a pastel pink cable-knit sweater with a heavy fold-over neck that draped over her chest and the collar of the pale aqua puffer vest she had on. A pair of pink earmuffs was hooked around her neck. Her long blond hair was pulled back in a simple pony-tail. Her pink lips smiled often as she talked to her customer. Her fingers, poking out of tipless pink gloves, were long and unpainted.

Liege smiled. She had a thing for pink. And he had a thing for her.

He was so fucked.

She must have felt his intense surveillance, for she looked right at him. And though he knew she couldn't see him—not through the energy he hid behind—gooseflesh rose on his skin as he wondered just how deep she was in with the Omnis.

He wasn't certain he could extinguish the beautiful light that she was.

What was he going to do if he discovered she was an innocent caught in an Omni web? He'd looked up her social media footprint last night. It showed she'd worked here since graduating college with a degree in landscape design, six years ago. It even showed that she'd dated the owner's son off and on during that time.

Were they off now or on?

Liege yanked himself from that train of thought. Mutants and regulars didn't mix. Her relationship status was of no interest to him. They could never meet. He told himself his interest in her was because of her friendship with his daughter.

Kiera was always his first priority.

BRISCOE'S NURSERY was dormant now in the wee hours of the night. Liege had come back so he could do some reconnaissance, maybe discover what the Briscoes and the Omnis were up to.

A dense fog obscured his view of the lower half of the building. The moisture in it had crystalized and was sparkling in the glow from the streetlights.

Something moved close to the main entrance, rising from the fog to stare at Liege. The Matchmaker. The hairs along Liege's arms and neck lifted. He'd gotten the bastard's first message; he didn't need a reminder—he just wasn't inclined to act on it. Too much was at stake.

He wanted to confront the redheaded monster, but knew there was no point. What he was seeing was merely a projection, not the fiend's corporeal form.

Liege drew the fog around his Escalade and himself, using it for cover. He disabled the garden center's security system and cameras as he approached the front door of the nursery, then telekinetically unlocked the door, opening and closing it behind him without ever touching it.

The front portion of the main building was a retail shop, filled with garden-themed tchotchkes, books, and linens. On the left was a small greenhouse with potted and hanging houseplants. The air was thick with humidity and oxygen, rich with the scents of dirt and living organisms.

Liege moved toward the back, where the offices were situated off an L-shaped hallway. The first office before the hallway turned a corner belonged to *her*. His daughter's friend. The Matchmaker's target. Light spilled from the small space—not light as a human would see it, but light from an energetic glow, like that of an aura.

Summer Coltrane.

Hers was a rare energy indeed. A powerful one, something he sensed could change his life. How perfectly the Omnis had architected her for him. He was drawn to her space as if compelled to come closer. Was that because of the Matchmaker's influence? The very hint of a compulsion made Liege doubt himself.

He stepped into Summer's office, into the field of her energy. It surrounded him, slipped inside him, filled all the hollow places he'd kept hidden from himself and his team. The sensation was unlike anything he'd experienced as a mutant or a human.

A psychic's pot of gold.

It was far too easy to believe she was his lifemate, but it was a mirage he had to resist. A gift of the heart was the best poison of all—perhaps the only poison—that could affect him.

Liege looked around the small office, wondering

about its occupant. When he let himself move beyond the feel of her energy, his other senses kicked in. There was a faint hint of roses. The desk was cluttered with stacks of papers and books. A deep shelf nearby held large scrolls of paper. He wondered about the human female who used this space. He checked for any pictures of her that he could find, but there were none. There wasn't anything of a personal nature at all in the space, other than the sweater that hung on a hook behind the door.

Liege lifted the soft knit fabric and held it up, realizing the woman who wore it was tiny—in comparison to him, anyway. He brought it to his nose, burying his face in it, scenting her own unique essence and the rose perfume she wore.

He stuffed her sweater in his coat pocket, then left her office to wander around the remaining offices.

The next door opened to a long conference room. No alarming residual energy lingered there. The next office was empty. He went to the next one and stopped cold.

His enemy had been in here. Recently. Brett Flynn. Liege shut his eyes, shocked by the confirmation that the Omnis were close to the woman the Matchmaker said was his.

Wait—she was not his woman. For all he knew, she was bait to get him here. She and the Matchmaker could be colluding with the Omnis. Liege would have to surrender and enter their game if he wanted answers.

Whatever the truth was, the Matchmaker wasn't going to let Liege off with a warning. He never did for any mutant.

Liege looked at the nameplate outside the office door. Clark Briscoe. The son Summer had dated.

Fear was heavy in the room. What had caused so palpable a reaction in the kid?

Flynn liked fear. It sustained him, but he couldn't manufacture that emotion on his own. Perhaps he hadn't been able to even as a human. He'd been a psychopath as a human, a trait the mutant shift only intensified. Liege suspected that whatever a human was before being changed, he became more of as a mutant.

Liege knew Flynn went on binges of sex and fear, lusting for sensations he couldn't generate himself, feeding off them from the humans he possessed.

Liege left Clark's office and went into the last room at the end of the hallway. He felt the energy of many regulars in there, couples and individuals, all of whom had come into this room in the last few weeks. Standing still, he sifted through the residual energy signatures, searching for the ones that had attracted Flynn.

This office belonged to Douglas Briscoe, Clark's father and owner of Briscoe's Garden Center. Flynn had been in here, but Douglas wasn't his target. Clark was.

Why? What did Clark have to offer Flynn? Why didn't he use Douglas too? And was it a coincidence that he had come to this garden center where the woman meant for Liege worked?

No. There were no coincidences. Flynn knew what he was doing. Liege expected he could feel the same thing the Matchmaker did—that Summer and Liege were lifemates.

Liege needed to come back when Clark was there to get a better read on what the kid was doing messing around with Flynn and the Omnis.

Summer's former boyfriend would never survive them—no regular could.

## 2

___

Two nights later, outside the college town's only bus stop, Liege watched his target snare his prey with the simple tool of a handwritten sign that read, "Women's Shelter."

A woman with a small satchel in her hand and fear all over her face went right to the guy. They started up a conversation. He didn't immediately drag her off to his car. No, he knew how easy it was to allay her fears by showing no interest in her at all, pretending just to be the driver the shelter had ordered.

He was smooth, like he'd done this before.

After a few minutes, when it appeared no one else from the bus was going to join them, he led the woman to his car.

Liege followed them to an abandoned church on the north side of town. Most of this small city was beautiful—a booming town full of landscaped shopping centers, corporate complexes, tidy neighbor-hoods, and wide roads with dedicated bike lanes. But every town had a scrappy part that was a holdover from the old days of less comprehensive urban regula-tions. The church was in one of these areas.

The guy went up to the front door, unlocked it, and went inside, leaving the woman in the car.

Liege pulled into the church's weed-filled lot. He could feel his enemy here. Flynn's energy was strong, more concentrated than it had been around his conscripted driver.

Liege walked over to guy's car, opening himself to the woman's energy. Her fear ripped through him, as did her will to live and to protect herself. Liege sent calming energy back to her. It was inexcusable that he was about to manipulate her free will, but it was imperative that she cooperate so he could keep her safe while what was coming went down.

He opened her door and reached a hand to her, sending her a compulsion to comply. "Will you allow me to take you to the real women's shelter?" Being new to town, she couldn't have known this wasn't the real shelter until they got here. God, they were so gullible, these women. Desperate, young, not worldly at all.

Liege helped her out of the car, then reached inside for her bag. He walked her over to his Escalade and got her settled inside.

"I'll just be a minute," he said. He set an illusion over his SUV, making it appear to be a garbage dumpster to any eyes that might see it. He went to the guy's parked car and got inside, pulling the shadows over him for cover. The guy came back outside, a big smile on his face. Liege lowered the window.

"I know it's late," they said, "but they're happy you came." He opened the door and stepped back, waiting for the woman to come out. Liege grabbed the guy's hand and yanked him down, banging his face on the edge of the door—knocking him out.

"I'll bet they are," Liege said as he got out of the car and stepped over the guy's body. He didn't kill him for the simple reason he was an unwitting accomplice whom Flynn had compelled to do what he did. Let him wake there in the parking lot, a sign for the women's shelter in his car, and no recollection of how he got there.

Liege drew his energy close to himself so the beings inside wouldn't be alerted to his presence. It was just old habit. The things he was about to face weren't humans anymore. Nor were they wild animals. They were a bastardization of both, more monster than anything else.

Seven of them were inside.

He opened the door and stepped into the nave. Faint illumination from the distant streetlights filtered into the room, but Liege didn't need it to see. What waited in there would have been horrifying to the woman. The monsters were spread about the space, eyes glowing orange. They were waiting for their prey, sitting on overturned benches, straddling a banister, standing on the altar, or climbing the support beams, all of them roosted on different perches like vultures.

These things were nothing but optimized predators. He doubted they even took much joy from the harm they did, doubted they felt much of anything. The gargoyle grins they wore weren't smiles at all but defects of the mutation process. Their skeletal structures had been altered, by design or malfunction, Liege didn't know. Their arms were lengthened, their legs shortened, their backs hunched. Their mouths protruded from their faces. Extra skin on their faces was rucked up in tight, batlike folds that led to mashed noses with wide-open nostrils. A scattering of wiry, black fur on their boarlike hides clothed them.

These beings belonged to Brett Flynn and bore his stink like a pot of stew made from rotten meat. Liege scoped out the situation, making several battle plans with various contingencies, all within the space of a breath.

He decided he didn't have the luxury of indulging in a physical fight while there was a woman who needed rescuing outside. Best take the most strategic approach. He conjured a telekinetic pulse that blanketed the room, aimed at every organic being in it. Ordinarily, unshielded beings dropped like flies as their brains turned to liquid. Liege had become expert in manipulating that tool. He could emit a minor pulse that delivered a light shock or a full pulse that destroyed organic matter.

He did the latter now, but only managed to gain

the monsters' full attention. Liege hadn't yet encountered one of these beings that was capable of such higher-level skills. Someone had to be shielding them.

So, it would be a physical fight. That worked too. Liege drew two knives from his thigh holsters. The knives were long and wide, with rubber grips and metal hand-guards. The steel blades had serrated edges toward their bases. Acier had made the blades specifically for Liege; he'd crafted a pair for each of the men according to the needs of their fighting styles.

The room exploded into movement. Liege jumped back a step, sending out an image of himself running in a different direction. The mirage tricked three of the monsters. They chased after it, slashing their clawed fingers, drawing blood of their own, which caused a frenzy of motion. In seconds, the three were fighting each other. None survived.

That left four still coming at him. Liege ran into their midst, somersaulting between two of them as he slashed at the arteries in their necks. He knelt to dodge the razor-sharp claws of two more and cut their femoral arteries. The loss of blood barely dazed them. Given how fast the monsters regenerated, nothing less than multiple catastrophic wounds would put them down.

Liege rolled backward and got to his feet, imposing an illusion on two of the monsters that made their peers mistake them for him. They attacked each other, doing his work for him.

One remained standing after all the carnage.

Liege threw one of his knives into the monster's uninjured eye. He shook his head, trying to dislodge the long blade as he fell to the ground. Liege pulled his head up and sliced his throat.

The immediate threat now ended, Liege let his energy slip through the rest of the building, searching for any others who were trying to hide. These were the only ones here.

Liege went from monster to monster, severing heads. If he left the monsters substantially intact, they might survive to fight again, especially if their puppet master got them on life support quickly enough.

No, he wasn't taking chances. He went out to his SUV to grab a body bag and a small medical kit, then returned to the destroyed nave. From each fallen mutant, he collected a vial of blood, storing it in its slot in his case. He knelt by one of the mutants to have a closer look at the monster. He lifted its hand, examining it. The structure was different from that of a normal human. The bones were bigger, the fingers longer and curved, as if holding an invisible ball. The nails were many times thicker and pointed, which accounted for the wounds Liege had suffered in the fight. What were these beings? An error in the lab or an intentional creation? Liege snapped pictures of them.

He and his men needed answers. They were fighting an uphill battle to put an end to the modifications the Omnis were forcing on regular humans. But until he could find the experts that the Omnis were hiding, the best he could do was to collect and store the critical samples they'd need for their research.

He looked over the trashed space. Blood was spattered everywhere. Why had Flynn brought the woman here? To teach these mutants to hunger for the kill, like dropping a puppy into a dogfight?

The only consolation he could think of—and it wasn't much of one—was that she wouldn't have lived long after encountering these beasts. Her suffering would have ended fast.

He and his men intercepted as many of these attacks as they could, but it was a numbers game they were losing.

Liege suppressed from humans the discovery of any evidence of himself that he may have left behind in here or outside. He didn't care about hiding it from the Omnis. They would feel his energy anyway, and he doubted they would leave the place intact. No, they'd clear out the bodies and torch it.

He was glad the Omnis were leaving the war in the shadows where it belonged, but how much longer he could keep regular humans from learning about it, he didn't know.

He returned the medical kit to its case, dropped the body bag full of heads in his SUV's cargo area, then took out a gallon of water and rinsed the blood from his hands and face. He dried himself off with a towel then got behind the wheel. His passenger was where he'd left her, still in the grips of the trance he'd put on her.

He drove across town to the real women's shelter. Parking out front, he sent the woman a mental compulsion to leave his car with her bag and to remember nothing about the time between when she got off the bus to this moment. He sent the director, who lived at the shelter, a summons to open the front door and let the woman in. She did just that as Liege drove away, but he knew she would have done so even without the compulsion he'd issued.

His daughter never turned away a woman in need.

LIEGE DROVE BACK to his fort, which was way out on the plains east of town. The sprawling adobe structure had been built atop the entrance to a Cold War missile silo Liege had acquired years ago. He went down several flights of stairs to that subterranean structure. It now housed research labs, quarters for visiting scientists, offices, and conference rooms.

All of them were empty at the moment. Liege had considered bringing in academics for the research he needed to have done. While many were tops in their fields in the different branches of nanobiotech, none had ever been involved in a human trial. It was possible they could reverse-engineer the samples he and his team collected, but the research they would be doing broke global ethics standards, and he couldn't risk letting the knowledge of what was happening in the dark world of mutants spill out into the world of humans.

No, he needed scientists already working in the human modification experiments. Omni scientists. They knew the enormity of what they were dealing with; there was no way they would risk contaminating the world of regulars with their knowledge once he freed them from those who held them.

So for now, Liege and his team froze the heads, bodies, and blood samples of the ghouls.

He marked the blood vials with the date and place of collection, then put them in the freezer. Two of his men, Guerre and Merc, came in with their own samples. Acier and Bastion were still in the field. Liege didn't need the lab's dim light to see his two men were as cut up as he was; he could smell the blood of their wounds.

Liege set his bag of heads on an autopsy tray for Guerre and Merc to package for the freezer.

"I've never seen mutants like the ones we've been fighting lately," Merc said, his Australian accent heavy in his anger. "We need to focus on snagging the scientists the Omnis are hoarding so we can find out what's going on."

"Whatever brand of mutations they are using lately is creating monsters instead of super soldiers," Guerre said. "I think their tech broke, and they're making deviants instead of fully transformed humans."

"Yeah. Vicious killing machines," Merc said. "And

who knows how long the Omnis can keep control of them. Sooner or later they're going to start showing up in public places."

"We're making a dent in their forces," Liege said. "We have to keep up the fight until we can turn a corner or find the Omni scientists we need."

"Bullshit, we're not making a dent," Merc argued. "They're popping out these monsters like candy from a factory."

"Do you think the human males who become these monsters volunteered for this?" Guerre asked. "Or are they more victims in the Omni's march toward hell?"

Liege shook his head. "Both, maybe."

THE NEXT MORNING, Liege backed his black Escalade into a spot at a coffee shop just off the local university campus. He stayed put for a moment, sifting through the various visual aliases he employed when he went anywhere in public. One never knew when hell was going to break loose; it was a best practice for changed beings like him to always be camouflaged so that eyewitness reports would never place him near the scene of whatever crazy shit might go down.

Not that he expected trouble today. None of the Omni fighters ever came here. The newly turned couldn't tolerate the frenetic brain noise from the regulars, and the mature fighters rarely had down-time. And the monsters were only let loose at night.

Liege selected the image of an average-height white man with blue eyes and straight brown hair. It would let him fit right in with the crowd in NOCO; a black guy his size and height generally stuck out, and that was never a benefit for a changed being.

He went inside the coffee shop and ordered his Americano. The menu had a kitschy name for the simple drink he ordered; he never used their terms, preferring instead to force the staff to translate his order.

One of the TVs was reporting news on an abandoned church that had burned down overnight. Arson was suspected.

He paid the bill, holding his hand out for the change, which he dropped in the tip bucket. The clerk made eye contact with the middle of Liege's clavicle, which was how Liege knew his illusion was working. Had he been the average-height guy he was projecting, the clerk would have been looking right at his eyes.

Too bad the coffee shops in the U.S. weren't full service like many were overseas; here he had to wait to take his own drink to his seat.

He looked over to see if his favorite booth in the back corner was open. It wasn't. Three kids from the university were sitting there with books open. He sent them a mental compulsion to move to another spot. They exchanged confused looks, then gathered their things and crossed the shop to an open table.

Liege picked up his coffee and went to the recently vacated booth. He pulled a small leather journal from his chest pocket, removed the sterling silver fountain pen from its loop, and incremented the last number by seven, jotting down the number 264 and yesterday's date, then stared at it a moment.

He'd begun his journal ten years ago. It had twenty lines per page, two-sided pages. At two columns per page, writing in small print, he'd only used four double-sided pages out of the fifty available.

He sipped his coffee and wondered if his current journal would last him the rest of his life. He couldn't imagine having a shelf of these logs, but maybe that was how it was going to go, especially at the rate his enemies were growing their forces.

He leaned back in his seat. Maybe it was odd that he kept a manual tally of his kills when he could remember everything about the dead, like their height, skin color, hair color, eye color, good teeth, bad teeth, missing teeth. Their age, not so much. They were all about the same, weren't they? The mutants, anyway. Twenties to mid-thirties, even if their bio age was forty-five or sixty or more.

Of course, most of his kills this past year had been monsters—more than ever before. For them, raw tallies made sense.

He sipped his coffee, holding the murky brew in his mouth, savoring the rich flavors of the beans. This shop had suppliers from across South America. The owners were knowledgeable about each producer's annual harvest and the weather conditions, altitude, and other factors that affected each crop's flavor. Their expertise in bean selection and the attention they paid to proper roasting was impressive.

It was all a science. Like everything in life, including him and his men. They were just science experiments, gone right or wrong, depending on which side of the line you stood on. The Omnis would argue gone wrong, but that was because Liege and his men were on a mission to eliminate them.

Or, at least, the evil among them.

He looked at his journal and sipped his coffee. So what if he didn't want to take his kills casually. Even though he could remember everything in exquisite detail, all of his own aliases—those assigned to him and those he self-assigned, and every moment of the training camp that was part of the medical trials he and his men had been tricked into being part of, he still feared he might forget. Or might stop caring.

Death had come easy in the jungle camps.

It still came easy, but it shouldn't be unacknowledged.

He shut his journal and swept the coffee shop with a slow glance. He liked the human noise clogging the air. It forced him to sharpen his focus since it took an effort to filter out the pandemonium or sift through it for a thread that might interest him. He could slip into the mind of anyone here, feel the texture of that person's life, his or her hopes and dreams, experience the exquisite detail of their emotions. Humans jumped from emotion to emotion. It punctuated their days and tortured their nights.

Sampling it made him remember what he'd once been.

He and his men lived an isolated existence, with humans but always separate. Rarely did he show himself out in public. His energy was powerful and always needed to be tempered. If humans felt him and saw him, he'd attract too much attention.

The isolation made him a non-thing now. Not human, but not an automaton either. He was focused on his mission, ruthlessly so, but there wasn't a day that passed that he didn't miss what he'd lost.

It was almost time to go see Summer. He wondered if she'd be entry 265 in his journal.

## 3

——————

Acier and Bastion's favorite bar was in the heart of Old Town Fort Collins. Close to the university, it was frequented by kids letting off steam from their intense studies.

Liege didn't have to search the crowded room for his team; their energy trail led right to them—and to the women fawning over them.

Bastion had two females flanking him. Guerre stood alone. Merc was oblivious to the brunette trying to connect with him. Acier had his arms around a woman who was straddling his lap, her high heels caught in his chair rungs.

A wave of irritation slipped through Liege. So much for keeping a low profile.

But really, it wasn't their fault. Standing over six and a half feet, all of them stuck out like sore thumbs, anyway. Liege was black—one of only a handful of dark men in the room. Bastion was a jovial

Frenchman who loved being the center of attention. His black, curly hair was pulled back into a man bun, but his beard and his build said there was nothing feminine about him. His boisterous laugh was infectious. He'd probably be dancing on the bar before too long.

The social setting did nothing to take the edge off Merc's attitude. His curly blond hair and warm-toned skin made him a magnet for college girls. Too bad the Aussie had a chip on his shoulder the size of his home country.

Guerre, a serious introvert, didn't make social connections. The Canadian liked being with the team, but as their resident healer, he was highly sensitive to external energies. He kept a shield around him that pushed humans away.

Acier was a law unto himself. With his shaggy, dark hair, blue eyes, and trim beard and mustache, the man played his bad-boy good looks like a finely tuned guitar.

Liege sent the women a mental compulsion they could not ignore. *Leave us.*

As soon as they pulled away, Bastion's head lifted. He glared at Liege. Merde, he said, using their psychic network for communication.

*Not like it would matter, Bastion,* Liege replied.

*To me,* non, *but to them it would be heaven,* Bastion answered, kissing the tips of his bunched fingers before spreading them wide.

Acier exchanged a grin with Guerre. *His humility*

*knows no bounds.*

*This is not true,* Bastion complained. *I merely wish to keep alive what it was like as a regular. It was good to feel* something. *I want that again.*

Liege ordered a whiskey from one of the wait-resses—more for cover than enjoyment. The modifications they'd all undergone prevented them from being the recipient of even a mild high from the liquor.

*Two more labs burned today,* Merc said. *The authorities haven't identified the bodies found in the wreckage.*

*The Omnis have been busy covering their trail,* Bastion said. The Omni World Order had been growing their power since their Second World War, and was now its own dark nation, existing in secret in every country across the globe. The Omnis were who had changed the five of them into the mutants they were now.

*We don't know if the people who died in the fire were the researchers or someone else,* Acier said. *The Omnis have been taking the scientists off the grid.*

Liege sipped his whiskey. The room was throbbing with a song that had more bass than tune. He was glad they didn't have to speak audibly. *I hope they've at least preserved their research somewhere.* Their research was far too powerful to submit for a patent—they would have to expose too much information in the application. If it was lost with the scientists, then it was gone for good.

*My FBI source knows about an Omni World Order hideout in an abandoned missile silo outside of Denver,* Guerre said. *It's under FBI control at the moment.*

The agent Guerre had cultivated was a regular and had no idea that Guerre was in his mind, harvesting useful info. Liege was impressed with Guerre's technique, but that was, after all, why they'd been changed. *You, Bastion, and Merc need to get in there. See what they were using that site for. Maybe they had a lab there, and if so, there might be something that will lead us to the researchers.*

Liege stared at his drink as he made a mental scan of his friends. Despite their persistent sense of being outsiders among regulars now, all of them were managing to keep their shit together—except Merc. He'd been so different in the training camps—irreverent, funny, a rebel through and through. He was more killer than human now. It would be nothing for the Aussie to end his own suffering. Liege met Guerre's deep blue eyes. Guerre was keeping an eye on Merc.

Liege dropped his gaze to his whiskey. They were so close to turning a corner in their secret fight against the Omnis. They just needed a break in their hunt for the researchers involved in the medical trials where he and his men had been changed.

And...they needed more fighters. Liege had teams in Europe, Africa, and South America, but his Legion was spread thin.

He wondered what new complication the Matchmaker had brought him in the person of Summer Coltrane. Maybe the lifemate curse was only a thing if you believed in it. He closed his eyes and slipped back into the feel of her energy, her scent, her easy smile. He hungered for her in a way he hadn't for a woman even when he'd been a regular.

He packed all of that away, out of the reach of his men. No point sharing his misery until he understood what it meant for all of them.

But he knew right now that fucking curse was working on him.

*Flynn is in town,* Liege said.

Bastion nodded. *I can smell him on you. Like bacon fried on an overheated diesel engine in a sweet antifreeze sauce.*

Liege laughed. *You must be hungry. The bastard smells like shit to me. Remember that scent.*

Bastion shook his head. *I could never forget it, even if I wanted to.*

The fact that evil had a scent had been one of Liege's first discoveries after he came to grips with his altered state of existence during the medical trials. He sipped his whiskey, then looked at Bastion. *You know, if you hadn't become a mutant, you would have made a great chef.*

Bastion was insulted, making his French accent heavy as he said, *I am a great chef. It's unkind of you to insult me. You can make your own breakfast in the morning.*

*I'll have to, anyway. You're heading down to that missile silo.*

Bastion shrugged. *So we'll all go hungry.*

Liege tried not to laugh. *I can make eggs.*

*You can slaughter eggs,* Bastion countered.

*Well, you won't be there to make love to them, so…* Liege looked at Acier. *I want you to keep an eye on one of Flynn's guys. Clark Briscoe out at the big garden center on the north side of town. I was in there last night. Flynn's energy was heavy there. Don't know what he and Flynn are working on, but we need to watch them closely.*

*Let's finish this and put an end to him,* Merc said.

*No,* Liege nixed that. *He's not a small player. He's running an op. We need to know what it is and who's overseeing it.*

*Copy that,* Acier said. *Now can we have our women back?*

Liege nodded. Without any verbal invitation, the females returned to the table. He stared into his glass. The same mods that had reengineered Liege and his team into perfect warriors had also rewired their hormones, negating their natural libido. Obviously, the researchers who made them thought a soldier's sex drive was his worst liability. A switch had been flipped somewhere in their genetics that rendered casual sex wholly unsatisfying for any mutant, which made what Liege felt around Summer all the more intriguing.

Urban legend among his kind whispered what sex was like when they found their true mates. Supposedly, it was explode-your-head extraordinary. So far, none of them had found their soul mates, so none could corroborate that.

Liege could sense Acier's arousal as he kissed the

woman straddling his lap. Acier hadn't come out of the same training camps as the rest of them at the table. The weapons maker had sought Liege's Legion out, a lone mutant hunting for a pack. There was safety in numbers. He'd fit right in, though, and had been a valuable part of the team, but Liege wondered if his mutations were the same as the rest of theirs.

A FEW NIGHTS LATER, in a subterranean depot station, Merc and Acier stepped out of a door marked "Private" and followed Clark Briscoe into a public hallway. Well, as public as any of the space in the secret Hyperloop system was.

Acier had been watching the younger Briscoe for a few days before he made his move. This particular Hyperloop depot was below the grounds of the Denver airport. Merc, Guerre, Bastion, and Acier had spent the last several months mapping the labyrinthine tracks of the Hyperloop as it crisscrossed the nation and even went north and south of the border. New tracks were being put down all the time, so their work was ongoing.

At the moment, Merc knew only specially permitted users were allowed aboard—politicians, celebrities, even crime lords who didn't want their movements known or tracked.

There were no cameras down here, and very few

travelers either. People coming through here were bypassing public travel grids, so they had an understanding that there was no guarantee of personal security. Those who were worried about it provided their own bodyguards.

No one made eye contact. No one wanted or needed witnesses, which suited Merc just fine. Though it didn't really matter. He and Acier had camouflaged their appearances and jammed any recording devices that might be operational.

Clark summoned a private Omni tube. There was a burst of air as it entered the station and slowed to a stop. The side door lifted up. Merc and Acier boarded the same tube. Clark spoke the destination code as he entered, then sat back in his seat and fastened the seatbelt.

At two thousand miles an hour on the vacuum train, it was a short ride to Des Moines from Denver. Merc looked at Acier, but didn't break their communication silence. Clark was under Flynn's control; neither of them wanted his handler to notice them.

In Des Moines, they got off at another private Omni terminal. An elevator led up to a parking garage. Clark got in one of the company cars. Merc and Acier stole a vehicle and followed him into a gritty area of downtown. They had no idea what his objective was, but it soon became obvious he was going hunting.

There were plenty of neighborhoods offering easy

pickings. Low incomes. High unemployment. High dropout rates for public schools. This was strictly a stats game. All cities had people struggling to survive. Des Moines was no different from any other urban area, but there was one thing it offered that Denver couldn't: it was a long way from Fort Collins. No one would connect Clark to a string of missing Iowa kids —thanks to the Hyperloop. And there were plenty of them looking to make some easy cash in exchange for beer or dope or whatever it was they craved at the moment. Food, maybe.

Merc watched Clark slow down and eye all the white-skinned, blue-eyed females—confirmation he was on an Omni errand.

Acier changed the observable appearance of their borrowed vehicle several times so that Clark wouldn't realize he was being tailed. They stayed a car length or two back, keeping space between himself and Flynn's energy covering Clark. If they were discovered, the whole thing would end before it had really begun.

Clark turned back toward the city, to an area packed with off-campus student housing for one of the local universities. It was a crisp autumn weeknight, but kids were still moving about, some jogging, some walking to and from local restaurants. There was a blond girl jogging, wearing earbuds and outfitted for the cold evening.

Clark turned down the same road she did. He drove around the block once, then backed into an alleyway ahead of where the girl's run would take her.

Merc parked and waited. The woman ran past them, then slowed from a jog to a walk, eventually stopping at the alleyway. She turned to face the dark corridor. This was worse than watching the heroine of a horror movie do the very thing the entire audience was screaming at her to not do.

She walked into the alley.

A minute later, Clark drove out of the alley with a passenger in his back seat. When Merc pulled forward to follow them, he noticed a faint blue light in the alley; the girl's phone had been left on the ground.

Liege had been clear in the orders he'd given the two of them: do not interfere. Follow and observe only. Merc knew the reasoning behind the order— they couldn't take down this module of Omni criminals if they didn't know where these stolen girls were being taken. And since the Omnis likely had several operators like Clark in use, they needed to know more about what was happening.

It helped to think that Liege believed the women were being pulled into a program like the one that had changed Merc and the team. Liege thought the Omnis were modifying these women to enter into some sort of service for the Omnis. Or to further their knowledge of how the latest nano modifications affected females.

What Merc most feared was that it was only a short leap from modifying females to modifying pregnant women—or even their living fetuses. Or the very worst—feeding them to the ghouls.

He hated the Omnis with a passion that couldn't be overstated. Liege was forever trying to convince him not all Omnis were bad, but as far as Merc was concerned, the only good Omni was a dead one.

Clark drove back through some older, more troubled neighborhoods. A young woman wearing a thin hoodie instead of a coat was walking from a corner store, carrying two bags of groceries. Clark's car slowed then stopped. Merc saw Clark lean across the passenger seat to talk to the woman. She shook her head at first, then went still. She set her groceries on the sidewalk and got inside Clark's car.

Shit. How many women was he going to take tonight? Merc and Acier followed Clark back to the parking garage above the Hyperloop depot. Clark got out of the car and escorted the blond into the office building. Acier followed them.

*Liege,* Merc said via their mental link, *Clark has two females. He's using Flynn's energy to entrance them.*

*Describe them,* Liege said.

*They're both young. Early twenties, if that. The one he's taking down to the Hyperloop is blond. Acier is going with her. I'm sticking with the one in his car—a brunette.*

*Copy that. Good luck to both of you.*

After a few minutes, Clark returned to his car. Merc kept his borrowed vehicle hidden from Clark, though in his trance state, it was unclear whether he'd be aware of anything around him. How long had Clark and Flynn been tag-teaming like this?

Merc followed Clark on a circuitous route into an industrial area full of unused brick warehouses. He had a bad feeling about what was coming. Clark got out of the car and made the girl in the back seat go with him. Flynn had put her in trance as well.

Merc parked around a corner. He picked up the short-barreled shotgun he'd set on the front passenger seat and slipped the strap over his neck and shoulder.

Liege was partial to knives, but Merc liked the shotgun Acier had built him. Over his opposite shoulder, he wore a leather belt with a dozen magazines filled with double-aught buckshot cartridges. At close range, a round from his shotgun would blow a nice chunk out of any Omnis he encountered.

Maybe even an Omni-controlled human.

He followed the two into the dark building. Most of the building's glass windows were gone, lying as sharp rubble that was mixed in with the crumbling pavement all around the building. The ground crunched as Merc walked to the entrance. The double metal doors hung askew at the entrance. He stepped inside, then let his senses scan the space.

Mutant senses were stronger than a regular human's, which he was grateful for now. Merc's vision, even in a dark environment like this, was as crisp as if he were wearing night-vision goggles. Nonetheless, he couldn't hear, see, or smell Clark, the girl, or anyone else. But he could feel their energy signatures. They were here somewhere. He went deeper inside the dark space, moving around concrete pillars and huge pieces of abandoned steel machinery.

Clark and the girl weren't alone in here. There were others, too. The ghouls. Damn. At least a half-dozen of them hiding, waiting, stalking him.

Merc went back to the entrance. He sure as hell wasn't collecting heads tonight. And he didn't have vials for blood draws. He was going to take a stand just outside the entrance, pick them off as they came outside.

Clark came out of the warehouse, holding his captive's arm as he kept her in front of him. He smiled at Merc.

"Good to see you again, old friend," Clark said. It was his mouth moving, his voice, but not him speaking. "Still as serious as ever, I see."

"Flynn. What are you doing? Leave Clark and the girl alone."

Clark shook his head. "You and Liege's Legion are so uptight with the changes we underwent. You're all still trying to be human, forcing yourselves to live by the old rules. Lighten up, man. Accept what you are —a monster. You aren't shackled anymore. You're absolutely free. Enjoy it. I am." He yanked the girl's arm.

The trance she was in wasn't comprehensive—she was still aware of her surroundings. It was just a behavior-limiting compulsion to keep her from running or screaming. Merc could feel her terror. She was so pretty, so young, and so afraid.

Merc shared his situation with Liege, using Guerre's nonverbal technique for communication in which he gave Liege access to everything Merc himself knew about his situation without slowing himself down by using words. Killing Clark was not optimal because Flynn would just jump into a new patsy, and it would take time for them to find out who he was using.

Liege didn't hesitate. *Take him out. Save the girl.*

Merc raised his shotgun, but before he could shoot, the deviants burst from the warehouse, spilling around Clark and the girl but focusing on Merc.

"You can take Clark out," Flynn said, speaking from Clark's mouth, "but you know as soon as you do my friends here will shred the girl." Clark laughed as he licked a corner of his mouth. "What to do. What to do."

Clark put the girl in the back seat. Waiting to be sure she was out of range, Merc took the shot as soon as Clark straightened. It hit a deviant who'd leapt in front of him. Everything broke loose then. Merc had to focus on the monsters charging him. He dropped several of them, but not before Clark got away.

More of the monsters spilled out of the empty warehouse on the other side of the alley. Merc emptied his magazine, ejected it, replaced it, and got two more shots off before they overtook him, forcing him to switch to hand-to-hand combat. Besides their razor-sharp nails, those fuckers had fangs. He used Liege's recent trick of projecting an image of himself onto a couple of the beasts, confusing them, leading them to attack each other. When no more came at him, he picked up his empty magazine and jogged around the corner to the car he stole...the unusable car. Deviants had stomped all over its roof and hood, wrecking it.

Merc hurried out to the road. He was going to have to take another vehicle. He jogged along the wayside as he waited for a car to come by. Running wasn't going to get him where needed to be, but action was better than inaction while he waited for a ride. After a couple of miles, a truck came along. Merc compelled it to stop and forced its driver out. He wiped the driver's memory of him and the carjacking, then hurried down the road, on the trail of Clark, Flynn, and the girl's energy signatures, which he could follow like a dog on a scent.

Flynn's energy had distinctive essences. It was sweet and sour and slightly rancid. Unique to him, but then, every energy signature was unique to its owner, more so than any other biometric measurement.

Merc drove out of town, following Flynn to farmland outside of town. He drove until the road switched to dirt. No streetlights brightened the way. Farmhouses were few and far between out here. There was an area of dense forest, and beyond that, a field of drying corn that hadn't yet been harvested.

She was in there. He could feel the girl's energy. Flynn's too, though it wasn't as strong. He'd left the girl here. Merc parked and went into the cornfield. A cold breeze rustled the brittle leaves.

He almost tripped over the girl in his rush. She was lying on her back, staring up at the starry sky, her face frozen in terror. Her clothes had been slashed open. Clark had ejaculated all over her. Though it was Clark's semen, it was Flynn's ecstasy Merc felt.

This was the medical trials all over again. Flynn had brutalized too many women to count, leaving their bodies for Liege's team to discover.

Merc held his hands over the girl's body, testing her life force, which was too weak to sense. *Guerre. I need you. Help me help her. Her body's still warm.*

*Put your hand on her left shoulder.*

Merc did that, flattening his palm to her skin. Guerre's healing heat came through Merc's palm. Light glowed from the energy Guerre was sending into the girl. Merc could feel it slipping in, through, and around the girl, but it had no effect. He felt Guerre begin to pull back.

*No. Don't stop. You have to save her.*

*I can't, Merc. She's gone. Her spirit is no longer in her body.*

*Guerre. Just do it.* Merc's hand went cold as the light ended.

*I'm sorry,* Guerre said.

No. Merc sat back on his heels. The breeze chilled the tears on his face. He tried to straighten the girl's clothes, but there wasn't much left to work with. He drew his hand over her face, easing the frozen look of terror from her features. There was no visible wound that had been a clear cause of death, but that's how it was with Flynn. Rape and terror were his signature techniques. The girl had probably had a heart attack.

Merc remembered finding corpses like these all over the jungle where their training camps had been. The villagers chalked it up to various superstitions being visited upon them. Flynn was the embodiment of Satan.

None of the mutants who shared their strain of modifications had the ability to feel sexual satiation. They could orgasm, but it brought no relief or joy. Flynn had long found satisfaction in the intense fear he generated in his victims, but now, it seemed he'd also found a way of enjoying sex—by absorbing what the man he possessed was feeling.

It was a new and particularly devastating form of torture that had to end.

Merc forced himself to his feet. He'd wanted so badly to save this one, but he'd failed. Again. The cornstalks slapped him in the face as he stumbled away from her. How long before her body would be found? The carrion would eat her or harvesting equipment would chop her up first.

Her loved ones might never have answers.

She deserved better than that. He stopped and looked back at her, her body obscured by the desiccated cornstalks. A primal scream ripped from his throat. He spread his hands wide, his palms up, his fingers open and straining. A burst of energy broke from him, blasting into the field, bending the cornstalks to the ground, creating a huge circle around the girl.

They couldn't help but find her now.

ACIER GOT onto the same Hyperloop pod as Flynn's girl. Her trance was heavy. He knew she wasn't aware of being on the pod in the secret Hyperloop tunnels. She fastened her seatbelt, then calmly waited, her hands on her lap, her eyes staring straight forward.

He thought of redirecting the pod to a different depot, taking her where the Omnis couldn't get her, and then returning her to her home.

But he couldn't do that.

She was only one female of hundreds—perhaps thousands—going missing from the human world. He could save the one, but then he'd not be able to save the many.

Acier got out of his seat and went to kneel in front of the girl. He took her hands and looked into her vacant eyes, trying to break through the trance that held her.

He slipped into her mind, feeling for the edges of her reality and the one Flynn imposed. The line was there, but holding it was no easy task.

Each time he touched it, Flynn's energy pushed

him away. Acier made his energy feel like hers so that it seemed she was resisting Flynn's control. Inside her mind space, Acier left her a message.

*I will come for you. I will come for all of you. When you can, when you surface, call my name. Acier. Just in your mind so no one hears. I need to know where they take you, where you end up. Remember, call my name. Acier. Acier. Acier. Remember it. Acier. Say it to me so I know you know it.*

"Acier." Her voice was sweet.

Screw Liege. Maybe they couldn't save any of the humans the Omnis were taking, but he could save this one.

*No, you can't,* Liege said. *Stay the course. Let her lead us to the rest of them.*

*Fuck you, Liege.*

*Yeah. I am fucked. We all are. Stick to the mission.*

The pod came to a stop at its destination—the depot under the Denver airport. Acier hid himself as the doors opened. He followed the girl out of the pod and up into the main terminal. She moved with purpose toward an exit. Acier kept pace with her until a flood of people widened the gap between her and him, more and more people clogging his way.

Acier felt for the girl's energy signature, but it was suppressed by Flynn's. That would still have been enough to let him tail her, but Flynn spread his energy among dozens of blonds milling around him.

When Acier pushed free of the crowd, the girl was gone.

Fury whipped through him, sucking energy from

all around, funneling it into a shock wave that sent a surge of power a hundred feet around him, blanking out arrival and departure screens, stopping baggage belts, and darkening lights.

What the fuck good were all his enhanced skills if he couldn't keep track of one regular girl?

## 4

———

Summer sat in her old Subaru wagon an extra few minutes in the garden center's parking lot. It had taken the entire short drive from her studio apartment to the office for it to warm up that morning. She sipped her coffee, which was still hot, in no hurry to step out into the crisp October air.

She loved her job—or rather, she loved what she did for a living, just not where she did it. A change was coming. She could feel it, and that alternately excited and terrified her.

After taking her last sip of coffee, she left her steel cup in its holder and got out. A hard frost blanketed everything in a sparkly sheen. She wrapped her scarf another time around her so it covered half of her face then grabbed her messenger bag and went to the side door of the shop.

As soon as she stepped inside, she heard shouting from the direction of the offices. Dread slipped through her. Not again. Mornings that started with visits from her boss's partner were never good. And there were too many of those days lately.

It was clear the bosses were upset, but why? Business the last two quarters had been up significantly over last year.

Summer caught the eye of one of the sales floor staff. Jada waved her over. "Set your stuff down in here and help me water the ferns," she said. "It'll keep us out of the way until the dogs of war are done fighting. I don't like running into their partner."

Summer set her coat, hat, scarf, gloves, and messenger bag down. "Me either. They sound especially upset today. I wonder why?"

"Something about quotas and missed delivery expectations, but honestly, I'm trying not to listen. Don't want to be called to a witness stand."

Summer chuckled, but it wasn't really funny—Jada's fear felt like a very real possibility. She picked up a water sprayer and started a row over from her friend.

"Just stay out of sight," Jada said. "You're never yourself when Brett's here."

Summer had no problem complying with that suggestion. She disliked the Briscoes' business partner with an intensity she'd never felt for anyone else.

After a while, things went quiet. Summer spent a few more minutes tending some houseplants in the small greenhouse attached to the retail shop, her ears straining for more sounds coming from the office area. A half-hour passed without any new arguments.

Deciding it was safe to go to her office, she gathered up her things and left the greenhouse for the shop—just in time to run into Brett Flynn. She would have scurried back to the greenhouse, but it was too late—he'd already seen her.

Brett looked like a Scandinavian athlete. Tall and broad-shouldered, with blond, straight hair and blue eyes, he was the sort of man many women fell for. And perhaps Summer might have, had there been any humanity at all in his eyes.

She glared at Douglas and Clark Briscoe, father and son—owners of Briscoe's Garden and Landscape Design Center. Both were tense. Clark had scratches on his neck and face. He held a wad of tissues to his nose. She looked at Brett, wondering if their meeting had gotten physical—or were those injuries left over from one of Clark's infamous bar fights? If it was from Brett, why would the Briscoes be in a partnership with such a thug?

Brett paused in front of her, blocking her way. "Hello, Summer." He tilted his head to the right then the left, assessing her, his eyes digging into hers.

Every instinct Summer possessed urged her to hurry past him—just get away fast. She didn't, though. Maybe because she was curious about what was going on. If the business hadn't met some expected sales goal, did that mean Brett was going to take things over? She could never work for him. Perhaps that had been the change she'd felt coming.

Brett stepped closer to her. "I'm always surprised by how beautiful you are." He stroked the backs of his fingers down her cheek and neck. Summer jerked back before he could move his hand lower. He produced a card and handed it to her. "If you ever decide you'd like to have dinner with a man who is dependable, call me."

Summer shot Clark a glance, not entirely surprised her ex didn't jump to her defense; he'd never had much of a spine. She adjusted her coat so she could take the card, which she ripped in half and dropped to the floor. "I don't have dinner with bullies."

Brett's eyes widened, then he leaned his head back and barked a sharp laugh. He looked back at Clark and his dad. "She has more balls than either of you."

Summer gritted her teeth when his focus settled on her again. His eyes were cold as he bent over and picked up the torn pieces, dropping them into the waste bin at the cashier's station. "This one we keep." He glanced over his shoulder to the Briscoes. "Read me?"

Douglas nodded.

Brett stared into her eyes. Summer felt a strange sensation; he'd invaded her physical space earlier, crowding close to her, but this feeling was more than that.

"I'll pick you up at six on Friday," Brett said.

Summer had no desire to go out with him, but for some reason, she couldn't say no. Still, she tried to sidestep his invitation. "I'll be working late tonight."

"Not Friday, you aren't."

"Then pick me up here at seven."

"I'll pick you up at your apartment." Brett's smile was frosty. "Surprised I know where you live? Don't be. You're my employee."

Brett left the shop. It took Summer a long moment to shake off the weird pall that overcame her. Why hadn't she told Brett what he could do with his dinner invitation?

She glared at Clark and his dad. "That was unacceptable. If this is a new normal, I'm quitting."

Douglas sent his son a glare. "There's no reason to expect it will ever happen again. Isn't that so, Clark?"

Clark pulled the wad of white tissues from his nose and looked at the red stain on it. "Yeah. I'll take care of it. Sorry, Sum. Just go out with him. Keep him happy. I need a little time."

"Time for what?" Summer asked.

"To turn things around," Clark said.

LIEGE FOLLOWED Summer from the garden center to a restaurant off the main road through town. He'd been trailing her all week, trying to figure out which side of this war she was on.

She'd filled his mind ever since the Matchmaker

had pointed her out. She was at the epicenter of whatever Flynn had going on—the bastard had been at the garden center earlier that day. He'd hidden his energy well. He was getting stronger. Liege hadn't felt him until he'd gotten near the woman. Liege had broken every speed limit on his drive into town after that. Good thing he could evade cops; they'd only slow him down.

Unfortunately, Flynn had already left by the time Liege got to the garden center. The woman was flustered, her aura dotted with spots of gray—the putrid touch of Flynn's energy. Liege had stood inside Summer's small office, only feet from her. He'd tried to cleanse the taint Flynn had left, but it was entrenched. It would take more than one cleansing session to rid her of it.

*Don't mess with the regulars.* Liege's core tenet whispered through his mind. He ignored it. He wasn't messing with her so much as keeping another mutant from messing with her. Not at all the same thing.

And now here he was, watching her go into a restaurant. An unfamiliar stab of jealousy spiked through him at the thought that she might be meeting a date for dinner. That brought him up short.

Jealousy. It was a vile human emotion rich in destructive feelings. A weakness. He couldn't be jealous of her. He was a mutant. By the very definition of his modified existence, he couldn't feel lust or desire—it had been architected out of his wiring. He and his men had been turned into super soldiers, capable of being nearly invisible to human eyes, able to infiltrate any building, tail any enemy, eradicate any threat. Their libido had been sacrificed in the same rewiring of their neural networks that gave them their enhanced skills, making them virtual eunuchs.

So how could he be feeling what he was? And if he was really uptight about it, he should just slip into her mind and find out the truth.

He got out of his car, intending to follow her into the restaurant. Another woman hurried over to her in the parking lot. They hugged. They were about to go inside when a third woman called out to them from a few cars away.

Liege knew her voice, knew who she was before he ever looked at her. He should have felt her energy, but he'd been absolutely consumed with his focus on Summer.

He watched as his daughter joined Summer and her friend, exchanging hugs and laughter. They were having dinner again. Was this a weekly thing for them?

Liege watched them enter the restaurant. He stood outside for a long time. The cold October air cut through him. He shoved his hands in the pockets of his wool peacoat. Not only did he have a ghost relationship with his daughter, but now, apparently, he was going to have one with his woman.

His life was all kinds of awesome.

SUMMER WALKED across the icy parking lot of a suburban steakhouse and pub, glad she and her friends had agreed to meet for their weekly dinner someplace outside the crowded area of Old Town.

Their meetup was one bright spot in a day that had started bad and ended worse. Summer couldn't help wonder what Flynn had meant by his "this one we keep" comment. Were the Briscoes going to have to scale back their operations? Did that mean she would be demoted from her current position as landscape designer—albeit a junior one—to sales staff?

She sighed. Though she'd been in her current job for a long time, it had been a struggle to prove her worth every day. She'd dated Clark while they were both in the horticulture program at the university. He seemed different then, though her girlfriends had never really liked him. He'd gotten her hired at his father's nursery center after their graduation. Unfortunately, it turned out that instead of the promised job of a junior designer, her position was in reality more as Clark's gopher, doing the jobs he wasn't interested in or taking over the implementation phase of jobs he'd designed. Sometimes, and these hurt the most, she was handed landscaping jobs that were too complex for Clark, which she was expected to design *on his behalf.*

She'd gotten some industry experience in her current situation, but maybe it was time to move on. Especially if Flynn was going to be more involved in day-to-day operations of the garden center.

The problem was, thanks to her non-compete agreement, a new position meant moving to a design center a minimum of sixty miles away, making her commute horrendous, at least for the two years of the non-compete period. Her car could barely make it across town—there was no way it could manage a lengthy commute.

Warm air blasted over her as she stepped into the pub. It was a small, dimly lit space with a central bar and tall booths around the perimeter. The wood floors, booths, and paneling were stained dark, meant to simulate the decor of an old English pub. The wait staff and bartenders knew the three of them, since the pub was one of a handful of their preferred weekly meetup spots.

She took her coat off and stacked it in a pile next to Ashlyn then settled in the booth next to Kiera. They placed their orders with the waitress. Though the restaurant billed itself as a steakhouse, it also had tasty vegan and vegetarian options, so it was the perfect spot for the three of them.

Their waitress returned a few minutes later with a tropical delight for Ash, a glass of burgundy for Summer, and unsweetened iced tea for Kiera.

Summer nearly snatched the wine glass from the waitress. If ever a day needed an after-work drink, this one certainly did.

Ash and Kiera exchanged glances. "Rough day?" Ash asked.

Summer nodded, then told them about her run-in with her boss's business partner.

"He *touched* you?" Kiera was furious. "What did your boss do?"

Summer stared at her drink. She knew what her friends were going to say. "Nothing. So I told him that if that was a new normal, I was out of there. He said it wouldn't be." She shot a glance at Ash and Kiera. "Clark had a bloodied nose when he came out of the meeting. I was terrified."

"You've got to leave," Kiera said.

"Yeah, babe," Ash said, "the writing's on the wall. They're in bed with some bad mofos."

"I wouldn't even go back," Kiera said. "Just call them in the morning and say that after what happened yesterday, you've decided to resign."

"They have me by the short hairs with that non-compete," Summer said.

"So leave your short hairs with them and get your ass to safety," Ash said. "They aren't looking out for you. Or even for their business, not with a business partner like that one. He's probably from some Mafia family."

"Can a Swede be in the Mafia?" Summer asked.

"Yes," Kiera said. "Look, your non-compete may have been invalidated by that creep's unwanted advances and their failure to protect you. But even if it is still viable, sixty miles is not that far. People commute from here to Denver every day."

Summer took another sip of her wine. "It's almost

winter, the worst time of the year to go looking for a job in my field."

"Maybe it is, maybe it isn't," Ash said. "But you should at least try."

"Briscoe won't give me a good reference."

"Right. He isn't going to now, and it's unlikely he will a year from now, so cut your losses and move on," Kiera said.

Summer held Kiera's gaze. Kiera was the calm one of their threesome. Something about Summer's situation fired off Kiera's substantial protective instincts, which made Summer much more nervous about returning to work the next day.

Kiera wrapped an arm around Summer's shoulders and hugged her. "I'm sorry. It's just that I fight this fight every day. Women don't see the danger around them. We're too trusting. We yearn for peace. We want to believe in the authority figures around us. For some reason, we don't fight as hard for ourselves as we do for those who abuse us." Her warm brown eyes connected with Summer's. "It's a pattern I know too well."

Summer knew Kiera wasn't exaggerating her situation. She'd built her career around helping at-risk women restart their lives and currently ran a halfway home for women in difficult spots in their lives.

"All right, you two. I will." Summer smiled at her friends. "But I can't quit until I have something else. I'll put some feelers out and get my résumé updated."

Their meals came, giving them a welcome a break from the topic.

"I've been dealing with something odd too," Kiera said. "I keep having women show up at my center under strange circumstances."

"Like what?" Ash asked.

"I always accept drop-ins. No one has to have an appointment to come to the center. But lately I've had women come who can't remember anything after arriving at the bus stop in town. They're often brought by a black SUV. They don't even remember the driver or the ride from the bus stop to my place."

"That's weird," Summer said.

"Were they drugged?" Ash asked.

"No. I've taken them to the hospital to be checked over. They're fine. Just dopey, like they just woke up."

"That is odd," Ash said. "Have you talked to the cops?"

"No. Because there hasn't been any crime committed."

They went silent for a little while as they thought through the implications of what might be happening at Kiera's center.

A cold wind came in from the front door. Summer looked over to see who was holding the door open and why. A tall man, reed-thin, with wild red hair, was staring at her.

The hostess asked him to come inside or stay outside, but either way, close the door. He came inside. He stumbled toward their table, but turned abruptly to sit at the bar. Still, he stared at Summer.

Ash leaned forward and whispered, "What's that guy's problem?"

Summer shook her head, returning her focus to her meal. "This day couldn't get any weirder." She shifted slightly so that she didn't see the man even from the corner of her eye. Kiera continued to monitor him, and when her eyes widened, Summer knew the guy was doing something else crazy.

A long shadow fell across their table. "It's you!"

Summer looked up. The odd guy was standing over them. He had a fist raised in the air. "It's you! You're the one they're looking for. You're the next to go. Beware. Beware!"

Summer wanted to run from the table, but the man was blocking her way. He grabbed her arm, yanking her up to her feet as he shoved his face close to hers. Summer pushed at his chest. Before things could get worse, two men from the bar knocked him down. One kept a knee on his spine while the other checked him for weapons. She slumped back into the booth.

It was a relief that he wasn't armed, but even pinned on the ground, the man was spewing a barely intelligible warning about the end of the world and kept screaming that she was the cause of the end.

Cops came in, wrangled the guy to his feet, and took him out of the restaurant. One of the cops then started over to their table. He stopped short, stared into the middle space between them, then changed directions and followed his peers out of the restaurant.

Summer realized she was squashing Kiera, who had an arm around her shoulders and her other hand holding her wrist. Summer scooted away a bit, but still stayed close to her friend, feeling terribly unnerved. Why had that guy singled her out? What was it he was trying to communicate? A warning?

The restaurant's manager came over to their table, an apologetic look on his face. "I'm so sorry for that. Are you all right, ladies?"

Summer checked her friends' shocked faces. They all nodded. "Have you seen him before?" she asked.

"No. He's never been in here before, as far as I know. He didn't hurt you, did he?"

Summer rubbed the arm he'd grabbed. "No. I'm fine. We're fine."

"Well, I'll be comping your meals tonight. Again, I am so sorry that happened."

Summer shook her head. "That's not necessary. Really. It wasn't your fault that he did that."

"Still, it's important to me that our clients know we take their comfort and safety seriously. It's the least we can do."

After the manager left, Ash let out a nervous giggle. "We've broken the code to ladies' night, my friends."

"How's that?" Kiera frowned.

"Hire a clown to come in and rattle some cages,

then boom! Free dinner!"

"Not even funny." Summer rubbed her arms. "I don't like clowns."

The interruption had stolen her appetite. For the next half-hour, she picked at her food and made small talk. The manager kept his word about comping their meal, but they left the waitress her usual tip.

Frosty air surrounded them when they stepped outside. After quick hugs goodbye, Summer made her way to her car, wishing its heat worked better than it did. She unlocked it, got inside, and quickly locked it again. Frost had formed on the windshield, which was odd. It was a crisp night, but not bitterly cold. Well, there was nothing for it. She was going to have to sit and wait for it to defrost before she could go anywhere. She contemplated getting out to scrape it off, but that guy's weird rant had her rattled. It was safer to stay in the locked car.

For a few minutes, to distract herself while her car was warming up, she flipped through her social media. When she looked up, the redheaded man was there, standing in her headlights.

"They're coming for you. Be warned. You are the next one."

Summer's instinct took over. She put her fist on her horn and let its scream rip into the night.

He came around to her window and banged his fist on it then leaned close—so close his warm breath clouded the window. "Remember this. Liege is the only one you can trust. Liege. Remember his name."

Summer saw the door to the restaurant open as two men came running out. The man saw them too. He pointed at her and shouted, "Remember. Liege." Then he disappeared. It wasn't like he took off. No, he actually just disappeared. One second, he was standing at her door, the next, no one was there.

The guys from the bar showed up. She got out of her car, frantically looking around.

"You are all right, miss?" one of the men asked.

"He was here. That guy from the bar." Summer felt a warm moisture on her face and realized she was crying. She swiped her fist against her cheeks. The white cloud of her breath was obscuring her vision. The men were looking around. When they focused on her again, they shook their heads.

"Sorry. Really. He's not here now," one of the men said.

"Look, we can call the cops again. Or call a ride for you," the other guy said.

Summer drew a shaky breath and released it slowly. "No. It's okay. He is gone." She stepped to her car. "I'm just going to get home. I'm good. He was on foot. He can't follow me home. Thanks. I appreciate your fast response. Go back inside before you freeze."

The long delay had at least let her car warm up. The men stood by as she backed up and drove out of the parking lot. God, what had happened? She'd seen a man disappear—right in front of her eyes. Poof! Gone. He didn't walk away. He'd flashed out.

Her drive from the restaurant to her apartment

wasn't long. She went slowly up the alleyway, using the high beams to give the area a good once-over. No flame-haired man anywhere, no furtive figures dashing about.

She pulled into her spot and moved quickly from her car, up the stairs, and into her apartment. She locked the door, then leaned against it.

She kept the lights off for a minute as she peeked outside to see if she'd been followed. Ten minutes passed before she took her first easy breath.

She flipped the lights on. Standing in place, she swept a glance around her studio apartment. She couldn't see that anyone was there. It didn't feel as if anyone was there. But just to be safe, she made a physical pass around her place to be sure. No one under the four-poster bed. No one under the futon. No one in the tiny kitchen, or the big closet or the bathroom.

Finally, she pulled her coat off, hung her keys up, then took a seat at one of the three barstools at the kitchen's peninsula counter and let her mind slip back through all that had happened that night.

She'd had one glass of wine. One. It wasn't like that had messed with her head. Several people had seen that redheaded man, so she knew he was real.

But how had he disappeared?

Maybe he was a magician and had played a trick on her.

Sick people were everywhere.

# 5

----

Liege felt his bed dip as Bastion plopped down on it. He kept his eyes closed, refusing to acknowledge his friend.

"Good morning, *mon capitaine*," Bastion said in his unique patois of English and French. He took a loud slurp from a cup of coffee.

The coffee tempted Liege to rouse. The other three were in his room too. So much for sleeping in.

"What time is it?" Liege asked, keeping his arm folded over his eyes.

"It is now," Bastion said, whose cheery nonsense always made him seem like a big puppy to Liege.

"Two thirty," Guerre said.

"In the afternoon. Time to tell us about your female," Acier said.

"And we have to talk about last night," Merc said.

That roused Liege. He unfolded his arm from his

eyes then squinted at the light in the room. His fucking friends had opened the drapes.

Merc's experience with Flynn and Clark had kept Liege up long into the night. He wasn't sure Merc would get back to the fort in a timely way. Sometimes, after similar incidents, they lost track of Merc for days.

It didn't help that Acier had followed the other female back to Colorado, only to lose her in a crowd at the airport.

Bastion slurped his coffee again. "*Oui. C'est vrai.* You never hide anyone from us, Liege. Until this female. Why do you shield her?"

Acier held up Summer's sweater. Liege grabbed it and stuffed it back under his pillows then threw the covers off. He stomped over to the chair where he'd left his jeans and pulled them on over his gray boxer briefs, zipping them but not fastening the top button. He walked barefoot from his room, through the two hallways, down the spiral stairs into the kitchen, the guys trailing behind him. The concrete floors would have been brutally cold if it weren't for their radiant heating.

He poured a cup from the coffee maker, then faced Merc and Acier. "About last night. We have to keep going. We'll save the ones we can, but we have to keep Flynn in our sights."

"We don't even save a quarter of the ones the Omnis take," Merc said.

"They aren't our objective," Liege said. "Any we

save are a benefit. We have to bring down the bigger machine."

"I don't care about the bigger machine," Merc said. "We can take it apart piece by piece until it can't stand on its own."

"There's more at stake than a few hundred civilians." Liege faced Merc.

"If those civilians don't matter, what does?" Merc countered.

"Keeping the modifications out of the general population. That's all that matters at the moment."

Merc shook his head. "That's fucked up."

"It is what it is." Liege met Merc's hard eyes. "We need the scientists the Omnis have taken. We need more fighters. We aren't equal to what has to be done as it is."

Bastion slurped his black brew again and winced. "This is disgusting," he said, taking Liege's focus off Merc.

Liege glared at him. "It's a custom blend. I buy it directly from the roaster locally. It's top-notch."

"And then you prepare it in this aberration of a machine. You could at least use your espresso machine."

"I like it already made when I wake up." He'd set it up before crashing last night, thinking he'd get up around noon. In all fairness, it was a little overdone. "Make yourself an espresso if you don't feel like suffering."

"Quit bitching, Bastion," Merc snapped. "You always have to be the center of attention."

Bastion gave the Aussie a feral grin. "At least I'm not a drama queen."

Merc scoffed. "You are the queen of drama queens."

Bastion's eyes narrowed, and he slammed his coffee on the counter. "Who are you calling a queen?"

"How about you two go play outside and let the adults talk?" Guerre suggested.

"Forget it." Bastion waved his hand. "I get grouchy when premium coffee is mistreated like this." He shrugged. "And besides, maybe I am a queen. I have yet to try it."

"Yet to try it, shit," Merc mumbled. "You were born to it."

"About the woman?" Acier prompted.

Liege met their weapon-smith's dark blue eyes. What was empty in him was empty in all of them. So much had been taken from them. The lives they were living. Their futures. Their humanity.

The coffee helped focus Liege. Ever since the medical trials, he and his men had a twenty-four-seven connection, though they'd all developed the ability to compartmentalize parts of their thoughts. Liege had obviously failed to do that sufficiently with Summer; his attraction to her had come without warning.

"I saw the Matchmaker," Liege said, staring into the black liquid in his mug.

"*Non*," Bastion hissed. "When?"

"That night I was supposed to meet you guys at the bar," Liege said. "About a week ago. I saw him again outside the place where my intended female works—at the Briscoes' garden center."

"Shit," Merc growled.

"What did he look like?" Acier asked.

"It was just a projection of him. But he was tall, skinny, red-haired. His eyes glowed red."

"So it's true," Acier said.

"Maybe." Liege shrugged. "Or maybe the Omnis have learned how to use the legend against us. I don't know that I believe the woman is my lifemate."

"You saw her?" Guerre asked.

Liege nodded. "When I ditched you that night. She was at a restaurant just down the street. She's a friend of my daughter's. They meet up for dinner on Wednesdays." He looked at each of his men. "She fits the Aryan profile of the perfect race the Omnis seem to prefer. She's either already in bed with them or is slated to become one of their victims."

"Fuck that, Liege," Merc said. "Get her out of there."

Liege sipped his burned coffee. "The Matchmaker's pairing is a death sentence for the human female. If she's really my lifemate, then I can't connect with her—I can't be why she dies. I don't want to love her and lose her. I've come to wonder whose side the Matchmaker's really on. He never pairs Omni fighters with their mates."

Guerre switched his coffee out for a beer. "How does he know who to pair up, anyway? How does he find our mates when we can't even find them ourselves?"

"Right." Liege nodded. "How does he do it? And does he do it to weaken us? If we resist his edicts, he ends us."

"But if we give in, he ends our mates," Guerre finished for him.

"So maybe the Matchmaker is an Omni," Acier said.

"Are there any couples who've survived the curse?" Guerre asked.

"There are a few whose ends haven't been met yet," Liege said. "I don't know how much time they're given to be together. Honestly, I thought it was more urban myth than truth, until I saw him myself—and saw the woman he meant for me."

"How did you know she was yours?" Merc asked.

"She was covered in a white light."

Guerre hissed in a sharp breath.

"Maybe that was a new Omni trick," Bastion suggested. "A diversion, something to distract you so you get off Flynn's trail."

Liege nodded. "I'm still considering that possibility, especially given the fact that she works where she does. But what if it's real? What if there's some energetic synergy that the Matchmaker can see? What if some Omni operative can see it too? What if it's not the Matchmaker's curse, but an Omni mission to deprive us of our lifemates?"

"Same outcome," Merc said. "Your girl and your heart both die."

Acier straightened. "If she's your true lifemate, then we'll guard her with our lives."

"It's true." Bastion slapped a hand over his heart. "Her life before ours."

Merc and Guerre nodded.

The air left Liege's lungs in a sharp exhalation. "I almost don't want to find out."

"But you must," Bastion said. "We have learned to accept what we are, but what we are isn't what we were made for. She could give you back what was taken from you."

Acier agreed. "And if you've found your lifemate, then it's possible we will too."

Liege sipped his now-cold coffee. He walked away from the guys and went to look out the window. It was just the beginning of October, but already the sky had taken on that gray autumn tint. Looked like a storm was rolling in. The prairie surrounding the fort was dry and barren, desperately in need of a good rain. Or snow. The sun was still shining south of the fort, making the northern sky look black and the blooms of the rabbitbrush glow a bright yellow.

It would be safer—for him, for Summer—if he kept away from her.

Guerre knew his thoughts. "If you resist, you will die. We can't afford to lose you."

"And if I give in, she dies," Liege said.

A thought hit him as he looked out the big kitchen window: he could hire Summer to design the fort's landscape. It would bring them into close contact, satisfying the Matchmaker. And it would give Liege time to read her, time to see if she was an enemy or not.

"I like it," Acier said, responding to Liege's unspoken idea. "What's her name?"

"Summer Coltrane. She's a landscape designer at the garden center. It could work."

Merc nodded. "Bring her here. We can keep her safe."

"Maybe we can see what it is about her energy that works with yours," Bastion said. "And then we can use that for our own benefit."

Liege narrowed his eyes. "She's not to be an experiment."

"Of course not," Guerre said, "but if we can figure it out, we can share it with the rest of the Legion. If we can get to them before the Matchmaker does, we might subvert his curse. But how are you going to handle your daughter?"

"Yeah. Kiera thinks you're dead," Merc said.

Liege frowned. Connecting with Summer presented nothing but problems. He'd stayed away from his daughter ever since he got out of the training camps. He'd been declared dead by the Army long before that. And given who and what he now was, it was safer for her to continue to know nothing about him. "I may have to tell her."

"She won't understand. Who does?" Acier said. "If it weren't for you freaks, I wouldn't still feel human." He looked at Bastion. "And I'm fairly certain one of us already isn't human."

Bastion slapped a hand to his heart. "You wound me."

Acier laughed. "You could always keep your truth hidden from both females. It would be easier that way."

"But what if Summer is my lifemate?," Liege said. "That means I would have to maintain the ruse the rest of her life. Not an easy thing to do, even if, as a human, she dies long before I do."

The room went silent. Bastion stared at the wall. "I don't want to live forever. At least not alone."

"Outliving our children and grands and greats." Merc shook his head. "I don't want forever either."

"I don't think living forever is something we have to worry about," Liege said. "I'm more concerned that we live long enough to ensure a peaceful transition as life as transformed humans becomes widespread." He thought about his options for a moment. "I will reach out to her. But be warned that I don't yet know whose side she's on. Flynn's been hanging around the garden center where she works. His energy is darkening hers."

"Foiling his interests is always a win for us," Acier said.

"A better win would be to take him down," Merc said.

Liege nodded. "Agreed. And as soon as we know more of what the Omnis are up to with the civilians they're taking—and what his role in their schemes is, we're done with him."

"And in the meantime," Acier said, "connect with your woman and get her out of Flynn's reach. We've got your back."

Liege looked at Guerre. "How are things looking in the Omni silo?"

"It's crawling with Feds. They've cleared the Omnis out—and most of the civilians who lived there."

"Does it connect with the Hyperloop system?"

"Don't know yet. That place is huge. Far bigger than the Titan missile silo it was built on. An Omni leader named King used it for his base of operations. It's a big break. I need to spend more time there."

"Okay. Take Acier with you." Liege looked at Bastion and Merc, who didn't like being left behind. "All of you. Go figure out the lay of the land. It's rare we have an Omni stronghold ripped open for us."

## 6

Summer was still at work late that afternoon when Clark stepped into her office. She ignored him, keeping her focus on the project she was working on—merchandising for spring.

"Sum," Clark said.

She'd always hated the way he shortened her name. Funny—it didn't bother her a bit when her friends did that. "Yeah?" She didn't look away from her screen.

"You have to get ready for your date."

"I'm not going. I already canceled with Brett."

"No. You are going."

The tone in Clark's voice finally forced Summer to look at him. His face was tense. "What is it with you and him?" She leaned back in her seat. "And why does it fall to me to repair your bridges? And why is your face all scratched up? You have a fight with a bush?"

"Forget my face."

"I'd like to."

"I'm being serious, Sum. Dad and I need help. Brett's a partner. It's political. A game. We all have to play our parts."

"I don't. I'm only an employee, not a partner." Wasn't that the very same thing he'd thrown at her when she wanted more challenging assignments in their design shop? Or a raise? Or asked to go to some trade shows for their industry that he and his dad always attended?

"Look. I get it." Clark lifted his palms. "You're more important to us than we sometimes show."

"Uh-huh. Brett can find his own damned dates."

Something snapped in Clark. He pushed into her tiny office, grabbed her coat and messenger bag and shoved them at her as he yanked her arm, trying to drag her into the hallway. "I ask nothing of you. Ever. This I need you to do."

"Fine." She snagged her stuff, then went back into her office to sign off her computer and collect the rest of her things. "Fine. I'll do this. But this is a onetime exception."

"Whatever."

"If Brett even shows."

"He texted me that you canceled. I told him I would make sure you're there for your date. I got you an extra hour. Go home." He looked at his watch. "You don't have much time to get ready. He likes people to be punctual."

LIEGE TIGHTENED his seatbelt and kept his foot on the brake as he waited for the impact from the car behind him. It came with a sharp bang and pushed his vehicle a couple of feet farther down the turn lane. He put his big SUV in park then got out and glared at the blond woman behind him who was now standing next to her Subaru wagon, looking dazed and mortified.

Summer Coltrane.

If this were a normal day and a normal encounter, he'd try to put her nerves at ease with a smile or a joke.

But this wasn't a normal day. She was a potential enemy, and he'd orchestrated this accident.

Cars behind them honked, but he ignored them. It took a moment for them to realize the cause of the delay. Then, without further drama, they pulled around and made their turns from the next lane.

Summer's hands started flapping about like birds whose legs she held pinched in her fingers. "I didn't see you! I mean, I saw you, but I saw you make your turn. You were gone. You'd turned."

"Obviously, I hadn't."

Her eyes widened at the sound of his voice and probably the rest of him. Liege didn't try to hide himself from her this time. He had the same effect on many people when he showed his real self. He was tall, dark, big, and spoke in a rumbling baritone.

"Oh my God! I'm so sorry. Are you all right?" she asked.

He looked at her straight blond hair, watching the breeze finger through it. He didn't need the glow from the street lamp to see the freckles on her pale skin. Her eyes were a warm blue. Her brows and long eyelashes were darker than her hair, but still a tawny butterscotch. Her face was a nice oval shape. She wore no makeup, but a tinted balm gave her lips a faint pink glow.

He closed his eyes and breathed her in, connecting his energy with hers, trying to read her, setting hooks in her mind he could use later. She went quiet. The whole world around them went still and silent.

He was in her, a dark shadow looking for secrets.

Only there were none.

She was as pure inside as she appeared from the outside.

Soft hands took hold of his forearms. "I'm so sorry. You'd better sit down before you fall." She drew him down to the curb and knelt in front of him on the pavement.

He stared into her eyes, shocked at the wave of relief that washed through him upon finding she wasn't in lockstep with Brett Flynn. But he could smell Brett's energetic stink on her.

"I'm calling an ambulance." She pulled her phone from her pocket.

"No." He pushed her phone down. "I don't need an ambulance."

"You almost fainted."

He smiled at that. "Not even close." His gaze moved over her face. He asked, though he knew the answer from the scan he'd just completed, "Are you hurt?"

"No." She flapped her hands again. "Just shocky. I'm so sorry. I really didn't see you still there."

Of course she hadn't—he'd projected the illusion of his having already made his turn.

She stopped flapping and stared at him, frowning. "You seem so familiar."

"Do I? Must have one of those faces."

She shook her head. "There's nothing common about you, but I feel I've seen you before."

Liege had been right about her sensitivity—he'd felt her sensing him many times over the last couple of weeks. He longed to spend more time with her right now, but it was rush hour, and they were in the way.

"Let's just exchange our info and call it good." He stood and gave her a hand up, then gave her his insurance info, which used his current human alias: Sam Garrick. They took a pic of each other's info.

"Can you drive your car, or should we call someone for you and get a tow truck?" Liege asked.

She glanced back at her car with its wrecked bumper. "I think it'll be okay. I don't have far to go.

Oh my God! I'm late." She looked at the time on her phone. "Really late."

A car honked at them. The driver looked like he was going to try to squeeze past them in the turn lane they were clogging. Liege gave the driver a hard stare. The driver stopped, then backed up and went around them.

He and Summer swapped info.

"Thank you for being so nice about this," she said.

"We'll tell the cops and our insurance companies that it's my fault. I started to go but stopped."

Her eyes filled with tears. "No, it's my fault. I was behind you."

He reached out and gripped her arm. "You sure you're okay?" He sent her a wave of calm energy, helping to settle her. As soon as he touched her, he knew what she was late for—a date with Flynn.

She took a long breath and let it out slowly. Her shoulders relaxed. "Yeah, I'm good. Sorry for ruining your evening," she said.

"You didn't." He gave her a nod, then got into his SUV and made the turn that had started the whole encounter. He watched in his rearview mirror to make sure she was good. After a couple of blocks, she turned off.

Liege sent an illusion over his SUV, making it seem he was driving a white minivan. He followed her home, parking on the street instead of the narrow alley where her garage apartment was.

He shielded himself as he walked into her alleyway. A limo was parked out front of her apartment. Liege didn't need to send out energy feelers to discover who the car belonged to; its owner was standing beside the back passenger door, talking to Summer.

Flynn. Evil personified. His aura was gray and black. Some of it's darkness slipped into Summer's energy field, threading more gray into her shimmering aura. He was imposing a compulsion on her.

To do what?

Liege waited quietly at the corner, hiding himself from everyone, especially Flynn, as Summer jogged up the steps to her apartment.

Five minutes later, she came out wearing strappy black high-heeled sandals and a flowery, summery dress. Not at all seasonally appropriate. And no coat.

She'd been forced to go with Flynn. Liege slipped into her mind, causing her to pause on the bottom step of her staircase.

*Do you want to do this?* he asked.

*No.*

*Then don't. I'll deal with Flynn.*

*I don't want anyone hurt.*

Flynn noticed her hesitation. He sent a look around them, but his gaze never settled on Liege. A cold wind came down the alleyway, tossing the edges of Summer's skirt high over her thighs. Liege felt his body tighten.

*Get in the car and out of the weather. I'll be near if you need me.*

*Who are you?*

*A friend.*

Liege could feel the trance she was in. She had to fight for her own words. And though they'd spoken just a short while ago, she didn't recognize him. He wondered what Flynn's interest in her was. Did he know the Matchmaker had selected Summer for Liege?

Either way, Liege had no intention of letting Flynn harm her. Flynn, like all changed fighters, had no use for women or sexual liaisons of any sort. He just liked the energy of their fear. There was a real possibility that Flynn meant to do to her what he'd done to so many other unsuspecting females.

No way was Liege going to let that happen to Summer.

He followed them into Old Town. The limo let them out at a new, upscale restaurant. A truck ahead of Liege was about to park, but Liege sent the driver a compulsion to move on down the street, letting Liege slip into the empty spot outside the restaurant where he could wait. He didn't go inside. He didn't need to in order to monitor Summer. So far, she wasn't feeding Flynn her fear, which made Liege proud of her.

Liege closed his eyes and experienced Summer's date through her mind. Flynn put his hand on the table, palm up, waiting for her to set her hand in his. She didn't. Flynn's anger was barely contained. Liege felt the order he gave her to hold his hand, felt

Summer's resistance, felt her hand move against her own impulses to settle in Flynn's.

She looked at the menu. She was a vegan, Liege realized. Or maybe a vegetarian. There was only a house salad available for her to eat.

Flynn looked around the room. Liege knew he was checking to see if Liege had come to save his woman. So that answered his question from before. This whole show was a ruse to draw him out.

Flynn ordered for both of them without even consulting Summer. She didn't counter him—it seemed she couldn't at the moment.

She looked utterly miserable. Flynn ordered her to speak, but she still didn't. She was there in body but not in spirit. And holy hell, did she have some spirit.

Their meals arrived a few minutes later—big New York strips for both of them. Flynn dove into his steak. It was half gone before he realized that Summer wasn't eating hers. He ordered her to eat her supper.

Liege smiled. Compulsions were one thing, but when they butted up against the hard line of a personal belief, they could only go so far. No amount of forcing was going to make Summer eat that steak.

It was then that Flynn introduced pain into Summer's brain. Gentle and brief at first. Son of a bitch. Flynn knew Liege was near, monitoring Summer.

Summer rubbed her head.

"Eat and it will stop," Brett said in a soft voice.

"I don't eat meat," Summer replied.

"You'll do as I say."

Summer cried out, holding her hands to her head. Liege sent that pulse right back into Flynn's brain. His enemy jumped then laughed.

"So the game's on," Flynn said, grinning.

"What game?" Summer asked.

"I wasn't talking to you."

*Hurt her, and I will end you tonight,* Liege warned him.

*You've tried before and failed, many times. I wondered how long you would hide behind the woman.*

*You know better than to mess with the regulars.*

Flynn smiled. *I could kill everyone in here without a care in the world. It's you who wants to keep us hidden from the regulars.*

*Then go ahead and do it,* Liege suggested. *Out yourself and us. Start worldwide pandemonium.*

*Soon enough. Soon enough. Be patient, dear friend.* Flynn leaned back in his seat and sipped his wine, studying Summer over his glass. *Are you claiming this one? I find that interesting. Why this female? What is it about her that tempts you? Her white skin? Her beautiful flaxen hair? You've chosen well. She'd make a perfect Omni vessel. Perhaps that's why I like her too. I don't want you to soil her.*

*I'm coming in to get her. You will not make a scene.* Liege froze the entire restaurant as he entered, keeping them from seeing him take Summer. He shrugged out of his coat as he approached their table.

Flynn smiled at him and popped a bite of steak into his mouth, then began to choke on it. He stood up, holding his hands to his throat as Liege carried Summer out to his SUV.

Sometimes, in the heat of a crisis, even the changed forgot the special skills they had access to. Flynn dropped to his knees. Liege released the freeze he'd put on the occupants of the restaurant. Someone went over to Flynn as Liege backed out of his parking spot.

Summer remained in a sleeping trance the whole way back to her place. Liege carried her up the stairs and into her apartment. He set her on her bed, removed her sandals, then pulled the covers over her. He slipped into her mind and pushed Flynn out of it, freeing her from the bastard's grip. Liege blocked her memories of what happened tonight and transitioned her into a deep slumber.

He hated himself for violating his main tenet that the changed don't mess with the regulars, but he had no choice. She was in the thick of things, and whether she knew it or not, she needed his protection.

## 7

Summer stretched beneath the covers of her bed. The air was crisp in her apartment, but she was warm. In fact, she felt amazing. Rested, clear-minded. Her sleep had been the best she'd had in a long time.

She tossed the covers off and sat up, then froze. She was wearing one of her summer sundresses. She frowned, trying to remember why she was dressed as she was—and more importantly, why had she worn it to bed?

Brett Flynn. God. Clark had insisted she go out with him. She covered her eyes as she remembered trying to ditch Brett. Then her rush home. The accident and the tall, gorgeous Sam Garrick, whose SUV she rear-ended.

When she got home after that, Brett was already there, waiting for her in his limousine. After that, things got fuzzy. She thought he'd picked this dress for her. But she couldn't remember if he'd been in her apartment. Her memories were so scrambled.

They went to Old Town. A steakhouse. She remembered the steak she'd ordered. Why had she done that? He'd tried to force her to eat it. She couldn't. She just couldn't. Brett had gotten angry. Everything else after that was a blank.

Had he raped her? She did still have her underwear on—not that that was an indicator of anything, but rapists rarely redressed their victims. God, what had happened? Had she been roofied?

She crossed her arms and bent in half as she sat on the edge of the mattress. Oh my God. What if he had drugged her? What should she do?

She grabbed her phone from the nightstand and punched in Kiera's number.

"Hey you," Kiera said in her usual friendly way. So normal. Summer started crying. "Summer? Honey, what's up?"

"I think I was roofied last night."

"What? What happened? I didn't even know you were going out."

"Remember that creep who's one of the Briscoe's business partners that I told you about?"

"Yeah. You went out with him?"

"Yeah."

"What were you thinking?"

Summer put her hand over her mouth. The fight to not cry meant she also couldn't breathe. She got lightheaded before her body took things back over, forcing a gasp from her and freeing her tears.

"I'm on my way over. Keep talking to me."

"I'm so ashamed."

"I shouldn't have hollered. It's not your fault." Kiera paused. "How do you feel?"

"I felt great, until I saw that I was in bed in the outfit I wore out last night. He came in my apartment. He was here, and I don't remember anything."

"Okay. Look, I'm going to take you to the women's clinic. They have a sex-assault examiner on staff. They'll get you right in. You haven't showered, have you?"

"No."

"If you can wait, don't pee either. They'll need a urine sample. Don't brush your teeth. Stay exactly as you are. Go grab an outfit to change into after the exam. I'll make the call, then I'll be right there to pick you up."

"It's probably nothing, Kiera. Like I said, I felt fine until I realized there was a chunk of time I have no memory of."

"That right there is why we're doing this."

"But what if it's nothing?"

"Then we'll fucking celebrate the fact you weren't raped. There is no shame in this, Summer. The shame is his."

Summer started crying again. "I'm scared, Kiera."

"I know, baby. I got you. Let me make that call to the clinic. Then I'm calling Ash."

"Okay." Summer hung up. She went into her closet and put together an outfit for after the exam. She slipped into a pair of faux-fur-lined boots, then sat on her bed and waited for Kiera.

She didn't have long to wait. Kiera burst through the door, took one look at Summer, then went all business. Kiera's calm, assertive behavior was reassuring. She took Summer's hand and drew her out of the apartment and down the stairs, never leaving her side. "Ash is stuck in a meeting. She's sick about it. I told her there's nothing she can do and that I've got you. I told her we'll call when you're done with the exam. They can take a fair amount of time." Kiera opened the passenger-side door of her blue van, then put Summer's bag and purse in the back seat and hurried around to the driver's side.

The drive to the clinic took only a few minutes. Kiera parked and grabbed Summer's stuff, then took her hand again.

"Kiera, I really can't afford this. We should just go home."

"The state pays for rape kits. You won't be charged. We're doing this. If it's nothing, I'll buy you an ice cream. If it's something, I don't know. I guess I'll buy you a huge fucking sundae."

Summer huffed a shallow chuckle at that bribe, as if she was a child. "I'd be lost without you, you know. And Ash."

"I know. And I know you'd do this for Ash or me, so shut up and let's get through this."

"You've done this before."

"It's my job. We get a lot of women at the center in your exact spot. It's all good. We'll have you set to rights in no time. After this, I'll take you home so you can shower."

"After my ice cream."

Kiera laughed. "Right. After that."

THE NEXT COUPLE of hours were a blur. The clinic took urine and blood samples, did the physical exam, built the rape kit, then did the interview.

At the end of it, the doctor met Summer and Kiera in her office. "Good news and bad news," she said as she sat behind her desk. "There's no apparent evidence that you had sexual intercourse last night. And you aren't exhibiting the usual aftereffects of the common date-rape drugs like ketamine, gamma-hydroxybutyrate—or GHB—and Rohypnol. Those have a very short half-life, so if you've been drugged, it may not even show up in the samples we took."

"If she wasn't drugged, then what accounts for her loss of memory?" Kiera asked.

The doctor nodded. "And that's the bad news. We may not know what happened to her last night." She looked at Summer. "I would like you to rest today. I can write a note for work, if you like. You can resume normal activities tomorrow. If these symptoms reappear, you should visit your regular physician."

"So it's nothing," Summer said. "Not rape. Not drugs."

"I'm not saying it's nothing. There are always new drugs, new hybrids showing up. And we don't know what happened to you in that window of time you can't account for. I want you to be aware and vigilant about what you do and who you do it with. Let's see if something happens again. If you have any fears or concerns, we have counselors here. And if you have more problems, come see me if you don't want to see or don't have a regular physician. We'll have to wait for the final word from the labs. I'll call when those reports are back."

Summer stood. "Thank you, doctor."

They went out into the waiting room. Ash stood up, looking pale and angry. She held her arms open. Summer stepped into them and started to cry again.

"I don't know why I'm crying so much," Summer said. "There's nothing wrong. No rape. No drugs."

"And no explanation," Kiera added.

Summer straightened and wiped her eyes. "But we are getting ice cream."

Ash laughed. "So good news and better news. I like that."

They left the clinic. "I'm sorry I wasted everyone's time," Summer said. "I scared you for nothing."

"It wasn't for nothing." Ash wrapped an arm around Summer's shoulders. "You did the right thing getting yourself checked out. And we're always here for you."

Summer caught the look Ash and Kiera exchanged. They were both worried. So was she. She still couldn't explain the lost hours she'd experienced or the weird pall she'd been under during her dinner with Brett.

"Ash, go back to work," Summer said. "I don't want you to waste your leave on this. You're saving up for your big trip."

"Don't worry about it," Ash said. "I'm due a ton of comp time for all the overtime I've been working. I'm free this whole afternoon."

"Why don't you take her home, Ash?" Kiera said. "Summer, you can take that shower I bet you're craving. I'll stop for ice cream and some food, then come straight over."

Summer nodded. Kiera hugged them both, then took off. Summer slumped into the passenger seat of Ash's Volvo.

Ash gave her a worried smile. "Can I ask you something? Not a judgment, just genuine curiosity."

"Sure."

"Why did you go out with him? You said he gave you the heebie-jeebies."

Summer sighed. "I don't know. He's important to the Briscoes. Clark said it was critical to them to keep him happy and that I was the only one who could do it."

"Clark's a dick. Since when do you do what he wants?"

"I wish I hadn't." Summer felt her tears well up all over again.

"Forget it. Let's talk about something else."

"Kiera had to promise me ice cream to go to the clinic."

Ash laughed. "Kiera always knows the right thing to do or say. She's a force of nature."

"She is. I love you guys."

Ash reached over and squeezed Summer's hand. "We feel the same. I'm sorry I put you on the spot. It could have happened to any of us."

"I doubt that. You guys are too savvy."

"You have no idea how easy it is to be taken advantage of, even from those we trust."

They reached Summer's place. She wasted no time in grabbing another change of clothes before heading to the bathroom.

"Hey, Summer," Ash called out, "stay in the shower until the hot water runs out. I'll get some tea going."

"Thanks, Ash." Summer washed her hands, scrubbed her teeth, then stripped and climbed into the shower—the thing she'd wanted to do since she woke that morning.

She stood in the hot stream of water, letting it wash over her, rinse last night off her. Emotion flooded her. She still didn't understand how she'd even been talked in to going out with Brett. It was like she wasn't even in control of herself.

She let her tears mingle with the warm shower stream. A vision of Sam Garrick rose to her mind, unbidden but welcome. He was fearless, kind, protective—at least, in her mind he was. She didn't even know him, but something about him stood out to her. Strange the images she pulled to her when she needed to borrow their strength. Right now, Sam was what she needed.

She closed her eyes, imagining him in the shower with her. He poured soap on her scrubby ball, then rubbed it over her back in slow circles that eventually covered her whole back. Summer dipped her head, loving the daydream. He lifted her arms, stretching them out to the corners of the small shower stall. This time, it was his hands rubbing soap over her arms, massaging her muscles from her shoulders down to her fingertips.

When he was done, she was wavering in the hot stream of water. He pulled her back against him and wrapped his big arms around her.

*It was I who brought you home. I took you from Flynn.*

His words slipped into her mind, a welcome answer to the mystery. If only that were true. She lifted her hand to touch his arm, but nothing was there. She was alone in the shower. Of course.

Except...her back and arms were soapy.

She leaned her forehead against the blue tiled wall. Her mind was fracturing.

Just the thought of that made her straighten. She had to fight it, whatever this was. She had to keep herself together.

She poured shampoo into her palm and lathered up her hair, then did the rest of her shower protocol, finishing with another hard scrub of her whole body.

When she got out, she covered herself in a rose-scented lotion then pulled on a T-shirt and a pair of sweats. She grabbed a pair of thick, fuzzy socks and pulled them on, then went out to the main room of her studio apartment. Ash was sitting at the counter, her hands around a tall mug. The scent of Earl Grey tea was coming from her steaming cup.

"Ready for tea?" Ash asked.

"I am. That smells great."

"Feel human again?"

"I do." Except…there was the little matter of Sam. She missed him and wished he was there with them. So foolish. She'd never see him again. It was a car accident, not a meet-and-greet.

But she *craved* him.

Kiera arrived with subs and ice cream. She put the ice cream treats in the freezer, then cut the subs and served them. She stood at the counter and ate hers.

Summer found she was starving. She dug into her veggie sub and polished off half of it before a thought hit her. "Oh my gosh. Work. I never called in this morning."

"It's winter," Ash said. "They can do without you for a day or two."

"Yeah, but I should have called them." Summer dug her phone out of her purse and called Clark. "Hey. It's me," she said when he picked up. "I'm sorry I didn't call in sooner—"

"Didn't expect you to. Brett said you'd be taking the day off."

A cold chill poured down her spine. "Brett doesn't have the right to speak for me."

"How'd your date go last night?"

"Horrible. Look. I'm not feeling well today. I'll be in tomorrow morning, though."

"Yeah, that works. See you then." Clark hung up.

Summer dropped her phone on her bed, which Ash had made with fresh sheets while she was in the shower.

Ash and Kiera exchanged glances. Summer returned to her seat at the counter and took another bite of her sub.

"I think you should quit that place," Kiera said.

"I agree," Ash said.

"I can't just quit. I have bills. Rent." Summer stared at the second half of her sub. "But I have been getting my résumé together."

"Honestly, waiting tables would be better than going back there." Kiera gave her a dark look. "There's more at stake than just your happiness. Something's not right over there. That Brett guy is bad news."

"And if they're using you to keep him happy…" Ash didn't finish that thought.

"I know," Summer said. "You're right, but this is such a lousy time to look for another job in my field. No one's going to take on new hires off-season. And I have that stupid non-compete."

Ash frowned. "There's no way that could hold up in court. Not after what happened last night."

"I just need some time to get my head together. Make a plan." Summer took a sip of her tea. "You guys are right, though. I'll get on it. I don't want to go back there."

## 8

Night came so early this time of year. Summer couldn't wait until the days were longer, but it was just the beginning of the dark season. The girls had left hours ago. They'd been with her the whole day. She was grateful for their company, but now that she was alone, there was nothing between her and her demons.

She triple-checked that the front door was locked. Holding her phone in case she had to dial the cops, she went through her apartment, obsessively checking any place a man could hide. Why, she had no idea— she just needed to know she wouldn't be violated again. Her entire space was clear. She shut off the lights and got into bed. For the first time in all the years she'd lived in that studio, she felt too exposed. She pulled the covers over her head and listened to the muffled silence. The air got hot and thin. She couldn't stay under there long.

Pushing the covers away, she looked around her room. A streetlight at the corner of her alleyway cast the shadow of skeletal tree branches from the cotton-wood that stood between it and the garage.

The thought of returning to her job made her physically ill. Kiera was right. Waiting tables had to be better than returning to the garden center. At least while Brett was still a partner. No, that wasn't true. She was over the Briscoes altogether. They'd never treated her as if they valued her. She needed to take the lessons she'd learned, be grateful for her experience, and move on.

She dreaded facing that tomorrow. She turned on her side and tucked her knees up close. Try as she might, she couldn't close her eyes, didn't dare risk falling off to sleep.

After a while, she decided to do something she had never done, find a more defensible spot where she could feel safer: her closet.

She grabbed two pillows and her phone, then went into her closet. She dragged her rolled-up sleeping bag down from a shelf and spread it out on the floor, then closed and locked the door. She had nothing to prop up against it to slow someone who might want to kick it in.

God. She was crazy. But she had to do it, just for one night. She'd get a full night's sleep and in the morning, her mind would be clearer.

She switched the light off, then climbed into her flannel sleeping bag. It had a pleasant, familiar scent.

Campfires and fresh air. She shut her eyes, and her thoughts turned to her favorite daydream of late—Sam Garrick. The poor man had no idea how she borrowed him for use as her friend and protector and potential lover. Pretending he was with her helped ease her nerves. Besides, she was never going to see him again, so he'd never know.

LIEGE PARKED around the corner from Summer's apartment. He'd come to town as soon as she summoned him. He wondered if she knew she'd drawn him to her through her intense thoughts.

Being with her in the shower earlier had nearly wrecked him. She was shattered. Her friends had stayed close the whole day. But tonight, when Summer had curled up to sleep and pulled him in with her, she felt the same attraction he was feeling.

He sent his energy ahead of him, into Summer's quiet apartment. She was alone. He unlocked her door then locked it behind himself. The dimly lit space wasn't a visual challenge for him—a quick glance around it showed she wasn't in her bed. The sheets were rumpled. Maybe she'd just gotten up to use the bathroom. He hid himself behind an illusion and walked into the short hallway. The bathroom was empty, but the closet door was closed. And locked. He flattened his hand against the door. Closing his eyes, he slipped into her mind. She was asleep, but restlessly so. He sent calming energy into her mind, letting it flood her body, giving her complete relaxation.

When he sensed she was deeply asleep, he unlocked the door. She was asleep on the floor. Remorse cut through him. He and Flynn had done this to her. Kneeling next to her, he eased her pillows from under her head and set them on top of her, then he scooped her up, sleeping bag and all, and carried her to her bed. He laid her on top of her covers, still in her sleeping bag, then settled next to her on the mattress. He took a couple of her pillows and propped them up behind him. Then, gently lifting her head, he set the other pillows under her head.

Before he could pull away, she grabbed his arm and pulled it against her chest. In her dream state, she opened up to him.

*I'm glad you're here,* she said, unaware she was actually communicating with him.

*You called me to you.*

*You feel so safe to me,* she said.

He wasn't safe. Far from it. Damn the Matchmaker all to hell. But Liege would protect her. He'd gladly make her his life's mission. As soon as he thought that, he realized he hoped she didn't want that—for her own good. He was already a ghost in Kiera's life—he could ghost Summer as well, but he hoped, for her sake, she could forget him. Find a nice, regular guy and have a normal life.

What he was doing here, with her right now, broke the rules he'd set for his men. Never mess with the regulars. The unchanged had to be respected. They needed the freedom of never learning about men like Liege, his team, and their enemies.

But Flynn had already broken that edict, hadn't he? And now, without knowing who he was or why she was fascinated with him, Summer was calling him to her.

Despite the wrongness of it, he loved that it was he she turned to in times of stress. And they hadn't even been properly introduced. Yeah, weirdly, he was old-fashioned. The younger guys picked on him about his hang-ups. Whatever. He was the way he was, and he liked himself that way.

Summer shifted to her side and wrapped her arm around his waist, tugging herself closer, burying her face in his waist.

No amount of meditation was going to tell his cock to stand down, so he ignored its throbbing and hoped Summer didn't start exploring him in her sleep.

Earlier that day, when Summer was in her shower, her summons had nearly undone him. She was crying and alone, ravaged from her interactions with Flynn —and with Liege, if he were honest with himself. But still she called him to her. He'd had her pour body soap on her big scrubby, then he rubbed it in little circles all over the tense spots on her back. She'd let him massage her arms, from shoulders to wrists. They were such skinny arms, nothing like his. He'd wrapped an arm around her waist and another across her chest in the shower, pulling her against him, letting her lean on him. He'd kissed her temple, hoping all the while that he'd fully shielded her from the huge hard-on she'd caused.

*Sam, snuggle me,* Summer said, trying to tug him down toward her, even in her deep sleep.

Liege moved lower on her bed and turned to face her. She moved up against his body, her head resting on his arm. Sleep immediately let her slip away from him.

Sam stroked her straight, soft hair, his dark hand a stark contrast to her pale mane. He lifted it to his face, rubbing the silky strands across his cheek. He now knew where that delicious rose scent of hers came from—her body wash. He would never again see a rose without thinking of her.

His Summer.

Sam closed his eyes and let himself drift into a light sleep. He couldn't stay the whole night. He had to slip out before she woke. It would scare the hell out of her to wake with him actually in her bed rather than just there as a figment of her imagination. Of course, he could hide himself from her, but it felt like an invasion of her privacy.

She nuzzled her face against his chest. He'd thought she was asleep, but her active mind startled him. *Make love to me.*

A shiver ripped through him. *No.*

*Why?*

*Because we don't know each other yet.*

She sighed. He grinned.

*You are so old-fashioned,* she complained.

*Respect never goes out of fashion.*

*But I'm dreaming. I can do anything I want. I want you.*

She moved up a bit on the bed, bringing their faces level. *Can I kiss you?*

*You're supposed to be sleeping.*

*I am sleeping. Of course, or you wouldn't be here.* Her lips moved as she thought those words, feathering against his mouth. *So about that kiss—*

*Yes.*

*Will you kiss me back?*

*Try it and see.*

Her head was on the pillow next to his. He smoothed her hair away from her face. She reached up to palm his super-short hair. He felt her smile against his lips. Then she kissed him. Her lips were thinner than his, her mouth smaller. All of her was smaller. He returned the kiss, holding her head in his hand. Their lips parted, and their tongues touched. She groaned.

He was afraid she was close to waking from the stimulation, so he deepened her sleep trance.

*Mmmm. I like the way you taste,* she said.

*Yeah?* He kissed the side of her mouth.

*Yeah. I've been thinking about you and this and us so much since the crash. Is that crazy? I think I have a crush on you. Make love to me, Sam.*

*No.*

*Why?*

*Because you're sleeping. I want you awake when I make love to you.*

*What difference does it make? This is just a dream.*

He didn't answer. He couldn't—their tongues were wrestling.

*I'm going to call you,* she said.

He smiled. *What are you going to call me?*

*No.* She held her hand to her ear as if it were a cell phone. *Call you.*

*And say what?*

*And say,* Hi. I'm that blond chick who hit you. I need you to come over and fuck me.

He chuckled. *That's not how it's going to go.*

*Please?*

*No. First we'll have a date. Well, not really an official date. More like a getting-to-know-each-other dinner. An un-date.*

*Tell me you don't have a three-date rule.*

*No, it's more like a* never *rule.*

*Why a never rule?* She frowned.

*I don't do casual sex.*

*Why?*

*I don't enjoy it.*

*Do you want sex with me?* she asked.

*Yes. So much. We are going to be lovers.*

*You promise?*

*Yes. After we've gotten to know each other.*

*I'm a quick study.*

He laughed quietly. *Go to sleep. You're safe with me.*

She snuggled closer, resting her head on his chest and pushing her leg between his. She folded her arms between them. He had to keep himself from rubbing her back out of fear he'd get her started all over again.

Everything he'd said to her tonight was the truth. They were going to be lovers.

There was no way he could walk away from her while Flynn was stalking her. And now having connected with her, he'd tied her fate to his.

He would protect her. The Matchmaker be damned.

SUMMER HAD A PROBLEM. Several of them, in fact. She was crushing on a man who didn't exist. And she was about to quit a job without a fallback option.

She pulled her winter coat on and slipped her messenger bag over her shoulder. Her purse was already in her bag. She sat at her counter, delaying starting her day.

Last night had been wonderful—or it would have been, had it been real. Her dream about Sam Garrick —or rather, her made-up version of him—had been just the thing she'd needed to get through a terrible night following a terrible day.

She looked at the folded sleeping bag she hadn't put away. She couldn't remember moving from the closet back to her bed, but evidently she had some-time during the night.

Her dream about Sam holding her had seemed so real that she was actually startled when she woke to find he wasn't there.

And even now, fully awake, she still felt the need to draw him close to her, take him with her to work, pull strength from him for what she was about to do.

She felt a passing shot of guilt over conscripting his spirit for her own uses. It was good that she would never meet him. She'd practically mauled him last night.

Wasn't it odd that he'd spoken in a way she never did? He was just a make-believe stand-in, but he'd said things like "respect never goes out of fashion" and had refused to engage in her full fantasy until they knew each other better.

Thinking of her pretend Sam gave her momentary ease, but she still agonized over what her resignation letter would say and whether she should mention in it the problem she'd had with Brett. Seemed like she should in case she ever had to battle the Briscoes over enforcement of their non-compete.

She wasn't a savvy businessperson. She ought to consult with a lawyer, but there was no way she could afford that. Kiera had coached her on what to say and not say. Summer folded her arms and bent over. Her whole future rested on the outcome of her confronta-tion with the Briscoes today. She was a creative; she just wanted to design gardens, not carve a spot in the power structure that defined her professional life.

*Be strong. I'm with you.* Sam's baritone voice rumbled through her mind. Great. On top of everything else, she was splintering into multiple personalities.

It felt as if he was laughing at her. She laughed at herself, too. It was kind of comical.

*And overly dramatic,* Sam added. *Go fight the dragons. Don't let them win.*

SUMMER WENT straight to her office. No one stopped her. No one started up a conversation. She wasn't certain if the Briscoes were even in yet. She opened her laptop and started drafting her resignation letter. The final version did include Brett and being forced to go out with him as the reason for her resignation.

When she finished, she went looking for Clark's dad. Douglas was in his office. She knocked on his doorjamb. "Got a minute?"

"Sure thing." He looked up and smiled as if nothing in the whole world was wrong. It was a jarring contrast to her mood and made her question everything she was about to do.

*As it was intended to. Continue on, Summer. You are not in the wrong.* Sam's voice was reassuring. It was as if he was actually right there with her.

"I need to give you my resignation letter." She handed it to him.

He scanned it, his good mood quickly fading. His eyes blazed as he looked up at her. "I can't accept this."

Of all the reactions Summer had expected that was not one. Her brows lifted. "You don't have a choice. I spent yesterday at a women's clinic getting a rape kit drawn after my 'date' with Brett. Next step will be a restraining order against him. He won't be able to be here when I am. And since he's your business partner, that won't work out very well."

"But he likes you. He said your date went well."

"It didn't."

Douglas's face hardened. "What was the result of the rape kit?"

Summer didn't tell him there was no clear evidence that she'd been raped. It didn't matter. She had no complete recollection of that night. And the parts she could remember were fuzzy. He'd clearly drugged her. Maybe he hadn't been able to take the night to the conclusion he'd desired, but that didn't absolve him of his nefarious intent.

"It's out at the lab at the moment."

"I'm sure this is all a misunderstanding. I'll call him. He can come in and explain himself."

"I won't be here when he does."

Summer left his office and went into hers to start gathering her things. She heard Douglas go into

Clark's office. He closed the door, but their voices were elevated.

A few minutes later, both Douglas and Clark came to her office. The scratches on Clark's cheeks and neck looked even more numerous than they had yesterday.

"Summer, we can see that you're upset," Douglas said. "Rightfully so. We need you here. We're only weeks away from our last big push for the year. We won't be able to replace you in time."

Summer rearranged some stacked papers. "That's your problem."

"Look, you want to avoid Flynn. We can make that happen. If he's going to be here, we'll tell you ahead of time. If he comes when you're here, you can leave. We'll help you stay clear of him."

She gave that some thought. If they'd give her that, then she could take the time she needed to get another job. She wouldn't have to be in a panic about making ends meet.

Summer glared at father and son. "You will not use me to placate him. I don't care if he's happy. I don't care about him at all."

"We won't," Douglas said, giving his son a hard look.

Summer faltered. She knew Kiera would be furious, but she had to look out for her own future—and Kiera wasn't going to pay her bills. Besides, change wasn't something Summer was comfortable with. She'd negotiated something she could live with in the short term, and it bought her time to do a proper job search.

"We'll see how it goes for a little while," Summer said. Maybe she had overreacted to everything. "If you keep your word and I never run into Brett again, it may work out."

They looked relieved. Summer felt exhausted. She had no idea if she'd made the right decision or if she'd just agreed to worsen her hell.

## 9

------

Liege now knew so much about Summer—where she lived and worked and worked out. He knew she smelled like roses. He knew her crappy fifteen-year-old car had still not been repaired from their collision; she'd had a friend tie the hanging front bumper to the frame instead. He knew her credit was a hot mess, her apartment was spotless, and she hated her job but loved her work.

More importantly, he knew her energy signature's feel and sound.

And he knew he had a dangerous interest in her that bordered on addiction, and that if he didn't get another dose of her soon, his life would go off the rails.

Tonight was Wednesday, the night she met with her girlfriends for dinner. Less than a week had passed since the accident. He'd shadowed her most of that time, but tonight, he wanted something more. He wanted her to see him. After she'd agreed to stay in her job, she'd closed her mind to him. It was almost like she'd made the conscious decision to buckle down and soldier through the hard times ahead of her, leaving him—her imaginary friend—behind.

The most recent cold snap had passed, making this evening's forty degrees feel balmy. Summer and her friends were going to one of the Old Town restaurants this evening. He didn't know which one, but he knew she was near. He started down the sidewalk, savoring his anticipation of running into her.

The night was black and clear. Fairy lights sparkled on the spines of the bare locust trees lining the main drag in Old Town. More people were out than usual on a weekday evening. Liege shoved his hands in his pockets of his peacoat, keeping a casual appearance despite his every sense being trained on Summer.

Beyond her weekly dinner date with her friends, she had almost no social life, which surprised him, given how bubbly her personality was. Even now, with nearly a whole block and a dozen people between them, he could hear her laughter—not because she was loud, but because his senses were entirely focused on her. They were walking toward each other. His heartbeat deepened in anticipation of seeing her.

"Sam." Summer's voice slipped through him.

Liege lifted his gaze, letting himself slowly home in on the woman who'd taken over his mind. He gave her a little smile and stopped walking. "Summer."

"I didn't expect to see you."

"Likewise."

"This is my friend, Ashlyn. Ash, Sam." Summer winced as she added, "The guy I hit." He nodded at Ash, and politely ignored the way her eyes were walking all over him. "You're a long way from home."

"I came for dinner. It was here or Cheyenne, and here's a little closer. Hey, why don't I buy you both dinner? I could use the company."

Ash smiled. "Thank you, but I have plans." She pushed Summer forward. "Summer doesn't, though. She could use a date. She never has any." Ash glared at Summer. "Any good dates, that is."

"But we have reservations," Summer said.

"Another time, then." Liege was relieved that he didn't let his disappointment show.

"Nonsense. We're boring," Ash said. "We always have dinner on Wednesdays. Why have boring when you could have Sam?" She took Summer's arm and pushed her toward him again, then started off down the street. "Bye! You two have fun!"

Summer looked chagrined, as if she'd been forced on him. "Are you sure you want to have dinner?"

"Oh, yeah." He smiled. "I'm starving. And it's just dinner, not a date."

"An un-date." Summer blushed.

"An un-date?" Liege repeated, frowning. Had she remembered that from the night they spent together?

"Yeah. A not-a-date date." He didn't need the

pale light from the streetlamp overhead to see the color in her face. He smiled. She did remember.

"I know just the place." Summer turned back the way she'd come. They went down a side street.

Liege slowed his pace to match hers. "Excellent. I was just going to walk the streets until my stomach decided the right place to stop."

"It's vegetarian." She looked at him to see if that was a problem.

"Even better. I get two dinners tonight. One with you. One for my stomach."

She stopped. "Oh. Yeah. I didn't think. You probably eat three times what I do."

Liege smiled, thinking he could eat her too. "Doesn't matter. You pick. My treat."

"There's a pub down this street, too. They have great burgers."

"Do they have something my little vegan friend can eat?"

She laughed. "They do artisan salads."

"Then I vote for that choice."

"I'm not entirely vegan, I just don't eat a lot of meat." They started walking again. "I was just telling Ash about you before we ran into you."

"Oh. Well, she was very gracious, considering I'm the one who got you jammed up."

"No. It wasn't about the accident. I was telling her about *you*. You've been on my mind a lot."

"Oh." He looked at her. "And you still came to dinner with me."

"I wanted to see you again."

"Why?"

"Something about you." She looked up at him. His nerves heightened. "I think it's your eyes. They're beautiful."

He chuckled. "I've been called a lot of things in my life, but beautiful isn't one of them."

"Sam, I know this is just dinner—and I'm perfectly happy with just dinner—but, out of curiosity, are you married?"

Liege shook his head. He liked her directness. She could have spent the evening walking all around that question without hitting it head-on. "I'm single. How about you?"

"Same."

She caught his arm and drew him to a stop. Though she wasn't touching his skin, her energy spilled into his. He felt an electrical charge whisper through him, carrying his awareness of her to every cell in his body.

"Look." She pointed at a small garden in the front of a teahouse. "I did this."

He leaned a little in her direction, hoping to catch a hint of roses. "What did you do?"

She waved her hands out over the little urban garden with its frozen plant skeletons. "This. The teahouse wanted a flower garden for their patio. I gave them the design and installed it. It's been three years now. This was the first absolutely stunning year. The rosa rugosa hedge on the side provides a nice privacy screen from the alley. And for three weeks in the spring, it's a brilliant fuchsia color. We used a mix of perennials, annuals, and flowering shrubs to bring color to the garden from early spring to late fall." She sighed. "Everything's past its prime, obviously. I wish you'd seen it in the summer."

"I can imagine how it must have looked." He saw it, actually, in her mind's eye, vibrant and flourishing. A work of art that was alive and ever-changing. "You really did this?"

"Yeah." She folded her lips between her teeth. He knew she was waiting to be cut down, something he could never do, not when he felt what this meant to her.

"It's like a painting. You should do this for a living."

"I do." Her face fell a little. "Well, it's what my degree's in. Landscape architecture. I have a job at a nursery, but it's not going quite as I planned."

"Why's that?"

"The senior designers don't give me any of the challenging contracts. And I don't like some of their business practices." She shrugged. "It's okay. Everyone has to pay their dues, right?"

"There's a difference between paying your dues and having your genius throttled." He held her gaze until she blinked and looked away. "I could use some landscaping out at my place."

"Oh?"

"I just had it built. The construction's finished, but

it's a little austere without some landscaping." He'd talked about this with the guys, and the more he thought about it, the more it felt like the perfect solution. Of course, she was only one of many women the Omnis had cast their nets around. There was no way they could save them all, but this one, he would for damned sure.

They reached the pub. Liege opened the door for her. It was still early for the dinner crowd, and being midweek, the place wasn't as busy as it was on the weekends. It had an intimate atmosphere with its high booth backs and dim lighting. Music provided a nice cover for most conversations. Liege smiled at Summer, pleased to share his evening with her.

She blushed a little. He imagined how she'd look in his bed. Her fair skin would probably turn red from the neck up when he did to her what he'd been thinking about.

That was a sight he looked forward to observing.

And it was a thought that brought him up short. He wanted Summer. He *wanted* her. He hadn't had an ounce of hunger for a woman since he was changed…until Summer.

He must have given her an odd look, for a shadow slipped over her features. "You don't really need to buy me dinner."

"Sure I do. It's the least I can do for wrecking your car and now taking you away from your friends." They placed their orders. "So why is it that you don't date very much? You're a beautiful woman, and you seem kind. You're obviously intelligent and have a deep passion for what you do."

Her brows lifted. They were a deep honey color, darker than her hair. "You know that from our two interactions?"

"I'm an observant man."

"I don't do casual dating." She shrugged. "And you have to go through some casual dates to find a guy worth seeing more than once."

Their drinks arrived. Unsweetened iced tea for her, beer for him. She didn't do casual dating, but she was sure up for casual sex—but then, maybe that was only with men she thought were imaginary.

"Sounds like you know what you're looking for, and you're not finding it."

"I know what I want. To be honest, I thought I was close to having it, but it didn't work out. Now, I'm just focused on my work. I want to move up in my field, on my own merits." She sipped her tea. "Time for you to be in the hot seat. Why are you still single?"

"Guess I wasn't ready to settle down. Spent time in the Army, then hooked up with a private security company. I've recently left all of that. I bought some land here, built a place. I'm rethinking my options. Maybe open my place as a B&B on the ecotourist route."

"Wow. You've covered a lot of ground in a short bit of time."

Liege smiled. It was a lifetime, really, but he knew

she was going by his visual age, which wasn't much older than hers.

"So, your property is way out there," Summer said. "Why would a guy like you isolate himself like that?"

"Peace and quiet, I guess. I've had enough excitement to carry me for lifetimes."

"What kind of house did you build?"

"A fort."

Her brows lifted. "A what?"

"I assembled elements of several pioneer trading forts—updated, of course, for modern use. I've wanted one since I was a kid. I was considering opening my place for an ecotourism stop. It's highly efficient, wholly off-grid. It has a multi-tier water reclamation system and makes use of passive solar light for heat. I have wind turbine trees and solar panels with weeks' worth of battery storage."

Summer's eyes went wide. "That's amazing."

Their meal was delivered—her vegan tofu steak salad and his huge T-bone. They looked at each other's meal and smiled.

"And yet, with all that eco-innovation out at your place, you drive a gas-guzzling SUV. I swear that thing felt like a tank when I hit it."

That's because it was. Bulletproof top to bottom. He didn't tell her that, however. "Sometimes, it's all about comfort and security. I never know when a flighty blond driver might get behind me."

She gasped, but there was a small hint of humor

in her eyes. "That was uncalled for."

"True." He laughed. "My apologies. Is your fake cow good?"

"Delicious. How's your real cow?"

"Delicious."

Their convo was easy the rest of the meal. Talking to her felt as if Liege was reconnecting with an old friend, which only wove her threads deeper through his psyche. He wanted her, plain and simple. Except it was neither plain nor simple, actually. She was the secret sauce he'd craved his entire life. But having her came at a high price.

Control.

Everything came down to self-control.

But his need for her was like riding a bucking bull. On steroids. Wrestling it to the ground was going to be fucking hard.

If not impossible.

Did she feel it too? She said she'd been thinking of him since the accident. She'd even talked to her friends about him. And that wasn't because of any influence he'd exerted over her. He'd tried to stay out of her mind, especially once she closed herself off. If they were to connect, he wanted to know she came to him of her own free will.

A little while later, when they'd both finished, he paid the bill, then led her out of the restaurant. The temperature had dropped considerably. He held her jacket for her. Her long blond hair was caught inside it. He wanted to help her rearrange it, but if he touched her right then, he didn't know where he'd stop.

He shoved his hands in his pockets. "So where to? Your car, or do I escort you back to your friends?"

She smiled up at him. His eyes traced the soft curves of her lips. "You don't have to do either."

"Of course I do. It's dark and you're a beautiful woman alone."

"Fort Collins is safe."

"Safety is an illusion. Humor me."

She shivered. He didn't mean to scare her, but it was just as well to remind her to always be alert.

They walked to her car. Slowly. Liege loved that she seemed no happier about their evening ending than he did. When they got to her car, he nodded toward her temporary bumper repair. "You haven't gotten it fixed yet."

She winced. "No."

"Problems with your insurance company?"

"No. No, they sent me a check. I just used it for something else."

"Let me take care of it for you. I can pick it up while you're at work."

Her eyes widened. "Why would you do that?"

"Because I was the jerk who caused the whole thing to begin with."

"Well, no. But thank you."

"It won't pass inspection."

"True, but I have a few more months before then."

"Money tight?"

She huffed a quick laugh. "Always."

"Then take the landscaping job out at my place. I'll work with you directly."

That suggestion shocked her. Her mouth made an O and her pulse sped up—he could hear her heart beating faster. "I can't. I need my job. Yours won't last forever, and what will I do after that?"

"Find another. I'll provide a good recommendation."

"No. But thank you."

"Fine. I'll hire the company you work for. Which landscape place is it?" Of course, he knew the answer, but she didn't know that.

She told him.

"That's one of the big ones."

"Yeah."

"I'll ask for you specifically."

She shook her head. "Won't matter. I don't get to assign myself to jobs yet. By the way, how large is your place?"

"I have a thousand acres."

"Yeah. They're going to take that one for themselves. Especially if you're opening an ecotourist destination."

"Bullshit. I want you." That was no lie. He wanted her in all the ways he could have her, from his bed to his life and back again. "I'm the customer, right? I get what I want."

She sighed. "Come in. Talk to them. I'll at least

get a commission for finding you."

He grinned. She was going to get a whole lot more than that. "We'll start there. And don't worry. The job's yours."

~

SUMMER WAS reluctant to end their evening. She could go see if the girls were still at the restaurant—whether they were or weren't, it gave her an excuse for a few more minutes with Sam.

"I changed my mind. I do want to see if the girls are still eating."

He smiled. "I'll walk you there."

Summer locked her car then fell into step with him. The restaurant wasn't very far, so she kept their pace slow to lengthen their time together.

This was crazy. She'd never met a guy who made her feel this way. She didn't want to be apart from him—how could that be when they'd only spent a few hours together? She'd never felt this in her time with Clark or any other boyfriend.

"So is this Wednesday dinner a regular thing for you guys?" Sam asked.

"It is. We started it a few years ago after Kiera's husband died in Afghanistan. She was despondent. Ash and I had to find a way to bring her back to the land of the living. So we forced her to come out with us, and we've done it every week since."

"You're a good friend."

"We're like family now. We share everything."

They'd reached the restaurant. The outside court-yard in the front was bordered by a low wall. Summer stepped up onto it. It was maybe a foot high. She held her arms out to balance herself. Sam reached a hand up to steady her. She stopped and faced him, realizing they were the same height now.

She didn't want to go inside yet. His hand was warm and big. She reached for his other hand, which he didn't hesitate to offer, and said, "Thank you for dinner."

"Thank you for the company."

His outer layers were beige—a knit hat and wool peacoat. The light color complemented his dark complexion. His hair was cut super short—she couldn't see it now, but she had at the restaurant. He had a strong face. Dark brows arched over his eyes in the shape of a boomerang. His high cheekbones, wide jaw, and long chin gave his cheeks the look of a lean predator. His nose was straight, narrow at the top, wide toward the bottom. Women would kill to have lips like his.

Under her inspection, those lips tilted up at the corners, pouring a strange warmth through her. "When will I see you again?" she asked.

So much for playing hard to get.

"Depends. Are you working tomorrow?"

She nodded. "Ten to five."

"I'll be in when it opens."

"You're coming to Briscoe's tomorrow?"

"I have a landscape designer to hire."

She smiled, but then reality slapped her back down. "They really won't let me work with you." Or maybe they would after everything that had happened. They owed her one.

That thought sent her mind spinning through the terrible events of a few days ago. Sam's hands tightened on hers, drawing her attention back to him.

"I'm a persuasive kind of guy. I'll handle them."

He said it in a way that almost made her believe him, but he didn't know the Briscoes like she did.

The light from the restaurant behind her sparkled in his eyes, making them seem to glow. There was so much unsaid between them—hopes and dreams and questions. She had the bizarre desire to tell him about Brett and how she'd called Sam in to her the night after her examination at the women's clinic, but then she'd have to confess how she'd perved on him, and that likely wouldn't lead to a real first date.

"Hand me your phone," Sam said.

She unlocked it and handed it to him. He punched in his number, then added it to her contacts.

He handed it back to her. "Call me. Anytime. For any reason."

Summer couldn't describe the feeling of safety that that invitation gave her. It was like she wasn't alone anymore, which was ridiculous, because she had Kiera and Ash—she wasn't alone, anyway.

"Good night, Sam."

"Night, Summer. I'll see you tomorrow."

She nodded, then tore her eyes away and headed down the wall to where it ended at the path into the restaurant. She jumped off and looked back at him, but he was gone. He moved fast for a big guy. She went inside the restaurant. Her friends were waiting for her. Ash waved when she walked inside. Summer slipped into the booth next to Ash, who gave her a quick hug.

"I was hoping you'd come give us an update," Ash said.

Summer giggled. "I think I have a crush on him. No, I know I do. He's so nice. I wish you could have met him, Kiera. He's like the last nice guy on Earth."

Kiera wrinkled her nose. "Great. Just my luck you get him. You know you're supposed to save the brown ones for me?"

"Oh, hush," Ash said, laughing. "You have a whole sea of vanilla to choose from."

"So does Summer's Sam, apparently," Kiera said.

"Besides," Ash said, "he's not brown. He's not even milk chocolate. He's pure cacao."

Summer felt her face turning bright red, which made her friends crack up. "He's not cacao either. He's sweeter than that."

"Mmmm. Bittersweet baking chocolate, then," Ash said, laughing.

Summer waved that away. "It's got nothing to do with chocolate or vanilla or any other yummy flavor," Summer said. "Sam's just nice. Really down to earth —but still eccentric. He built a fort for himself way out east. He's thinking of opening it for a stop on some ecotourism route."

Kiera looked impressed. "Sounds like he's got money."

"And he's over thirty. That's good," Ash added.

"And single," Summer said.

"That could be good or bad," Kiera said. "Is he divorced? Does he have kids?"

Summer shook her head. "I don't know. We only got to the single part."

"Quit fussing, Kiera, and be happy for her," Ash said. "Look at her glow. Whether it'll work out or not is something she'll discover, but for now, sounds like it's off to a good start. Summer, take your time with him. See him in all his moods—his best and his worst —before you decide to jump in with both feet."

"Don't worry," Summer said. "He's not going to be another Clark."

"Speaking of that jackass, how are things going?" Kiera asked.

Summer saw the disapproval in her eyes. She had updated both of her friends the day she almost quit. Kiera didn't say anything though. "You'll be glad to know I've sent my résumé to a handful of other design shops. The Briscoes have kept their word about keeping Brett away from me. Sam offered to hire me to design the landscape for his fort."

"Wow." Ash looked impressed.

Kiera asked, "Are you ready to head out on your own? That might not be a bad idea. Indie designers have a lot of freedom, but also need a lot of infrastructure that you don't have in place yet, like a nice savings cushion for any dry spells between jobs."

"I could wait tables between jobs. Actors do it."

Kiera shook her head, which made Summer laugh. They were such opposites, she and Kiera. Kiera was obsessively over-prepared for every contingency in her life—and she was lucky as hell. She'd found an angel investor who was really an angel. He wanted to give back to the community without drawing attention to himself. He'd kept his identity hidden from Kiera, but he always came through with anything she needed.

Summer had no such angel in her life. But she did have two of the very best friends a girl could ever hope to have. They were always there for her, no questions asked. Or maybe some questions, but never judgment.

Summer reached for their hands. "I love you both, you know. I've been sensing for a while that a change was coming. I didn't know what it was. But I think I do now."

"You think it's Sam?" Ash asked.

Summer nodded. "Sam. A job change. Both, maybe. But something big seems close."

The waiter came over with the receipt for their dinner payment. They slipped out of the booth and put their coats on. Outside, the three of them went toward their cars. Summer's was the closest.

"How have you been feeling, Summer?" Kiera

asked.

"Much better now that Sam's in the picture."

"Don't go too fast." Kiera gave her a worried look. "Let it be what it will be."

There were fewer people out walking about now that evening was moving into night and the temperature was even colder than before. A man was coming up from behind them, moving fast with big strides from his long legs. The girls stepped over to the side of the sidewalk to give him room to pass. He paused just briefly beside Summer and hissed a warning in her ear.

"Liege. Run to Liege." He quickly resumed his walk.

Summer gasped. She recognized his red hair poking out from under his knit beanie. He was the same man who had accosted them at their dinner last week, the one who'd singled her out afterward. He'd said something about a "liege" then, too.

Ash started after him, shouting, "Hey!"

The man turned around and walked backward. "Remember that. It's going to matter."

Kiera grabbed Ashley before she could rush the guy.

"Wasn't he the one at the restaurant last week?" Ash asked.

"Yeah." Summer swallowed. "After we left that night, he showed up at my car."

"He did?" Kiera asked.

"Yeah."

"Why didn't you tell us?" Ash asked.

"I didn't want to worry you. I honked my horn until someone came out of the bar. That scared him off." Well, not off, exactly. He'd just disappeared.

"Was he screaming that same nonsense as he did in the restaurant?" Kiera asked.

"Yeah," Summer said. "And something about a liege, too. I have no idea what it means."

"I don't like this," Kiera said. "Once is an oddity, three times is a pattern."

"We should go to the cops," Ash said.

"And tell them what?" Summer asked. "That we keep running into a weirdo?"

"Look, come stay at the center, where I can keep an eye on you," Kiera said.

"Or come crash on my couch," Ash offered. "You shouldn't be alone right now. First that weirdo, then your awful date with Brett, and your problems at work, and now the weirdo again. And you said yourself you're having premonitions of something big coming."

"Not premonitions," Summer said. "Just a feeling. It's all good."

Kiera sighed. "Fine, but if you change your mind, we're here for you. Call or text us when you get in tonight."

Summer smiled. She gave each girl a hug. "I'm so glad you're my friends."

"Yeah, we kinda like you, too," Ash said. "We'll be waiting for a text."

# 10

—————

"**M**ay I help you?" a salesgirl asked Liege as he came into the garden center's main building the next morning.

"Yup. I have an appointment with one of your landscape designers."

"Junior or senior?" she asked.

"Neither. I'm meeting Summer."

"I'll let her know you're here, Mr...?"

"Sam Garrick. No need. She's expecting me." Liege felt Summer's energy nearby. The soft rub of her life force deepened his craving for her.

"Sam?" Summer's sweet voice had him spin around. She stood there, rolls of architectural drawings in her arms, a pencil behind her ear. And shadows under her eyes.

She hadn't slept well last night. He could tell she was full of anxiety about this morning. Rage danced in his mind, but he forced himself to be calm. This was not the place to lose the control he'd carefully cultivated for so long.

"Hi." Liege gave her a smile.

"You came."

"I told you I needed your expertise."

Her smile started slowly and ended brilliantly, lighting her face. He was instantly hard.

And then regret took over her features. She leaned close and said in a lowered voice, "It's not going to work out. They won't let me handle your account."

Liege's face hardened. "Then fuck them. Come with me now."

She gave a quick shake of her head. "I just want to see their expressions when you ask for me. My life will be complete after that."

"That bad, huh?"

"Dreams come in all forms."

An older man came out of the back office area. He sent Summer a harsh look. Liege felt it bruise her spirit. She had no protective barriers up; all that she was, all of her beautiful glow, was offered up to anyone who came into her sphere of energy.

"Summer—I think you have some work that needs your attention?" Douglas Briscoe said, nodding at her armful of papers.

"I do." She didn't move.

Liege was glad she stood her ground. He held out a hand and introduced himself. For a fact, the elder

Briscoe was in the Omnis up to his neck. Gray dots clouded his aura. It was interesting that he was still a regular. Couldn't be that high-ranking in the org, then.

"Thanks for meeting with me," Liege said. "I've come to hire a landscape designer. Word is that Summer's the best in town."

Douglas's chuckle was awkward. "Well, that's great. She brought you here, so she's redeemed herself. Unfortunately, she has other things to do here that will have her too busy." He gestured toward the back offices, inviting Liege to follow him.

Liege took Summer's elbow to draw her with him. "How will she learn if she isn't given the opportunity to do so?"

Douglas frowned. Liege wondered if he felt the compulsion Liege was projecting to the older man. "Yes, that's true. Summer,"—Douglas looked at her —"do join us."

Summer's tense gaze hopped between Douglas and Liege. "Of course. I'll just put these down. I'll be right there."

Liege looked back at her before entering the conference room. She was grinning ear to ear and blew him a kiss.

Liege leaned his head back, eyes closed. He suddenly no longer had any interest in this charade. He'd deal with the Briscoes on his own terms. He just wanted to get Summer away from them, tucked away at his fort, where he could more easily protect her. He felt his eyes burning, as they were wont to do when his raw nature awakened.

He blinked to settle himself. His glowing eyes would take this convo to a whole other level.

The younger Briscoe was already in the conference room, befouling it with Omni energy. Liege looked at son and father, seeing not their physical bodies but the auras clinging to them. Gray twisted with black. He should end them both right now, add them to his death count.

Summer woke him from his blood reverie, startling him with the cool touch of her hand on his where it rested over his folded arms. Only two truths gave him ease: she would be in his bed very soon, and the Briscoes would soon be dead.

He smiled at her. A frown whispered across her brow. He knew she felt the killer coiled within him. She was deeply sensitive. He gave her a hard look. There was little redeemable about those tainted by the Omnis—regulars or mutants. Both weren't much more than functioning automatons. He hated that she was forced to spend any time at all near these evil men. He decided to end the meeting before it had begun, and sent the senior Briscoe the compulsion to accept his terms for the landscape design without further discussion.

"Summer," Douglas said, "Mr. Garrick would like you to draft a design for his landscaping project. Anything on your desk that is outstanding can be handed over to Clark to complete."

Summer looked at Douglas in shock.

Liege forced more words out of Briscoe's mouth. The guy was easy to use—he and Douglas were like a ventriloquist and his doll. "Mr. Garrick is to have your complete focus for his project. When did you want to start?"

"This morning," Liege said.

Summer frowned. "But—"

Liege stopped her before she could resist. "We'll work out the details, Summer. You can keep them updated, once we have things ironed out." *Update them over the phone, from my place, where you're safe from them*, he added to himself.

"Right." Summer smiled. "Let's go. I'll just grab my things and meet you out front."

After the meeting, Summer's head was spinning at the easy way Sam had handled his request for her to work his account. Really, there had been no discussion at all.

As expected, Clark followed her to her office. "I can drive us out there. I'd like to see this property." He frowned and rubbed between his brows as if fighting a headache.

Summer stacked some things she'd need as she surveyed Sam's property—a sketchpad, sharpened pencils, an eraser, a catalog of plants, a measuring wheel, and a long measuring tape. She looked around her office, trying to think of anything else she'd need.

"I think this could be a lucrative deal," she said.

"Exactly why I think I should be there."

"It's exactly why you shouldn't. He made it clear who he wanted servicing his account."

"Just make sure that's all you service."

Summer straightened. "Excuse me?"

"You heard me."

"You're out of line, Clark. You long ago lost your right to influence my private life."

"I could fire you."

"I wish you would. I have a whole notebook of these conversations documented." She put everything she'd collected into a messenger bag, including her purse. "You've been digging a deep hole for yourself, so it's a full notebook."

Clark hissed and rubbed the heels of his palms against his temples. He was clearly suffering from a headache that looked like it was becoming a migraine. Even his eyes were watering. She felt a flash of sympathy for him as he backed out of her office.

"Maybe you should get yourself checked out," she suggested. "You don't look good." She nodded toward the scrolls of designs she'd left on her desk. "Those are the projects you'll need to take back over. I have notes entered into the system detailing what still needs to be done on each of them."

He nodded, but she wasn't really sure he was still aware of her. She went out through the offices and into the retail area. A couple of the sales staff were chatting near a register.

"Jada, you mind checking on Clark in a bit? Looked like he had a migraine coming on."

"Can you die from migraines?" Jada asked.

"Probably not." Summer swallowed a chuckle. "Just check on him in a bit, okay?"

Jada leaned close and whispered, "Can I do it after he drops dead?" They laughed, then Jada said, "Of course I will. And I'll text you."

"Good plan. Don't know how long I'll be." Summer handed her a sticky note with an address and Sam's number on it—her standing policy when visiting new clients. "I'll see you tomorrow."

"Good luck! Text me to let us know when you leave there."

"I will." Summer stepped out into the sunshine. Man, it felt wonderful getting away from the office. She looked at Sam and smiled. Suddenly, all of her problems seemed behind her.

All except one. Her car.

"So, I'm about an hour northeast of here," Sam said. "You can follow me."

"Um, Sam? I'm not entirely sure my car can make it there and back. I think I better rent a car for a day."

"No need. Hop in. I'll drive. And I'll bring you back this evening."

"You sure? That's a lot of driving."

"Not a problem. We can stop for a coffee on our way out of town if you like."

"Oh my God. It's like you read my mind."

They got in his Escalade. "Let me guess," he said. "You like a coffee that's sweet and has more syllables than a cat has fleas."

She laughed. "Actually, no. I like a double-shot Americano. No cream. No sugar. I like mine black and bitter like I like my—" *Oh God. Please, please don't let him have caught what she almost said.*

He arched a brow at her.

"I'm so sorry. I didn't think."

He shook his head. "I, for one, am glad that's how you like your men."

"I'm an idiot."

"Why? We have the same taste in coffee." He looked at her before making a turn. "But I don't do men."

Summer leaned back in her seat and tried to reset. The last thing she needed to do was screw this deal up. It could be her first big break.

"So what's the story with Clark?" Sam asked after a while.

"What do you mean?"

"He looked at you like he owned you."

"Oh. Yeah. We dated for a while. He got me this job after we graduated from the university." She looked at Sam and smiled. "Talk about learning your lessons the hard way. My friends warned me about him. They never liked him. He was always so charming. Until he wasn't. I thought he was the one. I thought a lot of things, but none of it worked quite how I expected it would."

He nodded. "I hate learning lessons like that."

"Wasn't a bowl of cherries, that's for sure."

"Why don't you leave the garden center?"

"It's a small industry. Everyone knows everyone. If I leave on bad terms, the Briscoes could make it hard for me to find another position—if and when one ever opens up." She looked at his hard profile. He was so clear-minded and forthright. He probably never waffled like she did. "And there's a little thing called a non-compete that I signed. If I leave, I can't work anywhere within sixty miles of Fort Collins. I like living in Northern Colorado. I don't want to go to Denver. Or move out of state." That was one thing that never wavered for her. "I'm determined to make my mark as a landscape designer. It'll be a struggle anywhere. Might as well take a stand and fight here, where I want to be. This area is growing like crazy. I want to help it grow in a beautiful and sustainable way."

He nodded and sent her a quick look. "I like that you're doing what matters to you—despite the assholes around you."

They hit a drive-through coffee stand, then made the long trek out to his property. Didn't take long to leave the last neighborhood behind them. Soon even the ranches grew sparse. The vegetation changed from the forced lushness of the suburban lots to the brown fields recently harvested, to the treeless grasslands of the prairie. They crossed the last highway that ran in a north-south direction between Wyoming and Colorado. And still they drove east. After a long while, they turned north off the two-lane highway onto a dirt road. The land became contoured, moving over and around small hills and dry creek beds. Much of the acreage was open grazing, so small dots that were black cattle spotted the range far into the distance.

She looked at Sam. He really was way out in the middle of nowhere. "You said remote, but there's nothing here. This is almost a moonscape."

"High mountain desert prairie. Beautiful, isn't it?"

"If you like wind and dirt."

"I do."

"What drew you to come out here?" He seemed to be a wealthy man. He could have bought property anywhere in the world. What made a sane man pick such barren land to homestead?

"Besides the low cost of the acreage and the huge amount of land available?"

"Yeah."

"I bought an old military missile silo and needed to build a home on top of it."

"You what? Why on earth would you want one of those?" She was glad she'd left Sam's address with Jada. Summer knew if she didn't check in later, at least one person would follow up with the law. If she disappeared, someone would be on it quickly.

"Let's just say I'm an extreme prepper."

"You think the world's going to end?" She chuckled as she said it, but the look he gave her sent a little shiver down her spine. He was serious. He did think the world was going to end.

God, why oh why did she rely so heavily on her gut instinct? She'd been so desperate to have a meaty job that she'd jumped at this opportunity without giving it enough thought. "You promise to bring me back to town tonight?"

He looked at her and grinned. "I guess right about now you're thinking I'm a weirdo serial killer or something."

"Are you?"

"Maybe."

"Don't joke about this, Sam."

"I did promise to return you to the real world tonight. But if you get scared and want to head back earlier, you can always call for backup."

She looked at her phone. Of course, no cell coverage.

He laughed. "You scare easily."

"Well, yeah." Oh, fuck. He was giving off a really weird vibe, too, the farther out they went.

It seemed they drove north for a long while before he made another turn to the east. Summer caught herself making mental notes of the scant few land-marks she saw on the off chance it would help later. Really, she was just scaring herself. Didn't help that there were only desiccated remnants of old cedar stumps, shallow ravines, and miles of barbed wire for landmarks.

They cleared another hill, and then she saw it. His fort. She gasped. It was massive. At least the size of a city block. He really did have a fort out here.

He pulled off the dirt road, then parked in a paved lot on the north side of his monstrous home. A big metal-roofed portico covered the lot and had several rows of solar panels on it. At least the parking area had some cover from snow and hail and all the other raw elements that everything out here was exposed to.

"Welcome to my home," he said as he put the SUV in park.

"Who all lives here?" she asked as she grabbed her stuff and got out.

"Me. Some friends. Occasional visitors."

She walked around to the end of his car. What wasn't he telling her? "Aren't you lonely living out here by yourself?"

"Sometimes the quiet is everything I need. Sometimes I need human company. When that happens, I go into town for dinner, like I did last night."

Summer walked beyond the parking area. The hill the fort was on let her see quite far in three directions. Way into the distance out east, there was prairie that had a pink shimmer. Even farther east were some big wind farms. A huge area was scraped brown by the oil and gas works going on. Wind buffeted her, tossing her hair every which way. She pulled it to one side and looked at Sam. "But what do you do here with all your quiet days?"

"Plan world domination."

She laughed. "I get it. It's none of my business." She looked at him. "I just worry about anyone being so alone."

His eyes were serious as he studied her. "I've only just built my fort. I'm not going to off myself anytime soon."

What an odd thing to say so casually. She was still contemplating his comment when he walked to front door.

The entry to the fort was an enormous arched blue wooden gate, big enough for giants to walk through. Black iron studs made a Z pattern on either half of the doorway. The gates opened outward, but there was a regular-sized wooden inset door that opened inward. He unlocked it at a keypad and held it for her, revealing a short, tunnel-like entrance framed by the fort's second floor above and the two wings on either side.

The thick adobe walls gave the corridor a solid feel. In front of them was a big courtyard. She looked around and saw so many neat nooks and crannies that she immediately wanted to explore, but she had to tamp down her excitement. This wasn't a tourist stop —it was a man's home. She had to be circumspect even though her mind was churning with possibilities for all kinds of garden touches. Collections of pots. Vines to grow up the portico supports. Even a garden plot for herbs next to the big Moroccan fountain in the middle.

"Come. Let's get some water, then I'll show you around."

They went through a French door set deep in the adobe wall to their right. The room looked like it would have been at home in Santa Fe, with its orange-beige adobe walls and a kiva fireplace. She set her messenger bag on a chair and looked around in awe. This was the biggest kitchen she'd ever been in. It was stocked with restaurant-grade stainless-steel appliances. There was a double oven range on one wall with a huge hood that went up to the ceiling. There were warming drawers and cooling drawers, two dishwashers, and a Sub-Zero fridge with glass doors. The cabinets were a dark taupe and had white quartz countertops. Several people could cook in there together without ever stepping on each other.

Summer knew Sam was probably secretly laughing at her. She wasn't used to such grand spaces. Even Kiera's kitchen at the shelter wasn't anything like this—and it was a big one too.

He handed her a bottle of water. His smile was soft, his eyes gentle. "What do you think so far?"

"I have so many questions," Summer said.

"Ask away. I may have some answers."

"Why a fort? Why adobe? Why here?"

"I've wanted a fort ever since I could remember. There weren't too many historical ones lying around anywhere, waiting for a buyer. Certainly not ones for sale, and if they were, they were in pretty rough shape. Plus, I'm a tall guy. Most of those were made for shorter men. And adobe has a nice feel. It's solid and grounding. The outer walls are four feet thick and have a specially designed metal spine, which helps deflect thermal and infrared probes."

That last was said with a smile. Her hand paused with her bottle halfway to her mouth. Was he serious?

"Why are you avoiding thermal and infrared probes?"

"I like my privacy."

"Oh."

"We'll take a walk around the outside of the fort, so you can get an idea of what I'm looking for. Was there a specific time you need to get back into town?"

"No. But speaking of which, I better text my friends so they know we got here safely." She said "we" in an effort to not offend him, but the implication was there. Something about Sam was heady and interesting, piquing her curiosity in an irresistible way. But there was also a countercurrent that gave her frissons of alarm now and then.

Really, what kind of person built himself a fort? Or bought an old missile silo? Or needed to deflect infrared probes?

She hoped he was just benignly eccentric. Maybe she should consider handing this job off to Clark... but that was dependent on Sam getting her back to the real world intact.

He gave her a Wi-Fi password. She connected and

sent off a text, then pocketed her phone. She slipped her messenger bag over her shoulder, then followed him back outside. The color scheme he'd used, the bright blue gates and warm beige walls, mimicked the color of the sky and ground, making the huge monstrosity of the fort fit in with its surroundings.

## 11

---

She and Sam walked a little way out front, then turned to face his fort.

"I studied dozens of historical adobe structures before coming up with the design for my fort," he said. "Of course, none of them had modern amenities, so that needed to be incorporated. And I wanted to be economical with the fort's power and water consumption, so I had to add an engine room for that purpose."

"You've thought of almost everything. But what about food?"

"Got that covered too. You'll see in our walka-bout. The entire south wing is a greenhouse."

"So what exactly are you hiring my company to do?"

"I want a garden. Everything right now is entirely utilitarian. A garden would soften that, make a nice place to wander and think." He spread his arms wide. "I'd like something surrounding the whole property."

"It would need to be xeriscaped, unless you have a deep well or are trucking in water. This terrain, as you already mentioned, is semiarid."

"Xeriscaping sounds good. I don't have an endless water supply."

"Even a dry garden will need a good amount of water for the first couple of years while the plants get established, but after that, they'd only need occasional watering, with a little extra in the driest and hottest months."

"I can accommodate that. If I have to bring in supplemental water for a while, I can."

She took out her notebook and started to jot some things down. "Tell me what you're looking for. Have you seen gardens you liked?"

His lips tilted upward. "I saw one in Fort Collins last night that blew me away."

Summer felt heat move up her neck. "I love that one too."

Sam looked at the fort and the barren grounds surrounding it. A stiff breeze was stirring up loose dirt. "I'd like something that complements the adobe structure. I loved many of the gardens I saw in Santa Fe and Taos."

"That's a similar climate to what we have out here, except they actually have more water than we do." She checked a chart on her clipboard. "The temperature here can swing wildly from thirty below in the winter to a hundred and ten in the summer, so whatever we plant, it'll have to survive those extremes."

"I'd like paths to wander through. Some sitting areas. Some shade structures. Maybe some water features. I love the sound of water."

"Right. Let me take some measurements and photos."

"I'll send you the dimensions of the outer wall."

"Great. How far out do you want the garden to go?"

"I think to about where we're standing. A hundred feet or so. Give or take ten feet."

"All the way around the fort?"

"I think so."

"Sam, that's going to cost you a fortune."

"Then it's lucky I have a fortune."

She shook her head. "Well, we can do this several ways. We can break it into quadrants and tackle each one sequentially. We could put in all the hardscape and then, in a future phase, put in the plantings. We could do some now and more in the spring."

"I want it all at once, in whatever way works best."

Summer gave him a bleak look. "This is one of the largest installations my company's done in years. They're going to take this away from me."

LIEGE FELT a wash of anger slip through him. "No they won't. They only get this job if you're the lead on it. Period. Of course, you could quit your job and work full-time on this directly for me."

Summer shook her head. "Except there's that non-compete with them. They'd nail me to the wall."

He smiled. She had no idea what he was capable of. In her eyes, he was a normal guy, though maybe a bit eccentric. "They could try, but they wouldn't get far." The shiver that rippled through her tingled his own nerves. He could feel she was equal parts fascinated and frightened by him. He had to remind himself he couldn't keep her, Matchmaker be damned. For her own wellbeing and his sanity, he should leave the fort until she was finished with the project. Just knowing that she was there and safe was all that mattered.

But that wouldn't satisfy the Matchmaker. And Liege's legendary self-control already couldn't get a handhold on his hunger for her.

"Forget measurements and note taking. You can do those later, on another visit. Talk to me about your vision."

She nodded and looked around, then tucked her notebook back into her messenger. "I'll draft everything up in a formal plan, eventually. I'm sure we'll go through several design iterations." She pointed to his two artificial trees that stood at the corners of his fort. "What are those?"

"Wind turbine trees. Each of the leaf sets turns with even a slight breeze, which creates energy that can be stored. They provide power when there's no sunlight—a nice backup should our batteries be depleted. I wish they weren't so obviously fake, but they serve an important function."

"We can do a treatment around them to soften them. I see another parking area on the east side. Which will you be using as a main entrance?"

He was still running with the cover story of opening a B&B for ecotourists, but how long could he keep that charade up? "The north gate will be the main entrance for visitors—my front door, if you will. There are two more gates on the east side, which you'll see in a few."

Summer cocked her head. "Are you going to be opening a restaurant? I'm trying to understand what will bring visitors to the oasis you're building."

Liege spread his arms wide. "This, all around us. This great, wide, empty nothing is what will bring them. There are several species of rare wildflowers around here that only bloom under extraordinary conditions. Some are endangered. We have herds of deer and pronghorn antelope, packs of coyotes that roam through here. We have raptor nesting sites and burrowing owls, which are a threatened species. It's a wild place to visit and reconnect with nature in a Zen-like setting."

"So I imagine you'll want a walled garden to keep the antelope and deer out."

"Yes. I like walls."

Summer clamped her jaw shut, but her smile still broke free. "I can see that."

"There's another reason people will come here. I'll show it to you if we have time."

"Okay." She nodded and looked around her. "Are you a draw-inside-the-lines guy, with all your walls and stuff? Or do you like curves and little surprises?"

"Curves. And surprises. I like wondering what's just around the bend."

"You can tell so much about a person by the garden they build. Doesn't matter if it's an epic one, like this will be, or a small urban patch. Personality always comes through."

"Interesting. I never thought about that."

"You're building your garden as a gift to others, you know. People will come here to heal."

Shit. She'd hit the nail on the head with that one. And she knew nothing about the rest of his property. He was one of only a few mutant team leads with a healer on staff. He looked away from her.

"I hope so."

He just wasn't convinced the healing that was needed could actually happen. But in an odd way, the garden gave him hope—something he hadn't felt in a very long while.

For the next hour, Summer talked to him about her vision, weaving an image for him that was rich in textures and colors. He saw everything as she imagined it, fresh in her mind. He didn't actually need her words, but her voice was sweet and delivered her ideas in yet another medium, letting him experience her plan in multiple dimensions—one visual and nonverbal, one audible and equally exquisite, both giving life to her vision. Taking them in simultaneously was nearly sensory overload.

If he weren't already craving her, he would have been blindsided by her effect on him. Hell, he still was.

She was soft, sweet, brilliantly creative. She was hope and kindness. She was everything he was missing in his life...everything he never thought he'd have.

How had the Matchmaker known she was perfect for him?

He should stop this. Fire her. Anger her so she would give this project off to the bastards she worked for. He was after them, not her. But it was too late. Having met her, having bathed in her voice and breathed her scent, he feared the last thread of his humanity would flame out without a connection to her.

He watched her move around the north and then west sides of his fort, waving her arms to indicate a certain spot for a plant or an architectural feature like steps or a path or a short wall. He saw what she saw. Every stroke of her hand was like the wave of a magician's wand, spreading color and beauty.

It was heady and humbling to the point of bringing tears to his eyes. Watching her was like watching God himself create the wonders of the world.

"What?" She stopped and stared at him.

He shook his head, not trusting his voice.

"Can you not see this?"

"I can."

She tilted her head, considering him. "You have such soft eyes."

He didn't, really. There was nothing soft about him. Not his body or his mind or his heart. Leave it to someone like her to see what he hid from everyone, even himself.

"You fascinate me," he said. "I have no idea what you're talking about, but watching you, I can see what you see." He looked up at the big wall of his fort. "For me, it's just a blank canvas, but for you, it's the finished product, plants thriving in this harsh environment. Color where there's only sun-bleached beige. Water flowing in this desert. You see beauty where I see harsh land."

He looked to see if he was making sense to her. He needn't have. He was in her mind and knew her response. He realized his words felt like a gift to her, and he saw what that looked like in her eyes; she was stricken, as if he'd pulled her soul out of her body to let the sun shine on it.

He swallowed hard. "I never thought about any of this before."

"If it's ugly to you, why did you choose this location?"

"Besides the silo?"

She nodded.

"Because I like the harshness. It's a raw part of

nature that we seem to ignore. I'm overwhelmed by your vision, Summer. I wasn't expecting so much could be done with this place. Water's scarce and the temps are often extreme."

She nodded and sent another glance over the scene she'd described for him. "Water is a scarce resource. We have to respect that and include that in our design. The plants I'm suggesting are highly drought-tolerant once they're established. A lot of what we'll be putting in here is landscape rocks, flag-stone, gravel, steps—hardscape. We'll build in some shade to help cool some areas and provide nice places to sit and linger." She smiled. "It's a tough space, but we can do it."

"When can you start?"

"I have a few other projects in progress that I have to finish first—or at least make sure Clark gets them done."

"Douglas said to give them to Clark."

She laughed. "I *am* the junior person that every-thing gets handed off to."

"I want to be your top priority."

She nodded. "I'll work something out."

"If you can't, I will."

"Do you always get your way?"

"Yes."

She shook her head. "Let's finish the tour around your fort."

They walked around to the south side. That portion of the fort provided a special function: it was where the pool and the greenhouse were located. The lower half of the wall was adobe, but the upper half, going up three stories to an arched ceiling, was all glass.

"Oh my God," she said. "I never expected this."

"It's for winter gardening. It isn't always easy getting in to town with the snowdrifts we get out here. And with our long winters, I'd like to still have fresh produce. There's a pool in there too."

"Wow. I need to see the view from in there. I was thinking this might make a great spot for a summer garden. Of course, we'll build it so that we can keep rabbits and antelope out."

"I think that would be nice. There's a great view of the prairie from inside. Let's definitely look at that before you go."

They went around the east side of the fort where the southeast covered parking was. The slope up to that level was steep. Liege reached over and took her elbow to help her up.

Summer looked back where they'd just been. "We should put in a retaining wall here. It can be tiered and either become part of the vegetable garden or full of colorful plantings that soften the wall."

"I like that. Want to see the pool room?" he asked.

"Yes!"

They went into the fort from the southeast gate, then went up to the second floor. The wide, winding stairs felt like something out of a castle. They went around the tower walls connecting the south and east wings.

A short hallway led them to a steel door, which Liege opened. Summer gasped as they stepped out onto the uppermost tier of a steeply graded room. Liege had hired a pool company to put in the pool and construct the terraces. Everywhere in the room had access to light from the windows. The glass triangles in the arched ceiling were frosted, letting in diffused lighting. Some of them opened automatically when the room became too hot, with inset screens that kept birds and bugs out.

At the moment, the space looked like an abandoned theme park ride. No dirt or plantings filled the deep troughs of each tier. The hardscape was softened by a fast-moving waterfall that slid and curved its way down to the long pool below.

"Sam." Summer wrapped her arm around his as she scanned the room, seeing all of its possibilities. "I want to do this room myself." She looked up at him. "Don't give this to my company. I don't care if you pay me for it or not."

"It's yours. And of course I'll pay you. You have a car to fix."

She laughed and jogged down several sets of staggered stairs to the lower levels. There were pathways and bridges over the artificial river. As soon as she got to the bottom, she came up a different way, running over several paths and laughing like a kid.

He smiled, watching her. She was everything he

needed. Joy. Light. Hope. And the fucking Match-maker had cursed her. And him, because when she died, so would he.

When she came level with him again, she threw her arms wide and said, "I love this room! I love it! What a haven this will be in the winter. Your guests will love it too."

He loved that she loved it. His friends had mocked him for putting this in the fort, but now he was glad he'd ignored them. Well, Merc and Bastion had, anyway. Guerre hadn't. He'd known a space like this could be healing. Acier was just glad to have a pool he could use.

"I have no idea what to do with this," Liege admitted. "There's good light in here, and it's temper-ature-controlled, so it's a perfect place for an indoor garden."

"It is. And it's tall enough that you could even have some date and coconut palms down below. You could have banana trees and some citrus trees. All kinds of food crops." She pointed to an area of the upper terrace. "You could have an herb garden there. And it wouldn't have to be all utilitarian. We can decide what you need for food and put in ornamentals around that."

"Good, because I was thinking of circulating the oxygenated air from in here through the rest of the rooms in the fort. The more plants we have, the better."

"That's a great idea." Summer took out her phone and snapped some pictures.

"Next time you come out, bring your suit. We'll go swimming."

She smiled at him. "If we do that, I won't ever want to leave."

*That would be okay,* Liege thought, but caught himself before saying it. He had to give her time. She didn't have the biofeedback that he did to jump from zero to a hundred as fast as he could.

"Okay." She shook off her excitement. "I need to grab some more pics. This is going to be so much fun! We can work in here when the weather's bad." She frowned. "Or maybe not. Maybe I'll have to save it for after the exterior work is finished so no one from the shop hears about it."

"You don't have to hide a damned thing. I'll take care of it, if it comes up."

She laughed and hugged him. The embrace was over almost as fast as it began, but Liege's heart skipped a few beats.

"I'm so glad I hit you," Summer said. "Well, not that I hit you, but that I ran into you. No, not that either. I'm glad we met. And I'm glad you wanted all of this work done. And I'm glad you have such a magical place here."

He chuckled. "You thought I was crazy."

"I still do, but I'm starting to like your kind of crazy."

How long would that last, he wondered?

"Will you show me around the rest of your fort?" Summer asked.

"Next time. It's a big place. And there's still one more thing I'd like to show you before it gets dark."

She put her hands on her hips and grinned at him. "Let's go."

They went back out to the carport. Instead of taking his Escalade, Liege opened the door of a Jeep that was in the same parking lot. She slipped her messenger bag over her head and set it on the floor in front of her seat then got in.

He started the car and pulled out of the covered parking, turning east on the dirt road that they'd driven in on. "Are you going to pave any of these roads?" she asked.

"Probably. If only to keep visitors from damaging the fragile terrain."

They headed toward the east then turned north on another dirt road. They drove over some rough areas where rain and wind had gouged out part of the road. After a bit, he stopped and put the Jeep in park. Summer got out before he could open her door. She gave him a curious look. At least she was no longer thinking he'd brought her out here to kill her and dispose of her body.

Liege started walking up a steep slope, following a path between two low hills. He couldn't wait for her reaction to what she was about to see. At the top, he reached down to her and brought her up beside him. He smiled when she gasped at the view.

They were standing on a ridge overlooking a wide ravine with several sandstone buttes. It was the perfect time of day to be there. The sun was behind them and low in the sky, painting the beige buttes in shades of orange and pink. The wind had stilled.

"Wow. Just wow." She looked back at him. "Is this part of your property?"

He nodded. "I'm working on a deal to purchase more of the surrounding land. I want to protect these buttes from being destroyed by oil works and wind farms. I have nothing against either type of operation, but I want to preserve the wildness of this site."

"I hope you're successful."

"I do too."

"I had no idea these were here. I've seen the ones south of here in the Pawnee Buttes National Grassland, but I didn't know there were more of them."

"There's a line of them dotting the region up into Nebraska."

Summer shook her head. "As if what you're doing back at your fort didn't make this a great place for visitors, this is the icing on the cake." She took a step closer to the edge.

Liege heard the crackling of the gravel and reacted before she even knew the ledge she was on was so unstable. He grabbed her around the waist and pulled her against him as a chunk of the edge crumbled away. He would have let her go as soon as he'd moved her back to stable ground, but her arms slipped around his and she leaned against him.

"This is a special place," she said.

He smiled over her head. Everything with beauty was special or magical or wondrous to her. And she made it so to him. He looked at their twined arms and hands, light and dark, content to have every last second she gave him. He drew a deep breath of her sweet scent. Roses. There absolutely needed to be sweet roses in his garden.

"I could look at this forever." She turned in his arms and put her hands on his chest. "I'm glad you brought me here. Maybe we could bring a picnic up sometime while I'm working on your place. If there's a warm day."

"Absolutely."

She smiled up at him. He stared into her eyes, wishing she would kiss him, but she pulled away, dashing that dream.

"I guess it's time to head back to town," she said.

"Sure."

They went back to his Jeep. "Do you think we could have some roses somewhere in your plan?" he asked.

"It's a harsh climate for them, but I'm sure we can find some drought tolerant ones. I'll do some research."

Summer was sad when they got back to Sam's fort. He was doing something truly wonderful here, and she didn't want to leave it to return to the real world.

"I have a favor to ask," Sam said as they parked.

"Sure, what?" Summer asked.

They got out of his Jeep. "Let me fix your car. Consider it part of your payment for working on my greenhouse."

"I don't know when I'm going to get to that yet. It could be a little while."

"I don't care. At least I'll know you'll have dependable wheels to get out here with."

She studied him a moment, wondering what it was like to have so much money that a thousand-dollar repair bill was hardly a blip to his budget. "If you're sure."

"I am."

"Then okay. And thank you."

"Do you have everything? I should probably drive you back to town."

"I'm good to go."

They stared at each other a long moment. Summer really didn't want to leave him. It was odd how much like her imaginary Sam he was.

## 12

Summer drove her broken car into work the next morning. Each time she slowed then accelerated, it had a brief hesitation. Whatever was causing that issue had predated her accident with Sam's SUV. She hadn't fixed her car after the insurance check came, partly because she needed the money for other bills, but also because she was debating junking it and buying the cheapest alternative she could find.

She felt bad letting Sam pick up the bill for the bumper repair. She decided when—if—she got to work, she'd tell him to forget about it. It wasn't worth repairing at this point.

She pulled into the landscape center's parking lot, relieved she'd made it. The morning was mild. Jada and a couple of other staff members were working out front, watering the autumn pots and refreshing the display of pumpkins and cornstalks.

Clark came out from the garden center, his coat on, keys in his hands. "Ready to go?" he asked Summer.

"Go where?"

"To this fort you're taking on. I want to see it. And you'll never make it in that beater of yours"—he gave her a disappointed glare—"which you have to know reflects badly on us."

That little dig stole her breath. If they compensated her according to the going market rate for her skill set, she could afford a new car. Before she could answer, however, a tow truck pulled into the parking lot and backed up to her car.

The driver got out and came over. "Are you Summer?" he asked.

"Yep."

He handed her a receipt and a business card. "Great. I'll get your car towed over to the shop. We're a little backed up, so I can't say for certain when we'll get to yours. You can call the number on that card this afternoon for a more exact schedule."

She signed the paper, feeling miserable. "Look, I know my friend put in this order, but I really don't think this car is worth repairing."

"Your friend?" Clark asked under his breath.

"Don't worry about it, ma'am," the driver said. "We can fix it. And Sam's already paid us, so let us do our thing. We'll get it back to you as soon as possible." He looked at her car. "Anything you need from it before I haul it away?"

Summer grabbed her messenger bag, then gave the guy her key.

The girls from the front desk were nosily watching everything, all while keeping busy straightening the front patio area. Jada was sweeping a display of furniture and clustered pots. She straightened and smiled. "Finally getting your car fixed."

Summer looked over at the tow truck. "Yeah, just not sure it's worth it."

"It's not," Clark commented.

Jada shrugged, ignoring him. "It'll be nice having it be dependable again."

"A bumper repair is a long way from fixing all that's wrong with it," Summer said.

"When will they have it back?" Jada asked.

"The guy didn't know. He said call the office later today. Looks like a week of buses are in store for me."

"I can pick you up," Jada said. "You've done it for me plenty of times."

Summer nodded. "Thank you, Jada. I appreciate that."

"Well. Now you'll have to let me drive you out there," Clark said, grinning victoriously. "You've got no wheels at all."

A car and a truck pulled into the parking lot. Summer looked at her watch. The shop wouldn't be open for another half-hour. Maybe these guys weren't aware of their winter hours.

A man got out of the truck and came toward

them. Jada said, "Good morning! Can I help you with something?"

"I'm looking for Summer Coltrane."

Jada smiled at her. "You are in demand this morning."

Summer nodded at the man. "I'm Summer."

He handed her a set of keys. "Sam asked me to drop off a truck, so you'd have some wheels while yours are in the shop." He touched the tip of his baseball cap. "Papers are in the glove compartment. If you have any troubles with it, just give us a call."

He got into the car that had come with him and waved as they drove off.

The truck was an extended-cab Ford F-150, in deep forest green. It looked brand new. Summer looked at the key fob in her hand, then swept her friends with a shocked gaze.

"I want a Sam," Jada said.

"I can't believe this." Summer shook her head.

Clark stepped in front of her, giving his back to Jada. "Our client is your 'friend' already? Looks more like a sugar daddy to me."

"You're disgusting, Clark. This is one of the biggest accounts we've landed. He clearly wants us to do his garden design."

"No, he clearly wants you—"

"I think you're jealous."

Clark's face hardened. "I think you need to watch yourself."

"Likewise," Summer said. She gave Jada an

aggrieved look, then stepped around Clark and went to the truck. "I'll be out at Sam's if you need me," she said to Jada and Clark, ignoring her ex's angry gaze.

She took out the journal that she kept in her messenger bag and jotted down Clark's latest harassment incident. He was stepping over the line ever more frequently. She hoped, when she finally did leave her job, that the things she'd documented would help her break her non-compete.

She tucked her journal away, then texted Sam. *Thank you. For the tow, for the truck loaner, everything. I appreciate it, I really do. I just don't think my car is worth fixing.*

*It's already done.*

She closed her eyes and drew a long breath. *Well, thank you.*

*Come on out.*

Summer smiled. *On my way.*

LIEGE WATCHED Summer work all afternoon on the west side of his fort. The days were getting so short now—she only had about an hour of daylight left. She was madly sketching something. She'd gone through pages of her sketchpad. He'd had no idea being a landscape designer was such a creative process.

At the beginning of the day, he'd brought her out a folding chair and table. He'd found a firm spot for the chair that worked with the angle she wanted for her sketch at that moment. A little while ago, he'd brought her out a metal travel mug of hot cocoa along with a fresh bottle of water.

She looked up once and saw him watching her from the windows in the living room—he'd forgotten to hide himself from her. For a long moment, they just stared at each other. He knew she was trying to figure him out. For his part, he was trying to absorb everything about her so that he could picture her in his garden long after his time with her had passed—as it would if the Matchmaker had his way. She would be a memory, but she'd be every bit as alive and vital as she was now. He wasn't ashamed for not looking away.

When the sun was low on the horizon, Liege became aware of Bastion standing near him and turned from the window.

Bastion shook his head. "I cannot believe that you have been given the greatest gift and do nothing but stand there staring at her. She is your woman, Liege. Why are you not spending your days in your room?" He huffed a sigh and threw his hands up, mumbling a string of French curse words as he started back through the dining room on his way to the kitchen.

Liege followed him.

"Americans have no passion. I assume your female is staying for dinner?" Bastion looked back at him. "You can at least feed her, *oui*?"

"Maybe."

"Maybe. You destroy me. If I ever find my female,

you will know it because you will never see me." Bastion opened the fridge and showed him the spread of fajita fixings. He opened the warming drawer. "I have sliced the flank steak I grilled for you. I also grilled her tempeh steak. The guys and I will eat in the game room, so we will not bother you. Much."

"Thank you, Bastion."

Bastion grunted. "It's your job to get her to stay." His eyes narrowed. "I don't care that it was the Matchmaker who pointed her out to you. She is your light. She is the one. Perhaps your only one for the entirety of your existence. Don't blow this chance."

"I can't corner her."

"It's not cornering her. It's loving her." Bastion pursed his lips, then shook his head. "Bah. Everything is here. Do what you want with it. I even have the rooftop deck set up with a fire going. I put a pitcher of margaritas in the fridge up there for you."

Liege stared at Bastion. "I didn't date much, you know, even when I was a regular. I didn't know how to impress a woman then and know even less now."

Bastion sighed. He came over and set a hand on Liege's shoulder. "It is good that you have me, then. I can give you the food and the setting, but I am no Cyrano de Bergerac. You must come up with your own words, *oui*?"

Liege smiled as his friend stormed out of the room. It would be fun to see Bastion in Liege's shoes. That was a sobering thought, however. The Matchmaker didn't give gifts; he gave curses.

Liege walked outside to fetch Summer. "Hey," he said as he came around the side of the fort.

She looked at him, then blinked at him as if just becoming aware of the hour and her loss of daylight. "Hi. I'm just finishing up."

"I can't wait to see what you've come up with."

"This is nothing formal. Just a guide for me to use in my planning software. Places have moods, you know."

He lifted his brows. She was hella sensitive. "I didn't know."

"Sometimes it comes from the people who live there; sometimes it's the land itself. It's in the way the wind sounds and how the sunlight looks and how shadows fall. It all tells a story. What I try to do as a designer is bring that story to life so that it's known, so others see it and feel it."

"Come inside. You can show me what this place told you."

She seemed to grow wary. "You aren't making fun of that."

"Why would I? Even if I can't detect the fort's mood, if you can, then that's a gift. Makes me even more certain I found the right person for this project." And for himself...

She tucked her sketchpad away, then stood and slung the messenger bag over her head. He desperately wanted to hold her hand, touch her. Instead, he busied himself with her folding table and chair. They entered through the north gate and went into the kitchen.

"I have dinner for us," he said.

"Oh." She shot him a quick look, then checked her watch. "Gosh, it is late. I lose track sometimes."

"You were in the zone."

"I shouldn't stay. I don't want to impose."

"I don't want to eat alone. And everything's already cooked. We can talk about your vision."

She smiled. He looked away so that she wouldn't see the light burning in his eyes.

"All right, then. I accept. I think I'll just wash up first." She set her coat and bag on a chair.

"Bring your coat. And the restroom's this way." He led her to a hallway off the kitchen. "I know I still owe you a full tour. I didn't want to interrupt your work today for it, since you were so focused, but there is one feature of the fort I want you to see now."

She handed him her coat. "Maybe next time I'm out here we can do the whole tour."

He lost himself in her eyes for a moment. "Right. The restroom is just there." He pointed into the large alcove under the tower stairs. "I'll just wait here," he said, standing at the foot of the wide stone staircase that bent around the wall of the tower.

When Summer came out of the bathroom, they went up to the rooftop area. Small lights on the stair risers lit their way. Liege could feel Summer's curiosity as she looked around them. At the top was a large landing. A glass corridor went around the second floor as it did below, connecting all of the rooms. In one corner, a spiral staircase went down to the kitchen. Just on the other side of that was a single-pane French door that led outside to a wide terrace.

True to his word, Bastion had started the gas fire in the firepit. Two free-standing heaters were glowing red. Blankets had been tossed over the L-shaped patio sofa.

"Wow. This is gorgeous!" Summer said.

The slope of the deck sent water runoff to a collection tank at the north end of the fort. Small lights were embedded in the lip of the concrete deck, filling the entire area with soft illumination. A metal railing with steel stringers came up three feet from the raised edge. Liege hadn't been up there in a while, but he knew the guys did a lot of grilling there.

*You see, I did everything,* Bastion said via their mental link. *The rest is up to you. Use your words, Liege.*

*Go away,* Liege said. *I don't need an audience.*

"This is amazing. Sam, what a gorgeous retreat you have here." She walked to the edges and looked out over the area where the garden would be. "This rooftop area adds another whole dimension to the design. I need to take into account what it looks like from up here."

Liege smiled. "That's what I wanted you to see." He took the margarita pitcher from the fridge and filled two glasses, then handed her one of them.

She took a sip then shivered as a breeze blew over

the fort. Liege grabbed one of the blankets and spread it across her shoulders.

"Thanks. I'm enjoying your project. It's the biggest I've gotten to do entirely on my own. I'm surprised you aren't hounding me for design specifics. Cost, timeline, etc."

"I can't wait to see it finished, but to be honest, I'm enjoying the process. I don't have any need to drive it to closure. I have faith you'll see this project through."

"I wish all my clients were like you."

He didn't. That would mean all of them were plotting ways to get her into their beds. Speaking of which... "Things still going okay with your ex?"

She shrugged. "He's a jerk."

"Agreed. So why work for him?"

"Well, technically, I work for his dad." She sighed. "We dated off and on in college. We were in the same master's program. I interned summers at his dad's landscape center. After college, Clark and I became more serious about our relationship—which had been an off-and-on kind of thing. Everyone around us was getting married, having kids, settling down. When his dad offered me a permanent position, I didn't hesitate. Their garden center is one of the largest and best connected in Northern Colorado. I couldn't have asked for a better place to start. But things don't always turn out like you expect. There was one other senior designer at the time we started. We were both assigned to assist him. But Clark moved up, and I didn't. And when that designer left, Clark moved up again, leaving me all the junk work. They even used my designs and presented them to customers as if Clark had made them. It didn't bother me much at first. After all, the back-office stuff behind a design should be invisible to customers. All they know is that they're hiring the landscape center.

"Eventually, though, it began to rankle. I worked twice as hard as Clark and got no recognition or bonuses for it. I started to network outside of the business. I volunteered to do garden designs for different organizations that were building homes for underprivileged homeowners or wounded vets or single moms. I guess word about my work was getting around. Douglas told me he wanted me to make it clear that I was doing my volunteer work on behalf of the garden center. I declined. He offered me a raise and promised to bring on an assistant for me if I would agree.

"Finally, I thought I was moving up, but he got me to sign that non-compete in exchange for the raise. Stupidly, I did."

"Those are often not enforceable. Your employers can't keep you from being gainfully employed using your area of expertise."

"I have a feeling the way they worded it, it would stick. It forbids me from working in my field for any company inside a sixty-mile radius of their garden centers for two years. That covers most of the Front Range, since they have several centers along it. I might have an out, though, after all the harassment

I've documented from Clark." She shrugged. "But I still expect a fight if I don't comply."

"When did you break up with Clark?"

"A couple of years ago. I was thinking we were headed toward marriage, but I caught him out with other women. After I broke it off with him that's when his dad gave him his first promotion."

"Bastard."

"Yeah. I've been dancing to their tune ever since. You really pissed them off demanding I handle your project." She smiled at him.

Liege grinned. "I'm glad."

"Clark had decided he'd drive me out here, since I didn't have dependable wheels and that reflected badly on the company. He'd no sooner said that than your courier dropped off the truck. It was perfect timing. For once in my life, absolutely perfect timing." She giggled.

The tinkling sound of her happiness transfixed Liege. Sometimes, things weren't only heard by your ears but by your whole soul. "That wasn't the first time—it was also perfect timing when you rear-ended me. Had anyone else hit me, we might not be about to share a delicious supper."

Her expression switched to something serious. "How do you do it?"

"Do what?"

"You aren't much older than I am, but you have your shit together. I'm like a twenty-eight-year-old teenager who refuses to grow up. If I did, I'd have parted ways with the Briscoes ages ago. I wouldn't now be living in the same studio apartment as I did in school. And I sure as hell wouldn't buy a gorgeous antique Uzbek carpet when I knew it would cause me stress paying my bills."

Liege shook his head. "We're different people. You can't compare us in that way. I bet that carpet was beautiful." He'd seen it, and it was pretty. "You're a creative. You have to surround yourself with beauty. It's the same to you as water is to fish. Buying that carpet probably gave you the strength to keep on the road you're on."

Summer swallowed hard. "I don't want to be on that road anymore."

"Then get off it. Do something different. Move to a different town and open your own shop. You have choices." She didn't have the freedom to do any of that, but he was stalling for time, trying to give her the chance to pick him of her own free will.

"My friends are here," she said.

"But your freedom isn't."

Summer broke eye contact with him, taking a sip of her drink. He wondered if he'd gone too far. He could feel her mind chewing on what he'd just said. He wished he could tell her not to sweat it because her future was as locked up as his; they were going to be a couple. It was an inescapable fact of nature.

"So when will you be opening your fort for visitors?" she asked, changing the subject.

"It already is. I've had a few couples stay here on

and off over the last few months." He gave her a smile. "Why don't we go back downstairs and have supper? I can't wait to see your sketches."

Back in the kitchen, Liege took out the dishes of fajita toppings that Bastion had made. Guacamole, chopped tomatoes, shredded cheese, sour cream. He took the sliced steak and tempeh out of the warming drawer, along with a dish of sautéed onions. "I wasn't certain how dedicated you are as a vegetarian, so I have flank and tempeh steaks. Will that work?"

"You just happened to have tempeh on hand?"

"No. I picked some up on my way home from dinner the other night. I figured, if I was lucky, you might stay for dinner one evening."

He felt her shock.

"That was thoughtful," she said. "Thank you. I sometimes eat meat, but it just doesn't light my fire."

He smiled. "Then I'm glad mashed soy does."

She laughed. "Can I help you with anything?"

"Yeah. How about grabbing the pitcher of tea and filling our glasses? Unless you want another margarita? But you do have to drive back to town tonight. On the other hand, I have plenty of guest rooms if you'd like to have another margarita."

She shook her head. "I didn't bring a change of clothes. I might take you up on that another time."

"Just say when. It might be easier if you stayed here some while you're working on my design. It would save a lot of time commuting."

"Thank you. I'll think about that."

They sat at the big kitchen island and fixed their fajitas.

"Tomorrow when you come, I'll give you the full tour. There are a lot of places besides the outside that need your expertise."

"Like the rooftop terrace."

"Right." They ate in silence for a bit. "You know, I did only contract with your company for the design plan. There's nothing precluding me from taking that and having a competitor install it. Even someone I pay directly. Like you."

"Sam—"

"The fort is more than sixty miles from their nearest garden center. They won't be able to invoke their non-compete."

"Oh my God." Her eyes were wide. "You're serious about having me work for you. You're asking me to jump from the pan to the fire—quit a job for an unknown."

He grinned. "Life's a wild ride, isn't it? Bet you didn't see that coming a few weeks ago."

"I didn't."

"Artists don't need security. They need creative challenges. Beauty. Options. Freedom."

"My friends would think I'd lost my mind."

"Just something to consider. I have plenty of room for you here. And I can double what you're making in your current position."

"All above board? A contract and everything? No strings attached?"

"Above board, with a contract, and no strings." Did he feel a twinge of remorse at that lie? No. He might have when he was still human. Now, he understood all too well the invisible world of energy that ran everything around them—the energy in which their fate was already written. "You don't have to decide tonight. Or even next week. It's going to take you a little while to finish the design. Decide then. If you say yes, I'll have a contract drawn up."

"Will you still cook for me if you become my boss?" Summer asked, giving him a crooked little smile.

He would do anything for her. That was the truth. He was her mate. There was nothing he wouldn't do for her. "Are you saying you're a poor cook?"

Her grin widened. "Let's just say you probably don't want to find out."

"We could include room and board in your contract. Then you won't have to worry about being fed out here."

"Geez. I'm such a charity case."

"I don't see it that way. I see it in terms of the trade we're making. Room, board, and pay in exchange for your expertise and labor." He stared into her eyes. They were like a midnight ocean in moonlight. He wanted to dive in and swim in her world.

Soon, he'd have some of her world surrounding his fort, a piece of her he could always keep with him.

One thing was for certain; he would never forget

her, just as she was tonight, in her youth, with her joy and confusion and hope.

After dinner, Summer insisted on helping clean up, which didn't take long at all. When the dishes were done, Liege wiped his hands on a tea towel and handed it to her.

"Want to show me your sketches?" he asked.

"They're very rough. I just wanted to envision what different parts of your garden would look like from eye level." She lifted a shoulder. "But I can show them to you if you like."

"I do. Grab your stuff. We can sit on the sofa to look at them."

Lights went on as they walked through the dining room on their way to the living room. Liege didn't even think about using his telekinetic skills, but he felt Summer's surprised reaction.

"Motion-sensitive lighting?"

"Yeah." Sooner or later, he was going to have to tell her he wasn't what she thought he was.

The living room had two full suites of furniture. He sat in the center of one of the sofas nearest to the dining room. She could pick a side, but either way, she was going to have to sit next to him. She set her messenger bag on the coffee table and took out her sketchpad, then settled in on his right side, close, like he'd wanted.

"Mind if I sit here?" she asked. "I want to point out some things as we go through my sketches."

# SPOKANE COUNTY
# LIBRARY
# DISTRICT

As of August
overdue fees are back.

Please return items
by the date due
to avoid any charges
to your account.

Thank you!

Spokane County Library Dist
Cheney Library
(509)893-8280

User name: THOMPSON, MYRA
KAY

Title: Liege
Author: Levine, Elaine
Item ID: 30922019
Date due: 11/12/202

WWW.SCLD.ORG

SPOKANE COUNTY
**LIBRARY**
DISTRICT

As of August
overdue fees are back.

Please return items
by the date due
to avoid any charges
to your account.

Thank you!

He looked into her eyes. "I didn't give you a choice. You had to sit near me."

"I could have stood behind the sofa."

True. Good. He was glad she still felt as if she had free will—he sure didn't. "Show me what you drew."

Summer sat next to him and opened her pad to the drawings she'd made outside his fort. These weren't the rough scribbles of an amateur artist—they were brilliantly detailed and delicately colored garden drawings done by a master. She could quit landscape design entirely and work only as an artist and still become renowned.

"Summer, this is incredible work. How can you say they're rough?"

She tilted her head and looked at the page. "I see everything they aren't."

He took the sketchpad from her. "I see everything they are. Can you really make my fort look like this?"

She moved to her folded legs and leaned against him as she began to point out different features in the garden that would give vertical interest, textural variety, spots of color, seasonal focus, architectural features, pathways, steps, etc. Every time she moved or flexed, his body tightened. He could barely focus on what she was saying for the fire he was fighting trying to calm his response to her.

He lifted his arm and set it around her so she could reach more easily to point out different plants and features. When they'd looked at all of her sketches, she twisted around to look at him.

"What do you think?" she asked.

"I love your vision. I want to buy these sketches and frame them."

Her gaze slipped from his eyes to his lips. "You do?"

"If you'll let me."

She dragged her eyes back up to his. He could scent the shift in her hormones, and it made him painfully hard. There were some aspects of being changed that he enjoyed; experiencing her arousal was definitely one of them.

She reached up and touched his face. His eyes never left hers. Never had a woman's touch felt so deliciously exciting as hers did right now. He let himself linger in that moment, fully aware their time was coming. There was only one shot at their discovery period; he meant to enjoy the slow build for as long as it lasted—and more importantly, as long as she needed.

Her eyes widened, and she yanked herself away from him, then scrambled off the sofa. Shit. That was abrupt. He stood and set her sketchpad down on her messenger bag.

"I'm sorry," he said, facing her.

She covered her mouth. "No. I'm sorry. I shouldn't have touched you. That was inappropriate."

"Why?"

"Because you're my client."

He tried not to smile. She had no idea what was

coming for the two of them. "Maybe I wanted you to touch me."

"Maybe I wanted to touch you."

"So no harm, no foul."

"This can't happen."

"Why?" he asked.

"Because I want you to respect me."

"I do respect you."

She nodded. "Good. I should go."

Liege shoved his hands in his pockets and nodded. "I can escort you out to the highway if you like."

"No need. I know my way out."

"It's dark out here. No streetlights."

She ventured near him to stow her sketchpad and sling her messenger bag over her shoulder. "That's why they invented headlights."

"Then I'll just walk you out." He led her into the glass hallway. Carriage lights were on in the short tunnel by the front gate.

"Good night, Sam."

"Night, Summer." He chewed the corner of his bottom lip as he silently regarded her. They were so close that he could feel her energy seeping into his. Likely she could feel the same whether she was conscious of it or not.

## 13

Summer did a video call with Kiera and Ash as soon as she got home. Ash's face was lit with excitement at her news. Kiera was less enthused—and not because of the late hour of the call. She was always the voice of reason and logic. Ash's response to any choice was always grab your parachute and jump off that cliff. Such opposites, Summer's friends. She told them about Sam's offer that she come work for him.

"He said he'll pay you double what you're making now?" Kiera asked. Summer nodded. "If he's as rich as you make him sound, he can easily cover that, because you make frickin' peanuts."

"And I bet his job will take most of a year," Ash said. "Look at it this way; you've got that dastardly non-compete to deal with. If you spend a year working at Sam's, then you'll only have to be away from us for another year after that."

Kiera nodded. "Let's wait and see what his contract looks like. If he really can pay double your current wage, then consider it. I have a lawyer I work with here. His specialty is family law, but he could still check out your contract for any gotchas. He'd do it for me."

"Oh?" Ash laughed. "Have you been holding out on us?"

"He's seventy, retired, and very happily married," Kiera said. "He volunteers for us. I'm desperate but not desperate enough to break up a marriage. Although I do adore him."

"Okay. Okay," Summer agreed. "I'll get Sam's design done, then go from there. I can't wait to get you guys out to meet him and see his fort. It's something else."

Ash chuckled. "He is too, if we're reading between the lines correctly."

"It's unprofessional, me falling for my client," Summer said. "There's just something about him. He's always on my mind."

"No, it's not," Ash said. "You're going to do a bang-up job for him, regardless of how things turn out between you."

"You can't be falling for him that fast," Kiera said. "You don't know anything about him. Maybe he got his money doing something illegal."

"We could buy a background check," Ash offered. "You know, under the guise of determining if he's a good financial risk as an employer."

"No," Summer said. "I have to go with my gut on this."

They chatted a little longer. When the call ended, Summer sat on her bed, feeling as if she were floating ten feet in the air. Without any plan or conscious thought, her life had taken a huge turn in an unexpected direction—a much better one than she would have even planned for herself.

Maybe that was what she'd felt coming.

Her gaze drifted to her beautiful Uzbek carpet, and she heard Sam's rationale for her. *You need beauty like a fish needs water.* He got her. Completely. How could a stranger tune in to her so quickly?

Two days later, Summer parked in the covered area on the north side of the fort. She went to ring the doorbell, but before she could, the inset door opened. Sam greeted her with a big smile.

"Morning," he said.

"Hi."

He stepped back to let her in then closed the door behind her. He gestured toward the kitchen and held that door for her.

"I was just washing up from breakfast. Are you hungry? I'd be glad to make something for you."

"I've already eaten, but thanks."

"Coffee, then?"

"Sure. That'd be great."

"Black, right?" He stopped and faced her. She almost ran into him. "You really don't do sugar, do you?"

"Only rarely. I love it, but it has a negative nutritional value."

He shook his head. "Never understood why something that tastes so good could be so bad for you."

Summer set her messenger bag on the tall seat next to her. "Tell me you don't look after this whole fort by yourself."

"For the moment, I do. I have cleaning staff come in once a week. I may soon need to hire a caretaker couple. Or maybe a cook and a housekeeper. I don't know."

"You'll definitely need them once you're fully open for business."

"Agreed." He looked at her bag. "Have more drawings to show me?"

"Not yet. I spent most of yesterday on the biggest garden—your west side of the fort. Today, I want to focus on your north and east sides. I think the southern veggie gardens will be the easiest to do."

He handed her a mug of coffee and refilled his own. "Before that, I thought I might start you off with a proper tour of the fort. When you're finished with the outside, you'll need to do our greenhouse. And then I'm sure we could use some work in the courtyard and the terraces." He gave her a curious look as one corner of his mouth curled up. "Did you think about my job offer?"

"I thought about it. I haven't made my decision yet."

"I understand. It's not something you need to move quickly on. But for the sake of argument, let's just have your design from the Briscoes cover the exterior space. The rest I'd like you to do as well, but we've yet to determine if that'll be through your company or directly for me." Sam set his coffee down. "Ready for a walkabout?"

"Sure." She smiled. "I've been dying to explore."

They walked from the kitchen to the dining room. The flooring in there, as in the kitchen, was a polished, stained concrete. He gestured toward the tower. "You know this corner. You've taken the stairs up to the roof. Besides the restroom, there's also an elevator and a laundry room." He gestured to his left. "This is the dining room."

Summer had seen the dining room when she and Sam had passed through it to the living room. It featured a long wooden table that was made from beautifully patterned rosewood. The narrow skirt around the table was heavily carved. A black strip of iron banded the whole table. Heavy wooden legs were made into trestles with the elaborate black iron scrollwork. Eight rosewood chairs sat on both sides. The two ends had wide wingback chairs in a paisley tapestry with heavy black iron nails on the wings and ends of the arms. The table had two expansion points for more leaves. Several additional side chairs sat around the edges of the room. They all had padded, coffee-colored leather cushions. On one wall was a long sideboard in the same Spanish-influenced design of dark wood and iron finishes.

There were no windows on the west wall of the dining room, but plenty of light filled the room from several glass blocks that ran in parallel rows in the ceiling.

Summer pointed to them. "I didn't notice those when we were on your rooftop deck."

"I wanted indirect light in here so that the sunlight wouldn't damage the art."

Summer stopped to look at one of the large pieces hung above the sideboard. It was a work featuring horses running toward a sunset that washed everything in a reddish glow.

Sam came to stand beside her. He stared at the painting, his hands behind his back.

"This is beautiful," Summer said. "Everything is. All the art. The room's furnishings. Did you work with an interior decorator?"

"No. I just like art and big furniture. One of the great things about building a fort is that I have plenty of wall space to display my collection. This piece is by a local Coloradan. She called it *The Last Goodnight.*"

"Why?"

"I don't know. She's Arapahoe, so I figured she was speaking to her heritage. There's something in her soul that yearns for what no longer is. We've talked about it over dinners and lots of drinks. I have several pieces of hers in different rooms."

Summer was shocked at the wave of envy she felt at the thought of Sam having intimate conversations with another woman—a reaction that was way out of line. She and Sam were nothing to each other but client and service provider.

"She and I are just friends."

Summer looked at him. How did he know what she'd been thinking?

"I love the way she sees the world."

He'd said the same thing about Summer.

He gave her an enigmatic look. "I love the way all artists look at the world. Each has his or her own unique view."

"Do you read micro-expressions?" Was that how he'd read her mind so easily?

"Sometimes."

"Hmm." She'd have to remember that.

They resumed the tour, moving in a counterclockwise direction, from north to south, around the ground floor of the fort. The living room was long, filled with more art. The walls had the same creamy-peach beige as everywhere else. The furnishings carried the Spanish influences from the dining room into the living room.

His sofas and armchairs were slip-covered in slouchy white linen. Two big, red Persian rugs gave the long room definition. The west wall had oversized windows and several single-pane French doors that opened onto a long terrace. It made the room seem like a wide-open loft space.

At the far end was an enormous entry to the next room. The dark, paneled wood was eight feet wide by twelve feet high, extending a few feet above the actual doorway. A carved mantel crowned the massive piece of woodwork. Its double doors were open now, showing fretwork that softened the rectangular corners and gave the entryway the look of an arch. The dark ash-brown stain highlighted the Moorish carvings and decorative iron studs. Summer ran her hand over the beautiful patterns.

What was even more shocking than the door itself, was the fact that the room beyond it had a matching entryway. It was like standing between two mirrors and seeing an infinity reflection.

Impressed, she gave Sam a look of awe. "Where did you find these?"

"I imported them from Morocco."

Through that grand entryway was a large billiards room. A home theater was connected to the billiards room. Each room was more luxurious than the next. Sam had to be going for a five-star rating for his unusual B&B.

A glass-sided corridor went along the perimeter of the courtyard, so one could walk from one side of the fort to the other without being exposed to the elements.

"Winters are so long here that we couldn't have the rooms connect directly to the courtyard. In the summer, these glass doors slide open. The corridor protects from wind and rain, too."

Because of the greenhouse that sloped down the whole southern wing, there were no bedrooms on that side. Instead, an indoor shooting range and an armory were tucked up next to the greenhouse.

They came to the southeast gate, which was just as large and formidable as the north gate. There were several bedrooms on the east wing, each with their own bathroom and walk-in closet. Before they returned to the north wing, Sam pointed to a corridor that led to the northeast covered parking area, but that one didn't have its own huge gate.

More bedrooms were at the end of the north wing. Sam's den was there, right next to the mechanical room. They took the stairs in the glass hallway up to the second floor.

Except for the rooftop deck above the dining room, the rest of the second floor was taken up with bedrooms. Sam pointed out his room, which was above the kitchen. He also pointed out the rooms his friends used. One of them lived in town but sometimes stayed at the fort, so he had a room too. All the bedrooms upstairs had access to the terraces that went around three sides of the fort.

"You've seen the greenhouse, so that's basically it," Sam said.

"This place is huge. Twenty-one bedrooms."

"It is."

"I guess you're ready for a lot of guests."

"I hope so."

"What you're doing here, with your extreme self-sufficiency, is like equipping a home on Mars." She was going to ask Sam to show her the silo, but for some reason, when she spoke, different words came out of her mouth. "I'd love to see the mechanical room."

"I'll show you," Sam said as he returned to the same staircase inside the glass hallway they'd used before.

Summer frowned as she followed him. She did want to see the engine room, so it didn't really matter that she'd asked to see that instead of the silo, but it was weird that she'd misspoken.

The stairs went straight down to that room on the ground floor. Inside were several large cisterns of white and gray water, along with a complicated water filtration system. Gray water from baths, showers, and sinks was collected, filtered, and then circulated to the toilets. Black water went straight out to the septic tanks. Sam explained that while he did have a well, as much water as possible came from the collection systems on the roof and went through an extreme filtration system to become potable. Plumbing was already in place so that filtered gray water could be used on the grounds outside the fort.

They went into the next room, one that was kept cool. It housed the servers that ran parts of the fort along with the batteries that stored the energy collected by the solar panels and the wind turbine trees.

The whole system was extremely efficient and

made great use of the natural resources that let the fort be self-sustaining.

Sam took her through a final section that housed a huge generator and a small chest freezer.

"That's an odd thing to have here. Why not put it in the kitchen?" she asked.

Sam looked at her a long minute. He seemed to be battling with himself before he unlocked it and lifted the lid. She peered inside and was shocked to see trays full of blood bags. They were grouped into five bunches labeled Bastion, Merc, Guerre, Acier, and Liege.

*Liege.*

Summer's breath got stuck in her chest.

*Liege.*

Was that who the crazy guy had meant? Had to be. Liege was too unusual a word to be a coincidence. She looked up at Sam, suddenly quite wary of him and the fort.

"We have to store several units of our own blood, my friends and I," he said. "We can't risk getting regular transfusions, should we find ourselves in need."

"Why?"

Sam squared his jaw. "Years ago, we underwent some intense medical trials that altered our chemistry. Those changes remain with us even now."

"What kind of changes?" Summer asked.

"Physical and neurological."

"Is that even allowed?"

He shrugged. "No idea if it was legal. We are what we are now."

"Vampires?"

Sam stared at her a long moment, then busted out laughing. "You think vampires are real?"

"I think there are some troubled people who like to think they're vampires."

"Not us."

"Which of you is Liege?" Summer's heart throbbed so loudly that it was banging in her ears.

"I am."

She frowned. She really wanted to get out of the engine room and back into the sunlight—preferably on the side of the gate where her loaner truck was.

"Why don't we head back to the kitchen?" Sam asked, leading Summer back to the main entrance of the engine room.

"So what is it that you really do? And don't tell me it's ecotourism. You wouldn't need a chest full of blood if that were true."

They crossed the short tunnel forming the north entrance to the fort and went into the kitchen. "We do a lot of things. I run a security business, but we're also activists."

"What kind of activists?" Her eyes widened. "Ecoterrorists?"

"No. We're pushing back against the organizations that changed us."

"So this fort really is a fortress."

"Not really. Not with the weapons available today.

It wouldn't survive a direct hit. It's just a good place for us to let our hair down."

"You say 'us,' but I've never seen anyone else here but you."

"My friends are often here. This is their home base."

Summer's mind was buzzing with questions. And fear. She needed to put space between her and Sam so that she could think. She faked a startled jump, then retrieved her phone, pretending she'd just received an alert.

"Oh, no." She shook her head and pocketed her phone again. "I'm so sorry, but I just remembered there's a thing I'm supposed to go to this afternoon and I still have some work to do to get ready for it. I shouldn't have come out today."

"Oh," he said. "Sure. A thing."

She grabbed her messenger bag. "I'm such a dingbat sometimes. I'm sorry I interrupted your day for nothing."

"I'm not."

She left the kitchen and scurried ahead of him to the front gate. "I've got plenty to keep me busy. I've already started on the formal designs for your place."

"Thank you." He opened the front door in the gate for her. "Promise me you'll finish them, Summer." Something in his voice stopped her and made her turn around. "At least that. Don't hand it off to the Briscoes."

"I won't." She looked up at him. She didn't want

to go. Even now, even knowing he was involved in something sinister, she wanted to stay near him. Sometimes, someone's path in life crossed yours and left it changed. That had been Sam for her.

He held out his hand. She took it. Hers was so much smaller than his. His was warm and strong. She didn't want to let go, but the gesture was quickly over.

"Thank you," he said. "I'm looking forward to enjoying the garden you'll design for me."

She nodded. "Goodbye, Sam." It was goodbye. It had to be. It couldn't be good being around someone whose secret work was dangerous enough to need a stocked blood bank.

"Goodbye, Summer." *For now.*

Those last words echoed in her mind. She felt them as clearly as if he'd spoken them, but perhaps her subconscious mind was just acknowledging the truth—she wasn't finished with him yet.

He was Liege, the man the crazy guy had warned her about. Or urged her toward.

How could that be possible?

Life had been much easier when she thought that crazy guy was just some random nut. This part of his rantings had been true, so what did that mean for the rest of what he'd said? That she was the one "they" wanted—that she was in danger?

And what was she going to say to her friends? Sam was Liege and everything that scary guy had spouted was true? That Sam was running secret missions from his fort with an invisible team?

Missions dangerous enough to require a stock of blood?

That would not go over well, even with Ash, who usually thought the most outlandish choice was the best one.

Summer couldn't say anything to her friends.

Despite the promise she'd made to Sam—Liege—whoever or whatever he was, maybe she should hand this whole project over to Clark, quit her job, and live off the grid for a while.

LIEGE SHOVED his hands in his pockets as he watched Summer pull out of his covered parking area and head down the dirt drive that led off his property. He walked into the sunshine beyond the covered parking, watching her truck until it went over a hill and disappeared.

He knew it wasn't the last time they'd see each other. He liked to believe it wasn't fate that the Matchmaker had tapped into to bring them together. No, he much preferred to believe it was simply science, that they'd at last found someone with chemistry that matched their own. The latter still left them with free will. The former stole every choice from them. She could no more quit him than he could her. That was chemistry.

And fate.

The north entrance opened and closed. Liege

pulled his thoughts away from Summer and tested the energies fast approaching him. Bastion and Guerre. Liege knew why they'd come. He'd been expecting them to pop in. The problem wasn't that they were here or why they were here, it was that until he heard them just now, he hadn't even known they were home.

Both men came to stand near him. Neither attempted to break into his focus on Summer, but their arrival had already done that.

"She's gone?" Bastion asked.

"Yeah."

Bastion set a hand on Liege's shoulder. "I'm happy you found her, my friend. But why did you let her go?"

"She's feeling overwhelmed and a little scared," Liege said. "She's fighting what her spirit already knows."

"Did you tell her about your changes?" Bastion asked.

"Not in detail. It's a frightening concept for the uninitiated. I thought I would break it to her slowly. Add to that the fact that she and I have clicked the way we have, well, she needs time to adjust to her changed future. And she believes she still has the freedom of choice—she's clinging to that. So for now, I have to leave her in peace, which is just as well. We have other things to focus on. Like the Omni silos."

Guerre nodded. "You need to get down and see them. The Omni shot caller running the place had it built out like a palace."

"*Oui.* A Baroque extravagance the Sun King himself would be proud of," Bastion said.

"Who's this shot caller?" Liege asked.

"A man named King," Guerre answered. "The gilded public places hid the dark belly of what the Omnis were doing there. They had a full prison below, complete with torture rooms. Many of the servant quarters made it clear they never saw the light of day."

"Did they have labs there?" Liege asked.

Bastion shook his head. "None have been discovered yet."

"That silo aligns with dozens along the Front Range, from Denver south to Colorado Springs." He looked at Guerre. "On your map of the Hyperloop system, is there an access point under that silo?"

Guerre nodded. "There is a tunnel that runs below the Omni silo, but whether the two are connected, we don't yet know. It's a maze in there."

"We need to find out," Liege said. Summer needed time, and he needed space if he was to give her that time. Digging in to this mystery was a good distraction.

## 14

S ummer didn't return to the office that afternoon. Nor the next couple of days. Her work on Sam's place had been cleared and given a high priority; the office didn't need to know if she was working at the fort or from home.

She didn't want to go in to the office.

Her life had gotten so tangled up. She really should hand this job off to Clark, but she didn't for all the reasons that had led her to take it in the first place. The challenge. The prestige. She could always hand the finished work to Clark to deliver to Sam, but she didn't want to do that either. Sam was excited for this project. He loved being a part of it. Cutting him out of his own project wasn't what she wanted to do.

She pushed that from her mind—nothing had to be decided right now. Best focus and get the job done. Sam had sent her the outside dimensions for his place, which she entered into the same design software she used at the shop. This was her own version of it—something she'd purchased for her private use in the volunteer projects she took on.

Hours passed without her being aware of how much time she'd been working on the project. Her phone rang.

Sam.

She stared at the buzzing phone.

*Answer it*, Sam's voice said in her mind. Man, her mind was still channeling him like an imaginary friend. Funny how soothing the thought of being so connected to him was.

She took the call. "Hi."

"Hi. I wanted to let you know that I'm out of town for a bit," he said.

"Oh?" Such a useless response when what she really wanted to know was where was he going and how long would he be away and would he be safe while he was there?

She had to remind herself they were nothing to each other. He'd hired her to do a job. She was his contractor, and he was her client. That was it. That had to be it.

So why didn't it feel like that's all there was to them?

"Feel free to come by the fort if you need anything for the project—more photos or measurements. No one will be here."

Great. She felt a little embarrassed about her

extreme response to learning he was Liege. He'd never been anything but exceptionally polite to her. She'd avoided contacting him for the last few days, and now she wasn't going to get to see him for a long while.

A little niggling whisper of doubt still persisted—would it be safe for her to go there?

"You'll be safe. It's a low-crime district out here." He chuckled. "The town has, what, a population of a dozen?"

Geez, it was like he read her mind. Summer didn't want the call to end…she didn't want to be apart from him, and once she hung up, she would be. "Vampires scare me."

"Is that why you left?"

"No, I had a thing."

"Mm-hmm."

"Zombies scare me, too."

"No vamps, no zombies are out here. No ghosts, either. Just me and my friends."

"Your *invisible* friends."

"I wish I could stay so you wouldn't be afraid."

"I'm mostly afraid of you."

There was a long pause. Then Sam said, "Yeah, that doesn't hurt."

She squeezed her eyes shut as she felt his pain. "When you come back, will you tell me what's going on?"

"Ignorance is bliss, Summer."

"No, it's not. It's dangerous and complicated."

"It is dangerous and complicated, and I don't want to drag you into it."

"Are you a criminal?"

Sam sighed. "You can call me anytime while I'm away."

"You aren't going to answer my question."

"It isn't an easy one to answer."

"It is. It's quite simple. Yes or no."

"I'll text you the codes for the front and southeast gates."

"Sam, do you know a red-haired man?"

He hissed in a sharp breath. "Why do you ask?"

"I keep running into one. He told me about you. He told me that you alone were safe."

"Hmm. Heed his warning."

Did he know the guy she was talking about? "How can I heed it when I don't know what's going on?"

"We'll talk when I get back. Until then, I think it's best if you spent as little time as possible in the office. The Briscoes aren't safe."

"What does that mean?"

"You've been getting a strange vibe from them. I can hear it in your voice whenever you talk about them. Trust that vibe. Trust your instincts. I'll check in with you when I can."

He hung up.

Summer stared at the phone. The silence in her apartment was thick.

She'd never felt so alone before.

Liege, Merc, Bastion, and Guerre arrived at the site the FBI had reclaimed from the Omnis. Liege didn't like being so far away from Summer, but Acier had stayed in town to keep an eye on the Briscoes and be near her should she need help.

The silo palace was below a scrappy stretch of ground out on the plains well east of Denver. An eight-foot-high chain-link fence topped with razor wire enclosed an acre of land. Inside the fence were a couple of mobile offices, outhouses, dozens of government vehicles, and a battered steel building.

Outside the fence was a pile of junked cars and other bits of scrap metal. Guerre parked next to the junk heap and set an illusion over their SUV to make it look like the rest of the scrap pile. They camouflaged themselves and walked right past the guardhouse.

Guerre led them into the steel building, straight over to an elevator. He hit a button that went down several floors. The doors opened. An FBI agent sitting behind a folding table looked up and frowned— exactly the reaction Liege had expected, since he knew regulars couldn't see them.

Bastion had begun emitting a mild electromagnetic pulse as soon as they arrived. It wasn't strong enough to fry electronics, but it did cause enough interference to incapacitate recording devices.

Liege felt his and his men's tension at being back

in an Omni stronghold. Didn't give much relief that the FBI now controlled the site, since he knew there were Omnis embedded with them. He did a mental check of his men. Bastion and Guerre were calm and felt responsive via the mental link the four of them shared. Merc, not so much, but that was nothing new. He needed to pull his shit together.

*Fuck off, Liege,* Merc snapped via their mental link.

Liege smiled. *Just checking your status.*

Merc came even with him. They were both the same height, so they stood eye to eye. *I'm here, aren't I?*

*Are you?*

Liege had dragged Merc out of the jungle in South America. He was half-mad then and mostly mad now. Not with any jungle fever, since they couldn't contract illnesses. Liege stared into Merc's eyes. No, this was an ailment of his spirit—much harder to heal. The devil that rode Merc had everything to do with what he'd lost, what he'd gained, and the unequal balance of that exchange.

Liege figured a person could only fight reality so long. At some point, you just had to surrender. Liege hoped Merc reached that point soon—and without too much collateral damage.

Guerre moved on to a gilded ballroom that had been converted into a base of operations. Desks were set up across the space. Signs were posted on tall metal stands with various abbreviations for different governmental agencies.

They stopped at a wall that held diagrams of all

the levels and spaces discovered so far in the silo complex, with a map to each. The place was huge. And as he'd suspected, it connected to other silos in a long line down the plains that bordered the eastern side of the Rocky Mountains.

*Guerre, you and Merc explore the lower levels. Find out if the Omnis had access from these tunnels to the Hyperloop system below us.*

They took off. Bastion remained with Liege and was now grinning at him. *Admit it. I'm your favorite.*

Bastion's heavy French accent always took Liege a second to translate. *You are not.*

*Impossible. Otherwise you would have sent me with Guerre.*

*Merc's good with the EMF pulses. Almost as good as you. Guerre and I can do them, but with an effort that will take away from our focus. We had to split up.*

*Bah! I know all this.* Bastion waved that away like the old news that it was.

Liege sighed. *I've been riding his ass. Figured he could use a break from me.* Besides, Liege thought, Guerre had an odd way of grounding people, a skill none of them had quite figured out. New abilities were still appearing for each of them. Liege had long ago learned to accept the skills that showed up when they showed up.

*What have you found that's interesting here?* Liege asked Bastion.

*There are dozens of apartment suites, offices, meeting rooms,* Bastion said. *This space was heavily used right until the Feds took it over. We also found prison cells that might have been used as torture chambers.*

*Let's go there.*

Bastion led the way through a maze of hallways and stairwells that cut through the subterranean palace. He opened the door to a guardroom, then gestured toward the cells down a hallway. Ten of them in a line. Liege cleared his mind, opening himself to the energies that had been there—many of them recently. The cells were called "pens," as if the humans they contained were animals.

When he got to Pen 9, Liege stopped. That cell was significant, but he didn't know why. He went inside it. There was a four-foot-wide ledge rimming a sunken floor in the middle of the room. The gray cinderblock walls were austere. There were a couple of sets of chains with cuffs on one side of the wall. The light overhead was housed in a metal cage. There were no windows. The only egress was the door he'd come through.

The pen had been tossed. A tall steel cabinet sat by the door on the upper deck. Its doors had been jimmied open and hung on slack hinges. Bits of a broken wooden chair were scattered around.

Liege went down into the middle of the shallow pit and opened himself to the energy that remained. The emotions that hit him were elemental. Fear. Anger. Anguish. Determination. Hatred. Hope. In his mind, Liege could feel water spilling into the pit, water that would be electrified by a lever on the wall.

Liege climbed out of the pit and picked up a leg of the broken chair. He could feel the energy of the man who'd been shackled to it, the energy of a woman who loved him. He was surrounded in here, sentenced to die.

But he hadn't. He'd survived and killed his enemies.

He was the War Bringer.

Liege looked up to see Bastion watching him from the door. Liege handed him the chair leg and waited while he sifted through the remnant energies.

"The War Bringer."

Liege nodded.

"He's who brought this palace down," Bastion said.

"Find him. We need him."

## 15

A few days later, it was time for Summer's weekly meetup with the girls. She considered canceling, but that would be the first time she'd done so in a long time—and would set off red flags for her friends. Besides, they'd just bring dinner to her apartment anyway, so begging off wasn't the way to avoid them.

Summer parked next to Kiera, who had just left her van and was walking across the parking lot. Summer realized Kiera didn't recognize her temporary vehicle.

"Kiera!"

Her friend turned and smiled as Summer hurried over to her. They hugged, then Kiera frowned. "You got a new car? Finally?"

"No. This is a loaner, since mine's in the shop."

"I thought you weren't going to fix it."

"I wasn't, but Sam is. He arranged this loaner for me."

Kiera's brows lifted.

"He feels guilty for the whole accident thing."

"Huh. Imagine that. A guy taking responsibility for his actions."

Summer laughed and looped her arm through Kiera's as they went into the restaurant. "I hit him, remember?" She often worried Kiera's day job was making her bitter. But how couldn't it? Running a shelter for women was not something for the faint of heart.

Ashlyn waved to them from the front of the restaurant. Summer relaxed and let go of her tensions, deciding to enjoy the distraction her friends provided. She hugged Ash, who looked to be bursting with news. Tonight's rendezvous spot was a non-chain Italian restaurant that had recently opened in Old Town. Ash had called in a reservation, so they wouldn't have to stand in the crowd of hungry people waiting for a seat.

The restaurant was dimly lit and decorated with warm red and white gingham. Italian folk music played softly. Ash flirted with the waiter who had a lovely Italian accent.

"So spill, Summer," Ash said after they gave their orders. "Did Sam give you that contract?"

God, Summer had completely forgotten about that. It was probably never going to happen now—and that thought filled her with crushing regret. "Not yet. I'm taking your advice and going slowly. First, I'm just focusing on getting the landscape plan finished. Then we'll see."

Kiera and Ash exchanged looks.

"So the Briscoes are letting you take the lead on Sam's design?" Kiera asked.

"They are. Sam worked that out with them."

"Good," Kiera said. "That's great."

"He went to bat for you." Ash nodded sagely. "He wants you."

"Yeah, well," Kiera said, "he doesn't get to have her just because he wants her. She's capable of standing on her own. This is a great break, Summer!"

Ash laughed. "Of course she's capable of standing on her own. That goes without saying. It's the lying under him part I want to hear about."

"I'm being professional, Ash," Summer said. "I don't want to jeopardize anything."

Ash looked crestfallen. "Oh. Rats. You had such a crush on him."

"I still do. I just don't know if it's going to work out. And I don't want to make a fool of myself."

"But he is repairing her car," Kiera said to Ash.

"Oh. That's a good sign," Ash said.

Summer looked at her friends and sighed. "I'm afraid to get my hopes up. What if it doesn't work out?"

Ash reached for her hand. "Won't be the first time. Probably won't be the last time, either. You'll still have us and our Wednesday nights. So really, if it doesn't work out, nothing changes."

Kiera smiled. "My mom used to say that boys were like minutes. Wait sixty seconds, and another will come along."

Summer thought there'd never be another one like Sam, but she smiled at the advice. "I told you about Sam's fort—well, I got to see it this week."

"And?" Ash asked.

"It's huge. A complete blank canvas. And he has a thousand acres that it sits on."

Kiera looked shocked. "He wants you to land-scape all of that?"

"No. Most of it he's keeping as natural space so it can be a stop on an ecotourism circuit." Was that a lie too? Had he been truthful in anything he'd told her? "Did you know there's a ravine with buttes out there? He owns the whole thing. And he's trying to buy more of the land surrounding his."

"I thought it was just barren grassland out there," Kiera said.

"It is, but he sees it as beautiful."

Ash grinned at Kiera. "And because he sees it as beautiful, it's beautiful to her."

"I can see what he sees in it. There is beauty in its rawness. He has a pool in his fort," Summer said.

"Oh? When can we go?" Ash asked.

Summer did need to get back out there to take some additional measurements. Bringing the girls with her gave her a sense of relief. "Well, he's out of town for a little while. I could text him and see if he'd mind if we crashed his place."

"Don't you think you're jumping the gun a little?" Kiera asked. "You only just met him. And you just said you wanted to go slowly."

"He gave me the code to his gates and said stop by whenever. And I do have to take some more measurements." She smiled. "What do you have planned this weekend?"

Ash giggled. "I will clear my schedule for a pool party!"

"Just the three of us, not a whole party." Summer gave Ash a dark look that made her friend laugh.

Ash's eyes went wide. "I'm a bad influence."

"You are. But we love you," Kiera replied.

"So what's your news, Ash?" Summer asked.

"Well, I settled on my trip destination—a tour of coffee plantations in South America."

"Oh, I would kill to join you on that," Kiera said.

"There's room for both of you. I haven't bought my tickets yet, but I need to get them pretty soon."

"I can't now that I have this big thing with Sam," Summer said.

"I don't blame you. But what's your excuse, Kiera?" Ash asked.

Kiera looked at both of them. "Problems. There are more women missing."

Summer gasped. Kiera was a calm, drama-free person. This wasn't idle talk. Something odd had been going on for months.

"How do you know they're missing?" Ash sipped her wine. "Maybe they've just gone into hiding. I mean, you run a shelter for high-risk women. Maybe they thought you couldn't protect them."

"That's what I thought at first, especially when it was just rumors I was hearing—nothing actionable. But now I have names of women who've stayed at my shelter before who've just vanished."

"Hand the info to the police," Summer said.

"Ask them to do a well check," Ash suggested.

Kiera nodded. "I will. The people living at the addresses that I had for these women never heard of them. If I can prove they are missing, then maybe we can bring in some big guns to investigate it."

"Have you talked to other shelters—here and elsewhere?" Summer asked. "Maybe they've been noticing a similar trend."

Ash nodded. "And if this is widespread, the authorities have to do something."

"I'll make some calls in the morning," Kiera said.

Summer put Sam out of her mind for the rest of their meal. She decided to hold off saying anything to her friends about her discovery that he was Liege. She didn't know what it meant yet, so there was no need to alarm them. It probably meant nothing.

When the meal ended, they divvied up the bill. A picture fell out of Kiera's wallet as she opened it to get her credit card. Summer picked it up and was about to hand it to her, but stopped. The man in the image was Sam. Summer looked closely at the pic.

Yes, it was Sam. But the picture itself looked to be decades old. The edges were frayed and white.

"Kiera, why do you have a picture of Sam in your wallet?" Summer asked.

"Sam? Let me see that." Ash took it from her. She stared at it, then shook her head. "This isn't Sam. Not at all."

Kiera took the pic back. She swept her thumb over the image. "This is my dad. Remember when I told you about what my mom had revealed while she was in hospice? That my dad wasn't my dad? This man was. I wanted to go find him, but I learned he died about ten years ago—in Afghanistan." Summer saw the sorrow that darkened Kiera's face just briefly. She'd lost her husband there just five years ago.

"Anyway," Kiera continued, "I never got the chance to meet him." She tucked the image away, but even with it out of sight, it still weighed heavily on Summer's mind.

Sam was Kiera's dad's doppelgänger.

SUMMER FLOPPED on her bed when she got home later that evening. Trying to not think of Sam was exhausting. She checked her phone again. Doing so had become a reflexive action. Take a breath, check her phone. Work a half-hour, check her phone. She was nothing to him, just a designer he'd hired—one who'd pretty much cut him loose the last time they were together. She couldn't expect he'd have the same infatuation for her that she did for him.

She fell back on the mattress and stared at the ceiling, seeing only the big bamboo ring that supported the mosquito netting she'd draped over her antique four-poster bed. It gave her sleeping space a bit of definition in her little studio…and it let her pretend she was someplace tropical, far from where she really was.

What kind of danger was Sam really dealing with? It wasn't like they were in a war zone or a place filled with gang violence. They were in Northern Colorado. Sure, it had remote parts, but they weren't dangerous areas, just a little desolate.

She sighed. She'd been working on Sam's design for most of the week. So far, she hadn't said anything to Clark about handing the project back over. Maybe she would keep on with it. She would find out more about Sam and what he was working on when he got back. She'd probably overreacted to the discovery that he was Liege, jumping to an emotional conclusion that had no bearing on reality.

Her phone buzzed. She nearly jumped out of her skin.

*Hi.* It was him! Sam was texting her.

She sat up and stared at her phone, trying to play it cool. *Hi.*

*Did I wake you?* he asked.

*No. Just got back from dinner with my friends.*

*You ok?*

No. She missed him. That was the truth. How could she freaking miss him when they'd only known each other such a short time? *Yeah. You?*

*Good. And I'm fine.*

*You're up late,* she said.

*Yeah.*

*Work going ok?* she asked.

*It is. I miss you.*

Summer's jaw dropped. He said the words she'd longed to hear. *I was just thinking that about you,* she texted. There. She'd admitted it, and it was the truth despite the way she'd left the fort the last time they were together. *I'm making good progress on your design.*

*Can't wait to see it.*

*How much longer will you be away?*

*That's unknown at this point.*

*Would you mind if I took a couple friends to the fort when I go back this weekend? I need to take more measurements.*

*Not a problem. I'd prefer you weren't alone, anyway. You have the codes. Help yourself to the place. Give them the tour.*

*Can we use the pool?*

*Can you swim?*

*We all can. But if you have water wings, maybe we'll use them—Dad.*

*I am so not your dad it isn't even funny.*

What did that mean? A shiver slipped through her as she thought about the different implications of his statement.

*How's the work on your car going?* he asked.

*No updates yet. He said in the beginning that it could be a few weeks. Sorry it's taking so long.*

*I'm not worried about it. You have solid wheels to use in the interim.*

Silence. Neither of them texted for a moment. Summer was wondering what to make of their conversation. She was glad he'd been thinking about her.

*You've been on my mind like crazy,* he said.

They were so attuned to each other—he always said the very thing she'd thought. *Why?* she asked.

*I'd like to get to know you better. You're not just a designer I've hired. You're someone special. I like how the world looks through your eyes.*

*I haven't seen the world. I've never been out of CO. Well, the states around here, but that doesn't count.*

*Where do you want to go?*

Summer gave that some thought. *Everywhere. My friend's going to visit coffee plantations in South America.*

*Alone?*

*Yeah.*

*Not a good idea. SA's a dangerous place for a woman alone.*

*She's an intrepid world traveler. She'll be fine.*

*Can we have dinner when I get back?* he asked.

*Depends.*

*On?*

Her heart pounded as she asked the question that had been on her mind a while. *Is it an un-date or a date?*

*A date. Def.*

*Were you married before?*

*No.*

*Why not?*

*LOL. You want me to be single, but you don't want me to be single?*

*No. That's not it. Except for the danger stuff and the weird blood bank, you seem like the catch of the millennium, and I can't figure out why you're still in the dating pool.*

*Maybe I was waiting for the right person. Hookups aren't fun. And it seems everyone else has already found their perfect other, so I stopped looking. And then one day, a beautiful blond rear-ended me and my life changed. Fast. Like I fell over a fucking cliff.*

Summer smiled then chewed her bottom lip as she reread his words. *I wish you were here.*

*Me too. So dinner?*

*Absolutely. Pick me up. When?*

*Don't know yet. Not for a while. Have fun at the fort with your friends. Want me to order up food for you?*

*Sam, you're out of the country. Or somewhere. Where are you?*

*Amazing what a credit card can do,* he texted, bypassing her question.

*We'll pack a picnic. Don't worry about us.*

*I do worry. I can't not think about you, Summer. I love your name, BTW.*

Summer smiled at her phone. *My parents were hippies. They still are.*

*Gotta go. Get some sleep. You need anything, you let me know.*

She squeezed her eyes shut. If she and Sam did date, it was going to be one helluva ride.

SUMMER DROVE in to the office at the end of the week. She needed to borrow a couple of reference books from the Briscoes' library. She didn't intend to stay long, but when she ran into Jada, she had second thoughts about being there at all.

"What is it?" Summer asked, reading the stress on her friend's face. "Oh, God. Is Brett here?"

"No. Something's up with Clark. Something bad."

"Like what?"

"I don't know. I hadn't seen him in a few days. Honestly, I'm thinking of calling the police, but I don't know what I would say. I asked his dad if everything was all right, and he about bit my head off. So I'm dodging him today. We all are."

"Okay. I'll check it out and let you know what I find."

"Be careful."

"I will."

Summer set her things down in her office. The company's library was in the conference room. Fortunately, she didn't have to pass Clark's office on her way there. She'd promised to check on him, but couldn't face that task yet. She scanned the rows of books, looking for the two that she needed for her work on Sam's job.

A shadow fell across the bookcase. Summer turned to see Clark standing close behind her. She moved a step away—and realized what Jada had been talking about. Clark's eyes were red-rimmed. His face and neck had even more scratches and bruises than they'd had when she last saw him. His hair was unkempt. His days-old beard was scraggy. His clothes looked—and smelled—as if he'd been living in them for several days.

He didn't greet her. He just stared at her. She had the impression that he was looking at her from far, far away.

"Clark, what's going on with you?"

"Nothing. Why?"

"Because you look like hell. And you stink. Go home. Take a shower. Change into something fresh."

"It's your fault. All of this. It's because of you."

That sounded perilously like the crazy talk coming from the orange-haired guy.

"I never told you to quit taking showers," Summer said.

Clark's eyes blazed with anger. He stepped closer, his mouth twisted open, but instead of the vitriol she expected to hear, out came a cry of pain. He doubled over and grabbed his head, whimpering.

Summer decided to forget about the books. Maybe the library had them. Before she could move away, Clark straightened again. His face was strained, the veins in his neck corded. His lips were pulled back from his teeth, and his eyes were watering.

Summer backed away from him.

"I will have you," he said through clenched teeth.

"No, Clark. You won't. You lost that chance a long time ago."

"I'm not Clark." He laughed.

Summer turned from him and rushed out of the conference room. She went to see Douglas, but he wasn't in his office.

She walked past the conference room on her way back to her office, peeking inside as she went by. Clark was sitting at the table, his head on his folded arms. Sam had told her to stay away, that the Briscoes weren't safe. How had he known about Clark's meltdown?

She had to get out of there—but that would leave Jada and the other staff members alone with a crazy Clark. What should she do?

*Go. It will be fine.* Sam's reassuring voice slipped into her mind. Perhaps it would be fine for Summer, but not for Jada.

Summer grabbed her things and went into the shop. She was just about to tell Jada to go home when Douglas came in. He looked harried.

"Douglas, something's not right with Clark," Summer said. "He's very sick."

"I know. I'm getting him help," Douglas said as he crossed the room.

Summer and Jada exchanged glances. "I don't know what's happening, but if Douglas leaves again without Clark, I want you to lock up and get out of here. Or call the cops on Clark."

"If I do that, I'll lose my job," Jada said, her voice just a whisper.

"Better your job than your life. Something is not right with Clark. Did you see all those scratches?"

Jada nodded.

"Look, at the very least, close up early, before dark. Have everyone find work to do in here. Keep together."

"I will."

"Call in sick for the next couple of days. Let the two of them run the front desk for a bit. Maybe it'll help Clark sober up."

"It's drugs, isn't it?" Jada asked.

"I don't know. He's not himself, that's for sure."

## 16

Summer opened her door and waved at Kiera as she came up the stairs.

"Smells delicious in here," Kiera said as she set her purse on one of the barstools in front of the counter. She came around and gave Summer a hug, then washed her hands so she could help. "I see you're going to make Ash eat healthily today."

Summer laughed as she looked over their picnic. Cut veggies with fresh hummus, apple slices with lemon and cinnamon, and homemade baked kale chips.

"Today and every day!" She hadn't exactly lied when she'd told Sam she couldn't cook—she could, just not what he'd want to eat. "So how did it go with the police?"

"None of the women I told them about had been reported missing. The detective I talked to said he was going to do a well check on them as a first step." She gave Summer a worried look. "I just don't think he's going to discover anything that will help us find them. It's like they've disappeared entirely. I mean, like their very existence has been erased. I called their employers and was told—by three different ones—that the woman I was calling about never worked there. I called their doctors' offices and was told they had to honor the privacy of their patients, but I did get one office to admit the woman I was asking about wasn't one of their patients. The detective called up their driver's licenses and no records were found. I had pictures of their driver's licenses, and yet they no longer exist. Something is not right."

"That's scary. How can a DMV record get erased?" Summer asked.

Kiera shook her head. "If it weren't for the copies I made of their licenses, I'd never have been able to get the police involved. The detective I spoke to said he thought the IDs I had might have been forgeries. Really, that was the only reason he was going to even look for the women."

"Well, you've escalated the situation up to the right people. The cops will be able to find them or determine what happened to them. Maybe something they were involved in caused them to go into witness protection."

Summer wondered if she should say something about Sam and her concerns about what he was wrapped up in, but Kiera was nothing if not fiercely protective of those she loved, and Summer knew she'd cancel their trip to the fort and pressure Summer to put distance between her and Sam.

Maybe that was advice she should follow without forcing Kiera to say it.

Kiera grabbed a celery stick. "If so, that's a black hole they won't be coming out of."

"I'm glad you and Ash are going with me out to the fort. Did you bring your bathing suit?"

"I did. Does he have a nice pool?"

"Oh, nice doesn't come close to describing it. It's at the bottom level of a terraced three-story greenhouse. There aren't any plants in there yet, so it looks pretty bare, but I can see how it will look when it's finished. The pool itself has a grotto you can only get into by swimming. It has waterfalls and jumping ledges. It's crazy. It looks a little barren without the greenhouse being completed, but it will be stunning when it's finished."

Summer and Kiera got their things loaded into Kiera's minivan. Ash pulled up just then. She brought her things over and gave both women a hug. "I made sandwiches and brought some chips."

Summer gave her a face. "You didn't trust me to make something tasty for our lunch?"

"That's not it at all. I knew you would." Ash giggled. "I just didn't want to be hungry the whole day, which I always am when I go swimming."

"I can't wait to see Sam's place," Kiera said. "You did clear it with him, right?"

"Of course," Summer said. "He's cool with it. I

will have to do a little work while we're there. There are some additional measurements I want to take, but I can do that while you're swimming."

Summer sat in the back, letting Ash have the front passenger seat so she'd get the best view of Sam's place. She couldn't remember the last time the three of them had taken a full day for themselves. It felt as if they were playing hooky from their normal lives. Kiera drove down the long dirt road that led, several miles in, to the fort. They cleared a low ridge, and there, on a hill, was Sam's huge adobe home.

"Oh my God. Is that it?" Ash asked.

"Yup." Summer felt unreasonably proud of Sam's place. He'd constructed something that would last beyond his lifetime—and hers. She wondered what people of the future would think about the man who'd built a fort centuries after such things were no longer needed. Maybe her gardens would still be thriving.

"He's crazy," Kiera said.

"I know," Summer agreed.

"But how cool is it to have a dream and make it happen?" Ash said. "I'm half in love with him myself."

Summer felt a cold chill of fear that her friend would get caught up in whatever it was that Sam was doing. At the same time, she felt a flash of jealousy that Ash wanted the same man Summer did. Hot and cold. She had to get a hold of herself.

Ash laughed. "I'm teasing. God. Kiera, did you see her? I think she wanted to kill me."

Kiera looked in her rearview mirror. "No fighting. There are enough men for everyone."

"Oh?" Ash raised a brow as she looked at Kiera. "So where are these mythical beasts?"

"Sorry, Ash." Summer felt contrite. "I sort of had a panic. You attract men like bears to camp food."

"Honey, you forget I've met your Sam. He only had eyes for you. I was an annoying gnat who insisted on being introduced to him."

"That's not true. He was polite. Turn here." Summer pointed to the drive that led to the north gate where the covered parking was. The sky was divided into polar opposite behaviors. To the north, dark gray clouds gathered ominously, but the autumn sun to the south was warm and bright, making the earth tones of Sam's fort glow.

"He lives here by himself?" Kiera asked as they got out of her van. "This place is huge."

Summer popped the back hatch. "He said he has a few friends who live here too, but I've never seen them." They grabbed their things. Ash and Kiera both carried the cooler while Summer entered the security code.

The inset door unlocked. Summer held it for the girls. They came into that short tunnel with the engine room on the left and the entrance to the kitchen on the right. In front of them was the beautiful fountain with its colorful Mexican tiles.

Ash turned to Summer. "I want to see everything!"

"You are a rotten houseguest," Kiera said.

"No, it's fine. Sam said I could show you around." Summer opened the kitchen door for them. That one room was more than three times the size of Summer's studio apartment. It had a huge walk-in pantry, a secondary storeroom for dishes, and a big eat-in area next to a small, southwestern-style kiva fireplace built into a corner of the adobe wall. A spiral set of stairs set in the front corner went up to the floor above.

There was a wide opening from the kitchen into the dining room. The girls went through the entrance that led to the stairs and utility area, then met up in the dining room and exclaimed over Sam's art collection.

Summer took them around the entire fort, saving the greenhouse for last. They went through the west wing, with its long living room and billiards room, which was paneled in dark wood and furnished in a heavy, masculine style. A faint hint of cigars lingered in the room—nothing so strong that it fouled the space. Summer sensed that room was one of Sam's favorite. The movie room had a huge projection system that used an entire wall for a screen. The theater-style seats had five rows of ten recliners each, with an aisle slanting down the middle.

They went by the bedrooms on the ground floor, which were furnished but uninhabited, then took a staircase up from the end of the glass hallway that went in front of the engine room. That was the one room Summer avoided. Just remembering that freezer of blood gave her the willies.

Upstairs, she showed the girls the rooftop deck that was over the dining room, then they went clock-wise to the bedrooms on the second floor.

"This place is mind-blowing, Summer," Ash said. "It's like a first-class private club. I would love to come here and veg out for a week. I can see your Sam spoiling his visitors."

The bedrooms on the second floor were on the north and east wings. Both were accessed on the courtyard side by glass hallways with big sliding windows that would give a lovely flow of air.

The girls peeked in a few of the bedrooms. All on the eastern side were furnished and looked inhabited.

They turned the corner to the bedrooms on the north side. "These rooms are all the same, but this last one is Sam's." She smiled at her friends as she opened the door to his room. There was nothing undone in his space. The room was full of different tones of brown—beige, tan, chocolate. One wall was covered with African masks, arranged in a tight column. A king-sized platform bed was made up with crisp white linens and a brown coverlet. Three rows of different-sized pillows in white linen stood neatly lined up.

White curtains hung in straight lines at the sides of French doors that opened out to a terrace. Ash stepped outside through the doors and onto the terrace that stretched across the whole wing.

Summer felt a warm glow as she stood inside Sam's room, not ready to leave. She went through his closet, sweeping a hand along the neat row of his suits and sports coats, then his orderly arrangement of pressed shirts and trousers, arranged by color.

"Your man's a little OCD," Kiera said.

Summer laughed. "See? You aren't the only one with that bug. And since I know how to deal with you, I'll be able to deal with him."

Kiera laughed.

Sam's shoes were arranged in a wide column of slanted shelves. "God, he's a clotheshorse," Summer said. "All of my shoes, clothes, and purses wouldn't even take up one section of his closet."

Kiera lifted her brows. "Thinking of moving in, are you?"

Summer gave her a little smile. "It could happen."

"Doubt it. He wouldn't like sharing his closet. He'll give you one of the other rooms."

Both girls laughed at that. They left Sam's closet and went into the large en suite. Here again, it was a study of masculine tones in different colors and textures. The floor was a beige porcelain tile. Immediately on her left was a small toilet room with a door. To her right was a long vanity made out of bleached wood. It had a black soapstone counter with two inset concrete sinks. The faucets for them came out of the wall. Mirrors set above each sink were in an industrial-style brushed steel frames.

The wall behind the toilet room was covered with

slate tiles. In front of it sat an ebony tub in curved, sleek lines. The faucet there, too, came out of the wall. The whole back wall was taken up by the huge shower tiled with wood-look porcelain tiles. The floor of the shower was covered in black pebbles. A wide bench sat against the back wall. Multiple showerheads were on the tiled walls, and rain showerheads were positioned over the two ends. Glass panels at least seven feet high enclosed the space.

The ceiling exposed the wooden beams of the adobe structure and wooden planking. The walls were painted a dark taupe.

Both girls were dumbfounded by the size, scope, and luxury of the room. "I want you to promise," Kiera said, "if you and Sam do hook up, that I get to use this bathroom at least once. Maybe twice. Once for a shower, once for a bath."

Summer laughed. "You got it."

On the counter by the sink was a bottle of cologne. Summer picked it up and brought it to her nose, closing her eyes as she remembered the faint scent she'd caught on Sam. Woodsy, citrusy. He never wore it very strong, just a hint.

God, she missed him. A shiver slipped through her, leaving her hot and cold, whole and shattered. Her eyes teared up.

Kiera reached a hand out to her shoulder. "What is it?"

Summer stared into her friend's warm eyes. "I think I'm in love."

Kiera's smile was a little sad. She knew, as Summer did, how very much out of Summer's league Sam was. "Have fun with it. Joy rides are okay."

"You don't think he could love me?"

"Everyone loves you, Summer. How could they not?"

"But not Sam?"

Kiera rubbed Summer's arm. "I'm jaded. I work with women whose loves turned them inside out. I hope he's the one for you. And I hope he falls for you as deeply as you may be falling for him."

Summer hugged her, then took her hand and led her out of Sam's room to the terrace. So far, the dark northern skies hadn't slid farther south. She pointed to the next two rooms and said they were the same as Sam's.

"Ash, we're moving on," Kiera called, but Ash didn't respond. They kept on their tour of the other empty rooms, then backtracked to the rooftop terrace above the dining room.

"Summer! Kiera!" Ash shouted as she ran to find them. She looked through the glass corridor and saw them waving at her from around the bend. She hurried over to them.

Summer frowned. "What is it? You looked scared to death."

"This fort's haunted," Ash said.

Kiera wrapped an arm around Ash. "Geez, you're ice cold."

"I saw someone. When you and Kiera were in

Sam's room, I saw someone in the hallway. One minute he was there, the next he just…disappeared."

Kiera and Summer exchanged glances. Summer pivoted and went back down the glass-enclosed halls. Another man disappearing. Like that redheaded guy had done that other night. She didn't see or feel anyone there.

"What did he look like?" Summer asked as she returned to them.

"Short, light brown hair. Big build. Gray eyes." She crossed her arms and rubbed them with her palms. "He was watching us."

"You know, it's funny—Sam specifically said his fort wasn't haunted, but maybe it is," Summer said. But why would he have said that particular thing?

"Well, no ghost is going to keep me from having fun with my two besties here today," Ash said. "Let's get our suits on and go for a swim before we have our picnic."

They went down to the kitchen and collected their things, bringing their packed lunch with them.

BAISE-MOI, Bastion said, *I'm going to follow them.*

Guerre gave him a dark look. *Stay cloaked.*

Bastion grinned. *They're going to the pool. Do you not want to see them swim? Perhaps they need a lifeguard.*

*You are a sick man, Bastion, spying on innocent women like a voyeur.*

Bastion laughed. *It is our nature now. It is what we've become. Today, I think I will play. Join me.*

*No. And don't mess with the cameras in the greenhouse or Liege will know you're perving on his female and his daughter.*

*Bah. It is not perving, merely curiosity.* Bastion went to the door, then paused and looked back at Guerre. *I wish—I wish the hunger hadn't been taken from us. I wish I could perv. I miss those days.*

Guerre nodded. He didn't laugh because he had the same sense of loss, though in some ways, it was easier not being driven by his body's needs.

Bastion was already in the pool room when Liege's woman and her friends entered. He stood off to the side, a silent witness. And since silence wasn't a first-nature thing for him, it was something close to torture.

The girls went into the female bathroom to change into their suits. He gave them their privacy, though he'd never admit such decency to the guys. Of course, he'd already shorted out the room's cameras, despite Guerre's warning.

Or perhaps because of it.

If Liege was as hooked into Summer as he said, Bastion would be hearing from him soon. He smiled. The girls came out of the bathroom in their bikinis. They'd rinsed off in the showers. Summer and Ash had long hair, blond and light brown, respectively. Kiera's had intricate ropes of dark curls.

They giggled as they stared out at the sweeping, tiered structure of the room, touching each other freely in that way females had of holding hands, slipping arms around shoulders and waists, leaning in to one another to laugh.

These ladies were tightly bonded.

Bastion closed his eyes and let himself slip away from his own awareness and enter theirs so he could sample their energy. Energy was different for every human and as unique as any other biometric identifier. Kiera was the somber one in the group. Ash was the playful one. And Summer—she was the creative one.

*Bastion. You bastard. Get the fuck out of the pool room,* Liege ordered via their psychic link.

*They're beautiful, Liege.*

*I'm not going to tell you again.*

*I am here and you are not. At least one of us should be able to enjoy them.* Bastion couldn't hide his humor from Liege, which he knew was incendiary.

*I will squeeze your brain until it pops.*

The pain started. Bastion cracked up. *No. Stop. You are making me laugh. It tickles.* He'd seen Liege do that particular maneuver on many of their enemies, but knew he wouldn't act against his own men.

*You okay there?* Bastion asked. Liege and Merc were exploring the Omni silo. Bastion was supposed to join them, but he and Guerre had instead decided to stay at the fort to observe the women.

*Yeah. The Omnis are close.*

*End them and get back home to your woman. She misses you.*

*You can feel that?* Liege asked, sounding surprised.

*Yes. Can't you?*

Liege sighed. *I want her to feel for me what I feel for her, but I worry I'm compelling her to have the reaction I want. I don't know what's real.*

*Stop overthinking it. I'm happy for you. Don't waste this chance with your Summer.*

*Release the cameras and get down here.*

Bastion sat on the edge of one of the empty planters above the pool. *Alas, I cannot,* mon capitaine. *I am their lifeguard. Let me take your spot there so you can be here with her.*

*I'll be done soon.*

## 17

Summer stretched. She'd come to the office late, hoping she'd miss Clark and his dad. She wanted to put the final touches on Sam's landscape design and get it turned in. Fortunately, everyone else had already left, so she was able to work uninterrupted.

Her phone rang. A jolt of excitement hit even before she looked at the caller ID. *Sam.* She took the call. "Hi."

"Hi."

"I just finished and submitted your landscape plan," she told him.

"Come out to the fort. Sleep over tonight. We can go over it in the morning."

"Sam—"

"I have a guest room. A dozen of them, in fact. You can pick your own." He paused. "Please."

The truth was, she wanted to be there with him.

"I'll pick you up," he said.

"No need. I know the way."

"I'm already here in town."

"Where are you?"

"By your truck."

"Be right there." Her hands shook as she collected everything she'd need for their morning meeting. She hurried through the offices and shop, shutting off lights as she went. She secured the front door, then looked for Sam over by her truck, across the parking lot.

The sun had set, and though dim light still lingered on the horizon, the parking lot lights had come on. He was leaning against her door. When their eyes met, he smiled. She wondered if he got the same shiver of excitement that she did.

She walked toward him, her speed increasing until she rushed into his arms. He caught her up in a tight hug. This wasn't the greeting of new friends. It certainly wasn't the greeting of a customer and a client. He'd asked her to stay over at the fort. Sure, he'd offered her a room of her own, but what did he really have in mind?

He set her back on her feet but didn't release his hold. Summer ran her hands up his chest. The man was as solid as a rock wall. She slipped her hands up his neck as his gaze bored into hers, his beautiful soft brown eyes that now looked hard and determined. Light flashed through them until he blinked and shifted so that the streetlights didn't reflect off them.

Summer wondered if his contacts did that. Did he wear contacts?

He palmed the back of her head and leaned down, touching his mouth to hers. As soon as their lips touched, Summer hit a combustion point. She couldn't get close enough to him—there wasn't enough of his lips or his tongue or his scent. His delicious scent. Woodsy. Citrusy. All Sam.

Never had Summer felt such an explosive kiss. Heat swept over her, through her, through him. She wasn't sure she was still touching the ground, and then she knew she wasn't when he turned and pressed her against the cab of her truck, his body between her legs.

"Your place or mine?" Sam asked, his voice ragged.

She cared only for the feel of his body against hers, the fevered touch of his mouth against hers. If he moved away from her, she thought it quite possible she would simply end.

"Here." Her truck or his SUV. She couldn't wait any longer than that to have him in her.

"Not here." He straightened, easing her to the ground between her truck and his body. "Your place. It's closer. I'll follow you."

Cool air slipped between them, restoring a fraction of her senses. She looked at him as she tried to right the world around her, then nodded. "Okay."

He opened her truck door. She threw her stuff inside and got in. He kissed her again. She smiled, happy to realize he was as hungry for her as she was for him.

He pressed his forehead to hers. "Hold that thought."

She felt cold when he left her, but everything inside her was on fire. She wasted no time getting across town to her apartment.

He parked in the alley next to her. She waited for him by the stairs, feeling a wave of nervousness about Sam seeing where she lived. She should have told him she'd grab her things and come out to the fort. But, of course, he was already in town.

He walked over to her, a warm smile greeting her.

"I should warn you, my place is small," she said.

His eyes studied hers. He stood near enough she could feel his heat. "I'm not judging you." He caught her hands and spread her arms out wide from her sides. "The thing is, Summer, you're all I thought about while we were apart. I played what tonight would be like over in my head a thousand different ways, and every one of them was humbling to the point of bringing me to my knees. To think a woman like you would give herself to a guy like me."

"What do you mean 'a guy like' you?"

"I am so in awe of you that I find myself lacking."

"How so?"

He kissed her and backed her up a step, then another. "We're opposites in just about every way possible."

She wrapped her arms around his shoulders,

feeling the little kisses he placed at the base of her neck. "It could work, though, right?" she asked.

"It does work."

Summer tightened her arms around his neck. "I want it to. I've never felt about anyone the way I do about you. And I barely know you. But I want to know everything about you. What were your parents like? What was your childhood like? Your first girl-friend. Your last breakup. Do you have kids? Everything."

She realized they were halfway up the stairs to her studio. She couldn't remember having taken any of those steps. "And other things, like where you got your money. How could someone only a little older than me be so rich?"

"Lots of ways."

She put a hand on Sam's chest. "Are you a criminal?"

He grinned. It was lopsided and sexy as hell. She leaned forward and kissed him, holding his face.

"That's it? That's your line?" Sam asked.

She nodded. "That would definitely be a line."

"You have several lines?"

"Don't you?"

"Only one."

"What's your one line?"

"It's that you feel like you resonate with me. We're vibrating in the same way."

She grinned. "Good vibrations? That's your thing?"

"Isn't it yours?"

She tilted her head. "I guess so. I always go by energy, how a thing feels, how it makes me feel."

"Exactly."

"Do you vibrate with many women?" She lifted her brow.

"No. I never have."

"Never?"

"Never. I've had my share of women, that's for sure. But I never resonated with any of them. Mostly, it's like eating your favorite meal—but without your taste buds to enjoy it. Being near you makes me taste again. I love that. I want more of it."

They'd reached her landing and her front door. Summer fumbled with her keys. She unlocked her door, then held it shut for a moment. Bringing Sam here was like bringing a man into her teenaged bedroom at her parents' house. She should grow up and get an adult place. Something with actual bedrooms. And a kitchen with a dishwasher.

Sam pulled her against his body. "We're going to fuck, Summer. Whether it's here, at my place, or on the way to my place, I don't care. Maybe all three. You are what I need. I don't care about your digs." He grinned as he moved her into her apartment. "And if you want to fuck in your room at your parents' place, I could totally do that too."

Summer gasped. All rational thought left as she realized she must have said that out loud to him. He was scrambling her wits. She covered her mouth with her hands. "I can't believe I said that out loud."

Sam smiled as he shucked his coat and knit beanie. "It doesn't matter. I thought it was funny." He helped her off with her jacket and tossed it over his. "You have a nice place here. I don't know why you were worried."

"I haven't even shown you around."

He looked at her then laughed, which was a little mortifying. There was nothing to show him around to —it was a one-room place with a bathroom and closet. Her face felt beet red. He lifted her onto her kitchen counter, then untied her boots and dropped them out of the way. He removed his own boots then stood and yanked off his sweater and the white tee underneath it.

Summer's mouth opened. Sam was huge. Of course, she'd known that, but seeing him now without his shirt drove that home. She stroked her hands over the tightly curled hair on his chest as he settled between her legs. "How are we going to fit?" she asked.

His face went serious. He helped her out of her sweater. "We'll fit. We'll go slow until you're comfortable."

"I don't want slow."

His hands were big and a bit rough, not soft-skinned as she'd expect for someone with enough money to hire out every task. What did he do with them that gave him callouses? He kissed her, smashing her face against his as he cupped the back of her head. She forgot her questions as they shared each other's breath. He tilted his head as the kiss deepened.

"I don't want slow either, but I refuse to hurt you. So we'll do what feels good." He caught her waist and bent slightly so that he could kiss her shoulder. She was ticklish like crazy, but his hands didn't tease. He scooped her off the counter and walked over to her bed. Kneeling on the handmade quilt, he set her down.

Summer scooted up to the pillows to watch him. The mosquito netting blocked her view as he went to his jacket and grabbed a few condom packets.

"You keep them in your jacket?"

"I hoped we were getting together tonight. I didn't know when or where, so I came prepared in case we didn't make it back to the fort." He looked at her jeans as he set the condoms on her nightstand. "Take them off."

She unzipped her jeans and arched her hips so she could pull them off. She kicked free of them, then scooted to the edge of the bed to rub herself against Sam's back, which was broad and layered in muscle. She nibbled his neck and ran her hands over his pecs. His small nipples tightened under her palms. He leaned forward and removed his socks.

He hooked an arm around her waist and pulled her in front of him so she was straddling him. He kissed her neck, her collarbone, then drew her chin down to kiss her mouth. They kissed for a long moment before he unfastened her bra and slipped it from her shoulders. He caught the sides of her breasts, looking as if he'd never seen anything so special. He held one and kissed it, then did the same with the other. He hadn't yet touched her nipples, and the omission seemed an exquisite torture. She arched her back, pushing her breasts forward. Smiling at her, he caught one nipple in his mouth and flicked it with his tongue.

"Sam—"

"Mmm?" He sucked hard on the taut peak, and she cried out.

"I said fast." She pushed him back on the bed and tackled his belt buckle, then opened his jeans and freed him from his gray boxer briefs. He was long and wide and delicious looking.

Liege stared into her eyes, then caught her around the waist and rolled over with her. Standing, he shucked his jeans and his boxer briefs, then helped her slip her panties off her legs.

He covered himself, then settled between her legs, easing his weight over her, holding himself on his elbows so he didn't crush her. He was nearly twice her size. She needed a moment to get used to the feel of him.

Or not.

She began to grind herself against him. He

pushed his hands under her head. He kissed her fore-head, temple, cheek.

"Sam. You make love like a tortoise. I need the hare right now."

He laughed. "Maybe slow's part of the fun."

"We can have fun later." She bent her legs, opening for him.

He rubbed himself between her soft folds, pressing against her clit, then, inch by inch, he pushed into her, slowly, so slowly, letting her get used to the feel and size of him.

Every bit of their joining felt incredible. She was unlike any woman he'd ever known. It was like she was his first ever. She was damned sure the first since he was changed that made all of his nerves tingle and his heart beat faster.

He not only felt her from his perspective, but he felt him from her perspective. Maybe that was what had been missing from all his other rounds of sex since his change.

When he was fully in her, he could feel her tension build. He closed his eyes and focused on their shared sensations, moving in just the ways that spiked her pleasure. Her pleasure was his pleasure. He knew, from their connection, what her body needed from his.

He went to his knees, still in her, and drew her hips up over his thighs, her legs draped over his. Holding her hips, he tapped against the sensitive places inside her. In this position, he had the added bonus of being able to see her face and watch her breasts as he thrusted. Her skin was so pale that he could see it pinken as blood heated her chest and neck.

He fingered her clit, sending her over the edge. She cried out and bucked against him even as her hands fisted the pillows beneath her head. Her inner muscles convulsed over his cock. And that was the last rational thought Liege had before gripping her hips and slamming himself into her, reaching, reaching for his own peak. When it came, his whole body braced for the impact of his release, which exploded from him, setting hers off again. She cried out with the intense pleasure of it. He lifted her up to sit on him. She wrapped her arms around his neck and gave herself over to the sensations pouring through her.

He almost came again.

He'd never been so close to doing that before. It was something he'd heard about from another changed guy when he was with his soul mate. Their bodies didn't need as much time to recover between orgasms as unchanged men, but it took being with the right woman to take them to that height of arousal.

Summer caught his face, holding his cheeks as she kissed him. "I want more, Sam."

He scanned her body and found it thrumming with unspent need, like he'd awakened something dormant in her that had burst into life. "I do too." He lifted her from him so he could ditch the old condom and put a new one on. He was still erect. She looked at his cock then met his gaze. She smiled then stretched, the motion sexy and teasing. She rolled onto her stomach, presenting him with her back, which was long and slim, her ass so nicely rounded. She wasn't very big, but her proportions were delicious.

And they'd fit together just fine.

He knelt between her thighs, pushing them apart. She looked at him over her shoulder as he lifted her hips and entered her.

He spread his hands on the white skin of her hips, watching himself slide in and out of her. She was so slick, so close. Wrapping an arm around her waist, he drew her upright. This position let him play with her clit while he kept his other hand on her breast.

Her orgasm hit fast. She gripped his thighs as she spun out of control. He gave himself over to the call of her body, wrapping both arms around her as his release cut through him.

When it was over, Summer was leaning back, draped over him, limp, sweating and panting. Shit. This was all new territory for him. He lifted her off him then settled her on the bed. Her hungry eyes followed him as he dropped the condom in the trash.

When he came back to her, he lifted her up so he could get them both under the covers. Lying on his side, he stared into her eyes and smoothed the hair from her face. Her hand slipped up his arm, to his shoulder, and back down. He caught it and kissed her fingers.

God, he loved her. The time he'd spent away from her had been hell. How long did he have, now that they'd been intimate, before the Matchmaker's curse set in? Or had that clock already started a while ago?

She smiled at him. "You look so serious."

He shook his head, at a loss for words.

She curled her hand around his neck and pulled him down over her. "Love me again."

He kissed the curve of her neck, her throat, pausing to hold himself against her face as he packed his emotions away and calmed the lights burning in his eyes.

He wanted to make love to her all night, but he would hurt her if they didn't slow things down.

"Not yet. We need to pace ourselves. We have all the time in the world to make love." It was a lie, but it seemed the right thing to say.

He carried her into the bathroom. He started the shower, then slid with her down to the floor. He left the water on cold—they were both still in this same fever of hunger and need.

She pressed her face against his neck. "What's happening, Sam? I can't get enough of you."

He squeezed his eyes shut. He knew what was going on. Though he'd never experienced it, he'd been warned about it. Now wasn't the right time to tell her he wasn't what she thought he was.

He appeased himself by telling her a half-truth. "I don't know." *How we deal with this.* "I have this insatiable need to take you over and over. Each time just makes me need more of you."

She nodded. "That's what I'm feeling."

"I think it's because you're fertile right now."

She pushed off his chest to stare at him. "What? How can you tell?"

"I just know." She looked tired. Her makeup was smeared around her eyes. He touched her cheek, watching as the water slipped down from her hair.

"I'm on birth control. I can't get pregnant."

"None of those systems are absolute. Nothing is, except abstinence, and I can't fucking leave you alone."

She nodded. "It's like a fever."

He smiled. "That's why we're here in ice-cold water."

She kissed his neck, his jaw. "If we go back to bed, I know I'll attack you. Has this happened to you before? It's like my hormones have gone haywire."

"It hasn't happened to me before. I feel what you feel. You're like an addiction to me."

"That's it exactly. Addictions kill." She leaned away to stare at him. He could feel her alarm.

"Let's get out of here," he suggested. "Go have dinner. Be someplace we can't have sex." He smiled.

She straddled his lap and pressed her palms against the wet tile behind him. Her breasts were in his face. She moved one so that her nipple rubbed against his mouth. He kissed it and grabbed her breasts, pulling her closer, sucking on them. She rotated her hips over his stiff cock, letting it rub against her thighs.

"One more time, Sam. Please."

He took two heavy breaths. His nostrils flared, and he shut his eyes. "No. We can't." He stood, lifting her with him. The cold water was doing shit to calm their burning libidos. He shut the water off and walked her out of the shower.

He grabbed a bath sheet that she had hanging up and rubbed it over her hair and body, then dried himself with efficiency.

"Where are your clothes?" he asked.

She nodded toward a closet that was across a short hallway from the bathroom.

He gently pushed her in that direction. She turned and leaned against the door, giving him a long look at her hot body. "How is it that you have so much self-control?"

He focused on his breathing. In. Slowly. Hold it. Out slowly. Pause. "I've been working on it a long time." He nodded toward the closet. "Come out dressed or I'll dress you myself."

She smiled. "You know where that will lead?"

"No. I will fucking dress you." He went into the main room and gathered up his clothes. He dressed quickly, feeling much more in control of himself with her out of his reach.

He made her bed, then went into her kitchen, trying to keep himself occupied so that he didn't crowd her in the closet.

There were open shelves above the counter that had stacks of white dishes. The stove looked like it was from the sixties. The fridge was turquoise and was either an original one from the same era or was a retro reproduction. He opened the door and realized it was an original. It worked in this eclectic place. She'd surrounded herself with an odd collection of colors and textures and shapes, and somehow, it all went together.

"Hungry?" Summer asked as she came out of her closet.

He closed the fridge, bracing himself before turning to look at her. He could still feel the electrical currents rippling through her in ways that were unfamiliar to her, ways that called to the same chaos in him.

"No. Yes. I was just admiring your fridge."

"I love it. I had it completely refurbished a few years ago. It came with the place, but I think we all fit in with it."

"We?"

"My things and I. I'd rather do without something than bring something discordant in to where I live."

Did that include men? "Did you pack a bag?"

She waited the space of a breath before answering. "Do you think that's moving too fast?"

"It's just a sleepover. I have a spare toothbrush if you don't want to bring anything." He kept the kitchen counter between them, giving her a little space. "The truth is, you have to come with me. We're going to have a hard time being apart, now that our energies have connected."

"What do you mean?"

"You'll see tomorrow when you come back to town."

She sat on one of her tall barstools. "This isn't normal, Sam. My friends have never had this reaction to someone. Maybe Kiera did. She loved her husband deeply. I didn't when I was dating Clark—or anyone I've dated."

"He wasn't the right one for you."

"You think we're the right ones?" she asked.

"I know it. But I'm willing to give you time to come to terms with it."

"Okay. I'll pack a bag." She started toward her closet, then paused. "What about my truck? Should I follow you so that you don't have to drive me tomorrow?"

"No. You can take the Jeep tomorrow. Or the SUV. Or you can work from the fort, which I prefer. We'll figure tomorrow out tomorrow. I have plans for you tonight."

"Want to order something in before we leave? I don't really feel like being around anyone but you."

Liege stared at her. He didn't either. "Sounds good." So much for eating where they couldn't have sex. Yeah. They wouldn't be leaving her apartment anytime soon.

## 18

They ordered dinner from two different restaurants. Summer had a vegan salad and Sam had a huge New York-style pastrami on rye bread. Fortunately, both deliveries came about the same time.

"I'm starving," Sam said as he sat next to Summer at her counter and unwrapped his sandwich, which looked to have about two pounds of meat in it.

"I missed you while you were away," Summer said.

"I missed you. You were never off my mind."

"I'm sorry for freaking out and running away that day."

"Why did you?"

Summer used her fork to push a bit of the salad around. "Twice lately during my recent Wednesday dinners, a strange man keeps making a scene, warning me about something that doesn't make sense and telling me you—or Liege—was the only one I could trust."

"The red-haired guy you mentioned."

Summer nodded, wondering how he knew that's who warned her. "Do you know him?"

"I know of him."

"So he isn't a raving lunatic?"

"Well"—Sam made a half-smile as he tilted his head—"yeah, he is a lunatic."

"Can you tell him not to come around me anymore?"

"Maybe. He's hard to get a hold of usually."

"Mmm. Are you ready to talk to me about what it is you're mixed up with?"

"No." He took another bite, chewing and swallowing before saying more. "I really don't. The less you know about it, the better. For you. For those around you."

"Is it illegal?"

He looked at her a long moment, then put his sandwich down and leaned against the back of his chair. He stared at the counter, then drew a deep breath. "Do you remember, when you were a kid, and you first learned that Santa Claus wasn't real?"

"My family never celebrated Christmas through Santa in that way. I grew up understanding he was a symbol of generosity, not a giver of dreams."

"Right. Your hippie parents. Then what about when you learned about sex and realized all the nasty your parents had done in order for you to be here?"

"Sex and reproduction was just another aspect of organic life. My dad was a high school biology teacher. My parents never got weird talking about it, so it was never something I learned to be uncomfortable about."

"Damn. Your parents had it figured out. Do they live in the area?"

"No. They're volunteering overseas, teaching at a school in Nigeria." She considered him a moment. "So you're saying that what you're doing is reality-shattering, if I'm interpreting your analogies correctly."

"Yeah. And I don't think I'm ready to shatter your reality."

"You already have. As soon as I ran into you."

Sam nodded. "I want to keep you innocent as long as I can."

"But those examples that you gave—in my life they weren't earth-shattering or innocence-shattering. They just added knowledge to my experience."

"What if what you think you know is not the only reality there is?"

Summer folded her lips between her teeth and ran her tongue across the seam they made. She stared at him. "You mean, like Earth really is flat, and we never went to the moon, and aliens are real?"

"What if mutant humans are real?"

"Mutant. Humans." She shifted her gaze from him to her salad. "Wow. I was not expecting that."

Sam took a couple more bites of his giant sandwich.

"Mutant humans," Summer repeated. "You're just gonna leave it there?"

"Yeah, it's enough for now, don't you think?"

"No."

"You trust me, right?"

She didn't like the sound of that. At all. "I'm not sure, honestly."

Sam leaned back in his seat, then rotated to face her. "Ten years ago, I was in the Army. My command volunteered me for an experimental program. I didn't know what it entailed until it was too late."

"Those medical trials you mentioned. What did they do to you?"

"Our bodies and brains were reprogramed. We became telepathic."

"Oh." *Telepathic. Huh.*

"You don't seem surprised," he said.

"I'm still digesting that." She was trying to stay calm, but it was hard when she was so close to him. "There've been many studies suggesting plants and humans can have a telepathic link. Are you saying you can communicate with people telepathically?"

*Yes.* The word whispered into her mind in Sam's voice.

She gasped. Had she just imagined that?

*No, you didn't.*

This couldn't really be happening, could it? "Wait, I wasn't ready. Say something else."

Sam smiled at her, making her see he'd already proved his ability.

She put her hands on her knees. "Okay, go."

*I think you're beautiful.*

Summer felt heat sneak up her neck. She couldn't have heard that right. "Tell me what you said."

"You heard me."

"No. We have to write it down. I'll write what I heard and you write what you said." *Just so neither of us cheats.*

"Just so neither of us cheats." Sam chuckled. Summer fetched a notepad and two pens from a kitchen drawer. He took a sheet and wrote something down. She did the same. They compared notes.

Word for word, they were the same.

Summer blushed. "I'm not beautiful. I have freckles and blond eyelashes."

"You don't get to tell me what is or isn't beautiful. It's a personal observation"—he shrugged—"a subjective truth, maybe, but it's my truth."

"Well, then, thank you."

Another thought hit her right then—had he actually been visiting with her the times she thought she'd conjured him up? Had it really been him? She shot him a worried look. His expression revealed nothing.

She wanted to die.

Mortification could kill, couldn't it? She squeezed her eyes shut. Could it do so right this moment?

God, where did she end and he begin?

She'd *used* him. He'd been in the shower with her. She'd *wanted* him in the shower with her.

"You didn't *use* me. You summoned me to comfort you. I was glad to be of help."

Summer covered her mouth with both hands. "I totally perved on you."

"Not totally." His smile was self-deprecating and a little crooked. "Not nearly enough."

"Oh my God." She moved her hands to cover her eyes. "I'm sorry."

"No apology needed. I should have resisted your summons, but I couldn't. I craved you." He got off his barstool and picked her up, then carried her over to the futon and set her on one side of him, her legs draped over his lap. "I still crave you."

She touched his face, letting her fingers trail down his cheek. His cheekbones were high, the line of his jaw hard, defined by the hollows of his cheeks. "Being near you has felt wonderful to me since the very beginning."

"You asked if what we're doing is illegal, and the answer is complicated, because what we've become isn't in the realm of normal. My team and I are searching for a way to reverse what was done to us."

"Can it be reversed?"

"I don't know. Maybe not."

"Are you"—she had to pause—"are you dying?"

"No. We just exist differently now. We're trying to understand our new normal. And we're hoping to stop it from being done to others."

"So are you like Superman? Can you fly?"

"No. But I have plenty of other tricks."

"Like what?"

"I don't want to scare you."

"It's a little late for that."

"I can manipulate your mind."

"Can you? How?"

"Like making you think I wasn't stopped in front of you the day we collided."

Summer gasped. "No, you didn't."

"That's why I said the accident was my fault. And it's why I'm getting your car fixed."

"Why would you do something like that?"

"Because I wanted to meet you."

"Why couldn't you have just visited with me at the garden center? Or followed me to one of my outings with my friends." Her eyes widened. "Wait. You did, didn't you? That night we had our first dinner?"

He smiled at her. "Guilty. Before that, I wasn't sure whether you were involved with the people I'm after."

"Am I?"

"Possibly. Though I now know you're an innocent. But the Briscoes are not."

"Am I in danger?"

Sam's answer wasn't fast in coming, and when it did, it was not reassuring. "Yes, though I don't know enough about the threat yet."

"So—answer this truthfully—did you hire me to design your garden as a pity assignment to assuage your conscience for tricking me into hitting you?" She faced him as an even worse thought struck her. "Are you a danger to me?"

"No. And yes."

"Which is it?"

"I will never intentionally hurt you. But the work I do is dangerous, and my enemies are ruthless."

"You sound like you're in a gang."

"I'm fighting one."

"Do you even need a garden?"

"I never thought I did until I saw your sketches. Now, I want your vision to be realized. I want to walk through something you created. I want something beautiful to give my eyes and my heart a rest from the fiends I'm fighting."

"Working for you is a dangerous thing."

"Yes."

"That's why you offered me double my current salary. And a place to hide."

"Yes."

Summer shook her head. "If you, with your strength, knowledge, and telepathy find the gangs you're fighting a challenge, they would crush me with no effort at all."

"True."

"Sam—I can't do this. I'm a landscape designer, not a fighter. I don't even know what it is you're fighting. Or who. Or anything."

"I know. I'm not asking you to be a fighter. I tried to stay away from you, but I couldn't. I tried to forget about you, but that's like asking me to leave half my body somewhere."

"Mutants." She shook her head. "How many like you are there?"

"Thousands. More being created every week."

"Does the government know about this?"

"Probably, seeing as I was active duty when I was forced into the program. After I was altered, I do know my command was told I'd died in the trials. Whether the Army ever knew the truth of what the trials were about, I don't know."

"So your friends are mutants, too."

"Yep."

"Thousands of them. How would I know if I'd ever seen a mutant?"

"You wouldn't unless the mutant wanted you to." Sam caught a lock of her hair and pushed it behind her ear. "Brett is a mutant, and not the good kind."

Summer gasped. "Oh, God. I went out with him."

"He did that to get to me. He knew I was already watching you."

"You were stalking me?"

"I was."

"That night—my lost memories. I wasn't drugged, was I?"

"No. He had you in a trance. He tried to make you eat steak, but even under his mind control, you wouldn't eat it. I took you out of there and brought you home. I watched over you that night and the next."

Summer frowned. "You moved me the night after I went to the clinic, when I was sleeping in my closet."

"Yes."

"How did you get in here?"

"I unlocked the door. Our neurological modifications gave us access to telekinetic skills too."

"No." Summer sat up and folded her legs under her. She didn't move away from him—for some reason, she couldn't tolerate any space between them. Her knees were pressed against his thigh. "Show me."

LIEGE SMILED. He mentally opened her front door, then closed it. He opened and closed the cabinets in the kitchen. He lifted the quilt on her bed.

"No." She leaned against him as he telekinetically moved things around her apartment. "If I just saw that without knowing you were doing it, I'd think my place was haunted."

Those were mere parlor tricks. He was hoping she'd not press for more exhibitions. That little display was more than enough for her for now. Too much too fast, and he'd seriously blow her mind.

"So that whole conversation we had about sex and dating really happened?" She squeezed her eyes shut and lowered her forehead to his shoulder. "I'm so embarrassed."

He wrapped an arm around her and moved her down to lie beside him on the narrow futon. "Why be embarrassed? I told you then we'd be getting together." He slipped his hand under her sweater, moving it to cup her breast. She arched into him. Her arms went around his neck, drawing him down to kiss her. She tasted so sweet. He kissed her upper lip, then her bottom lip, then caught her chin in his teeth. He lifted up to look at her, hardly daring to believe she was actually in his arms.

He stroked her face. "It's late. We should clean up. You've got work in the morning."

"I don't want to go back there."

Liege pulled her close. "Then don't."

"I'm worried about my friends who work there."

He frowned. "How so?"

"Clark has gotten really weird lately. Every time I see him, he has more scratches and bruises all over his face and neck and hands. Sometimes, when he looks at me, I'm not even certain he's in there. He's different. He gets migraines. He's sick. Inside and out. Douglas said he was going to get Clark some help, but I don't know if he's done that. What's Brett's interest in the garden center, anyway?"

Liege didn't want to tell her the whole truth, that Brett was using the Briscoes for his own sick jollies. "The people responsible for creating mutants like me come from an organization called the Omni World Order. They run several legit businesses up and down the Front Range here in Colorado and elsewhere across the U.S. and internationally. The Briscoes partnered with the Omnis through Brett. I doubt they knew ahead of time what they were getting in to."

"Can you help them get free of the Omnis?"

Liege stroked her hair, so silky and pale in his fingers. "After all the slights they've dealt you, you still care about them?"

"Clark's a jerk, but I never saw him as malicious. He and his dad use people—and I'm tired of doing their heavy lifting at the shop—but they don't deserve to become victims of a crime organization."

"If I can, I will." How could he tell her how far over the edge her friend Clark had already gone? How far was too far to be reclaimed?

## 19

Sam was awake when Summer opened her eyes the next morning. She smiled at him and reached over to touch him, wanting to be certain he was actually in her bed and not something she was imagining. He was reassuringly solid. They'd ended up in her bed again last night after doing the dishes and had decided to just stay in town.

She wasn't certain how she felt about his super abilities yet. She wondered about all that he'd been put through having those changes forced on him. It couldn't have been easy. And then to have the world told he was dead—what happened after that? How did someone recover from that?

"How do you feel?" he asked.

She was more than a little tender—they'd gone through all but one of the condoms he'd brought with him. "Sore. Scared. Happy."

He pulled her closer to him, wrapping his arms

around her, which was heaven. "That's an odd blend of feelings." He smoothed a bit of her hair from her cheek as he stared into her eyes.

"I'm glad you're here and not just in my mind."

"What are we going to do today?" he asked.

"It's a workday for me."

"I thought you finished the design?"

"I did, though I'll probably keep fine-tuning it. Why?"

"Because I want you to hand in your resignation notice. I'll go in and pay for the plan so I can be on-site when you quit."

"You can pay for it, but I'm not ready to quit. I've sent my résumé to several other companies, but no nibbles yet. I can't quit without a job."

"I'll hire you. Today."

"I'm not comfortable with that, Sam. I want to stand on my own."

"I'd be paying for your expertise. What happens between us is separate."

Summer sat up. "I don't want you to pay me."

"People with a specialized skill set hire it out all the time. It's how the world works."

"It doesn't feel right."

"If we were married, it wouldn't be an issue. What I have would be yours."

Summer's jaw dropped. "We haven't even had our first real date. You can't bring up the M-word yet."

"Yes, I can. Marry me."

"You don't have a slow mode, do you?"

He grinned. "Other than in bed?"

She leaned over his chest, bracing herself on her folded arms as she studied him. "And you wonder why you scare the hell out of me."

Still, he held his silence. He had that odd way of not filling awkward silences with a bunch of useless words. "Okay. I'll quit. And then I'll go find a fill-in job while I do my job hunt."

"No. I'll pay you in advance for the work you're going to do on my greenhouse."

"You're set on this."

"I am."

She straightened and settled by his side. "If I agree, it doesn't mean anything."

"It means you'll be designing the landscaping in my greenhouse."

"It doesn't mean we're engaged."

He smiled. "Yet."

"I want my own room at your house in case I stay over."

"Done." He folded his arms behind his head, looking supremely pleased with himself.

She sighed, then relented and kissed him. "I'm going to make some breakfast. Care for a frittata?"

"With bacon and biscuits and gravy?"

She laughed. "No. With artichokes, Kalamata olives, and feta."

"Sure. That sounds great. Got any coffee?"

"I do. But I don't have an espresso machine."

"We do at the fort." He caught her before she

could slip out of bed and rolled her under him. "Thank you."

She moved her hands over his big arms, moving up to his shoulders. "For what?"

"For not saying no to marrying me."

She opened for him, not caring whether he was covered. Neither of them did casual sex. And her birth control would prevent her getting pregnant.

"I don't have any STDs and can't get them." He pushed into her, reading her mind.

The feel of his hot length inside her sent shivers through her body. "How is that possible?"

"The nanos enhanced my immune system. I can't get, carry, or spread any illness."

That would take some thinking to digest, but right then all Summer could think of was how wonderful she and Sam felt together as she tugged him down over her body.

SUMMER FELT like a hot mess as she stood outside the garden center that had employed her for the past six years. It represented so many hopes and dreams, accomplishments and challenges. Her time there felt unfinished, but maybe it was just that she was unfinished.

Sam came to stand beside her, silently giving her the time she needed to focus on what she had to do. She nodded at him. His eyes weren't soft.

"I have your back," he said. "You got this." It was ridiculous how much stronger that assertion made her feel.

Summer left her messenger bag in the truck. Her arms were full of books she was returning to the garden center's library. She'd sent Clark and his dad an email to review and approve Sam's design, telling them he'd be coming in to pay for it that morning. She didn't know if Clark would even be there, given how messed up he was last time she saw him.

She walked into the garden center. Jada was at the register. They exchanged smiles. Summer would definitely miss her and several of the others she'd worked with for so long.

"Jada, Sam is going to pay for the design plan I did for him. I've already set up his invoice, if you'd like to ring him up."

Summer exchanged a look with Sam. *I love you.* His voice slipped into her mind, soft and sweet, like sun-warmed honey. Summer gasped. Sam laughed.

She spun on her heel and made a beeline for the conference room, where she dropped off the books she'd borrowed. She took the folded resignation paper she'd printed at home down the hall to Douglas's office. A quick peek into Clark's office showed he was sitting at his desk, staring blankly at the wall across from him. She looked away quickly, but not before seeing him slowly shift his gaze her way. His eyes were empty, and the void in them sucked her breath from her chest. She hurried to Douglas's office.

*I'm with you,* Sam said.

She looked over her shoulder. It wasn't Sam there but Clark. She squared her shoulders and knocked on Douglas's door.

He looked up and nodded at her, then stood and gestured toward the chairs in front of his desk. Summer didn't sit down. She felt pinned in the big office between Douglas and his son.

Didn't matter. This was the last time she'd ever be in this situation.

"I'm glad you're here," Douglas said. He turned his monitor toward her. A video segment was on a repeat loop, showing the passionate embrace she and Sam had shared last night. Summer was shocked.

*Damn. I forgot to take care of that. My bad. I'll do it now.*

"This is unacceptable behavior," Douglas began. As he spoke, the video twitched, then turned to digital snow.

"What is?" Summer asked him.

He gestured toward his monitor.

"I don't see anything," Summer said, feeling Douglas's shock when he looked at the feed he'd been watching on repeat.

She handed him her resignation.

He read it then shook his head. "I don't accept this," Douglas said.

"You don't have a choice," Summer replied. "Given the strange things going on here, I no longer feel that working here is in my best interests."

Douglas dropped the paper onto his desk. "Then I

accept. But don't forget that we have a non-compete agreement. I'll have your exit papers drafted this afternoon. You can come by tomorrow to sign them."

The thought of having to come back in to face them again shot panic through Summer's gut. She sent Clark a quick glance, snagging his hollow gaze. He backed away from her, opening a path to the hall door.

"Actually," Douglas said, breaking into her panicked thoughts, "don't worry about it. Any monies we owe you for unused leave will be in your last paycheck. And I've decided not to enforce your non-compete. Give me a minute to draft that up. You can sign it before you leave and that will be that."

Summer blinked, shocked at his turnabout. She nodded. "Great. Thanks. I'll just get my things from my office. Sam paid for the design I did. I'll wait out front for your document." That way, she could have witnesses.

She thought about offering Douglas a handshake, but she didn't want to touch him. Clark's soulless eyes followed her as she left the office.

The only personal thing she had in her office was her sweater. She went to grab that, but it was gone.

*I have it.*

*You have it?*

*I took it so I could keep your scent with me.*

Summer smiled, warmed by the freakiness of his instincts. She went out front to wait for whatever it was Douglas wanted her to sign.

Sam was standing beside the checkout counter. God, he was huge. She smiled at him. He smiled back. She walked right up to him and wrapped her arms around him. He hugged her back, then kissed the top of her head. For the first time in her adult life, she felt like she'd found her home.

"You did good," he whispered.

Jada was smiling at them when Summer pulled free. Summer went over to tell her the news that she was leaving. Jada hugged her. "I knew this day would come. I'm happy to see you spread your wings. Stop in now and then and give us an update."

"I will. Don't take chances with Clark. He's not right. Tell the others."

"I will."

Douglas came out of the offices with two sheets of paper. The handwritten text on both said exactly what he'd said to her: he wouldn't be enforcing their non-compete agreement, and all monies due her would be in her final paycheck.

They both signed both copies—with Jada as a witness.

It was so easy to step from one spot in life to the next. Bewilderingly easy. Why had she fought it so long?

She walked out with Sam, loving the solid feel of his arm around her shoulders. The sun was brilliant in the blue sky, and its warmth surrounded her.

"That wasn't as hard as I thought it would be. I

expected a ton of drama and a fight over the non-compete."

Sam took her hand. "Ready for your next thing?"

"I am." But with everything now being possible, she didn't know where to begin.

"Can we start with lunch?" Sam asked.

She laughed. "Are you hungry again?"

"Always. You pick, I'll buy."

They went to a local restaurant that specialized in breakfast and lunch. Summer ordered a veggie omelet. Sam ordered the whole works—with a biscuit and sausage gravy, which he'd been wanting since the breakfast she'd fixed for them.

"We may have to work on your food choices," Summer said. "I don't want you to have a heart attack."

He grinned and took her hands. "Maybe that's how it would work for regulars, but not me."

"Regulars?"

"Non-mutants."

"I'm a regular?"

"You are."

She leaned across the table to whisper, "Are there other mutants in here right now?"

"No. You make it sound crazy."

"It is."

"But it's reality."

She loved having him hold her hands, loved that everyone could see they were a couple. "Sam?"

"Sam I am." His eyes sparkled.

She laughed. "I think it's time you met my friends."

"I did meet Ash."

"I have another close friend—Kiera. We're really close, the three of us. I don't want us to change that."

"Why would it?"

"The girls and I, we do things together."

Sam looked into her eyes. Being with him filled her with the sense of comfort and calm. "I don't want to take you from your friends," he said. "Or your career. Or anything you like. I want to be an *and* not an *or*."

"So you're cool with meeting them?"

"Sure. We can have them out to the fort. Or meet up at a local place in town."

"Tonight's our regular Wednesday dinner. I'll see what works for them."

## 20

Summer had dinner warming in the oven, takeout from a nearby Italian restaurant, complete with a huge bowl of salad and their famous chocolate lasagna for dessert.

She sent a glance over the dishes set out on the counter. She didn't have a dining room table, and there were only three barstools at the counter, so some of them would have to eat on their laps on the futon.

Maybe they should have done this at Sam's place. Or at a restaurant. She'd wanted to host their first meeting at her place, somewhere familiar to everyone.

Sam came over and pulled her into a hug. She wrapped her arms around him and buried her face in his chest. "It's going to be fine," he said. "They're your friends. No need to be nervous. I'm glad they were open to doing this tonight."

"They've been wanting to meet you. I just have to warn you—Kiera runs a halfway house for women.

She deals with tough issues every day. I'm afraid it's made her somewhat critical of men."

"It's an important job she's doing."

Summer nodded. "Just go slowly with her. She needs time to warm up to people, and she's very protective of me and Ash. And Ash, well, she's the opposite of Kiera. She loves men. Seriously, loves them. She's going to flirt with you."

"I won't even notice. You're the only female I have any interest in."

"They're going to ask you hard questions."

"Bring it. I'm ready." He kissed her forehead. "I'm glad you have such fierce friends looking out for you —and you them."

"Most of our other friends have already settled down. I think that's partly why we bonded so thoroughly. We're the last single women our age in the whole town."

Sam smiled. "That's an exaggeration."

"Feels true. At least Kiera was once married."

Sam's brows lifted. "You mentioned she was a widow."

"She married right out of college. He was a marine. He died five years ago when his helicopter was shot down in Afghanistan."

Sam sighed and briefly squeezed his eyes shut. "That must have been hard for her."

"It was."

"Kiera's been through the ringer."

Summer nodded. "I really want them to like you."

"I can only be myself, Summer. They'll love me or hate me, according to their own preferences."

Liege was more nervous than he let on. This was the first time he would actually get to interact with his daughter. He felt a little guilty about the fact that he wasn't going to show his real face to her or Ash. He'd already hidden himself from Ash when he encountered her and Summer walking to dinner. He had to keep with that same cover—otherwise, he'd be forced to bring his daughter and Ash into the world of mutants. Of course, he hadn't realized at the time that that meant he'd have to hide himself from Summer's friends for the duration of their relationship.

Or maybe he'd done it because he was a coward and didn't want to face his daughter as himself.

Sam heard two people coming up the stairs to Summer's apartment. She shot him a tense glance as she went to open the door. The girls came into her living room on a wave of cold air. They took their coats and winter gear off, hanging it on a strip of hooks behind the front door.

Liege felt his heart banging around in his chest. Except for the years he'd disappeared into the Omni mutant program, he'd been involved in Kiera's entire life. Yes, it had been on the periphery, well out of her sight. He'd sent money to her mom, leaving it up to her as to how she wanted to explain the income he provided. He'd never asserted his rights as Kiera's dad, never interfered with the choices her mom made on her behalf. When Kiera's dad passed just before she was to go to college, Liege had set up an account with the money she'd need for tuition, room, and board. He'd lost track of her while he was in the trials, but when he got out, she was the first thing he checked out. At the time, she was trying to raise money for her women's center. Liege was her angel investor. He provided her center with foodstuffs for every Thanksgiving and Christmas. And the last two Christmases, he'd sent over piles of presents for the women and children in residence.

Kiera knew nothing of his involvement, of course.

He was proud of the woman she'd become. Maybe it made sense starting their relationship as friends rather than father-daughter, with all the garbage that came with that.

Maybe this would work out after all.

He smiled at her when she faced the room. Summer gave both women hugs, then took their hands and led them the few feet to where he was standing.

He shook hands with both of them. As Summer had predicted, Ash was all smiles and Kiera all glares.

Summer poured glasses of Chianti for everyone. Kiera sipped hers, watching him over the rim of her glass.

"So, Sam. You and Summer, huh?" Kiera said.

Liege smiled at Summer and drew her to his side. Shit. His daughter was one tough female. "Yup, me and Summer."

"This happened fast," Kiera said.

"Did it? Seemed slow to me," Liege said. "Took us weeks to get together."

"Why don't we have a seat and chat for a bit before dinner?" Summer suggested. She led Liege over to her futon and sat on it with him. Kiera joined them on the futon. Ash turned one of the barstools to face the room.

"We loved your fort, Sam," Ash said. "That pool is amazing."

"Glad you could get out there," Liege said. "It'll be even more amazing when Summer's finished with her plan for that room, and we get everything installed."

"What is it that you do, Sam?" Kiera asked.

"I'm a consultant in the field of physical security."

"What is that, exactly?" Kiera asked.

"Keeping people and places safe."

"So you're a bodyguard?"

"Not me, but that's one of my company's verticals."

"Enough of the grilling," Ash said with a smile. "I'm sure Kiera's already done a background check on you. And I'm sure you passed her inspection or we wouldn't be here."

Summer gasped. "Kiera!"

"Can't be too safe these days," Kiera said.

"What I really want to know," Ash said, "is why a fort? I mean, it is gorgeous, and a fort does make sense out on the plains where the wind can be harsh. That courtyard gives terrific protection from that. But why a fort?"

"That courtyard makes its own ecosystem, too," Summer said. "It stays milder a few weeks longer in the autumn and warms up a few weeks earlier in the spring. I'm going to have fun designing the garden in there."

"I did love that fountain," Kiera said. "I bet it sounds wonderful on a summer night."

Summer smiled. "Sam said he always wanted a fort, ever since he was a kid…"

Liege mentally stepped back from the women, listening to them converse. Their auras looked like a room full of flowers. They complemented each other perfectly—and accepted each other completely. It was rare to find such harmony among humans, and it was humbling that they let him into their circle.

But what would happen if they discovered the truth of his lies? He'd been bending the truth for so long that he no longer had any angst about it, until now, when the woman he loved was besties with his secret daughter. And neither had any idea what a monster he was.

"Ash," Liege said, glad to turn the conversation away from himself, "what is it that you do?"

Ash smiled and her eyes twinkled. "What is my

job? Or what am I?" She tilted her head. "Why is it that we define ourselves by our employment?"

"It tells us something of our affinities," Liege answered. "But I'll go with what are you?"

"What am I?" Ash asked the girls.

"An adventurer," Summer said. "An intrepid world traveler."

"Summer told me you're going on a tour of coffee plantations this spring," Liege said.

"I am. Have you ever been there?"

"Many times. Are you going with a tour company?" he asked.

"No. I'm doing my own thing. I tried to get Summer to come with me, but she won't leave your side. And Kiera can't leave her world, not now."

"Why's that?" Liege asked.

Kiera gave Ash a dark look. "There have been some odd things happening lately."

Summer reached over and took Kiera's hand. "Tell Sam. Maybe he can help." She looked at him and said, "This is at the shelter she runs."

Kiera gave him a measuring look. She seemed on the fence about Summer's suggestion before finally relenting. "I can't explain it. Some women have been showing up at the center without having any understanding of how they got there."

"Is it unusual to have drop-ins at your center?" Liege asked.

"No. And we were expecting each of these women, but they arrived hours later than planned—

hours they couldn't account for. Then there are others who never show up at all. When I call to see how they're doing, their numbers are disconnected, email fails, letters return unopened."

Liege had put a protection on his daughter's center, making it off-limits to the Omnis, but that didn't mean they couldn't do a runaround, intercepting women before they could get there. "How long has this been going on?"

"Months. I went to the cops about it. There's a detective looking into it for me."

"I'd be glad to have a look too," Liege said. "I have access to other resources the cops may not have."

"I doubt you'll find anything. The detective I'm working with checked out the IDs I gave him. He said they were fake. He thinks the women they belong to are up to nefarious things." Kiera shook her head. "I met them. I worked with them. They are real people with real issues. You can't fake the fear they had. And after they left the center, they just disappear?"

"I'll come by anytime to chat with you."

"Take him up on that, Kiera," Ash said. "The cops haven't been any help at all."

Kiera met his gaze. "Okay. Let's do that."

Summer kissed his cheek. "Thank you for helping Kiera. She's hasn't made any headway on that."

"I'm happy to help," Liege said. "Did you tell them your big news?"

Summer's eyes got big. "No. You guys—I quit today. The Briscoes let me out of their non-compete."

"That's great news," Ash said.

"It is," Kiera said. "I'm glad. Clark has gotten so weird. What's next for you?"

"Sam's place. I have a ton of work to do there."

Kiera gave him another of her hard looks, silently warning him he better not disappoint Summer. Liege smiled inwardly. His daughter was good people.

The rest of the evening moved too quickly. When Kiera and Ash were leaving, he and Summer stood near while they put their coats on. Kiera shook his hand.

"I can come by the center tomorrow to talk about your missing clients, if that works for you," he said.

Kiera nodded. "That would be great. I'd really appreciate the help. Summer can give you directions to the center."

Ash took his hand in both of hers. Her eyes were sparkling.

"I have friends in Colombia who own coffee plantations," Liege said. "If you like, I'd be happy to put you in contact with them. They're safe places to go on your tour."

"Sure!" Ash said. "I'd love that! It was great getting to visit with you, Sam. Summer has been gushing about you for a long time."

## 21

Liege parked in the lot next to his daughter's shelter. He and Summer had stayed at her apartment another night so that they could have this meeting.

Summer looked as tense as he felt—though for different reasons. She was worried about Kiera and the women she'd reported missing. He was worried about that and letting his daughter down.

If the missing women had been sucked into the Omni world, it was unlikely they'd ever be heard from again. Even if they survived the tests the Omnis were probably running on them, the mind control exerted over them would prohibit them from returning to mainstream life.

The real issue was bigger than a few missing women; the Omnis were a threat to human communities worldwide.

Liege felt Summer's small hand slip into his—a

reminder that she was counting on him to help Kiera. He might not be able to find these particular missing women, but perhaps the details surrounding their disappearance would help him learn more about the Omni program that was in play.

Liege was familiar with the layout of Kiera's shelter, since the foundation he'd set up for her had brokered the deal to buy the old school building and grounds. The mix of classrooms and offices was easily adapted to building-out studio suites, small apartments, common areas, and the classrooms that comprised the center. The compound had been behind a tall stucco wall that set it off from the street. In the remodel to make it a shelter, Liege had made sure that the wall completely enclosed the property. It wasn't a perfect defense, but it could slow down an attack.

A staffer greeted them and led them to Kiera's office. Kiera hugged Summer and shook his hand, then invited them to sit at her small conference table, where two stacks of folders had already been set out.

Kiera put a hand on the shorter pile. "These files are of women some of my current and former clients have asked me to check in to. I have not met them, but I trust the women who reported them missing. They wouldn't sound false alarms. They provided photos of the women, addresses, emails, phone numbers, social media info—everything they knew about each of the women they'd lost contact with. None of the women in this stack can be found. I've visited the addresses of those who are local, talked to their neighbors, called their phones, sent several emails, did online searches for them—all to come up empty-handed."

She moved her hand to the other pile of folders. "The women in this stack have also vanished—the difference is that I've met these women. They stayed here. I have copies of their driver's licenses. I know they exist, but even when I talk to their spouses and families, it's like these women were never associated with their own families. No one knows them or they haven't been seen in years—even when they were here just months ago."

"Summer said you went to the police about this," Liege said.

"I did. When I had names and contact info but no actual proof they ever existed, as with the women in this stack"—Kiera indicated the shorter pile—"the cops said adults have the right to lose themselves, that we're talking about abused and at-risk women who probably felt it was safer to do that than stay in their current lives. The cops refused to go looking for them."

"And about the women you'd known? What of them?"

"Since I had copies of their IDs, the cops did more thorough searches—at least to the extent that they identified that some were faked. They determined the women with these IDs either didn't exist in the system or the IDs had been stolen from actual people."

"But you don't buy that?" Liege asked.

"Of course not. These women were desperate. Their husbands or boyfriends were violent and powerful." Kiera looked from him to Summer. Liege knew she doubted they'd believe her. "They didn't fake their IDs," Kiera said. "Why would they? How would they even know to do that? But it's like they were erased. Just wiped out of existence."

Summer leaned forward. "Tell him about the women who've been showing up without any recollection of how they got to the shelter."

Kiera nodded. "There have been several of them over the last few months. They all came here on the bus. They remember the bus ride, then the next thing they remember is being inside the shelter. Nothing between those two stops."

Liege knew of a half-dozen women he and his men had retrieved from the grasp of the Omnis, but he couldn't tell Kiera that they were responsible for the gaping hole in the women's memories. He still hoped he could keep his war with the Omnis and what the Omnis were up to a secret from the rest of humanity.

"How many women has this happened to?" Liege asked.

"Thirteen so far."

That was more than his team had intercepted. Was someone outside of his team helping them? Or had those women fallen prey to the Omnis during the time of their missing memories?

"Are these women healthy?" Liege asked.

Kiera stared at him, then her brows twitched. "No. Half of them developed fevers shortly after arriving. Three of them later died at the hospital. I now know that anyone arriving with memory loss has to go immediately into quarantine until I can get them checked out. None of their blood tests have ever revealed anything infectious, but I can't take chances with our other residents. One of my clients is still in the hospital." Kiera's eyes narrowed. "How did you know they were ill?"

"I didn't," Liege said. "But fevers can cause foggy memories. Tell me, did you also have women you expected to show up who didn't?"

"Yes." Kiera knew he was onto something.

He nodded toward the file of women whose identities had been erased. "Have any of the women with the lost time also been erased?"

"All of those who were sick."

What if the Omnis were taking them, altering them, sometimes returning them to their families or regular lives, but in a way that shielded them from anyone looking for them, letting them die or recover as they would? If they survived, they would become candidates for future harvesting into an Omni program? Or maybe the Omnis were feeding them to their packs of deviants to rouse their bloodlust, like they'd done with the woman Liege had rescued a few weeks back.

"I'd like to visit the woman from your center who's in the hospital," Liege said.

"Sure." Kiera got her phone out. "I'll call and let her know we're coming."

Liege shook his head. "Don't. If she's being observed by people with malicious intent, we don't want to alert them to our arrival."

"You don't think I'm crazy." Kiera's surprise filled that statement. "Other than Ash and Summer, I haven't been able to get anyone to take me seriously. Without hard evidence, no one will open an investigation. I was about to take this story to an investigative journalist. Mine isn't the only women's shelter experiencing these anomalies."

"I will help you get to the bottom of this, but it needs to stay quiet for now." Liege followed that up with a mild compulsion that she keep this a secret for the wellbeing of the women involved. Truthfully, this needed to be kept a secret for the safety of all humanity, but he'd take an incremental win for now.

Liege drove Summer and Kiera over to the hospital where the center's newest client was. He sent an EMF pulse to disable the tech equipment at the security station, forcing the guards to do a manual pat down. The compulsion he issued made the guard overlook the knives he always wore.

Kiera visited here each day, so she went straight to the woman's room. The bed was empty. Liege could feel the energy of the Omnis who'd come to take the woman. It was fresh—they'd just missed them.

Kiera looked around, checking for her client. The bathroom door was closed.

"Don't bother," he said. "She's gone. Give me a minute. She might still be in the building."


SUMMER EXCHANGED worried looks with Kiera. Hopefully, they'd find the woman before whoever it was that Sam was fighting was able to get her out. She stepped to the door to see which direction Sam took —and saw him disappear.

*Disappear.*

Just like that red-haired guy had disappeared that night outside the restaurant.

"Oh, God," Summer said.

"What?" Kiera came to stand beside her at the doorway.

"He disappeared," Summer said.

"Yeah, he's trying to find her."

"No. I mean *disappeared*. Like vanished."

"He has long legs. He moves fast."

Summer shook her head. She'd seen what she'd seen. He was there one moment and gone the next, but Kiera was rationalizing the whole thing.

Before Summer could argue about it, Kiera hurried out to the nurses station to ask about her client.

The man frowned at Kiera but did a quick check

of their systems. "We have no one here by that name."

"Was she transferred out somewhere? Or was she released?"

"No, ma'am. There's no one in our system by that name."

"That's not possible. I've been here every day this week. She came in to my women's shelter with a fever. I brought her here myself three days ago."

"Maybe you have us confused with another hospital?" he suggested.

A woman came over to stand behind the man. "Is there a problem?"

"Yes. I brought one of my clients here earlier this week, and she's vanished from your system. She was in that room," Kiera said, pointing to the room.

"What's her name?" the head nurse asked.

Kiera told her.

She looked up the name. "No, he's right. We don't have any current or recent patients by that name."

"I see." Kiera nodded. "Of course." She turned away from the desk and started for the hallway to the stairs.

"What do you see?" Summer asked, following her.

"She's been erased. We didn't get here soon enough. We missed her by just hours."

Summer had to jog to keep up with Kiera's angry strides. She was about to text Sam that they were leaving, but of course he was already in her mind.

*I'll meet you out front,* he said.

*They have no record of Kiera's client,* Summer told him.

*I'm not surprised. I'm finished here. I'll drop you both off then see what I can do.*

Sam was standing out front, waiting for them. Summer felt a little of the stress lift away as soon as their eyes met. How could that be after seeing the man disappear right in front of her eyes?

What was really going on? Was he a magician? A hypnotist?

Kiera and Ash said Sam looked completely different from the way Summer saw him. How was that possible?

What was real and what wasn't? How was it that she couldn't trust her senses anymore?

"She was there," Kiera said, folding her arms as she glared at Sam.

"I believe you," he said.

"Why? I have no proof to offer about any of this."

"Let's get out of here." Sam started the SUV as they walked over to it. "There are roughly a hundred thousand people missing in the U.S. at any given moment, Kiera, if you combine those reported missing and some number of those who are unreported."

"These women didn't just disappear. They're completely gone. Nonexistent. Vanished."

"Maybe," Sam said. "Maybe they've just been moved from one set of systems to another."

"What are you saying?" Kiera asked.

"I'm saying we're dealing with sophisticated human traffickers who know how to cover their trail." He looked in the rearview mirror at Kiera. "At least until they ran into you."

"Can you help her with this?" Summer asked.

"Yes. But it's going to take some time."

Kiera sighed. "At least we're doing something." She frowned. "What are we doing, exactly?"

"I have your files. I have to ask you to leave this in my hands," Sam said.

"Trust you?" Kiera scoffed.

Summer knew trust wasn't in Kiera's wheelhouse. "Yes."

"I can't just leave it with you," Kiera said. "For one, you and I have no history. I've only just met you. For two, we're talking about the lives of women who came to *me* for refuge. I've failed them. How can I help anyone if I can't protect them?"

"Because I'm the only one who can help them. You've done what you can on your own. I'll take it from here."

"I can't pay you." They were pulling up to the shelter.

Sam stopped in front of the main entrance. "I don't need your money."

Kiera shook her head. "This could get expensive. You said yourself it's going to take time."

"I'll update you as I have more information. In the meantime, keep your head down. I don't want you to disappear as well. No more asking questions."

Kiera was shocked. "Is that a threat?"

"Not from me," Sam said. "It's nothing for these people to erase anyone, especially someone who stands in their way."

Kiera got out of the SUV. Summer rolled her window down. "You coming with me?" Kiera asked her.

"No. I'll call you later."

"Okay. Sam, thank you for anything you can do to help me with this. We're the only ones who know they ever existed."

Summer didn't say anything as Sam drove her over to her apartment. He parked, and she got out. He got out too and walked with her to the stairs.

"You really think you can help her?" she asked.

"I think I can find the traffickers who took her clients. Whether I'll be in time to help her clients, I don't know."

Summer folded her arms. "How is it that you can do what the authorities can't?"

"I have special skills. These traffickers are the same ones who changed me and the guys. We've already been on their trail."

"You didn't tell Kiera that."

"No. The less she knows, the safer she'll be."

"She wouldn't agree with you on that."

He pulled her into his arms. Summer kept her arms folded between them, but she did lean against him. He felt so solid.

"Sam"—she leaned back to look up at him—"I saw something at the hospital. I saw you disappear."

He nodded. "I'm sorry I scared you."

"You don't deny you did that?"

He pulled free and moved back a step. And then right there, right in front of her eyes, he vanished. She reached her hands out and felt the air. He'd been there just seconds before and was now gone. Gone.

"Sam!" she shouted. His arms went around her from behind. She startled then turned to face him. "How did you do that?"

"There's a lot I have to tell you, but now is not the time. I have to move on this new lead before the trail goes cold." He kissed her forehead. "Stay here. I'll come back for you tonight."

## 22

S ummer watched Sam get in his SUV. When their eyes met, she couldn't look away. For a moment she thought he'd change his mind and spend the day with her, but he drove away.

What had she gotten herself mixed up in? She saw again the way he walked out of the hospital room, shifting from corporeal to invisible. He'd done that again just minutes ago. Was he a ghost? What kind of alternate reality did he live in? And what were the implications of that for her? Or for her friends? She was convinced he wasn't showing his real self to Ash and Kiera—but how could that be?

The truth was that it really didn't matter. His enemies were scary—she sure didn't want to get mixed up with them. But Sam had protected her from Clark when he'd gotten so strange. She had no doubt Sam would protect her from the people he was after too. She could deal with anything as long as she had him beside her.

She made a cup of tea, then settled down to work on the design plan for Sam's greenhouse. She sat at her kitchen counter until she finished her tea, then moved to the futon. By the time she decided to pour another cup of tea, the shadows were long outside. She checked the time. Four thirty-five p.m. She was torn between waiting a little longer for Sam to come back or just heading out to his place. She thought he might pop into her head with the answer, but he didn't.

She wasn't sure texting him right then was the right thing to do either. What if he was stalking his enemies? A text on his phone might alert not just him but others. She heated the water for another cup of tea, then went back to her project.

The next time she looked up, it was fully dark outside. She better pack up and head out to the fort. She wanted to be there when he got back. She took a quick shower then pulled on a pair of black yoga pants and a baggy sweater over a white tee. She was just slipping on her hiking boots when the lights in her apartment went out.

She finished tying her boots, then went into the living room where the fuse box was. It didn't take much for the system to be overloaded. It was just odd that it had happened when she didn't have a bunch of things running at once.

She found her flashlight and checked out the box,

but none of the fuses were flipped to the off position. She moved the curtain on the front door to see if her neighbors' lights were also out. They weren't.

She backed away from the door, feeling the pall of fear slip over her. The hairs lifted on her neck. She grabbed her messenger bag and slipped it over her head then opened her front door, remembering her keys at the last second. They weren't hanging up where they usually were. She had to go back into the apartment to get them from the counter.

When she turned to leave, her way was blocked by a large man. No, not a man. A thing. A horribly disfigured being whose face was distended and twisted like a gargoyle's. Its eyes glowed yellow like the reflective irises of an animal—only there wasn't any light shining on him to make them glow.

Summer gasped and jerked back a step. It still was able to reach over to her with its long arm. It ran the side of his sharp nails along the surface of her cheek. Its lips were pulled back from his teeth as he did so, revealing huge apelike canines.

She couldn't quite believe what she was seeing. The thing wore no clothes, but thick hair covered its body.

And the smell. God, the smell.

She tried to rush around it, but it moved fast, keeping itself in front of her. She spun around, thinking to make a run for the bathroom, but there was another of the beasts behind her.

That one's teeth were bared in a fiendish smile as

it pointed one finger and drew it down her arm. The sharp nail cut through her sweater, through her skin, leaving a bloody trail. All of its focus was on the line of blood that trailed its nail. Summer watched it too, frozen in some kind of suspended animation. When it finished gouging her arm, somehow Summer broke free of the blur she was in. The thing snapped its teeth, then drew its arm back, its clawed hand open as its arm arced down to slash her neck.

Summer screamed. She screamed and screamed, her eyes closed, as she couldn't bear to witness her own death...a death that never came. Sam was there. He fought with the monster, rolling it over before the thing screamed in pain as Sam's knife made strategic cuts in the beast's flesh. The first beast Summer had seen was jumping around the two of them, making the floor rumble and shake.

Summer's legs gave out. She slumped to the ground, then tried to drag herself out of the way. Another beast came into her apartment, standing tall enough to block her doorway. It looked at the two fighting Sam, then looked at her. Its head tilted to one side before it dropped to all fours and came over to her.

There was enough light from the streetlight outside for Summer to see the fur on its hunched back standing in clumped spines. With one hand, she dragged herself across her living room as the monster stalked toward her. She backed into her dresser. She was only feet from her bed—maybe she could crawl under there, but then the monster set a heavy hand on her belly, holding her in place. When it leaned down to sniff her, she could see the rucked folds of the skin on its face. It didn't look as if its lips could cover its teeth. Its black nose moved in spasms as it sniffed her wound then her belly then her throat. Its breath was hot and foul. Summer was shaking violently as its jaw opened and its long tongue licked her skin.

She tried to scoot away, to get under her bed, but the claws of the hand the monster held on her belly kept her in place. It reared his head, letting out a roar like something a lion might do, then lunged down on her with those deadly canines flashing.

Before it made contact with her throat, however, its weight was yanked away from her. Sam lifted it straight up and slit its throat, cutting so deeply that he sliced right through the spine, dropping the monster's heavy, lifeless body to the ground beside her.

Two more monsters pushed into her apartment, followed by a man Summer had never seen before. Tall, big, dark hair pulled back behind his head, and a shaggy beard.

"We got this, *mon capitaine*," the man said in a heavy accent. "Take care of your woman."

Sam dragged the monster's corpse aside then knelt next to Summer, blocking her view of the door. Sounded like another man had arrived. She could hear more fighting, screaming. Something heavy dropped on her truck, triggering its alarm.

She made the mistake of looking at her left arm—

and the blood seeping from it—then sent Sam a panicked look. Her breathing was too fast and too shallow. She tried to lift her hand to him, but didn't have the strength.

"Stay with me, Summer," Sam ordered her as he sliced through the fabric of her sweater and tee. "Stay with me, babe. I got you. Guerre, help me help her," Sam said. Who was he talking to?

The pain eased up as he worked on her. She had to be going into shock. She felt her body relax, her breathing even out. She almost felt like she was floating. Was she dying?

Guerre. She knew the name, but how? Oh! From the freezer of blood units. He'd had a section in there.

Sam put his hands on her bare shoulder, one over the other, as if he was going to do chest compressions. Summer closed her eyes as a sense of peace came over her, then heat. It started at her shoulder and went down her upper arm to her elbow. She opened her eyes, wanting to tell Sam the pain was barely there anymore. Maybe she was dying. A warm yellow light came from Sam's hands.

What was he doing with a glow stick?

*It's not a glow stick. Guerre is healing you. Be calm. We have you.*

Who was he talking about? His invisible friends?

She closed her eyes and drifted to sleep.

≈

THE NEXT THING Summer was aware of was the gentle rocking of a car in motion, the hum of an engine, and Sam's strong arms around her. She opened her eyes, still under the influence of some medicine that made her calm.

Sam's arm tightened around her. He brushed the hair from her eyes. "Hi."

She let her gaze move over his beautiful face. He looked frightened. "Hi."

"We're almost to the fort."

She tried to sit up, but his hold was firm. "I'm fine, Sam."

"You will be. You will be fine."

Something in the way he said that made her think the opposite was true. She checked her wound, which was wrapped up in one of her T-shirts. Her whole arm felt numb. "It doesn't hurt anymore."

"That's because I'm shielding you from the pain. Guerre will work on it more when we get to the fort."

Summer suddenly wondered who was driving them. She saw the big guy with the wild hair in the driver's seat and sent Sam a questioning look.

"That's Bastion."

"Funny. I thought your friends were invisible."

The man in the driver's seat laughed.

They pulled into the northern parking lot outside the fort. Sam lifted Summer and carried her out of the SUV. Lights were on, banishing all shadows. The huge gate opened by itself as they approached. She hadn't realized it was automated.

*It's not,* Sam told her.

Oh. Right. His super skills.

Sam carried her into the fort. The door to the glass hallway on the left opened, also on its own. Sam took her up to his room. Another man was already there. Guerre.

He nodded at her. His gray eyes were somber. He was clean-shaven, his ash-brown hair neatly trimmed in a cut that was short on the sides and longer on top.

Summer looked around the room for the tray of medical implements that would be needed to stitch her arm back up, but she didn't see one.

"Sam, I need to go to a hospital."

He shook his head. "Guerre is our healer."

"I need stitches." In the light, she could see that Sam had cuts all over his body. His clothes were covered in blood. "So do you. Is Guerre a doctor?"

"No, but he heals all of us." Sam looked at himself. "Most of this isn't mine." He nodded at Guerre, who left the room. "We need to wash the fight off us before he works on us."

"I don't think I can."

"I've got you." He helped her take her T-shirt and bra off, then knelt to remove her boots and socks.

"What were those things?" Summer asked as Sam helped her to her feet. He slipped his hands under the waistband of her leggings and pushed them and her panties down. She set a hand on his big shoulder to steady herself as she stepped out of them.

"Monsters." He quickly checked her over for more injuries.

"Monsters aren't real."

"They are now." He stripped out of his clothes.

"We should go to the police. They need to know about those things."

"Let's talk about this later. You need to conserve your strength."

"But my neighbors are in danger."

"No they're not. We shielded them from observing the fight. They neither saw nor heard it. Merc and Acier are at your place cleaning up. Now close your eyes. I'm uncovering your arm."

She felt a little tugging and pulling, but nothing acute as he unwound the tee he'd covered her arm with. "I feel kind of woozy."

"I've got you." Sam wrapped an arm around her and helped her through his closet into his bathroom. He settled her on the edge of the tub so he could get things ready, then quickly turned the shower on and grabbed a couple of towels and a washcloth. Warm steam soon began to fill the room from the many showerheads on one side of the double shower.

He went back for her and helped her to her feet.

"We have to talk," she said, but worse than woozy, she really felt as if she were about to fall asleep while still standing.

"Relax into me. I won't let you fall. We're just going to do a fast wash, then Guerre will work on us."

Summer closed her eyes as Sam helped her into the shower. "But he's not a doctor."

"He's the doctor mutants like me need. He can heal humans too."

Summer leaned against his solid body as they stood under the gentle rain showerhead and let the half-dozen nozzles rinse them off. It was weird how relaxed she was. Her arm didn't hurt at all. She couldn't lift a hand to help as Sam ran the soapy washcloth over her body, paying special attention to her arm. He washed her hair, then rinsed her off.

His movements were clinical, not sexual, which filled her with raw emotion. She'd never had anyone care for her the way he did. She was defenseless, but he took no advantage of her. When he'd rinsed her thoroughly, he helped her to sit on the shower bench. She wanted to look at her injured arm, but she couldn't seem to do it. Instead, she watched him lather himself up. His body was perfect—he was tall and had broad shoulders, a lean waist, powerful thighs. If she weren't so numb and weak...

*Don't worry.* His heated words slipped into her mind. *We'll have all the time in here you want when you can make good on that thought.*

Summer giggled. *But not with Kiera.*

*What?*

*When I brought the girls here, Kiera fell in love with your bathroom. She made me promise she could use it a time or two.*

*Yeah, not with Kiera. She'll have to make do with the bathroom in her guest room.*

Sam finished and shut the water off. He grabbed a towel and wrapped it around his waist, then took the other and wrapped Summer in it. He carried her out of the bathroom. Summer leaned against his chest, listening to his heartbeat. She imagined she heard it beating out the rhythm of the words "I love you I love you I love you." She giggled again.

Sam used his mind to lift the covers away before he settled her on the bed. He tucked the blankets in around her body.

"Will this hurt?" Summer asked him.

"No. I'll keep shielding you from the pain."

He went into his closet and came out a minute later with his jeans on. Someone knocked at her door. Sam didn't say anything, but Guerre walked in. The healer looked at her, but it was as if he wasn't seeing her at all, rather seeing through her. He and Sam exchanged glances.

Summer still wasn't able to look at her arm, so instead she reached her good hand out to Sam. He got on the bed and lay on his side next to her. Holding her hand in his, he wrapped his other arm around her waist and held her close.

*I'm sorry you were hurt.* He kissed her forehead as Guerre put his stacked hands on her left shoulder.

*You were hurt too,* she reminded him, though a quick look at the numerous cuts and gashes he'd sustained in the fight showed they were farther along in healing than they should have been.

*This is nothing. I've had worse.*

*What's he doing?*

*He's healing you from the inside out, helping your body recover by running energy through it and your energy fields. Relax. I have you. You can even sleep.*

Summer felt the most curious sensation as Guerre hovered his hands over her wound. Heat. Comfort. Peace. The stress of her situation made her mind play tricks with her vision. She could swear she saw a warm yellow light come from Guerre's palms. He moved them from the cuts on her shoulder, to the start of her gash, slowly down her arm to the end of her wound. His hands never touched her—he kept them just inches from her skin.

Guerre's expression was one of complete concentration. Summer was mesmerized by his motions and the sensations his healing engendered. She lost track of time. She felt no pain. She closed her eyes, surrendering to the relief of sleep.

GUERRE LOOKED AT LIEGE. *I felt Flynn's energy in her wound.*

Liege nodded. He'd felt the same when he'd shielded her from the pain.

*He left something behind,* Guerre said.

*What is it?*

*I don't know. It feels malignant. We'll have to watch her to see how it affects her.*

*Thanks, Guerre. I appreciate your help.*

Merc and Acier were back and were down in the silo, waiting to debrief Liege.

*Go,* Guerre said. *She's sleeping. I'll stay with her.*

Liege and Bastion went down to the subterranean lab in the heart of the silo below the fort. The guys had returned with body bags. They put the corpses in the freezer drawers.

Damn. They were going to run out of space soon. They'd either have to quit collecting specimens or repurpose the extra lab space for more storage at the rate they were going.

"There were eight ghouls at Summer's place," Merc said, illuminated by the lab's pale blue lights. "We brought two back."

"They are making these things like sausages at a ballpark," Bastion said.

Liege frowned until he understood Bastion's reference. "Hot dogs. They make hot dogs at ballparks."

Bastion shrugged. "Is the same thing. Hopefully, we can soon learn something that tells us where these things are being changed."

"How's Summer?" Merc asked.

Liege shoved his hands in his front pockets. "Better. I hope. Guerre healed her. She was cut up pretty badly. She's resting now."

"Why go after her?" Merc asked. "Flynn has to know any harm that comes to her will just make us more determined in our hunt for him."

"Guerre said Flynn left something behind in her," Liege said.

"She was changed?" Acier asked.

Liege wasn't fast to answer that. It was unknown at this point if Flynn had poisoned, infected, or changed Summer. Perhaps he'd done none of those, just left his energy signature in her wound to throw them off guard.

"Maybe," Liege said. "But changed into what— we won't know for a few days or a few weeks."

Waiting to find out was like waiting to see if rabies would come after a bite from a wild animal…except with rabies, there was a prophylactic course of medication that could be started. With human mods, there wasn't any remedy.

There was nothing they could do but wait and see.

This was the Matchmaker's curse.

The silence in that sterile room was heavy with unvoiced fears. Liege knew that if Summer had been changed into a ghoul, there would be no return from that. He would have to put her down.

And that, likely, was why Flynn had gone after her —because of the pain her suffering would cause Liege.

"Go be with your woman, mate—while you can," Merc said.

Liege left the lab and went up the flights of stairs leading to the fort's ground level. The heated concrete was warm on his bare feet. He paused beside his bed, setting a hand on Summer's forehead. No fever. He slipped inside her to scan her body and her thoughts. She seemed completely at peace.

He crossed to the double French doors that faced north. The lights were off in his room; there was nothing to dissipate the glow of the moon that poured through the window panes.

Being a mutant had been easier when he'd not found his lifemate. Females had come and gone without triggering any emotion whatsoever. He looked over at Summer still sleeping peacefully on his bed. He refused to think about the worst possibility of what Flynn may have done to her. Only time would tell. It had taken him two weeks before he began to feel the effects of his modifications when he'd first been changed.

Dammit all to hell. They needed to find the scientists involved in developing the different human modifications. That knowledge was too valuable to leave in the hands of the Omnis.

## 23

Summer woke the next morning when the sun was high in the sky. Sam was next to her, lying on his side, an arm around her waist, just as he'd been when she went to sleep. Her waking stirred him from his sleep. His eyes opened, and all at once she remembered everything from last night.

Those horrible monsters. The way they looked and moved and behaved and smelled. They were more like wild things than altered humans.

The gash on her arm was healed. Only a long pink line remained to show where it had been. It was achy, but the pain wasn't as acute as a wound like she'd suffered should have been so soon after the injury.

"How long have I been asleep?" she asked Sam.

"A night."

"A night." She lifted her arm. "How could this have healed that fast?"

"Guerre tended to it."

Summer sat up. She remembered being wrapped in towels when she got into bed. Those were gone now. She got out of bed and walked naked into Sam's closet, before remembering she hadn't brought her clothes over.

*Bastion grabbed your bag before we left last night.*

It was there, sitting on a wooden bench in the middle of his closet. She pulled on a set of under-clothes, then took out a pair yoga pants and a sweater. She stepped into some flip-flops, then leaned against the doorjamb of the closet and glared at Sam.

"I need answers," she said.

He got up from the bed and came over to her. Last night, he'd just worn his jeans. This morning, he was already dressed in a tee and a beige sweater; he'd gotten up and gone back to bed.

"I need coffee. Bastion made breakfast for us. I'll answer all of your questions while we eat."

"With real answers. Not more mysteries that I can't understand."

"Sometimes mysteries are the only thing I have to offer."

Summer sighed. Sam seemed sad. She stepped into his arms, wrapping hers around his waist as she pressed her face to his chest. "I'm sorry."

He held her close. "You've done nothing that needs an apology. I should be apologizing to you. It's because of me that you were hunted and injured."

"I don't know that I can do this. I don't know how to do this."

Sam kept an arm around her as he walked her to the door. They went into the glass hallway and took the spiral stairs down to the kitchen.

Bastion had made ham and gruyere cheese crepes for Sam and plain cheese ones for Summer—both were waiting in the warming drawer, a bowl of fruit was in the fridge, and freshly ground coffee was waiting to be made into espresso.

"That smells like heaven," Summer said with a sigh. Sam made them both Americanos while she took their food to the table.

"Why don't we eat first?" Sam suggested.

"Agreed. You said Bastion made this for us?"

"Hm-mm. He's a helluva chef. I could hire out that job, but he enjoys doing it, and I doubt I could find anyone as talented as he is. How is your arm feeling?" he asked as he served the crepes.

"It's sore, but that's all. It feels like I pulled a muscle. Run-ins like mine last night are why you have to store your blood, isn't it?"

"That and worse."

*Worse.* That thought made her shiver.

Sam carefully steered their conversation to the mundane while they ate, but the juxtaposition of normal and abnormal made Summer's head spin.

After breakfast, they washed up, made another espresso, then wandered into the living room and sat at opposite ends of the sofa. "Okay. Now tell me what I need to know. All of it."

He regarded her for a long moment. "Do you trust me, Summer?"

She considered his question. "I trust you, but I don't trust your world."

"You know that I would never hurt you."

"Yes, I believe that's true."

The story Sam told her was fantastical, something out of some science fiction novel. He'd been signed up for the Omni studies by his command while he was still in the Army. His participation had been obligatory. He told her of the years spent in South America, training to use the mutations as they manifested. So many men died. So many failed to develop their skills.

He'd been reported dead to his unit, ending his life as a regular human. He'd lost his future with his daughter. He'd gone from one alias to another ever since he reintegrated with mainstream society. He and his team were always hunting the mutants who preyed on humans and searching for the Omni scientists who changed them.

Summer folded her legs and wrapped her arms around them as she listened intently to the story he told her. She realized how lonely he'd been, though she wasn't certain he'd admit as much to himself.

"So are you Sam...or Liege?"

"Liege is fine. Sam is fine. One is my name from

the dark world, the other is my name from your world."

"Which is the real you?"

"Both, but I have one mind, one heart." He paused. "One love."

She closed her eyes as she tried to block out his words. She couldn't. They reverberated through her body to her soul. She couldn't surrender to that, not yet, not when there were still so many unanswered questions.

"How long has this world within a world existed?" she asked.

"The Omni World Order goes back centuries. Its latest incarnation began after the Second World War, when they continued the eugenics effort started by the Nazis. They wanted to perfect the different classes of humans—servant, warrior, nobility. Advances in nanobiotechnology finally gave them the tools they needed to reach their goals in mere years, compared to what had taken generations before."

"What class were you modified to represent? Nobility?"

He stared at her, then blinked. She didn't think he was going to answer.

"Omni nobles can only be white. My team and I were made into super warriors. We were made to be ghosts, spies, infiltrators. We all came from military backgrounds. The modifications made to us were early ones. The Omnis hadn't perfected the enslavement of our minds yet. We grew strong, strong enough to fight our way out of the training camps. They hunted us, we hunted them—we've been at war ever since."

"Sam, that's horrible."

He shrugged. "It is what it is."

Summer reached a hand out to him. He caught her hand in his, forking his big fingers through hers. "What happened to your daughter?" she asked.

"She grew up. Went to college. Graduated. Got married. Became a widow. All without me. I watched over her as I could. But I couldn't do so in a way that would bring her to the attention of my enemies."

"Could you try to reach out to her now?"

"She thinks I'm dead. It's best if it stays that way."

"What if I connected with her for you?"

"You already have."

Summer's brows lifted. "I have? How?"

"She's one of your best friends. Kiera is my daughter."

Summer gasped and yanked her hand away from his to cover her mouth. She hopped off the sofa and stomped over to the opposite wall before facing Sam again. "How is that possible? You're about the same age as she is."

"Another side effect of the modifications made to us gave us rapid cellular regeneration. We heal fast. And we don't age. And those of us who survived the modifications even had our age reversed. I was forty-six when I went into the program, ten years ago."

"I knew you looked exactly like her dad." Summer

frowned at him. "But how is that possible? They don't see you the way I see you."

Sam frowned. "How did you know I looked like her dad?"

"Kiera has an old picture of you. One her mom gave her."

"She knows about me?"

Summer nodded. "But she and Ash don't see you the way I do."

"I mentioned to you that I have the ability to influence thoughts. I projected a different version of myself to your friends. I never expected the complication of my mate being my daughter's best friend."

"Oh God." Summer shoved her hands into her hair, grasping fistfuls as she paced back and forth. "If you can influence our thoughts, how do we know what's real? Like that mind trick—that thing you did yesterday at the hospital and at my place—how do you do that?"

"It can be done different ways, but the easiest is to compel your brain to see the space I'm in as it was when I wasn't in it."

"That's how that redheaded guy who told me to run to you disappeared that night I first saw him."

Sam's face tensed when she mentioned that guy. "Yeah."

"What else is in your bag of tricks?"

"I showed you some of it. The telekinesis, telepathy. We have heightened senses, strengthened instincts, stronger reflexes."

"Your eyes change color. Like they did last night. Like those monsters did too."

"Our eyes change to reflect our emotions. For the most part, I've learned to suppress those symptoms. Last night I was too angry to calm that reaction."

"How is any of that possible?"

"The rewiring that was done to our neural networks gave us access to neurological systems regular humans never develop. In addition to our psychic skills, we have a sense that deals with energy. I can see auras, and from them determine a lot about the person I'm reading. Auras are pure energy. But energy can be known in many ways. Some see it, some physically feel it, others just sense it, some smell or taste it, some hear it. I can smell and sense it."

Summer went still, trying to understand the deeper dimensions Sam existed within. She couldn't. She didn't have the energy sense, so she was blind to it.

"You do have the energy sense," Sam said. "You knew Brett was bad news. You have a strong sense of intuition. That's all fed by psychic and energy sensors that operate from your subconscious."

Summer looked away from him and did another round of pacing. What he said was going to take some time to digest. She needed to get back to what she could understand. "So what were those things last night?"

"They're deviant mutants."

Great. They were now in the land of confusion,

where even the answers she'd demanded needed more answers to make sense. "Deviant mutants?"

"Those creatures were once human men. I don't know why or how they were transformed into the things they are now. It's something new in the Omni World Order's suite of horrors. That's something we're trying to figure out now."

"How are you doing that?"

"I'm looking for the scientists who changed us or others in the Omni system who know of their research."

"I can't reject this reality, can I? I can't go back to life as it was before—"

"Before me?"

Summer stared at him. She didn't have the heart to answer that with words, so she just nodded.

"I can erase your memory of me, of the monsters, of all of this, but that won't mean you'll be safe."

"Wait a minute. You said you could erase my memory. That's what happened to some women at Kiera's center. Did you do that?"

"Yes. I had to. They were being fed to monsters like the ones that came after you last night."

"How long has this been going on?"

"My team and I were changed a decade ago, but it was happening even before then. The mutants who trained us had been changed well before that. Last night's monsters, however, are a recent twist."

Summer felt cold. She rubbed her arms and met

Sam's eyes. "I want you, Sam, but I don't want your reality."

He got off the sofa and came over to her. "I tried it your way. I tried to keep my world away from you. It didn't work. My world and I are a package deal."

Summer looked away from his warm brown eyes. She couldn't look at him while she was contemplating leaving him. "I guess I can't leave this fort if I want to be safe."

"You can't live inside these walls. No one can. Go and live your life. I will keep you safe wherever you are."

"I could buy a gun, do some intensive practice at the shooting range, be ready next time."

Sam squeezed his eyes closed. "That's not the life I wanted for you. You aren't a fighter; you're a creative. The world needs the beauty you bring to it. And unless you blow their brains out, a gun won't kill them. They regenerate tissue too quickly."

"So a head shot or a heart shot."

"A heart shot may only be sufficient to stun them, but it would give you time to exit the situation."

Summer nodded—a little too quickly. She could do this. She could survive on her own—she just needed to get a gun. "If I leave town, those things won't be able to find me, right?"

"They'll find you. They're everywhere. We've been fighting them all over the country. Other teams are dealing with them internationally. But I'll be with you."

"You can't be with me twenty-four-seven."

"I can. When I feel your fear, I can enter your reality and assist you."

Summer fought back a huge wave of emotion. She was at a decision point in her life. She'd never handled change well—it was why she stayed in Fort Collins after she graduated, why she was still in the same tiny studio apartment she'd been in as a student, why she'd worked for the Briscoes for so long. "You're asking me to jump off a cliff."

Sam nodded but didn't say anything.

"I need—I need time." The one thing he couldn't give, and the one thing she didn't have.

"There isn't a deadline on this, Summer. For me, the decision has already been made. It was made for me when I saw your bright glow. You are my only one. For as long as you live. For as long as I exist."

Summer's breath left her in a rush. She couldn't quite unravel his words—her mind had snagged on the image he sent her of seeing her inside an oval orb of shimmering white light.

She stared into his eyes, realizing she didn't have to articulate her questions—they were so much more eloquently stated nonverbally by simply thinking them.

Sam sent her an image, almost like a video, of him seeing nothing but her glow, then going in deeper to the colors that surrounded her—pink and green and a little gold, then deeper still to the version of herself she knew. He saw her like a flower pod opening in the warm sun.

He was so much more than just a human, too much for a mere human like her.

"I have to go," she whispered.

He nodded.

She hurried out of the living room and rushed up to his room. She thought about leaving her things, but she didn't know if she'd be back. She scrambled to pack everything and finish dressing. She hoped Sam wouldn't be waiting for her at the gate—almost as much as she hoped he would. She needed one last look at him, one last time to hold him, one last kiss.

She opened her door. Bastion was standing opposite it, leaning on the glass wall of the corridor. He didn't try to stop her, but his dark eyes were full of blame. "Your leaving will kill him."

Summer held her breath, trying to block the sobs she was fighting. She turned and rushed down the hallway to the stairs. Another man was there—curly dark blond hair and serious brown eyes. He said nothing. He didn't need to; his expression said it all.

Summer went past him and rushed down the stairs to the door at the end of the glass tunnel. Guerre blocked her exit. Sam was standing outside, waiting for her. Summer blinked and wiped away a stream of tears. "Be strong, Summer," Guerre said. "Fight for what you most desire and let the rest be damned."

Summer pressed the back of her hand against her

mouth and squeezed her eyes shut. She nodded. She felt cold air swirl around her body, chilling the salty tears on her face. When she opened her eyes, Guerre was gone. The door was open, and Sam stood on the other side of it.

She walked up to him. His face was stoic, his eyes empty. He held his arms wide. "I'm yours, Summer. Kiss me. Leave me. Do what you must. I will always be yours."

Summer pulled a ragged breath. "I'll return the money you sent me."

"I won't accept it." He handed her a set of keys. "Take my SUV."

Oh—right. She didn't have any wheels here. She stared at the keys in her hand, grateful Sam had helped her yet again. She turned from him and walked to the gate. The inset door opened. She paused at the threshold, her back still to Sam. She loved him. She was certain of that. It was the only thing she was certain of.

He moved to stand behind her. She could feel his heat as he braced his big arms on either side of the open door. *Love is an easy word for some, but not for me. Love is what I do and doing it is so much harder than the easy word it is.*

*I don't want to go.*

He wrapped his arms around her. *Then stay.*

A sob broke from her. She grabbed his hand and kissed his knuckles then pulled free.

LIEGE WATCHED Summer hurry to his SUV and drive off. He slipped inside her mind, felt the emotions tearing at her. He could calm them, numb her, but she needed to experience them in order to make her mind up about their future.

He refused to take that away from her.

Merc slammed the inset door closed then came at him, shoving him. Shoving him again. "You let her go."

Liege said nothing.

"You just let her fucking walk out of your life."

"I can't take her free will away from her. It's all she has left of her humanity."

"They'll eat her alive," Merc snapped.

"They will not. I will not let them." Liege looked over at Bastion and Guerre who'd joined them in the entry tunnel.

"None of us will let them harm her," Guerre said.

Merc put his face in Liege's and snarled, "Don't pretend that she isn't your light."

"She is my light."

Merc leaned back. "Then go after her."

Liege shook his head.

"We have to keep an eye on her to be sure she isn't going into the change," Guerre said.

"I will," Liege said. He would always watch over her.

## 24

S ummer cried the whole way home. Nerves were the only thing that broke through her wretched mood, sharpening her focus as she neared her apartment. She made a circle around the block once to make sure none of those monsters were around, then drove down her alleyway, past her apartment. Everything looked so normal. She drove around the block again and reentered the alleyway.

*Your apartment is clear,* Sam said, his voice slipping into her mind.

*Thank you.*

How could it be that her life had been so completely shattered, and yet the sun still shone, the big, bare-branched cottonwoods still swayed in the breeze? There were no monsters lying with broken backs where they'd been tossed off the stairs and balcony.

Nothing but normal.

And yet nothing was normal.

Two worlds were colliding, and she was at ground zero.

She got out of Sam's SUV and went up the stairs to her place. She would have to move. She'd have to get serious about another job. Maybe if she settled in another state, the monsters that had attacked her wouldn't come after her friends. Her staying here put them all in jeopardy. Sam had managed to keep his distance from Kiera, but Summer's friendship with his daughter would undo all he'd done for her.

She unlocked her door, wondering how it had gotten locked in the first place—before remembering their telekinetic skills. Last night's horrific fight hit her hard. She had no idea what she'd find when she opened the door. She hadn't even thought to ask Sam about that.

She slowly widened the door, sweeping a glance around her place...which looked exactly as it had before the attack.

*Is this real or a mirage, Sam?*

*The guys cleaned it up for you. There are no remnants of the monsters or the fight inside.*

She walked into her apartment with no small amount of trepidation. What if the things were inside, hidden from Sam? Could they do the disappearing act, too? Would she even see them if they came for her again?

She walked all around her place, looking everywhere, feeling her courage return as she faced her fears. As far as she knew, she was alone in her apartment.

She went into the kitchen and opened her cabinets, trying to get a sense of how much she would have to pack. She repeated that assessment in her closet and bathroom. She'd lived in the same place for so many years that there were stacks of things she kept but never used, mostly because it was too small to store everything properly.

Maybe she should just leave. All of it. Just walk out of there and start over somewhere else. No things. No friends. No Sam.

That made her cry again. She sat on her bed and stared at her front door.

She needed to get a gun, but what vendor should she go to? What kind of gun was best for the type of shooting she needed to do? How much would it cost?

There were only hours until sunset. She needed a weapon before dark.

Her phone buzzed with a text message. It was from Sam. He'd sent her an address to a building in an industrial park.

*I've told him you're coming,* Sam said telepathically. *He'll get you set up with a shotgun. I get all my weapons from him.*

Sam—

*Go. You'll want to be home before dark.*

Summer grabbed her purse from her messenger bag and hurried out the door. She drove across town, making only one wrong turn before finding the location of Sam's gun dealer.

There was no sign outside his entrance, only a street address. The door was locked. She lifted her hand to knock, but the door swung inward.

The outside light barely lit the shadowy interior. A tall man stepped back to let her enter. She only caught sight of the ink that spilled from his hoodie cuffs, over the backs of his hands and down his fingers before he closed the door.

"You're Liege's woman," he said, his voice rough, as if he used it infrequently. Was he one of them? "I am. I'm part of Liege's Legion."

"He has a legion?"

"Fuck yeah. We're all over the place." They walked out from the front room into a manufacturing space—some kind of metal shop. "Why did you reject him?"

"I didn't. I haven't. I just need time. His world scares me."

"Yeah, well, life scares me. It ain't like we can shut it off now, can we?"

Summer had so many questions. She held her hand out. "I'm Summer."

He took her hand and stared into her eyes. His blue eyes glowed slightly. He started to grin. "Nice to meet you."

He didn't offer her his name.

"Liege said you want an elephant gun to blow those deviant fuckers in two. I have just what you need."

He led her through the machinist area to a long shooting range with six different lanes. Resting on a table inside the room was a black gun.

Liege's friend nodded to it. "It's a twelve-gauge semiauto shotgun with a ten-inch barrel. Use double-aught buckshot in it, and those deviant motherfuckers will drop like flies. The magazine holds ten rounds. I built it myself. Let me show you how it works."

For the next two hours, he taught her how to assemble, disassemble, clean, load, unload, and switch out magazines. And then came the shooting practice. He had her repeat each step until she could do it in the dark—then he had her do it in the dark.

When their practice time was over, Sam's friend led her to another room where he stored ammo. He took down several boxes of cartridges and grabbed a long leather belt. He frowned, put the leather belt back on its hook, and took down a black nylon belt. "So you're a vegan. Liege said not to use leather."

He loaded four magazines into the belt, filled all but one of the cartridge slots, then wrapped it around her waist and adjusted it to fit. "Keep this near you at all times. When you're home, keep a round chambered."

"Don't I need to have a background check done? And get a concealed carry permit?"

"No. Regulars will never see this. And only a few mutants have been granted permission to observe it, most of whom you've already met. Come here tomorrow so we can do more shooting practice for you. I need you to eat, sleep, and breathe firing this shotgun. You hear a noise, you pick it up. You get the willies, you pick it up. Got it?"

Summer nodded. He ejected the chambered round and put it into the last cartridge slot on the belt.

The man straightened and set his hands on his hips as he glared down at her. She wondered if he was having a silent conversation with Sam—Liege. What should she call him?

"I've set you up with forty rounds. It's unlikely you'll get hit by a pack of more than six deviants. By the time you get one round squeezed off, the Legion'll be there to assist you. When I'm comfortable that you know what you're doing, I'll send you home with a few hundred rounds."

"Thank you." She picked up the bag with the shotgun and gun belt. "I didn't catch your name."

"I didn't give it." A muscle bunched in his cheeks. "It's Acier. French for steel. Seeing as I ended up supplying the Legion with weapons, I guess it fits." He opened the door for her. "Come back tomorrow. Noonish."

"Tomorrow, then."

The late afternoon shadows were getting long by the time she left Acier's shop. Sunset was less than an hour away.

*Your home is safe,* Sam said.

*Thank you,* Summer answered. *For everything.*

*Thanks aren't needed. It's my duty to you.*

*How many fighters are in your Legion?*

*Dozens, scattered around the country and the world.*

*Are any women?*

*No. They are men I met in my training camp plus a few that joined up later. There were no women there.*

*But you are open to women joining your ranks, right?*

His answer was slow in coming. *You are not to become a fighter.*

*But that's exactly what I'm doing, isn't it?*

She could feel his angst. *This is not what I wanted for you.*

*Me either. But I can't go back. I wasn't talking about me. Kiera would make a wonderful addition to your team.*

*She's my* daughter.

*I know. And I've never met a woman fiercer.*

*The Legion is composed of changed humans. Neither of you could keep up.*

*You could change us.*

*I cannot. It would kill you. But if there are changed females who are natural warriors, I'll see about having them join us.*

*I don't like "no" for an answer.*

*I just said yes—to your original question, anyway.*

*Acier is nice, but he's not you. Could you do my training?*

*Absolutely. I'll meet you there tomorrow. Tonight, keep your weapon loaded and near your bed.*

*Do you think they'll come back tonight?*

*No. But from here out, wherever you live, whatever you do, you must always be ready to defend yourself.*

SUMMER CARRIED the black duffel bag with her shotgun and gun belt to Acier's shop at noon the next day. The steel door opened as she approached and closed behind her. Acier stood in the doorway, looking pale and formidable. He had shaggy black hair, a neatly trimmed beard that followed his jaw to his ears, and a mustache that arced over his mouth. He was handsome but hard-edged. He made her nervous.

"You came back," he said.

She straightened her shoulders. "I find I have a strong will to live."

"Hm-mm." He walked out of the room. She followed him. "Liege is here. You called in the big guns. Didn't trust me?"

"I trust you fine."

He laughed, in a way that made her question her trust.

They went into the shooting range. Sam was there. Just the sight of him stole Summer's breath. She set her things on the table, uncertain how to greet him.

*Come here,* he ordered her.

She faced him then slowly walked over to him. God, she was glad he'd made it here today. She slipped her arms around him. He pulled her close and, cupping her cheek, bent to kiss her. His mouth was warm. Heat flooded through her body, warming everything that was cold inside her.

"Aw, fuck, Liege. I'll give you the room. Let me know when you're finished." Acier slammed the door behind him.

Sam drew back and stared into her eyes. The lighting was dim in the room as he and his mutant friends seemed to like it. "Summer, you need to know that you will not be harmed in today's training. The simulations we'll do will seem real, but you'll always be safe. Understand?"

"No."

"You will." *Acier, return.* Summer heard the silent order he gave his teammate.

Acier came back into the room. "So we doing this?"

Sam nodded. "Yes. Let's begin with static targets. She needs to warm up."

There was one lane lit by a low light. Summer stepped over to the platform and set her gun down so she could put on her ear protectors. She looked back at the guys behind her. "Don't you need earmuffs too?"

*No. We can contain the sound so it doesn't harm us,* Sam said. They watched as she went through the steps of unloading, checking the magazine, loading it, chambering a round.

Acier told her to take her position, then he

adjusted her stance and her hold on the shotgun, making sure her cheek was gently against the stock.

"You have ten rounds in the magazine and one in the chamber. Use them all. Remember to aim for the head, neck, or heart. Shoot when ready, Summer," Acier ordered her.

Summer shot at the target. The recoil banged her shoulder, but it didn't seem as bad as it had yesterday. She emptied the magazine. They repeated the practice at twenty feet, ten feet, fifteen feet. The paper targets she was shooting were made to look like the horrible monsters that had invaded her apartment two nights ago. They glowed in the dim light of the shooting range.

Acier and Sam both gave her suggestions and tips throughout the practice. She was tired, but feeling good about her progress.

"Now that you're warmed up, let's do a simulation," Acier said. He led them to another large room. At the back of it was a table with several boxes of ammo. "Reload your magazines."

She did. "I'm ready."

Acier grinned at her. "Sure you are. Remember, this is just practice. Turn around and face the room. Liege is going to set the scene. Close your eyes and keep them closed until I tell you." A short moment passed. "Right. Open your eyes. Remember to hold your weapon as I showed you."

"This is my apartment." Summer was shocked. It

was as if she'd been transported back to her place. Everything was exactly right. She heard a noise on the stairs outside. A stomping sound. Something banged into her door. It hit it again, so hard that it rattled the door before it slammed open and a red-eyed beast stood in the doorway. Fear turned Summer's insides to ice. The thing dropped to all fours and charged her. She screamed and dropped her shotgun as she turned to run.

Sam's arms went around her. The lights in the room went dim again. Everything was silent, except the rasping sound of her heavy breathing.

She shot a look over her shoulder. There was no beast. Her apartment had vanished. The room was just the big, empty space it had been before.

*It was all an illusion, Summer,* Sam told her.

She dropped her earmuffs, but even without them, her breathing was the only sound she heard. Her shotgun was floating a foot off the ground. Sam went over and retrieved it.

*Get a strap for it,* he ordered Acier. *This is a finely tuned weapon, Summer. Dropping it on the ground is the exact thing you don't want to do. For one, your enemy could grab it and use it on you. For two, even if it's empty, you can use it as a club. For three, if it's loaded, it could fire off a shot.* He handed the shotgun to Acier, who gave her a black look as he took it to put a shoulder strap on it.

Summer folded her arms as she tried to calm her shaking body. "They looked so real. I almost thought you'd taken me back to my apartment." She put her palms to her forehead and took a slow breath. "I can't deal with such a fast shift in reality." She glanced at Sam. "How did you do that?"

"I gave your mind a suggestion that you experience the environment of your own apartment. You created the mirage for yourself."

Acier slipped the strap of her gun over his head. "Hold your weapon facing up, like this, between your shoulder and head. Always, unless you're actively aiming at a target. There are other positions, and we'll practice them, but for now, do it this way. The strap will keep your weapon on you." He handed it to her and watched while she positioned it.

She looked around the empty room. "Do we have to do that again?"

"Paper targets are good for practicing technique, but your real enemy is your fear," Sam said. "We need to repeat this simulation until you're bored with it. Until you know without doubt that anytime you see a ghoul you can take it out. Until the horror they represent is no longer crippling because you know your own capabilities are stronger than your fear."

They exchanged hard stares.

"Alternatively," Sam continued, "you accept my protection and surrender yourself to my care."

"You won't always be with me."

"Not physically. But I can do as much to protect you from a distance as I can in person."

Summer gave that a quick thought. The truth was that she'd been self-reliant for years and didn't want to give that up. That was perhaps what she found most intimidating about entering Sam's world. If she could handle herself in his world, then she could meet it head-on.

Sam nodded. "Then we do the simulations."

"Okay."

"Righto," Acier said. "Take your places. The fun's about to begin. Summer, close your eyes."

Sam gave her a fortifying smile and nod. She could do this. She stepped a few paces from the guys and shut her eyes.

"Begin," Acier said.

Again, Summer found herself in her little studio apartment, standing in the living room area, facing the door. She heard the movement on the stairs outside, the heavy jumping as the beasts came up to her door, the banging into her door. Her heart was in her throat as the door gave way and the thing got inside. This time, she didn't hesitate. She blew a hole in its chest. Another monster leapt over the first and jumped into the room, then stood up and stared at her with its glowing red eyes. Summer shot the top of its head off.

She had no idea how long the simulation went on. She shot monster after monster, changing out her magazine twice. When she'd run out of ammo, they stopped. Again she was trembling.

Sam looked at her then Acier. "That's enough for today."

"You know as well as I do that the ghouls aren't

going to come at her that slowly. They aren't going to sit and wait to be shot. You went easy on her."

"It's enough for today. We'll pick it up tomorrow."

Acier cursed, then took her weapon to clean it. Summer felt numb. Cleaning and maintaining her weapon was another important aspect of owning a weapon, but she was right on the edge of being violently ill. She doubted she could handle one more thing that day.

Sam refilled her magazines, then loaded everything back into the duffel she'd brought and handed it to her. The bag was heavy. She turned to walk through the maze of Acier's shop to the front door.

Outside, the sun, low in the sky, spilled warm light over her chilled body. Sam kept pace with her.

"Summer, let me drive you home," he said, standing next to her truck.

She couldn't look him in the eyes. He'd given her what she wanted. Space. Time. Support. Tools. And it wasn't enough. She wasn't equal to the task at hand. She was shaking so much that her teeth were chattering. She shook her head, keeping her gaze on his chest so that she wouldn't see the disappointment in his eyes.

"No. I need wheels at my place."

"I'll stay with you tonight. You shouldn't be alone."

Again, she shook her head. "I have to be. Don't you see?"

"No. No, I don't. I see you suffering. I see me doing nothing to help."

"Not true." She flashed him a quick smile before staring at his chest again. "You've done everything. The rest is up to me." She felt the pain her words caused him. "Goodbye, Sam."

He didn't try to stop her as she got into her banged-up truck. She was numb as she parked outside her apartment. She knew without doing her own scan that it was safe. Sam wouldn't have let her be there if it weren't.

She locked the door behind her, then unpacked her shotgun and set it within easy grasp by the bed on her nightstand. She turned and faced her front door. There was no difference between the reality she now stood in and the simulation Sam had made for her at practice that day. For a second, she listened to hear the heavy steps on her stairs.

They didn't come. But then, it was still light out.

Summer untied her boots then stripped and walked into her shower. She stood there a long time, letting the hot water pelt her skin. She was numb, inside and out. Weak human that she was, she almost summoned Sam to join her. She yearned to feel his arms around her.

She denied herself even that relief.

She was no match for Sam's world. What arrogance had made her think she could stand with him and not always behind him? She knew she hadn't seen but a fraction of what his skills were, skills shared by his friends and foes alike—and the ghouls that hunted on demand for Sam's enemies.

After her shower, she brushed her teeth, put some yoga clothes on, then got on her bed and pulled her shotgun across her lap, staring at the front door as she waited for the monsters.

## 25

Three days later, Summer heard the girls coming up her steps. She'd been avoiding them for most of the week, but they took that as a silent plea for company.

When they'd texted they were on their way over, she'd told them she wasn't feeling like being social and asked if they could come next week. She had hoped that had been an end of it, but she should have known better. Her friends were too close to her to take "no" casually when that wasn't her normal mode.

Summer opened the door before they knocked. Cold air swirled around her bare feet. She closed it and glared at them.

"I'm not going out tonight," Summer said.

Ash held up a big brown bag full of takeout from a nearby restaurant. "No need. We brought dinner to you."

"I'm not hungry." Summer went back to the futon

and folded her legs in front of her, making herself just about as small as she could. When had she been hungry last? Maybe she was coming down with something. Out of the corner of her eye, she saw her friends exchange worried glances.

Ash set the food on the counter then hung her coat on a hook next to Kiera's. Kiera came over and set her palm against Summer's forehead.

"No fever," Kiera said.

"I'm not sick—well, heartsick, maybe." Summer tucked her arms around her middle. She looked over at her shotgun, which she'd left on the dresser next to her bed. She was curious about whether her friends would comment on it. Acier had said they couldn't even see it.

"Problems with Sam?" Kiera asked, sitting on the coffee table so she could face Summer.

She looked from Kiera to Ash, who'd gone back to the kitchen. "I love you guys."

"We love you," Ash said.

"What's this about?" Kiera asked.

These two women were Summer's best friends. What kind of life could she have if she couldn't be honest with her friends?

"Sam is Liege. Remember Liege? That guy the crazy guy told us about?"

"*Run to Liege*," Ash said, quoting him. "That Liege?"

"Yeah." Summer started to tear up. "I need you guys to believe me."

Ash left the food and came over to sit next to Kiera on the coffee table. She reached over and set a hand on Summer's knee. "Of course we believe you."

"Not just about that, but also what I'm going to tell you."

*Don't, Summer,* Sam said her mind. *Don't bring them into this.*

Summer wiped her eyes, ignoring him. "You're my best friends in this whole world."

"We are." Kiera nodded.

"We don't lie to each other," Summer said, as much for Sam's sake as her friends.

Ash and Kiera exchanged a look.

"Monsters are real." Neither of her friends blinked at that assertion. "They're real, and they're around us."

Kiera blinked. "Honey, how long since you last ate anything?"

"I'm not making this up. I'm not lying." Summer jumped off the futon, rushed to the front door, yanked it open, and jogged barefoot down the ice-cold steps. The girls were close behind her. She looked for her borrowed truck, but it was gone. In its place was her old white Subaru wagon.

"Your car's back," Ash said. "It looks great."

Yeah, it did. But the truck with the smashed hood was gone. "It's gone. Sam's truck."

*You were in the shower when I came by,* Sam said. *You can have the truck back after it's fixed.*

"I wanted to show you proof."

"Proof of what?"

"The hood was dented from where a fiend fell on it."

Her friends exchanged another of those looks. God, this was why she hadn't wanted them to come by. She wasn't ready to pack this away and pretend she hadn't seen and experienced what she had.

Kiera put an arm around her shoulders. "You hit a deer. That's all."

"A buck, probably," Ash said.

Summer shook her head. She pulled free of Kiera's arm and stepped away. "No. It happened right here. I saw them. Well, I didn't see the one that fell on the truck but I heard it fall, heard the alarm go off."

"You must have hit something but didn't realize it at the time," Kiera said.

*Leave it at that,* Sam said. *Let them think it was a deer. It would be a kindness. Do you want them to have the fear you have?*

*They're in the same danger I am,* Summer responded. *Those things will hunt them too.*

Fear and anger filled Summer with confusion and frustration. What if those things got to her friends? If they didn't know they were coming, then they couldn't prepare.

She wiped her eyes and slowly became aware of her feet freezing on the icy ground. "You both have guns, right?"

Kiera gritted her teeth. She took Summer's arm and guided her back to the stairs. In her apartment,

Ash grabbed a pair of thick socks from Summer's closet. She sat on the coffee table and pulled them on Summer's frozen feet.

"How long has she been here alone like this?" Ash asked Kiera.

Kiera shook her head. "Not sure. A few days?"

"We should get her to the hospital."

"No," Summer said. "The monsters will just come for me there. A lot more people will get hurt."

"What does Sam say about all of this?" Ash asked.

"He's one of them," Summer said. "Not a monster, but still one of them."

"Fuck," Kiera said. "I knew something was off with him."

"Kiera, he's your dad," Summer said.

Kiera gasped. She stared at Summer, then shook her head. "He's our age. He can't be my dad."

"He's fifty-six years old."

Ash reached for Summer's hand. "Honey, have you been out with Clark again? Or that Brett guy?" She looked at Kiera. "It's possible they slipped her something that's got her tripping now."

"I'm not tripping. I wish I were, then I could explain all of this. I'm not lying. I'm telling you what I saw."

"Monsters," Kiera said.

Summer nodded.

"Wait. Wait, you guys. Listen to this." Ash turned the volume up on the TV. There was breaking news about a local business owner who'd been mauled by what appeared to be a pack of dogs. The dogs hadn't yet been apprehended.

The victim's name was Douglas Briscoe.

Summer gasped. She covered her mouth, then ran to the bathroom and emptied her stomach. When the heaves stopped, she flushed the toilet and sat against the wall, shaking.

*Come to me,* Sam said. She ignored him and the corresponding urge to comply.

Ash came into the bathroom. Taking Summer's hand, she drew her to her feet and over to the sink. She turned on the warm water. "Wash up. It's all going to be fine."

"How? How is it going to be fine?" Summer asked as she glared at her friend through the mirror.

"It just is," Ash said. "It always is. It was dogs, not monsters, that did that to Douglas."

"We don't have packs of wild dogs wandering around town, Ash."

"Look, why don't you take a nice, long, hot shower? Kiera and I will be waiting for you. We'll get to the bottom of this. Maybe you should see a doctor. Kiera knows a few she's used through the center that she could recommend. We could even go with you."

"I don't need a doctor. I need you both to believe me."

Ash let go of a long breath. "We're trying to understand. Definitely something has you wrecked like this."

Summer pulled her sweater off, exposing her arm with its long pink scar that was still healing. "Look."

Ash gasped. "Summer—what happened? Wait. Kiera! Come back here."

Kiera joined them in the small bathroom. She was shocked at the sight of Summer's arm.

"The monsters broke into my house. They attacked me. Sam fought them off." She didn't tell her friends about Bastion and Acier, or whoever the other fighter was that night. Maybe she could keep their existence a secret.

"That looks like it was bad," Kiera said. "But if this just happened days ago, how is it healing so fast?"

"One of Sam's friends is a healer."

Ash and Kiera swapped shocked glances. All of a sudden, Ash bent in half and laughed like a crazy person. "Oh my God. That's the best Halloween prank ever. Evah."

Kiera started chuckling. She shook her head and went back to the living room. "Damn you, Summer. You got me too."

Ash straightened, though laughter still buffeted her. "Take a shower. Wash that stuff off." She smiled. "And don't forget we brought your favorite—sweet and sour tempeh and rice. And spring rolls." She closed the bathroom door behind her.

*Summer, my love—*

*No.* Summer stopped Sam before he could work his magic on her, melting her mind along with her resistance. *You are not welcome here. Get out of my mind.*

356

*You are protected, as are your friends. I will not let harm come to any of you.*

God, she wished he was there with her now. Her resistance was weakening. *I can't live an existence between two worlds. How will I ever know what's real and what's a mashup of your vision and my reality? I can't do this.*

*Bending reality becomes reality.*

*Not for me. Not for my friends.*

*Not for most regulars, which is I why I advised against telling them. Humans have an extreme need to be understood and heard. Mutants simply accept the void.*

*We aren't mutants,* Summer said.

*Which is why you should not have broached the subject.*

*I can't walk it back now.*

*I'll wipe their minds.*

*You'll do no such thing. They are in danger, and they need to know it.*

She felt Sam's resistance. *I can't leave it with their thinking you've either pranked them or are having a mental breakdown.*

Summer huffed a breath. *But I am, Sam. I am having a breakdown.*

*I'm coming for you.*

*No. I'm done. I'm out. It's over.*

*But you want me there with you.*

She scoffed at that. *I want a whole host of things that aren't good for me. Hot chocolate and cookies and pounds of candy and fudge. God, I love fudge.*

*I'll bring you fudge.*

*I won't let you in.*

*You can't keep me out.*

*You said you respected me.*

*I do.*

*Then respect my wishes.*

Summer waited for his snappy comeback, but he said nothing—as was his way on difficult topics. She didn't for a minute think he'd caved.

A man whose team had named him Liege wasn't one to surrender.

Summer stripped and got into the shower, standing in the hot streams of water, letting it ease her tension. Sam had said that mutants knew to accept the void—she supposed that meant the divide between human and mutant realities.

She had to embrace the void too. She was what she was now; she knew what she knew. She didn't have to convince anyone. Sam had said he would protect her friends. She believed he would. It was possible they would never have to discover the void themselves.

And that would be a good thing. Sam had been right about that.

Filled with resolve, she finished her shower, dressed, then went out to join her friends, who were still chuckling about her scaring them.

"I wish it had been a prank." She tugged the neck of her tee over to her shoulder. "Look. It's a real scar from a real wound."

Kiera then Ash both touched her skin. Their humor vanished as the horror of what Summer was telling them sank in. Their faces took on blank, china-doll expressions, as if they were desperately hoping she was still pranking them.

It was too much for them to absorb. Sam had been right. She smiled. "That was the best shower I've ever had. I'm starving."

Kiera and Ash swapped glances. Summer ignored them and looked through the containers for her favorites.

The girls didn't move.

"What?" Summer looked over at them. "You don't want me to eat it all, do you?"

"Um, Summer? Why didn't you tell us you'd been attacked?" Ash asked.

"I'm telling you now."

Silence from her friends.

"So you're not panicking about the attack anymore?" Kiera asked.

Summer looked at her friends. They hadn't been privy to the convo she'd just had with Sam. None of this could possibly make sense to them. She wished she hadn't said anything.

"Oh, I am. Just more quietly. I'm keeping it to myself." Summer took a bite of one of the spring rolls. "It's better that way, don't you think?"

"No, not if you're still screaming inside," Kiera said.

"Screaming inside lets everything still look normal on the outside," Summer said. "Normal is what counts, isn't it?"

"I still think you should see someone," Ash said as she moved into the kitchen and handed plates to the girls.

"Only if it's a mutant shrink." Summer laughed. "That does sound crazy. But that would be perfect." She wondered if Sam would comment on that, but he held his silence—as she'd asked him to.

"Okay," Kiera said. "Let's go with this." She looked at Ash. "Just because you and I haven't had the same experiences as Summer doesn't invalidate her experiences."

"True," Ash agreed.

"So, tell us about these mutants," Kiera said.

Summer shook her head. "I don't think so. I'm embracing the void." Funny how saying that made her feel as if she could find a balance, exist with a foot in both worlds. It made her feel closer to Sam.

"What void?" Ash asked.

"The void that exists between the way humans and mutants experience life."

"I'm sorry I made it difficult before for you to talk to us," Kiera said, speaking slowly and carefully, "but we're ready to listen now. You don't have to be alone in this."

"It doesn't matter. Sam was right."

"What was he right about?" Ash asked.

"That I shouldn't open the veil and show you the other reality," Summer said.

"You said we could be in danger," Ash said.

"Sam said he'll protect you." Summer looked at

Kiera. "He's not going to let anything happen to his daughter—or her best friends."

*Or the woman I love.*

Summer ignored that, though she felt the effect of his words like a soul caress.

Kiera dished some food onto her plate, careful to not pin Summer with one of the looks she was famous for. "In mutant reality, how is it possible that Sam's my father?" She shrugged as she looked at Ash. "I mean, what if it's true?"

"His body was rewired in a medical experiment that changed his neurobiology, his physiology," Summer said.

"Ah," Kiera said into the silence that followed Summer's answer. "But what does that mean?"

"It means his body learned how to heal itself and reverse its age. It means he heals very fast. It means all of his senses are heightened. It means his neural networks were revamped so that he has extreme use of his mental faculties. He can communicate telepathically, move things telekinetically. He has not just what we consider sixth-sense powers, but even a sense of knowing energy. He lives in dimensions we can barely comprehend. He's a mutant." Summer took a bite of her tempeh and pineapple.

*I like your summary of me.*

Summer blinked. "I love him, and I don't know how to be with him because his world is terrifying."

*You love me?* he asked.

*It doesn't need to be said. It's something that I'm doing*

361

That's what he'd said, wasn't it? That love wasn't in the words but in the doing?

*It does need to be said. I need to hear it from you.*

*Loving you doesn't mean we have a future,* she told him.

*Maybe not, but it's a place to start.*

The room was silent a long time before Ash broke the spell. "You make it sound possible."

"It's more than possible. It's happening, and it's my reality."

## 26

A knock sounded on Summer's door.

Her grip tightened on her shotgun until her fingertips and knuckles were white. This was it, what she'd been waiting for since the simulations several days ago. Her hands shook as she lifted the shotgun into position and aimed at the door. She watched it, waiting for it to bend inward as the ghouls broke into her place.

Wait. Ghouls wouldn't knock.

*Summer, don't shoot,* Sam said in her mind. *I'm coming in.*

Relief broke through her panic until she remembered she hadn't showered—or changed her clothes since the girls were there. Her place was a mess. She didn't want company. She'd been avoiding him, her friends, and her training for days. She sure as hell didn't want him to see her like this.

"Go away. I'm not here."

"Aw, honey, I know you're in there," Sam said through the door.

Of course he knew she was there. There were no boundaries between them...and she'd just spoken to him.

"I'm coming in."

"No. You can't. The door's locked." She heard a click as the deadbolt turned and the door opened. This was exactly what she meant about boundaries. She glared at him from the disheveled covers of her bed, still holding her shotgun in front of her, though now slanted upward across her body.

He stepped inside, took a long look at her, then sighed. The door shut behind him. She was never going to get used to his special abilities. He crossed the room and eased the gun from her tight grip then set it on the floor beside her bed. He scooped her up and carried her over to the futon, holding her on his lap.

Summer wrapped her arms around his neck and hid her face. She knew he could feel her shaking, which wasn't out of fear. It was just the adrenaline leaving her body now that he was here and she was safe.

He sighed. "I've been here the whole week." He sat quietly with her, rubbing her back in slow strokes. After a while, he said, "You are the bravest damn woman I've ever met."

She started to cry, shaking her head. "I am so scared."

"That's my fault. I should have eased you into those simulations."

"They needed to be real."

"But not fuck-you-over real. I'm sorry. I've fought so many of those ghouls that I don't think much of it."

She straightened and looked at him. He wiped her tears away with the pads of his thumbs. "I don't know how this works," she said. "I don't want to be a science experiment."

"Jesus." He looked at her ceiling, staring at it a moment before meeting her eyes. "You think I wanted this? Or any of my men?"

"Tell me. Everything. Start back at the beginning." She could feel his thoughts as he worked through what to say. In fact, he didn't even need to put them into words. It was like having a hearing person say the words he was speaking in sign language—she was listening in stereo.

"I don't know where to start."

"Kiera."

"I told you about her."

"You need to tell her you're her dad."

Summer folded her legs and wrapped her arms around them. Setting her chin on her knees, she wondered how things might have been different. Sam would have been a great dad. But maybe things had worked out how they were meant to. Kiera's struggle after losing her parents had set her on a path of helping others. What she did was important. Had things been different, perhaps she might not have turned to that work.

She looked at Sam as a frightening thought occurred to her. "Can you go back in time?"

He grinned. "No. Time is the same for us as for regulars."

"What happened in the training camps?"

Sam's face took on a faraway look. "We weren't told what to expect. Hell, we weren't told we'd been changed at all. Maybe the people running the experiment didn't know themselves what to expect. You often hear of the military breaking recruits down so they can build them back up differently, make them into warriors. I guess that's what happened to us. We all developed some similar and some unique skills. We're all different. We all have different abilities, just like regular humans."

"The regulars."

He nodded. "We began to change. Rapidly. Too fast for some in my group. Thirty percent of the group died within a short while. Didn't take long to realize that staying alive was the only purpose of our existence at that point. And staying alive meant killing the ones trying to kill us. We separated into two groups. Prey and predators. I knew what was happening had to do with one or more of the shots we received. We learned. We grew. And we stopped being prey.

"When we got out of the training camps, we weren't the men we'd been before. I was forty-six when I went in. I got out seven years later. I should have been fifty-three, but my physiological age had been reversed. I kept getting younger in appearance until I returned to how I looked in my mid-thirties. That, more than anything else, robbed me of my life. I couldn't resume my old existence. I lost everything. I sure as fuck wasn't going to tell Kiera, 'Hey, look—I'm your dad. And from here out, you better always look behind you because the monsters I'm hunting are hunting me.'"

His eyes were full of regret as his gaze swept over her face. He smoothed a lock of hair behind her ear. "I never expected to find you. And now I've put you in the crosshairs of my enemies. I will leave you alone if you ask it of me. But you have to know that for the rest of your life, or mine—which ever ends first—I will protect you. Because I love you and because your life, having crossed mine, will never be the same." He shrugged as he looked at her. "It's all that I can do. I can't un-love you."

Summer grasped his face in her hands. "I never expected to feel what I feel for you. It's so intense. It's as if you are so woven into me that anything that happens to you happens to me as well."

He nodded. "It's even worse than that. Because we've connected, because our energies have aligned with each other, we'll suffer if we're apart, like addicts jonesing for a fix. Disconnecting from each other could kill us." He studied her face. She could feel that he was fighting to find the right words. "I wasn't looking for you. I didn't want to find you. I didn't want to complicate your life. I didn't seek to harm you. I didn't wish for this."

Summer gave him a sad smile. "I know. The same goes for me. I'll get used to living a deeper reality than I ever knew existed." Moisture in her eyes made her vision waver. "I'll gladly do that. You know why?"

He shook his head.

"Because I love you. But I don't know how to do this, Sam. I don't know how to be me when I'm so connected to you that I don't know where either of us begins or ends."

"Some of that gets easier. You learn to be sensitive to the feel of energy. It's like knowing the scent of different flowers. You'd never get the smell of a rose confused with the scent of a carnation. Soul energies have their own markers. You can learn to sort them out."

"You'll teach me?"

"Yes."

"There's another thing we have to deal with," she said. "In ten years, I'll be almost forty, and you'll be, what, thirty-five? And in twenty years, I'll be almost fifty and you'll be thirty-five. And the next decade after that, people will think you're my caregiver."

Sam chuckled. "Sixty's the new forty, don't you know that?"

"I'm not joking." Summer wasn't amused.

"I know."

"It would kill me to see you turn from me for a younger woman."

"Says the twenty-eight-year-old woman to the fifty-six-year-old man."

"Sam—"

"Summer, I've wandered through my entire life alone. And then you came into it and brought with you everything that I'd been missing. Everything. Every fucking thing. You're like winning the world's largest lottery. How can I let that go? Please, don't ask that of me."

"Change me."

Sam's eyes went wide. "No. Fuck no. That could kill you. Even if I wanted to—which I don't—the researchers who changed me and the guys are gone or dead. For all I know, their research has been lost."

"Find someone else who can change me."

"We are looking for them, but even if we find them, I don't want you changed. It's too risky."

Summer thought that over…and rejected it. "Maybe you don't get to make that call. Maybe, if it's at all a possibility, we leave it on the table. Maybe I get some choice in all of this. Right now, you are so highly evolved that we're barely the same species. I don't know how we'll get through all the things that are different between us."

"How about we focus on the one thing that's the same: our love."

"A god and a human are ill-matched lovers."

He gave her a wry smile. "Star-crossed."

"Stay open to changing me."

"If what was done to me becomes mainstream, and if more progress is made so transitions are safer, yes, we'll leave it on the table. If this all goes away, the science is lost or buried or discontinued, then that's an end of it too. I don't hold out a lot of hope for that since we're already in a secret war over it. It's going to come out. It's going to wreak havoc in the world's balance of power. It soon will be the new arms race. Changed people will be harvested for research purposes. I don't want you caught up in that."

"I already am, Sam. There are no innocent bystanders in this."

"Can we agree to take this day by day?"

"Yes." She smiled at him, her first smile in all the dark days since she'd left him.

He shook his head. "You left, but you didn't leave me. And I didn't leave you. I just waited until you quit screaming before showing up."

"I don't think I have quit screaming yet."

He nodded. "That's okay. It took me years of mourning what I once was before I settled into being what I now am. A soul can scream for a long time. And then, one day, it remembers what sunlight feels like. And it starts to crave laughter. And it gets a peek at joy. And then it suddenly makes all of that its life purpose." He held her gaze a long moment. "You are my life purpose, Summer."

Summer held him tightly and let her tears come. This whole week she'd put herself through hell because she couldn't understand how he truly could be interested in her. She'd fought to set him free, set herself free, and it had nearly killed her.

He eased his hand over her hair. "You see us as unequal. And I see you as a miracle."

She shook her head. "No. You're the miracle. I just have a hard time believing you're *my* miracle. Good things like you don't happen to me."

She looked at him. He stroked his thumb over her cheek. "Day by day, yeah? Even if it's forever."

"I hope it is."

He nodded. "I didn't like the dark place you've been in this past week."

Summer sniffled. "I didn't want to give you up, but I didn't know how to deal with any of it. And there wasn't anyone I could go to."

"You have me. You have the guys."

"I'm not going to go whining to your friends about us."

"They're your friends too." He smiled at her.

"What about them? If you and I get together, will we be breaking up the band?" Summer asked.

Sam laughed. "The thing about being connected like we are is that when one of us becomes happier, healthier, stronger, we all do. They love you already— because I love you."

That was true. Acier had asked her about Sam and hadn't liked her response—she knew it was because he was protective of Sam and the others.

"How did you guys get together, anyway?"

"We decided there's strength in numbers. We opened our foundation, kick-started by an infusion of cash from a crime boss in Colombia. Brett Flynn had raped and murdered his daughter. It was an 'enemy of my enemy' sort of thing."

Summer could feel the flood of emotions that surged in him at that point in his story, all of them very human.

"Are you still connected to that boss?"

"No. Brett killed him in revenge for his support of us."

Summer shook her head. Her gut instinct had been right all along about Brett.

"Always trust your gut. Even for regulars, our guts react to energies we can't always understand." Sam smiled at her. "Feel like a shower? We'll stay the night here. You can pack some things in the morning, then come home with me. The rest will work itself out."

Home. Home with Sam. Home to her future. "It will work itself out, won't it?"

Sam smiled and nodded. "It already has."

SUMMER WOKE up with Sam spooned around her, his arms under her head and around her waist. He was home to her—not his fort or her apartment, but the man himself. She drew his hand up so she could kiss his fingers. He shifted behind her to kiss her neck and shoulder.

"Morning," he mumbled against her skin.

She smiled. "Morning. I love you."

"I love you."

They should wake up that way every morning for the rest of their lives.

"Are you sore?"

She remembered their very long shower last night —and the hours that followed it. "No."

He wedged a leg between hers, then slipped his cock inside her. "Good."

Shivers swept across her skin at the feel of his slow, comfortable thrusts. His hand moved over her thigh to her hip, her waist, her breast. She arched her back, angling her hips to feel more of him. He rolled her over to her belly, still connected to him, then spread her legs with his as he continued to thrust inside her. He braced his weight on his elbows, banging his hips against hers. His heat surrounded her, filled her. He moved to his knees, lifting her hips with him, taking her harder, deeper. One of his hands slipped between her legs to stroke her clit. Summer cried out as her orgasm ripped through her, prolonged by Sam's thrusts and strokes until he at last surrendered to his own orgasm.

They collapsed on their sides on the bed, his semi-relaxed cock between her thighs. "I'm glad you're here," she said.

He chuckled as he kissed her shoulder. "Me too."

She rolled over to face him, feeling a strange tension coming from him. "What is it, Sam?"

"You asked last night how you'd know if you were acting on your own will or under the influence of some external force," Sam said. "I'll show you."

"Okay." She smiled at him. He was intense this morning.

"Sit up and face me. Close your eyes. Now, hold your hands flat, palms down. What do you feel around them?"

Summer did that, concentrating on the sensations her hands were feeling. "Nothing."

"Keep your eyes closed. Now what do you feel?"

He must have slipped his hands under hers. They weren't touching hers, but she felt his heat. She couldn't tell if it was coming from her or from him, but it was a sensation that hadn't been there before. "I feel a slight heat, almost like a lingering warm breath."

"Is that your heat or mine?"

"I don't know."

"Now put your palms together. What do you feel?"

"My hands."

"That's too easy of an answer. How do you know they're your hands?"

"Because I can feel them. I know them."

"Can you feel from the left hand only?"

"Yes."

"And from your right hand?"

"Yes."

"So you know where you begin and end."

374

"I guess so."

He separated her hands then pressed his palm to one of hers. "And now?"

His hand was large, rough, and warm. "I feel your hand."

"Do you feel yours?"

"Yeah."

"So you can feel you and me at the same time?"

She nodded.

"When I attempt to enter your mind, you'll feel a soft sensation, like the heat between our hands. It's my energy penetrating yours. That push will always carry with it an undertone of the sender's energy. It might present itself as a peaceful visitor, but its truth cannot be fully hidden. Focus on the aftertaste, the bitter playback, like a cup of bad coffee. That sensation is what you must watch for; it carries the essence of the person attempting to connect with you. You know yourself. You know what's not you. You know what an almost touch feels like. What comes next is you knowing which is which, and that comes with practice."

Summer opened her eyes. Sam was there, sitting in front of her, his gorgeous brown eyes soft. She reached for his hands and twined her fingers with his. "I've tried to send thoughts to people before and never could."

"Without extreme training and practice, it's quite difficult to push a thought. It's easier to invite that person's energy into your own and then give them the thought."

"How did you learn this?"

"I had a teacher. But these mental practices, like any muscle, must be built up over time with continued use. That's why we were in the camps for so long. The guys and I had to develop our skills to survive the dangerous situations we were put in. I don't know if, had we been trained differently, in a different environment, we would have the skills we have now. There's something about survival that makes the brain kick into gear."

"So let's do a test. Push a thought into my mind," Summer said. She felt a need suddenly to lie back and bare herself to Sam. It felt as if she'd thought of that herself, except that hadn't been where her mind was headed just before she asked him to push a thought her way. She lingered a bit, feeling the thought and its compulsion, trying to sense the aftertaste of energy. It wasn't there—or she couldn't feel it yet.

Unable to resist the compulsion, she did lie back. She slipped her legs over his folded ones, then pulled the sheet away, opening herself to him.

The hunger in Sam's face was real as his gaze slowly grazed her body, but another emotion soon took over his features—regret. Sorrow.

She reached for his hands so she could pull herself up onto his lap, then wrapped her arms around his neck, feeling the heat of his body surrounding hers.

"Don't be sad," she whispered.

His arms went around her ribs as he buried his face in her neck. "I am as afraid of pushing my will over yours as you are. Sometimes, I can't help it. I want you so much. Every time our eyes meet, I want to stop the world and fuck you."

Summer ran her hand up his strong neck and over his soft, short curls. She kissed his temple and whispered, "I don't think it's a problem, Sam. I think it's a feature."

"How so? You said last night you didn't like the power imbalance between us."

"I'm still coming to terms with that. But I've never felt as connected to a lover as I do to you. I'm finding that experience rather heady. I like that you know me so completely. Every time you connect with me, you share a bit of you, which ties us together ever more tightly."

Sam sighed. He seemed unconvinced. He lifted her thighs and shifted the sheet, then slipped her down over his hard length. Summer felt her whole body tighten at the sensation of him inside her.

He looked into her eyes as he gently rocked her up and down his cock. "I want us, Summer. I want a life together. I want you to walk with me in this strange new world. I love what I see from your eyes. I love how you process life."

Summer stroked the sides of his face as she stared into his eyes. She'd never been complete until he held her in his arms. No wonder it had always been so easy to touch him, to stand near him. She kissed him, then soon forgot to kiss him as his movements inside her deepened. His thumb, touching her just where it was, threw her into an orgasm that made her gasp for air as she rocked against him. She wrapped her arms around his neck and felt his release come, felt his entire body stiffen as he lost himself in her.

As the edge of their passion settled, Sam leaned back on the bed and drew her with him, still buried deep inside her. His big hands stroked her back as he smiled up at her. "Give me today. Let me show you my world."

"Your world is my world." She frowned. "Isn't it?"

"No. My world's hidden. It exists in a secret part of yours, like something you only see out of the corner of your eye."

She nodded. She didn't have to ask if it would be safe—she knew it would be. "I love you."

He stared into her eyes. "And I you."

"Let's go on your adventure. But first another shower."

"Agreed."

## 27

Summer threw on a sweater and a pair of jeans when she got out of the shower. Sam was in the kitchen cooking them breakfast. In her closet, she took her satchel down and was trying to decide what to pack.

*Bring everything,* Sam said.

*I feel sad leaving here. Maybe we should keep it. It's nice to have a place to crash if we want or need to while we're in town. I have to leave some things. And I can't move in with you before we've even had our first date.*

*You have too many rules. Hungry?*

*Starving.* Summer left her empty satchel and went out to the kitchen. Sam had a big breakfast of eggs, bacon, biscuits, gravy—the works. "Where did you get all of this?"

"I went to the store while you were in the shower. Don't worry. I didn't forget my plant eater." He put a bowl of cut fruit on the counter.

Summer took the coffee he offered and sat on one of the barstools. "So what's the plan for today?"

"Our first date."

"For real? Where are we going?"

"I've been craving prime rib. And the place I'm thinking of has amazing salads, too. And Yorkshire pudding."

"Sounds delish. Where is it?"

"It's a surprise."

"Sam, I can't handle more surprises right now."

He stared at her. "I need to ask for your trust. I want to show you my world."

"Just tell me where we're going."

"San Francisco."

Her eyes went wide. "For dinner? Are we flying?"

"No. But you might want to wear comfortable walking shoes. And I promise to have you home by nine so you don't turn into a pumpkin."

"How can we go there and back by then if we aren't flying?" Summer narrowed her eyes as his comment snagged her thoughts. "Wait, tell me you don't turn people into pumpkins."

"I haven't. But I could impose the perception of being a pumpkin." He grinned, his white teeth flashing.

She shook her head. "What's the dress code?"

"Not fancy. Something you'd wear out to dinner with your friends."

"I am going out to dinner with my friend." She smiled at him. "My best friend."

"I like that."

They made small talk while they ate, then Summer looked at the clock on the stove. It was already past eleven. She had no idea they'd slept in that late.

"We didn't go to sleep till pretty late," Sam said as she hurried to get ready.

"I'd like to do my hair. Are we short on time?" She peeked out of her bathroom.

"No. No hurry at all." *I don't want to rush anything with you.*

Summer felt the impact of those words throughout her body. A shiver passed through her as she realized she may have found a rare, mythical creature...a man who would venerate his woman. Neither she nor Ash had experienced such a man. How many times, after bad dates, had they commiserated that no man was capable of being what they needed?

Too many to count.

In her closet, she slipped out of her clothes and changed into a matching pink lace bra and thong set.

But how would Sam be when he was exasperated with her? When he was in an overall bad mood? When she was out of sorts and picked a fight with him?

His answer was both mental and verbal. *I will be a god among men, I swear it.* "Are you going to put me to the screws for hours before letting me have my day with you?"

Summer jumped and let out a shocked "eep"

when she realized Sam was standing at her doorway. She held up the two outfits she'd been deciding between. "Sweater and jeans or a dress?"

"You do know San Fran is windy, right? I would love seeing your sweet ass, but I don't want to treat other men to that delicious sight."

She smiled. This was the best day ever. "Jeans it is."

She hung up the dress, then stepped into her skinny jeans and wiggled them up her legs.

"Jesus." Sam turned sideways and faced her living room, keeping his eyes squeezed shut.

Summer felt a hint of pain—from him. She went over to lean against him and run her hands up his chest, his neck, his face, forcing him to look at her. "What is it?"

He frowned. "I want you. We fucked all last night and this morning, and I still want you."

Summer felt a warm blush work up her neck to her face. "Me too."

"I can't seem to have a thought without you in it."

"That's how I feel about you."

"I know."

"Can we make this work?" she asked.

"We will. You're my one and only, Summer."

Summer gave him a quick kiss, then went back to her closet. She pulled on a white tank top and a beige cotton cowl-neck sweater over that. She moved past him and went into the bathroom to brush her teeth.

Sam still leaned against the closet doorjamb,

watching her. She smiled, foam filling her mouth. "Have you never seen someone brush their teeth?"

"Sure I have."

Summer rinsed her toothbrush and her mouth. Drying off, she looked at him over the towel.

"Does it make you nervous, me watching you?" he asked.

"Yes."

"But everything you do is so normal. I like that. No, I love that. Makes me feel normal."

Summer took his arm and pushed him forward. "Go sit out there and wait for me. This will go faster if I don't have an audience."

"Fine. But you don't need makeup. You're drop-dead gorgeous just how you are."

Summer turned on her curling iron, then poked her head out of the doorway. "Two words. San Francisco, Sam-I-am."

"That's three words."

Summer laughed. She moved through her makeup and hair in less than a half-hour. In her dressing room, she put on a pair of hiking boots, then fretted about whether she should bring a pair of shoes for the restaurant that were a little dressier. She dug out a drawstring backpack and slipped a pair of flats in it.

When she went into her living room, Sam stood up. She held her arms wide and turned around. "Will this do?"

"Absolutely."

She slipped her arms around his waist. "Sure you don't want to stay here?"

"I do want to. But I also want to show you my world. And you have to work tomorrow."

"For you."

His arms tightened around her. "I want my pool garden. The truth is that I want all of your days and all of your nights, and I'm not ashamed of how much I need you."

She loved how it felt to rest her head against his chest. She looked up at him. "Does it scare you to say that?"

"Scare me? Why would it?"

"To think that I have power over you."

"You have a thing about power."

"I guess I do."

"No, it doesn't scare me." He nodded at his overnight bag sitting on the coffee table. "Give me fifteen minutes to clean up, then I'll be ready to go. Why don't you finish packing what you want to bring to the fort for a few nights?"

She smiled. "I'm on it."

WHEN THEY REACHED the fort a little while later, the sun was already getting low in the sky.

"Are we really going to San Fran tonight?" she asked.

"Yup. For dinner and a bit of a walkabout."

"So...how are we going to do that?"

"There's a train depot under the fort."

That took her a minute to unscramble. "A train depot. Under your fort." She shook her head. There were no underground trains out here that she knew of. "And you think we can to take a train to San Fran and be back before nine p.m. tonight."

"Right." He grinned at her.

Summer shook her head as she looked away. "Fine. Keep your secrets."

"You'll see soon enough."

When they went into the fort, Liege's friends were standing in the courtyard, their expressions hard. She remembered their disappointment when she left, like there was a line between her and them she could not cross.

And yet these were men who voluntarily put themselves in danger when they had stepped in to fight the monsters who'd attacked her. They'd protected Sam so he could help her. They'd removed all traces of the fight from her apartment. She owed them a debt of gratitude.

She stepped close to the one called Bastion. Taking his hands, she stood on her tiptoes and kissed his cheek. "Thank you."

He smiled at her and pressed a hand to his heart. "*Bien sur.*"

The next in the row was Guerre, who'd somehow magically healed her. She gave him a hug. For a moment, he stiffened, then his arms went around her in a tight hold.

She moved to Acier next. Everything about him screamed brute muscle, except his eyes. She shook his hand. "I will keep practicing with the shotgun."

"Damn straight you will. And I'll help."

The last man she came to was Merc. She had seen him the day she left. Though she didn't know him at all, she felt the way he held himself apart even from his team. She gave him a big hug, one he returned.

Bending close, he whispered, "I'm glad you came back. You make him happy."

She blinked away tears. "Thank you," she said as she pulled away.

"Wait—why did Merc get a hug and I did not?" Bastion complained.

"He looked like he needed one," Summer said.

"And I don't?"

Summer laughed and went over to hug him.

"That's good. *Et maintenant, que voulez-vous pour le dîner?*" Bastion asked.

Sam slipped an arm around her waist. "We aren't staying for dinner. I'm taking Summer for prime rib in San Fran."

The men looked surprised but didn't argue, though they seemed to know what it meant in a way that she didn't.

"Have fun," Guerre said.

"Need company?" Acier asked.

"No," Sam said. "I got this." He handed Bastion

their bags, then led her into the glass hallway by the engine room. They went to the stairs in the northeast tower and went down several flights.

"Told you that you aren't breaking up the band," Sam said.

Summer smiled at him. "I'm glad."

He opened a steel fire door and led her into a sterile white hallway.

Summer hadn't been in this area of his fort. Were they going into the silo that he said was beneath the fort? "What is this place?"

"We're in the silo structure now. These are the labs I built for the researchers we've yet to find. We have offices, dorms, a conference room, a server room, several labs." A wave of tension entered his features. "We have everything we need, except the researchers."

Summer slipped her hand in his. "Where will you find them?"

"The Omnis have them somewhere in their vast infrastructure. I hope they're hidden. It's possible the Omnis have wiped them out, but I think that's unlikely. Their knowledge is too valuable to waste."

They went past a couple of large rooms that looked like morgues with long steel tables, carts of instruments, steel body drawers, desks, microscopes, and all the other accouterments needed to dissect a body. She shivered. Sam's hand tightened on hers.

They turned the corner and stopped at a bank of elevators. There were no biometric security panels either here or when they'd come into the silo. She was surprised at the open access this area had.

Sam smiled. "This area is restricted by energy signatures that we set. No one who shouldn't be here can be here—nor would they even know it existed. As far as the government knows, this silo was fully decommissioned and filled in with dirt and cement."

They stepped into the elevator. It serviced several floors—up to the fort and down one stop—but how far down that stop was, Summer couldn't tell. She was glad she hadn't seen this on the tour Sam had given her. This whole area would have sent her running.

Sam leaned against the back wall of the elevator and pulled her between his legs. "That's why we didn't come down here. Besides, at that point in time, I still hoped to keep you out of this part of my life."

Summer put her hands on his chest and gave him an admonishing look. "How could we be a couple if you had a whole side of your life you kept secret?"

"Spies do it all the time."

"But you aren't a spy."

"I was engineered to be one."

Summer slipped her hands up his chest, his neck, his face. She was about to pull him down for a kiss, but the elevator doors opened.

They stepped out into a short hallway. Sam faced her. "Summer, this is the dangerous part of our trip. I will give us appropriate cover, but I need you to keep calm, keep your emotions level."

That wasn't what she'd expected. What happened

if she failed? It would be like trying to hold her breath.

Sam smiled. "You can breathe. It's just that this Hyperloop system is not open to the public. The people who use it currently have high levels of clearance, special passes, or mutant skills. Do not expect any of them to be friendly."

"Can we still talk?"

"Sure, but let's do it via our mental link." *Ready?*

*No.*

*You wanted an adventure. Have you ever been to California?*

She shook her head.

*Good—it's one more state to check off on your list.*

They left the short hallway through another steel door, then entered a space that looked like many subway stations, with its tiled walls and arched ceiling.

The space was empty. She wondered if this was a private stop for this Hyperloop train.

*It is. It's restricted. We're the only ones who use it.*

After a few minutes, a pod slipped into the station silently, with a puff of air that smelled like earth. The door on their side of the pod opened. It was empty.

Sam drew her along as he stepped onboard. There were three rows of two seats—luxuriously appointed, high-backed seats that were slightly reclined. The door lowered behind them. Sam entered some command in the screen, then they both buckled into their seats.

"Hold on," he warned.

She tensed, but he relaxed. The pod shot forward in a smooth glide. The windows showed only a blur on either side of them. At the speed they had to be traveling, Summer thought she'd feel some G-forces. The pod had to be pressurized, for she felt nothing more than a floaty feeling.

"How fast are we going?" she asked.

"This pod can travel between two thousand and three thousand miles an hour."

Summer gasped. "How is that possible?"

"It's a vacuum tube. A Hyperloop."

"But they're only now beginning to experiment with those for transportation. And they don't go anywhere near that fast."

"Yeah, that's for show. They'll be bringing this to the public soon. They can't keep things like this a secret forever. The system we're on now was started ten years ago. It connects all major cities, airports, transportation hubs, and military bases coast to coast. It even crosses into Canada and Mexico."

"How is it that the Omnis were allowed to use this secret government conduit?"

"Money buys access. The government wants to benefit from the genetic advances the Omnis have made, so they have partnerships."

"How did you get ever get away from them?"

"We didn't. Our very existence is a lie. To the world, we died in the trials. Death was the only way out."

"But you got out."

"We did. And now we're taking down the ones responsible for our entrapment."

"The Omnis."

"The thing is, not all the Omnis are bad, and not all the bad guys are Omnis. Some work for our government and other governments internationally. The Omni World Order has a long history, dating back to the time of the Catholic Church's Inquisition. The OWO was established to support the advancement of scientific research, even when such undertakings often meant death to those doing the research and those funding it. The OWO was started as a means of protecting scientists and disseminating the results of their study to other scientists."

"What happened that caused them to change their mission?"

"Well, only some of them changed. Corporations are their modern-day patrons. They want to maximize the return on their investment, which means an end to sharing info. A perverted subgroup watched the so-called purification of the human race via the study and practice of eugenics at the turn of last century, which fed into the ideal of the Aryan race in Germany during the Second World War. That work continued in secret for decades using selective and sometimes forced breeding. But when molecular biologists made nanotechnology a reality, that was a game changer. That's the program that I got caught up in."

"But you're black. You shouldn't have been caught up in all of that, given their mission."

"It was early days. They needed guinea pigs. Disposable humans. They wanted men with certain skill sets and weren't picky about race or nationalities."

"Sam." It crushed her to think anyone could think of him as disposable.

"The joke's on them, though, because I survived. And I kept many of my men alive."

"Is it still going on—those tests?"

"Yeah, it is. They are continuing to perfect their formulas, but in illegal trials, often on kidnapped kids and young adults." He looked at her. "There's been a higher than average number of women, even pregnant ones, reported missing."

Summer gasped. Was it possible that accounted for what was happening with the women Kiera worked with?

Sam nodded. "I do think they're being taken into the Omni research programs."

"That's terrible." She took his hand, glad he was opening up to her. "So how did you all get your names?"

"In the trials, Bastion wasn't allowed to use his native language. Every time he said anything in French, they sent an electrical pulse to his brain."

"Like he was an animal."

"Yup. We were all identified by control numbers. Our past was completely wiped away. Obviously, no one thought we'd return to the lives we left."

"They took everything from you."

"When it came time to assign ourselves new names, Bastion thought assigning us French names was an under-the-radar revolt against the trial managers. I became Lige. Merc always spelled my name the English way—Liege—so that's what eventually stuck. Bastion claimed he was as strong as a fortress and would protect those who couldn't protect themselves, so that stuck. Merc—I'm not sure we ever did pin down the why of his name. Sometimes I think it's for mercenary, mercy, or mercurial. Any would fit him. Acier joined us later. He wasn't in the same medical trials we were. Calling him the French word for steel just seemed to fit him. And then Guerre, the gentlest of all of us. The kindest, too. He's a healer. Bastion thought he needed a strong cover name, so he called him War, or Guerre. He never lost his humanity—during or after the trials."

"Did you?"

"Eventually, I think. I follow different rules now, rules that keep me and my men alive while we strike back at the Omnis."

"Like you have trouble accepting boundaries."

He grinned at her. "Like that. Like sending you a misperception about the distance between our vehicles so you'd hit me so we could meet."

"I still can't believe you did that, except that I understand you differently now."

"When I first saw you, you had that brilliant white glow about you. I thought it might be an Omni trick."

"When did you first see me?"

Sam looked away. She waited for him to continue. "You mentioned that red-haired guy that threatened you."

She nodded. "Scared the bejeebers out of me."

"He came to me, too."

"Why didn't you say that?"

"His role in the mutant world is troubling. We call him the Matchmaker. He somehow finds the perfect match for mutant warriors among human females. His matches are both blessing and curse. If the mutant refuses the match, he dies. If the mutant accepts it, the human female dies."

A chill slipped through Summer's nerves. "What does that mean?"

"I don't know. Until he appeared to me, I thought it was an urban legend. I refused his gesture, offering my life instead. He didn't take it. I saw you that night, at dinner with Kiera and Ash. Because of the nature of the Matchmaker's message—and the fact that you worked at an Omni business—I couldn't help wondering if the Matchmaker caused you to have that glow, that maybe he was working for the Omnis, and that you were part of the charade. That's why I caused the accident."

"Are we going to die?"

"No."

"But how do you know? Don't you believe in fate?"

"I believe we make our own fate. My men and I are dedicated to keeping you alive. As far as the

Matchmaker goes, the jury's still out on whether he's an Omni. His curse may only carry weight if you believe in it."

"I'm scared, Sam."

"I didn't tell you to frighten you. I just want you to be aware of your surroundings, make safe decisions."

The pod slowed to a stop. She could see this depot was much larger than the one they'd used. Dozens of people were standing and waiting.

"We're here," Sam said, smiling at her.

## 28

They got out of the pod barely forty-five minutes after they'd gotten in. Sam led her out to the platform. She looked at the different people, wondering who they were that they were allowed to be there. Omnis, regulars, mutants— they all looked like normal humans, though maybe the mutants were the ones who were big like Sam. None of them looked at her.

*Why do they do that?* she asked Sam.

*Better to not be a witness to anything. Most regulars don't yet know how to lie undetected.*

*I hate it when you say things like that.*

*Because it's the truth?*

*No. Because it defies all of my norms.*

They took an elevator up to the street level, then came out a door that looked like an apartment side entrance. The sidewalk was on a steep hill. It took Summer a moment to get her bearings.

Sam held her hand and led her up the hill. A newspaper vendor caught her eye. She wanted to have a paper to show the girls as proof in case she ever did decide to share this story with them.

Sam smiled and said, "Pick one."

She showed one to the clerk, then started to slip out of her backpack so she could pay, but Sam was faster than she was.

"Is this really San Francisco?" she asked the vendor.

He frowned at her, then bounced a look between her and Sam. "You okay, lady? You need some help?"

"Is this San Francisco?" Summer repeated.

"Yeah. Has been all day. Will be tomorrow, I suppose."

Summer nodded and stepped away. She wasn't keeping track of which streets they crossed or which direction they took; she was too lost in her thoughts.

"None of this is real, is it?" she said.

"What do you mean?" Sam frowned.

"We're really still in Colorado. You've just implanted a vision of our trip here."

Sam did grin at that. "I sure could have, but I didn't."

"How would I know?"

"You wouldn't. That's what makes what I can do so dangerous. I could give you a false memory, change an existing one, or erase it entirely—it would feel as real as what you're experiencing now. Reality isn't what it used to be."

"Let's make a pact that you won't use your super-powers on me."

Sam didn't immediately agree. In fact, he didn't agree at all. "I can't."

"I don't give you permission to manipulate me."

"In any normal situation, where you aren't in danger, I agree. I will not step over that boundary. But if you're in danger, I have to be able to take you over in order to protect you."

"From what?"

"From attacks like what happened last week. Those are going to become more frequent, I'm afraid."

Summer pondered that as they continued on their way to the restaurant. The host seemed to know Sam. They laughed and made a joke. Summer wondered if it was real, or if Sam had caused the maître d' to behave like a friend.

How could she trust anything surrounding him? Or, for that matter, herself?

The steakhouse was full of old-city charm. The decor featured Tudor-style stucco and beam walls. The flooring was dark oak. The booths and chairs were upholstered in a rich red fabric. The tables were stained dark, matching the floor. The acoustics were perfect, letting quiet conversations happen all over the room without one running into another.

The restaurant specialized in prime rib, but they did have some seafood options, along with wonderful salad choices. Summer's stomach growled as she scanned the menu. Sam smiled at her.

He ordered a bottle of Shiraz, Summer's favorite wine. She didn't even pause to wonder how he knew —they were too connected for her to be surprised he'd discovered that on his meanderings through her brain.

After they placed their orders, Summer reached across the table for his big hands. "I have to tell you I'm having an existential problem."

Sam nodded. His eyes were serious. "I'm not surprised. Lay it out for me. I'll see if I can help."

"How do I know that anything I observe or remember or experience is real?" She lifted a shoulder to punctuate that concern. "I've always had a rich imagination. It's the place that I create my gardens from. It's where all of my dreams and daydreams come from. Even before you, my imaginary world sometimes crossed into my real world, but I always knew the difference between the two. I always knew what reality was. Now I don't."

"Here's the thing. Your understanding of reality could only be changed by someone like me. We'll work on knowing what's from and of you versus what's from and of another being."

"I don't have to be changed to do that?"

"No. The changes that my team and I went through made these neural networks stronger and more dominant. It took what was there and enhanced it. Even regular humans can empower the same networks that the nanos fired up for me, but it's something that takes practice and discipline and courage."

"I have those things. Pretty much."

"You do. So consider this. Let's say, for the sake of illustration, that everyone wears perfume. Everyone would then have a clear smell. When you hug someone, you get a hint of their scent on you. Energy is sticky like scent. It has its own signature. However it is that you as an individual sense energy, you'll begin to tell that everyone's energy—every animal, or thing, too—has its own energetic signature. When a changed person like me goes into your head, their energetic signature leaves a residue. That's what you can become aware of. If you find yourself doubting something about yourself, take notice of any foreign energy residue that lingers in conjunction with that thought. If you find that thought's been tainted, then you know it's not yours. Reach deeper into your mind for the original thought or memory, the one with your own energy signature, and you'll be able to tell the difference."

"Oh. So the original thought or memory stored in my brain is still there. Or does the act of insertion change the original?"

"No, the insertion basically just encapsulates the original. It steps in front of it so that's what your mind grabs first. Implanted thoughts are weaker than original thoughts. Unless they are frequently reinforced,

they age out, degrading over time. I think it imperative that you begin your training."

"How long did your training take?"

"Five years of intensive one-on-one and group
training under a master-level fighter. Two years of
field experience. Three years, now, of straight
survival."

"Wow. It's like becoming a doctor."

Sam nodded. "And that was with the assistance of
the nano injections during that first five years.
Without the injections, it could be a lifetime of study
and practice."

Summer swallowed hard. Was she prepared for
that? What if not doing it meant losing Sam? "Is your
master looking for new students?"

"No. He's gone into hiding. He may be dead."

"I thought you guys were immortal."

"We're not. None of us could survive a lethal
wound without immediate life support."

She looked deep into Sam's brown eyes, trying to
ferret out the words he wasn't saying. She had the
distinct impression he didn't expect to live a long life.

She prayed that if he didn't, that she wouldn't
either. Living without him would destroy her.

He kissed her hand, his eyes sad. "This is our first
date. Don't be thinking about our ending just yet."

"I love you."

His face hardened. "I love you."

Their food arrived. Summer let the topic rest

where they'd left it. She had a million unanswered questions, but that wasn't what tonight was for.

Tonight was for fun.

"Right. I'm wooing you," Sam said.

She huffed an empty laugh. "With your woo-woo powers."

He chuckled at that. "No. With my heart and soul."

"Oh, Sam." She met his eyes. "You're asking me to jump off a ledge and fly with you, but I don't have wings."

"Nor do I. Though my men and I were changed, we're sure as hell no angels. I bet I could find us some glider suits though."

"I don't want to live without you."

"Nothing says you're going to."

Worse than the thought of her aging and dying while he was still young was her living without him.

She smiled. "I think this first date is definitely one for the record books." She lifted her glass to his. After the soft clink of their glasses touching, she took a sip. "I was going to say I would never forget this, but that might not be true."

Sam didn't answer that. At least he didn't lie.

Summer stared at her grilled mahi-mahi. She forced herself to eat her expensive dinner. Sam had made a huge effort to bring her here to this place, from her world, through his, to hers again.

She felt tears well in her eyes, but she refused to

shed them. She forked a bit of fish and salad and made herself chew and swallow. They ate in silence for a while, polishing off their meal. She picked up the last bit of her Yorkshire pudding, which Sam had made of point of asking the waiter to prepare with butter instead of the usual beef drippings.

She realized he had become everything to her.

"Since we got here for an early supper," Sam said, "we can just make it to the wharf in time to see the sunset. Want to go there?"

"Sounds beautiful."

After they left the restaurant, Sam hailed a cab. He held the door for her, then slid next to her and gave the driver their destination.

"What did you think of the steakhouse?" Sam asked her. "Would you go there again?"

"It's so crazy to think we came all the way from Colorado just for dinner. But yes. It was delicious. I would go there again. Did you like your steak?"

"I did. I crave their prime rib now and then. Even Bastion, as good as he is in the kitchen, can't come close to what they do."

"Does he do a lot of cooking for you?"

"When he's around."

They reached Fisherman's Wharf. The crowd was surprisingly heavy, given the hour of the day. Tourists were moving every which way. There was a sign that said something about sea lions. She went a little ahead then turned around to wait for Sam.

Liege caught up to her. She grabbed his hands and started to rush him along as she jogged backward on the pier. He laughed and pulled her close, afraid she was going to run over other tourists. Though it was autumn, the flood of tourists hadn't ebbed for the season.

By his calculations, they had less than fifteen minutes before the sun would set. He smiled down at her, loving the feel of her in his arms, loving having this moment with her.

He kissed her, right there on the pier, forgetting to shield them from onlookers. When they parted, he knew she was as aroused as he was.

She leaned close and whispered, "Can you hide us? Right here?"

"I can, but I won't."

"Why? I need you."

"And I need you. Unfortunately, the sun won't wait for us. And I don't think a quick fuck will satisfy either of us."

Summer sighed and leaned her head against his chest. "You're a cruel man, Sam Garrick."

He kissed the side of her forehead. "Come on. Let's head to the end of the pier."

Summer took his hand, and they slowly strolled across the wood decking. The air had a salty tang that Liege loved. He could tell there were several shops she wanted to visit, but each time, he heard her tell herself no. Her finances were tight. He understood, but that didn't stop him from wanting to spoil her.

A weird sound caught her attention—like dogs barking. Beagles wailing. A bunch of them. "What's that sound?" she asked, frowning.

"Sea lions. They're just over there."

They reached the area where piles of sea lions were sprawled on several floating docks, watching visitors above them, barking at each other. Summer gasped then laughed. She put her foot up on the bottom rung of the pier wall to lean over and see more. Liege wrapped an arm around her waist. The evening's breeze caught her hair, waving it around like a silky flag. He leaned his face against her head, more enthralled with her than the wildlife.

The end of that pier was crowded with visitors wanting to watch the sunset. Liege compelled several of them to move away from the best spot, making room for him and Summer. He stood behind her and wrapped his arms around her. She leaned against him, holding on to his arms.

"This isn't the ocean," he said, "but the bay is gorgeous. Another time we can come back and do a drive up the shoreline."

"I'd like that. I like these adventures with you."

They were silent as they watched the colors of the fading sun wash across the water.

"Sam, how do we handle Kiera? She didn't believe what I said about you."

Liege sighed. He lifted his gaze to the salmon-colored streak rippling on the water. "I'll have to talk to her, I guess. Somehow."

"She already knows about you."

"I know. I listened to you tell her about me."

"No, not that. She knows her mom had an affair with a sperm donor."

"Sperm donor. Great."

"And she knows that her bio dad paid for her college. And that her mom asked her bio dad to stay out of her life."

"She knows all of that? And she's okay with it?"

Summer turned in his arms. "She would have tried to find you, but her mom said you were dead." She put her hand on his chest. "Do you regret not reaching out to her in her childhood?"

He nodded. "I promised her mom I'd never interfere. When her real dad died while she was in high school and money got tight, I sent extra money. I did pay for her college. She was a sophomore when I went into the medical trials. And once I was changed—and I'd met my enemies—I thought it was safer if I stayed away."

"You're her mysterious secret Santa each holiday."

He nodded.

Summer sighed. "She's going to be angry, you know. That you did all of this and didn't respect her enough to come forward."

"I couldn't risk it. She's very much a warrior. I like

that about her. But she isn't on equal footing with my enemies."

They stayed until the sunset faded away. Summer put her jacket on. Liege wrapped his arms around her. "Mind if we stop in some shops on our way back?" he asked.

"Are they still open?"

"They stay open late," he said.

"I'd love a mug. You don't mind shopping?"

"I think I'd love shopping with you. Pick anything you like. My treat. I'm sure they have fudge here somewhere."

By THE TIME they returned to the Hyperloop, Liege was carrying a shopping bag full of all the items Summer had admired on their stroll down Pier 39. It was early yet, but he was going to make good on his promise to have her back at the fort by nine p.m. He could feel she was tired. He shouldn't have kept her up so late last night.

She was quiet as they took the pod back to Colorado. She leaned her head on his arm and fell asleep. When it came time to disembark, he realized she had a fever.

Liege carried her across the depot to the private hallway and the elevator, which took them all the way up to the second floor of the fort. He went to his room, summoning Guerre as he set Summer on their bed.

Guerre set a hand on her left shoulder and went quiet as he sent his energy into her body.

Liege turned away and began pacing the length of his room. At last, Guerre separated from Summer. He looked grim.

"Her change is beginning."

## 29

Liege became aware of a car driving on the far fringes of his property. Nearly a week and a half had passed since Summer fell ill.

He left her with Guerre and went downstairs to the front gate. The car was still some distance from the fort, but he could feel his daughter's energy. She was full of emotions—fear, anger, worry, determination, love.

When she parked her car, Liege mentally opened the smaller inset door. Kiera walked through it. He stood back, a few feet in the openness of the big courtyard so the shadows of the tunnel didn't hide him.

His daughter was furious. Summer was right. She was fierce and brave, coming alone to confront him. He'd been expecting this visit.

She stopped only feet from him. "She's here. Don't deny it."

"She's sick. I'll show you to her." He turned and led the way to the stairs in the glass hallway that went up to the fort's second floor. They went into his room. Summer was lying so still in the middle of his big bed, her face flushed with the fever she'd been suffering.

Kiera sat next to her on the bed. She took her hand and rubbed it between hers. "Summer, I'm here. I should have come sooner. I'm so sorry." Summer was unresponsive. Kiera glared up at him. "What have you done to her?"

Liege looked at Guerre, surprised that he was hiding himself from Kiera. "I believe she's changing into a mutant."

Kiera's mouth dropped open as rage filled her eyes. "I can't believe you. It isn't enough that you take her from her life, from her friends and work and everything. But now you've done God knows what to her to make her this sick and you have the gall to say she's changing into a mutant. I'm taking her out of here."

Liege shook his head. "No. She's not going anywhere. No hospital could give her the care we can."

Kiera scoffed at that. She pulled the covers back. Instantly, Summer began to shiver. Kiera scooped a hand under Summer's shoulders and tried to help her sit up, but Summer's body was a dead weight.

"Help me," Kiera said, looking up at him. "Please, if you care anything for Summer, help me get her to a doctor."

Liege nodded at Guerre, who made himself visible and reached over to take Summer from Kiera and get her settled back under the covers.

Kiera stared in shock at Guerre. He did not look at her, but Liege could feel the strangest pull of energy between his man and his daughter. Perhaps Guerre was mentally communicating with her. Perhaps it was something else.

Liege walked to the door. "Kiera, I need a word with you." He gestured toward the hallway.

"I'm not leaving Summer," Kiera said.

"Just for a moment. There are some things I need to explain to you."

Kiera narrowed her eyes at Guerre, gave Summer a worried look, then followed Liege from the room.

"What I have to say, you don't want to hear," Liege said. "You won't understand it. And knowing it puts you in jeopardy. But perhaps you already are in jeopardy. I don't know."

Kiera folded her arms and glared at him.

"I know Summer has spoken to you about me, about my being a mutant."

Kiera's brows lowered. "Whatever head game you've been playing with her won't fly with me."

"And yet it has. For years."

"What are you talking about?"

Liege revealed his true appearance to her. She gasped and stepped away, backing up until she hit the cold glass of the hallway wall. "What are you doing?"

"I'm your father," Liege said. He wished there'd

been a better way of breaking the news to her. Or better yet that he'd never had to tell her at all.

"No."

He nodded. "Everything Summer told you was correct. I am a mutant."

Kiera shook her head. She squeezed her eyes closed and slammed her hands over her face.

"I would be glad to tell you everything, but I don't think this is the time for that."

"No. It's a game. You've learned how to deceive or to hypnotize."

"That is true. I am an expert in those things. But what I'm telling you is also true."

"This isn't real. It can't be."

"Your mother and I met when I was home on leave. She and her husband were going through a rough patch. They were separated—irredeemably so, she thought. We connected just for a weekend. It wasn't love. It was just a comfortable break from our regular lives. She told me about your dad and their inability to conceive. Though they'd been separated, they still had intimate encounters. They were still in love, but their hearts were broken. I left your mom pregnant with you. Your father never knew you weren't his, and your mom wanted it that way. Since I was active military and spending most of my time in dangerous engagements overseas, I couldn't parent you the way they could. They reconciled shortly after our weekend together. Your dad loved you as his own. You were his own."

Liege teared up as he thought of everything he'd given up so that he could have his life and Kiera could have hers.

"Your mom sent me letters and pictures. I sent her money every month. She and I made up a cover story about a distant relative who'd included your mom in her will to explain the money. When your dad died, I paid for your university expenses. I was forced into a medical research program shortly after that. I lost touch with your mom and you until a few years ago when I came back to Colorado." He stared at her. "It was I who funded your women's shelter."

"My secret angel investor."

Liege nodded. "I was changed in that medical research program, changed without my knowledge or permission. It took me years to survive what had been done to me, then the training to use my new skills, then the fight to get away from people who changed me."

Kiera shook her head. "This is crazy. This isn't real. You knew about my picture of my bio dad."

"Not until Summer told me about it."

"You faked what you looked like before. How do I know you're not doing it again? This is all some kind of a head fuck. What do you get out of it?"

"I never intended to fall in love with your best friend. I thought I could watch over you from a safe distance without ever being in your circle."

"Why? Why not do the right thing and come tell me you were still alive?"

Liege spread his arms. "Look at me. I look nothing like a man who is your parent should look. I'm in your age group. But beyond the complexity of hoping I could get you to believe I just had good genes, connecting with you puts you in danger from my enemies. They are dangerous and ruthless. I felt it was safer that you lived your life without the taint of mine."

"I don't believe any of this. How did you hide your true self from me?"

"I compelled you to see me as another man you had in your mind's eye—any black man. That's why you saw me differently than Ash did."

"Hypnosis."

Liege nodded. "Basically. We mutants have almost endless ways to bend your reality. We could be a danger to human civilization. The war we fight is to end these human modifications."

Kiera blinked several times as she silently regarded him, processing all he'd said. "I can't—can't accept this."

"Summer tried to tell you. I didn't want her to, but in the end I realized that I can't have her without also having you in my life. Which means the three of you have to be brought in."

"What happened to Summer, then? The truth."

"You saw the wound on her arm."

Kiera nodded.

"She was attacked by deviant beings we call ghouls. We're working under the theory that they infected her with nanos that started her change into a mutant being. The exact nature of these changes is unknown at this point. We're searching for a few scientists who would be able to discover that answer for us."

"Can it be reversed?"

"I don't know. Not without the blood analysis that needs to be done—and the experts to do that."

"Summer said you were rich. Can't you hire the experts you need?"

"Money isn't the issue. None of the scientists we could hire have ever been involved in human trials. Unfortunately, the ones who have have been taken by our enemies. We can't find them."

"But wouldn't Summer be better in a hospital where she can be properly monitored?"

"No. Her presence would put everyone in jeopardy if my enemies decide to go after her. The war I'm struggling to keep quiet would go public. And we don't know exactly what changes were made to her, so we possibly would be exposing her care providers to danger from her. She has what she needs right here. Guerre—the man you saw in my room—is our healer. He's capable of supporting her bio needs while she goes through the changes."

"How long does something like this take?" She shook her head and turned away. "Gah! Look at me talking to you as if any of this was real."

"It is real, Kiera."

She put her fists up to her temples as she pivoted

to face him. "What can I do to help?"

"There's nothing you can really do. Go back to town. This shift could take several weeks. Or it might be days. We don't know. She may not survive the change. And if she's been changed into a ghoul, I will have to put her down."

"Kill her."

Liege nodded, his jaw set.

"You would kill the woman you love."

"Should she become a ghoul, she would no longer be who and what she was. That change destroys the host. It's irreversible, as far as I know."

"I can't leave her here."

"You are more than welcome to visit her anytime. I think she would be comforted having you near while she goes through this. But I also will not be leaving her; she will not be alone."

Kiera began to pace. Liege patiently waited for her to find a way to verbalize her thoughts and concerns. It was odd that in the middle of Summer's hell, she was the bridge to his daughter. It was a gift, and he regretted that it took Summer's extreme situation to push him toward the truth he'd been avoiding all of Kiera's life.

Kiera stopped and faced him. "My missing women are somehow mixed up in this, aren't they? That's why you agreed to help me with them."

"Yes. The ones we delivered to your center, we did so after wiping their minds. They would have been taken into our enemies' world and either fed to the ghouls or used for more medical trials. Erasing their short-term memory was a kindness. Unfortunately, we missed some. We will continue our search for them, but we may never know what happened to them."

"I want to stay with Summer for a while today."

Liege nodded. "She would like that. You're welcome here anytime. Ash as well."

"So this is really true. Ash and I thought she was losing her mind."

"We could have handled this better. Being open with regulars is new territory for all of us. Secrecy has been our only protection for a long time." He went back to his door and opened it. "Come, I'll introduce you to my friend."

Kiera nodded at Guerre.

Liege caught the way their eyes lingered on each other, and frowned.

"I know you," Kiera said. "You've brought food and gifts to the shelter. You never stayed long enough for me to thank you."

"The gifts were from your father, not me," Guerre said.

"Well, thank you." She looked from Guerre to Liege. "Both of you."

LIEGE QUIETLY CLOSED the door to his room, leaving Summer with Guerre. He stretched and rubbed his neck. He was sick with worry about her transition. He hated leaving her side, but Guerre forced him to go get some food.

What if the Matchmaker's curse was manifesting right now? What if the time Liege had already had with Summer was all he'd get?

He paused at the spiral stairs that led down to the kitchen. Rich scents of bacon, potatoes, eggs, and coffee wafted up like a summons.

Bastion was belting out a French folk song at the top of his lungs. Liege knew asking him not to sing was a guarantee for increased volume, so he said nothing as he fired up the espresso machine.

"*Bon jour, mon capitaine,*" Bastion said cheerily.

At least he didn't sing his greeting, Liege thought with a sigh.

Bastion took food to the table then settled across from Liege. "I have good news."

Liege looked at him, waiting for him to speak.

"I have found the War Bringer."

That was good news. Hopefully the War Bringer could give them info on some of the researchers they were looking for.

"And, I have bad news."

"Bastion—"

"The War Bringer lives on a compound of fighters. They call themselves the Red Team."

"Are they like us?"

"Yes. And no. They are Omni fighters, but they are not mutants. Well, not all of them are changed. I need to scope them out before I make contact."

Liege gave him a hard look. "So why are you here?"

"Because no one feeds you when I'm gone and you need to eat."

"I've been eating." Liege stared at his plate, realizing that was probably a lie. He couldn't remember his last meal. Guerre had made a veggie broth for Summer. Liege had had some of that as he fed her.

Merc and Acier had been busy hunting ghouls—they didn't have time for domestic duties. Liege had seen little of them the past two weeks. They were keeping a close eye on Kiera for him. Besides the increase in ghoul activity, Flynn had gone quiet. He was probably cultivating another host.

"I haven't gotten inside the mansion yet. I only just discovered them, but I can already sense some who have come through there are mutants. One, I believe, is a female."

The fog cleared Liege's mind. "They changed a woman?"

"I don't know if they changed her or how she was changed."

"But she survived."

"*Oui*. Her energy is faint, so I don't think she lives there. When I finish surveying their compound, I'll get inside the house and learn more."

Bastion didn't ask how Summer was; Guerre kept them all updated on her progress. Liege wasn't certain how long no news would continue to be good news. He sipped his espresso.

Bastion's report gave Liege hope. Maybe the Wyoming fighters could be brought into the Legion.

$\sim$

SUMMER SLOWLY SURFACED. Without opening her eyes, she tried to determine where she was. The room felt different from her apartment. It sounded different. She could smell Sam's delicious scent all around her. It was more than his cologne she was smelling. It was him—the sweet fragrance of his skin.

Except for the soft sound of his breathing, the room was silent, but she could still hear it. The flow of water in the tubing of the radiant heat system buried in the concrete. The whooshing sound of the ceiling fans. The wind outside. Water in the pipes in the bathroom.

She wasn't in her apartment. She was at Sam's fort.

How long had she been there? Her body ached as she turned over to face him. She opened her eyes. He was on his side facing her, his beautiful face relaxed as he slept.

She reached over to touch his cheek, her mind filling with sudden knowledge—his love for her, his fear for her, his worry about her. His utter and complete exhaustion.

Summer swallowed, becoming aware of herself. Her mouth was dry. Her body ached. And she stank in a way she never had before, like she'd run a marathon, rolled in a pig sty, then gone to bed. She lifted an arm and sniffed her skin to confirm the smell was hers. Ugh. It was.

She tossed the covers off, in desperate need of a shower. She was wearing a white tee that came to her thighs. Had to be Sam's. Odd. She couldn't remember putting that on. She pulled it off and dropped it on the floor.

In the bathroom, she turned on the shower, then spotted her toothbrush in a stand next to Sam's. She loaded it up with toothpaste, then got in the shower, still scrubbing her teeth. She spat out the toothpaste and set her toothbrush down. Her own toiletries were in the shower, but she couldn't remember putting them there. She did remember packing them in her bag the day Sam took her to San Francisco. But that was it.

She poured shampoo into her palm and scrubbed her hair—twice. Cream rinse was next. Then she lathered up Sam's soap and scrubbed her entire body. Only then did she feel a little more human.

She dried off and put her lotion all over herself then, wrapped in a towel, went back into Sam's room. Her bag was sitting on one of the armchairs in the corner. She dug out a comfy outfit and dressed.

Sam startled then. She felt the shock that slammed into him when he reached his hand over to where she'd been and found the space empty. Before she could say anything, he jumped out of bed. His eyes met hers. She smiled at him.

"Hi."

He rushed over to her side and scooped her up into his arms, bringing her back to the bed.

"No! God, no. It stinks. I stank. I can't go back in there until we change the sheets."

His brows knitted as he looked down at her. He walked over to the other armchair and sat with her on his lap. "That's part of the change. Your body was expelling its toxins."

Summer buried her face in his neck and wrapped her arms around him. "You, however, smell divine," she said, kissing his neck, the corner of his jaw, his ear.

Sam pulled away. He stared into her eyes. She could feel his energy slip inside her body, scanning her. She sighed. After a moment, his hold eased, and he relaxed against the back of the chair.

Summer smiled. He was being so dramatic this morning. Or was it afternoon? The drapes were drawn.

"It's morning."

"I slept around the clock? I was tired after our trip, but I didn't think I was that tired."

"You've been asleep for two weeks," he said.

Her brows went up. "Two weeks?"

"With a fever. How do you feel now?"

"Fine. A little achy, but fine." She stroked his face then kissed the side of his mouth. "I'm sorry I scared you, but I think my stink woke me." She laughed. "I had to shower." God, how had she gone to the bathroom?

This time, she didn't have to wait for Sam to answer her—she saw it in his mind. He'd taken her to relieve herself. He'd bathed her. He'd sung to her and rocked her and cried over her.

Overwhelmed by his emotion, she wrapped her arms around his shoulders and held him tightly. "Why did you cry?"

"I thought I was losing you."

"What was wrong with me?"

"That monster that cut you also delivered something into your system. We still don't know what it was, but I'm beginning to suspect you were changed."

"Into what?" She straightened and looked at him. "Am I going to become a monster?"

"I don't think so, but we don't know the exact nature of what was given to you. We can only wait and see."

Wait and see. Something was happening to her body, and there was nothing she could do about it. Nothing.

She felt calming energy spill into her from Sam, taking the edge off her panic before it spun out of control. "We've all been through the change. We're here for you. Guerre has been monitoring you the whole time. Neither of us sense a deviant's genes in you." He ran his fingers over her cheek and jaw. "Kiera came by several times while you were out."

Summer was shocked. "What did you tell her?"

"Everything. I showed her my true self. I told her I was her dad."

Summer wrapped her arms around his neck and hugged him. "That makes me so happy. How did she take it?"

"As you can imagine. I told her she and Ash were both welcome to visit you, but Kiera convinced me later to leave Ash out of all of this. For now, at least. I don't think we'll be able to do that forever. And it may be the longer she stays out, the harder it will be to bring her in. Truthfully, I couldn't give any of that much thought while getting you through your transition was my main focus, so I let Kiera take the lead on it." He gave her a hug and kissed her forehead, letting his lips linger against her skin. "How do you feel?"

"Actually, I feel great. Less achy now that I've been moving around. And I'm starving."

Sam laughed. His eyes sparkled as he asked, "Are you still a vegan?"

"I was never a full vegan. I do think I could polish off a dozen eggs."

Bastion's voice slipped into her mind. *I'm making veggie frittatas, home fries, and fruit. Come down when you're ready. We'll have breakfast for dinner.*

She looked at Sam, shocked that she'd heard Bastion herself. He slipped a hand behind her head and brought her close for a kiss. "You're one of us now." He smiled against her lips. "I'll help you block out the others so we can have some privacy until you can do it yourself."

## 30

---

Summer slowly walked down the main drag in Old Town, one hand in Sam's, the other wrapped around his arm. The night was cold, but not brutally so. Fairy lights twinkled in the bare locust branches. Store windows were filled with seasonal decorations. A little snow lingered at the edges of the sidewalk. The night couldn't be more perfect.

She was happy. She smiled up at Sam. He stopped and faced her. "Do you remember what I asked you a few weeks ago?" he asked.

She felt the memory he surfaced—their first morning together. They were in her bed. She loved him even then. "I do remember. You asked if I was going to make biscuits and gravy with breakfast."

He laughed. "No. Before that."

She tilted her head, enjoying torturing him. "Oh.

That. That wasn't a question. It was more of an order."

He went to one knee. "Then I'll ask you again." He took a box from his pocket and opened it. "Will you marry me?"

Summer gasped. Their minds were so intertwined —how had he been working on this surprise without her knowing? She laughed and covered his hands with hers. She didn't need to see the ring to give her answer. "Yes. Yes, I will." She bent over and kissed him. She was laughing and crying.

Bystanders shouted congratulations as they went past. Sam got to his feet and kissed her. He took the ring from the box and slipped it on her. He kissed her fingers and said, "You make me the happiest man alive."

Summer hugged him, then looked at the ring. It was a thin rose gold band with an emerald-cut diamond. Simple and classic. "It's beautiful, Sam."

He smiled. "Kiera and Ash helped me pick it out for you."

"I can't believe I didn't know you were working on this."

He wrapped an arm around her as he led her back to the SUV. She'd been thinking they'd head out to the fort after dinner, but now she wondered if they'd even make it back to her apartment before she attacked him.

He held her car door for her. "Keep up that train of thought and I will find a place to hide us."

"Do it." She giggled, feeling his response to her words.

Summer was absent-mindedly admiring her ring on their way to her apartment when the most terrifying thing happened. She heard Kiera in her mind, pleading with Clark.

Gasping, Summer looked at Sam. Instantly, Kiera's mind was shut away from Summer. "What's happening?"

Sam paused traffic at an intersection and broke half a dozen traffic rules as he cut in front of several lanes of traffic and made an illegal left turn. Summer grasped the passenger door handle as he flew down the road.

"Where are we going?" she asked him.

"To Clark's garden center."

"Why?"

"He lured Kiera there."

Oh. God. This was the very thing both she and Sam were terrified of—trouble coming to Kiera because of them.

LIEGE PAUSED traffic again as he made a right turn. His tires squealed as he accelerated. *Kiera, you will not come closer,* he said into his daughter's mind.

*He has one of my clients. I heard her on the phone. He's hurt her.*

*I'll take care of it. I'm almost there now.*

Kiera still kept coming.

*Pull into the next parking lot.*

*No.*

*Dammit, Kiera. There's nothing you can do. I'll handle this. My men are on their way too.* Liege imposed a compulsion over her, but it failed to take. Her resistance was too strong.

Liege made a sharp left turn into the empty parking lot of the garden center. The streetlights were out.

*Wait for us,* Merc said, already driving to town from the fort with Bastion.

*I can't. Kiera's headed here. I have to put this down before she's hurt.*

*We're almost there,* Guerre said, riding in with Acier.

Liege parked and turned to Summer. "No matter what you see or hear, you stay put in this vehicle. I've camouflaged it so that it won't be seen by any of our enemies. I can't fight this if I'm worrying about you, and there wasn't time to get you home." He ducked his head and looked into her eyes. "You copy?"

She nodded, too frightened to speak.

Liege got out of the car. He locked the doors. It took only seconds to hone in on Clark's energy—or what was left of it. He was standing off to the side of the garden center, in a big area that was used for plant displays during the summer. Now it was just bare concrete, covered by crunchy autumn leaves.

Geez, Clark looked like the monster inside him. His face was bruised and scratched and grisly. His eyes were red-rimmed. His hair was filthy and unkempt, as were his clothes. His shirt and jeans were full of stains and holes, hanging on him by mere threads.

Liege remembered Summer asking if he could save Clark. He actually felt bad for the guy. A look at Clark's aura showed it was no longer gray with black spots, but black through and through. Whether that was his true energy or the corruption of Flynn's influence, Liege didn't know.

Maybe it didn't matter.

Clark was now a rabid dog and was going to have to be put down. The trick was figuring out how to do that when Flynn was in and all around him.

*Let him go, Flynn. He's done what he could for you. This fight is between you and me.*

*Oh, but he's been such a good pet. It will take so long to break another one in.*

*You're a coward.*

*And you're a fool. You'll die long before Clark does. I've been picking your Legion off, mutant by mutant, all around the world. At least I will have the pleasure of shredding your beloved fiancée tonight—right before your eyes.*

*That's not happening. Not tonight. Not ever.*

SUMMER REMEMBERED HER SHOTGUN BAG. It was still in Sam's SUV from their practice earlier in the day. She climbed into the back seat. She hadn't reloaded her magazines after practice. Her hands shook as she did so now, slipping the loaded magazines into their loops on the gun belt Acier had given her.

A car pulled into the lot. Kiera's van. Oh, God. Summer left the SUV and ran over to her. Kiera was crying and angry, shouting about Clark getting one of her women.

Summer didn't try to reason with Kiera, just dragged her toward the SUV. The damned thing wavered between being Sam's Escalade and looking like a big dumpster, the mirage he'd set over it. She had to focus on what the truth of it was before she could get the door open. "Stay here. Sam is here. His men are on the way—I can feel them. Don't leave this vehicle."

"You get in, too." Kiera grabbed at her, but before Summer could climb inside, a ghoul spun her around.

She mentally slammed the door shut, sealing the SUV off and letting it return to the mirage Sam had set for it. She leapt away from the SUV, rolled to her back and shot the deviant mutant that was about to fall onto her. Jumping to her feet, she shot another one.

Something out of the corner of her eye caught her attention. Sam was wrangling with two of the monsters. God, the sound of their growls sent shivers down her back. Suddenly, Sam shoved them back from him several feet. Summer aimed and fired, hitting them both at once, right through the top of their skulls.

Rhythm in a fight like this was key—she'd learned

that in her training simulations. The size of these beasts and their horrific appearance were the only superpowers they had in a fight. They could be bested. Summer stayed near the SUV, worried Kiera would try to break out and look for her client.

Another big SUV arrived. It parked, blocking the parking lot entry and breaking Summer's concentration. One of the beasts got close to her. Instead of slashing at her, it just stood quietly behind her, exhaling hot breath over her shoulder.

"Hey!" Sam shouted at it.

The thing turned and looked at him, then fell back as Sam's knife pierced his eye, stabbing into his brain. He went down. Summer fired a round into his skull to keep him down.

By that time, Acier and Guerre had also taken up defensive positions around the SUV. With their help, it didn't take long to end the rest of the beasts. While Sam's fighters were standing in silence, breathing hard and taking stock of the now-still battle ground, Clark, who had looked to be down for good, pushed himself to his feet. He walked in an unsteady and unholy stumble toward Summer.

Sam felt her horror and looked over that way. The hairs rose on her skin as she became aware of the energy blast Sam sent Clark. The top of her ex's head crumpled inward as his neck swelled like a balloon, then blood exploded from him. He slumped to the ground and lay unmoving.

Summer bent over and lost the dinner she'd just

had. When she straightened, Sam handed her a wet towel to wipe her face. She held it in place for a long moment, slowing her breathing as she sucked air through it.

Kiera got out of the SUV. Summer could feel her friend's horror, disgust, and disorientation.

"Clear the area," Sam told his men.

Merc stopped them. "I already did." He grabbed a blanket from the back of Sam's SUV. "Your girl's over here, Kiera. Guerre, we need you."

Summer hadn't even seen him arrive. This fight had to have run far longer than she realized for him to get here from way out east—even breaking every speed limit to do it.

Sam pulled her into his arms. Together they walked over to the area where the pumpkins had been on display out front of the garden center's main entrance. A woman was lying there in a pile of scattered straw, coughing and struggling for air. Her clothes were in tatters. Kiera cried out and rushed to her side. She leaned over her and stroked her face, telling the woman to look at her, that she was safe, that the horror was over.

Merc covered her with the blanket. Guerre knelt beside the woman and pushed the blanket aside from her shoulder. He set his hands on her, one on top of the other. Golden light began to shine along the seam between his palm and her skin. The woman became calm, then went limp.

Kiera wept. "No. No! Stay with us. I won't leave your side."

Summer didn't know how long they stood in a circle around Guerre, Kiera, and the woman. Only when Guerre finally sat back did Summer become aware of how she'd been holding her breath.

"She's going to be okay," Guerre said. "Her healing has begun. I've wiped her mind. She won't remember this."

Kiera looked up at him. For a long moment, they stared into each other's eyes. Summer wondered at the energy that was jumping between them. At last, Kiera nodded.

"I'll help you get her to the center," Guerre said. "I can stay with her if you like."

Kiera blinked away tears as Guerre lifted the woman and carried her to the van. She came over to take Summer and Sam's hands. "I'm sorry that I didn't believe you."

Sam wrapped his arm around Kiera and pulled her into a hug. "I'd rather your ignorance of this world than your knowledge. I thought I could keep it from you."

Summer hugged her next. Kiera was shaking.

"When did you get a shotgun, Summer?" she asked.

"After I was attacked. You're going to need one, too."

Kiera nodded. "Maybe so. Is it safe for me to take her to the center?" she asked Sam.

"Your center is safe," Sam told her.

Kiera nodded. "We have some talking to do."

"We do, when you're ready," Sam said. "Not tonight. Let Guerre take you home."

Kiera squeezed Summer's hand and felt her ring. "What's this?" She held up Summer's left hand and stared at the engagement ring a long moment, then covered Summer's hand with hers and nodded. "Good. I'm happy for you." She looked at Sam. "For both of you."

ACIER, Bastion, and Merc spread out to begin the cleanup duty. They brought one of the garden center's dump trucks over and loaded up the dead deviants. They let Clark lie where he fell. Someone would find him in the morning.

Liege faced Summer. There was so much to say, and yet none of it would matter if Summer rejected him now. He pulled away from her despite his desperate need for one more chance to run his hand through her hair, to feel her lips on his. Depending on her answer to the question he was about to ask her, he might have to let her go. He had to know her answer.

"This is what I am. This is all that I am."

She caught his hands and pressed them against her heart. "I don't understand this level of evil."

Tension knotted in the corners of his jaw. He dreaded her next words, wishing he could stop time and at least keep them here, where they were together and the end hadn't happened yet.

"You know I love peace," Summer said. "Not war."

He tried to pull away, but her grasp on his hands tightened. No rational mind loved war. Especially not the warriors who fought it.

She kissed one of his palms. "Without you, without what you do, there would be no peace. Darkness would win." She looked around them at the devastation his men were cleaning up. "The world needs you just as you are. And if you'll still have me in your life, I promise to be your refuge."

Liege choked on the sigh that broke from him. He grabbed her and bent his face down into the crook of her neck, trying not to let his ragged breathing get the better of him. "I love you, Summer. And I desperately need you in my life."

Her arms tightened around his neck. "Good. Because I would be lost without you. I love you, Sam."

He shook his head. "I didn't want this to be your life experience. I wanted you to live surrounded by peace and beauty."

"I like peace and beauty. And I like being able to fight when I need to."

Liege thought of the Matchmaker who'd brought them together. Had they bested his curse? Were they free to live their lives?

He stared at Summer, then dragged his gaze to

her temple as he brushed her hair from her face. "We'll keep training, yeah?"

"Yeah."

He pressed his lips to her forehead and said, "I want my garden."

Summer laughed. "Your garden will be the most spectacular ever built for a fort."

He put his arm around her and turned her toward the SUV. "Let's go home."

## 31

**B**astion stood outside a sprawling mansion in the middle of nowhere, Wyoming, keeping himself within his electromagnetic shield. He was only beginning his exploration of the compound that the Red Team used as their headquarters, but already he knew the property was lousy with cameras and sensors.

The War Bringer was here—the man who'd brought down the Omni silo fortress. This location was an unlikely site for the resistance against the Omni World Order. Bastion wondered why they'd chosen it.

Men weren't the only ones here. There were females and children as well. This place wasn't a stronghold—and yet it was.

Walking around the outside of the mansion, testing the feel of its energy, Bastion saw a strange orange light coming from the garage area. He moved in that direction. The orange light washed over him as he stepped around the corner, radiating from a fiend no mutant could hide from.

*The Matchmaker.*

The glow in his red eyes was chilling. He pointed a long, bony arm toward Bastion.

*Merde.* Liege's monster had now come for him.

Bastion looked up at the dark mansion. Somewhere inside was a woman meant only for him…a curse neither of them could escape.

# OTHER BOOKS BY ELAINE LEVINE

## O-MEN: LIEGE'S LEGION

LIEGE

## RED TEAM SERIES

(This series must be read in order.)

1 The Edge of Courage

2 SHATTERED VALOR

3 HONOR UNRAVELED

4 KIT & IVY: A RED TEAM WEDDING NOVELLA

5 TWISTED MERCY

6 TY & EDEN: A RED TEAM WEDDING NOVELLA

7 ASSASSIN'S PROMISE

8 WAR BRINGER

9 ROCCO & MANDY: A RED TEAM WEDDING NOVELLA

10 RAZED GLORY

11 DEADLY CREED

12 FORSAKEN DUTY

13 MAX & HOPE: A RED TEAM WEDDING NOVELLA

14 OWEN & ADDY: A RED TEAM WEDDING NOVELLA

## SLEEPER SEALS

11 FREEDOM CODE

**MEN OF DEFIANCE SERIES**

(This series may be read in any order.)

1 RACHEL AND THE HIRED GUN

2 AUDREY AND THE MAVERICK

3 LEAH AND THE BOUNTY HUNTER

4 LOGAN'S OUTLAW

5 AGNES AND THE RENEGADE

# ABOUT THE AUTHOR

Elaine Levine lives in the mountains of Colorado with her husband and a rescued pit bull/bull mastiff mix. In addition to writing the Red Team romantic suspense series, she's the author of several books in the historical western romance series Men of Defiance. She also has a novel in the multi-author series, Sleeper SEALs.

Be sure to sign up for her new release announcements at http://geni.us/GAlUjx.

If you enjoyed this book, please consider leaving a review at your favorite online retailer to help other readers find it.

Get social! Connect with Elaine online:
    Reader Group: http://geni.us/2w5d
    Website: https://www.ElaineLevine.com
    email: elevine@elainelevine.com

CPSIA information can be obtained
at www.ICGtesting.com
Printed in the USA
FSHW011955030921
84539FS